She Who Hears The

Sun

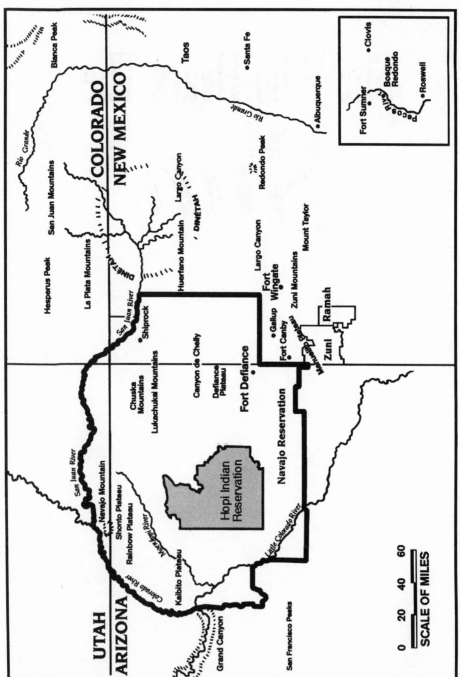

Map of Diné Bikéyah, Navajo country

She Who Hears The

Sun

A Novel of the Navajo

Pamela Jekel

KENSINGTON BOOKS
http://www.kensingtonbooks.com

KENSINGTON BOOKS are published by

Kensington Publishing Corp.
850 Third Avenue
New York, NY 10022

Copyright © 1999 by Pamela Jekel, Inc.
Mountain Chant is a stanza from "Blue Horses Rush In" Copyright © 1997 by Luci
Tapahonso. Reprinted by permission of the University of Arizona Press.

Library of Congress Card Catalogue Number: 98-075558
ISBN 1-57566-439-9

First Printing: August, 1999
10 9 8 7 6 5 4 3 2 1

Printed in the United States of America

For Jack,

Who helped me to see the ever-changing earth in all its beauty,
Who showed me how to slow down enough to feel its rhythms,
Who sat with me in silence, so my heart could fill again with love.

SHE WHO HEARS THE SUN

For long years I have kept this beauty within me,
It has been my life.
It is sacred.
I give it now that coming generations may know the truth.
I give it as the dew falls.
I give it as the sacred pollen.
This covers it all,
The Earth and the Most High Power Whose Ways Are Beautiful.
All is beautiful before me,
All is beautiful behind me,
All is beautiful below me,
All is beautiful above me,
All is beautiful all around me.
My days have been long.

—The Night Chant of At'ééd Jóhonaa'éí Yidiits'a'í

Prologue

▲▼▲▼▲

*A*s you ride down out of the Rocky Mountains, out of the highest
places of Colorado, you descend into a strange and beautiful country
which rests in a great bowl between the Colorado River and the Rio
Grande, known to the Indian peoples of the Southwest as the sacred
center of the earth.

Mesa Verde, Shiprock, Chaco Canyon, Canyon de Chelly, Rainbow
Bridge, and Black Mesa are only a few of the many shrines and dwelling
places of the Old Ones, the wandering nomads who would come to call
themselves, Dinéh, the People.

But they did not find this rugged, windswept land empty when they
came from the high reaches of the Colorado. The early Anasazi, or Cliff-
Dwellers, already had built large and complex cities into the high canyon
walls. The Hopi and the Zuni and the Pueblo peoples hunted the lands
and lived among its hidden springs. But the newcomers were determined,
quick to take the best of what they found and make it their own, and
willing to fight the more passive tribes and drive them forth. The Pueblo
called them by a name which meant "enemy"; the Hopi called them
Tasavuh, "Head Pounders," for their habit of crushing Hopi skulls with
stone axes. Finally they became known by the name which the Spanish
called them . . . the Navajo.

The Navajo came into this region of the Four Corners, where Colorado,
Utah, Arizona, and New Mexico touch, somewhere around 1000 A.D.,
into a vast semiarid desert of more than fifty-thousand square miles,
bordered on the north by the San Juan Mountains of Colorado, on the
east by the Sierra Blancas and Mount Elaine, on the south by Mount
Taylor and the Zuni Mountains in central New Mexico, and on the

*west by the San Francisco Peaks near Flagstaff, Arizona. This is roughly
the area of extended Navajo occupation today, except that they have less
than half the space they ruled a thousand years before.*

*It is a land of flat alluvial valleys where wide deserts of sagebrush
are dotted with groves of juniper, cottonwood, tamarisk, Russian olives,
and pinyon pines. It is a place of rolling upland plains and high deep-
pined mountains with vividly painted mesas. The rivers of this land
carve deep cool gorges and towering cliffs of spectacular beauty, but it
is a hard land, where the wind never stops and life is not crowded upon
life as it is in the swamp or the sea or the eastern forests but is, instead,
scattered in spareness and utter stark simplicity. Each blade of grass,
each bush, each tree or shrub has so much space around it that it stands
out bold and poignant against the hot sand and the barren rock. The
light here is so clear that it makes the eyes ache and water with its
brightness; life here is so rare and individual that each struggling cliff-
rose, each twisted, scabbed juniper seems to be a metaphor for survival
and freedom.*

The Navajo call it Dinétah, *the Land of the People. They arrived as
wandering family-clans of nomads, seed gatherers, and hunters, fierce
in determination but poor in cultural tools and inventions. By the time
the Spanish arrived in 1540, they had dislodged the stronger, more
culturally advanced Anasazi from their stone-and-mortar pueblos, had
beaten back the Hopi and Zuni, and had established themselves as "Lords
of the Soil" of this region, as they were called by the Spanish, largely
through the strength of their unity and the power of their religion.*

*They called their way of life The Rainbow, and their land, the Land
of the Rainbow, a brutal region of bottomless canyons, fierce rivers,
jagged mountains, and the widest vistas they had ever seen.*

Prelude

▲▼▲▼▲

Summer 1846

A raven with dusty wings flew down from the white sky and landed in the open adobe doorway with a quick buckle of wind and a rustle of feathers. He cocked a gleaming eye at the three women within who did not notice his arrival, so busy were they with the young girl between them. She was Pahe, granddaughter to the chief of the Red-Earth Streaked clan, Narbona, a plump, plain-faced stubborn girl who would live far longer than she then imagined and see more joy and anguish in her long years than all the years of her grandmother and mother put together.

Next to Pahe kneeled her mother, Ayoi Anílnéézí, The Tall One, who could imagine neither her daughter's life nor her own imminent death, remote as both seemed to her now as she sewed up the hem of Pahe's long blanket skirt.

Behind them both stood Deezbaa, Going Off To War, mother to Ayoi, grandmother to Pahe, who would one day be remembered for her enigmatic wisdom and her astonishing betrayal. For the moment, however, she was arranging Pahe's long black hair into the intricate strands and coils of the *tsiiyééł*, the hair bundle-style worn by Navajo women past the age of childhood. She pushed the hair up her granddaughter's neck and frowned at the result.

Three women: one old, one in the last of her child-bearing years, and one still a child. Three women who prepared for the homecoming of their kinsmen, as they did each evening as regularly as the sunset.

"You can pile your hair high as the yucca," her mother said to Pahe, standing and stretching. "But if you do not learn to keep your eyes respectful, there will not be a single man who asks your bride price at the meeting dance.''

Pahe stood before the great silvered mirror in her mother's hogan, holding quite still despite her delight. The mirror had been a gift to her grandfather from the Spanish Governor, Fernando Chacon, more than forty years and several wars ago. It was the only silver mirror for a hundred miles, and Pahe felt very proud that she belonged to the *Táchii'nii* clan, that her grandfather was such a powerful *Naat'áanii*, Headman, as to have such tributes paid to him.

She looked around the hogan, the place where she had been born, seeing it as if for the first time in the mirror. It was the same as most of the women's hogans in her clan, round and not very tall, built of earth and some wood held in place by square pegs, rocks held together by the hardened adobe mud, with the fire pit in the center and the door facing the east, as was proper. In the niches of the eaves, her mother had stored her jars of water, her cooking pots, her roots and herbs, her silver belts, blankets, and other treasures she had accumulated over the years of her marriage. Stores of food for the coming winter months, when they might be unable to walk about for many days at a time, were tucked into the rafters: bags of cornmeal, dried fruit, and pinyon nuts. With the fresh milk from the goats, the good mutton stew, and the *nanééskaadí*, the thick corn tortillas her mother made every day of the year, they always ate well, no matter how deep the snow.

She fingered the turquoise-and-silver beads looped round her neck. For the first time, she was wearing her grandmother's silver, the heavy jewelry that told all who saw it that Deezbaa was the wife of a *rico* headman. Pahe felt a whole new part of her life beginning.

Pahe studied her image in the mirror, trying to see her grandfather's hawk-visage in the young, soft planes of her cheeks. She was round and moon-faced, quite unlike her mother, with little of the fierceness of her clan evident in her eyes so far. She sighed and stood up taller, trying to see as much of herself as possible in the mirror. At least she could wear the silver, at least her hair was off her backside, two clear signals that she was finally a woman.

Her mother made as if to leave and then turned back at the door. Her grandmother continued to fidget with the skirt and jewelry that Pahe would wear for the first time at the great meeting dance at Chuska Mountain. The weight of her hair on her head made Pahe feel important. "Go back to your weaving," she said to her mother, attempting to close the door on her voice. "The man I choose will not wish his bride to keep her eyes lower than his leggings—"

But Ayoi pushed the door open again, clucking her tongue and shaking her head. "How did we raise such a headstrong ewe, Mother?" She ignored her daughter completely, pushing back inside the room, just to tease.

Deezbaa chuckled ruefully as she gave a final twist to the silver necklace, causing it to fall just right on her granddaughter's dark blanket, which served as her bodice. "She is of the *Táchii'nii* clan, born for Manuelito. She took it in with her mother's milk and her father's seed."

"How many other headmen will be there besides Grandfather?" Pahe asked, smoothing her hair carefully. As always, when her father, Manuelito, was mentioned, she thought of her own future. Her father, though young for a warrior, was already a leader, and one day, she knew, he would step into Narbona's footprints. No matter what she did, no matter who she married, she would always be granddaughter and daughter to important men.

"All of them," her grandmother said surely. "If your grandfather can make the trip, not a one will dare stay behind."

Her mother nodded in agreement as she reached out and patted her daughter's dark blanket skirt, a costume she had woven herself. "If Narbona can make the journey with his many years, the other *Naatáan*, Headmen, will have no excuse for absence. It is as your grandfather says: if the old ways are not followed, they will soon disappear and with them, the People." She grinned evilly. "But, of course, this will not matter to you, my daughter, for you will return to your grandfather's hacienda undanced and unpromised. Your suitors will take one look at your defiant gaze, listen once to your obstinate mouth, and they will flee like deer before the wolf." She sighed and rolled her eyes. "Your father will have to feed that mouth until he is old as Narbona."

Pahe laughed and cuffed her mother's shoulder gently. "He should be used to it, my mother, after near fifteen winters of union with you." Among the People, it was accepted custom that a man could have several wives, and her father had followed that tradition. His first wife, Juanita, lived in a hogan close by, and Pahe's half-brothers were as close to her as though they had been raised by the same fire.

All of the headmen that Pahe knew had at least two wives, sometimes three, and often they were related. Each had her own hogan, her own children, her own rights to the land, and her own flocks. The lands of the wives usually touched each other, though each grazed her own flocks on her own pastures so that the husband controlled land that stretched sometimes farther than he could see.

But the land was not really his to do with as he pleased. In that way, it was good that a man continue to love and respect his wife, so that the land might remain under his control. So far as Pahe could see, her father cared more for Ayoi than was usual. His sons teased him about the presents he brought her from trading trips, the scoldings he took from her good-naturedly.

Pahe knew that someday she would find such a man as her father for her own. And she would be a finer wife than her mother was, she told herself, with a face that smiled more often and a mouth less turned to scolding.

She spread her long colorful blanket skirt as she did when she was herding the goats into one corner of the corral, pretending to herd her mother out the door once more. Her mother wheezed and grumbled like an old ram, dodged her, and made as if to butt her from behind, as Deezbaa chuckled at them both. A faint bustle from a far corner of the sprawling hacienda made Pahe stop and listen intently. "My brothers have returned!" she cried out gleefully.

"You named her well," her grandmother chuckled. "No doubt, her brother's horse tumbled a small pebble before him, whilst he is still a half-day's ride away."

Pahe grinned and shook her head. "You two may stand here and gabble like turkeys, I am going to get the neck he promised me."

Her grandmother snatched at Pahe's skirt before she slipped from the room. "Not with my silver!" she scolded.

Pahe hurried to unloop the heavy jewelry from her neck, handing it over to her grandmother with a quick hug. "Do not worry, Grandmother, times are changed since you were a bride. Men do not wish their women to be so small and timid now, they wish them to be brave and fierce and meet their eyes with courage—"

"Tell us, O Well of Truth," her mother said mockingly. "Teach us of the ways of men and women, all that you have learned in your thirteen summers of vast experience."

Pahe flushed and snatched her skirt from her grandmother's hands. "Well, it's true, you have but to listen to your own sons. Hurry, they're coming!" She ran from the room lightly, calling to her slave to fetch her blanket.

Ayoi went outside the room to the inner courtyard and called to her own slave, "Has the hunting party returned?"

The small girl shuffled forward at her command. She was Zuni, and exasperatingly slow. "I have heard nothing, but the dogs are barking."

"Fetch my blanket, then," Ayoi said. "My daughter was right!" she called to her mother back in the room.

"She usually is," Deezbaa replied, gathering herself carefully and moving in a way that said she refused to be hurried, even for the return of her sons and grandsons after nearly a moon hunting in the northern canyons. "But do you think she is right about the young men today? Why, when I was a maiden—"

"It does not matter. She is Narbona's granddaughter. Even if she dances like an armadillo and stares like a rattlesnake, she will be desired. But if I tell her that, she will be even more impudent."

Deezbaa laughed lightly, pulling her blanket about her thin shoulders. "You are right. She will be made wife in two seasons, and mother before the year has turned."

Now they could hear the dogs barking and the faint, high cries of the slaves and the men left behind as they hurried to meet the arriving hunting party. "And the first in line, no doubt, to greet her brothers," Deezbaa added wryly. "Even if it is more seemly that she wait and greet them with her mother."

"Since she first drew breath, she has not suffered being overlooked with any gladness." Ayoi took her mother's arm. "Perhaps she is not so foolish after all."

The two women, grandmother and wife to the chief males at Narbona's hacienda, walked together with stateliness out of the sheltered courtyard, into the bright, open sun. A half-dozen Zuni and Hopi slaves clustered around them, as was usual whenever they strayed from their hogans. Now the dust cloud announced the return of the hunting party, and the slaves babbled and pointed. It was August, the Month of Expanding Seeds, and the sun was stark and white in the sky. No woman went outside without a blanket to shade her face from the dust and the heat, yet Pahe was at the corral, climbing up on the fence, her skirt up around her knees.

"Her brother promised her the neck of the first deer he took down," Ayoi said.

"And that is sufficient cause for her to climb the rails like a young boy?"

"Well, and you tell her, if you think she will hear you—"

"That one hears only what she wishes to hear," Deezbaa replied. She shaded her eyes with her hand. "They are heavily laden. Narbona will be pleased."

As though she had summoned him, the old man appeared then in the courtyard of his hogan, where he lived apart from the women's quarters and those rooms of his sons. It was to his hogan that the headmen came, to sit and smoke and talk and laugh or sit quietly for hours, for he was known to be a man of power and wisdom.

Narbona was bent and shortened with age, but his legs were still sturdy enough to hold him without the aid of a walking stick. He did not lean on the slave who stood beside him, and he wore his red head sash in welcome. As the horses drew near and cantered into the corral, he lifted his hand high in salute, and then turned to go back inside.

"I hope the Holy Ones favored them more than last time," Deezbaa said.

"They did!" Ayoi exclaimed. "Look. See how heavy the carry bags are!"

The women turned back to their courtyard then, to await the coming of their sons, as was seemly. They knew that at the next meal, they would hear the tales of the hunt, would see the deer or the bighorns, or whatever else the men had brought, and finally they would embrace and welcome the men home properly. But the first meeting would be with Narbona, and only the children would be expected to clamber over the corral, touch the hunt bags, and exclaim over the dead carcasses.

Pahe laughed and clapped her hands in delight when she saw her three brothers at the head of the line of huntsmen, their broad grins white in their dark faces, under their wide head scarves. Her older brother leaned down low over the neck of his horse and pulled her up on the blanket in front of him, and she rode with the hunters into the corral, sharing their triumph.

"Ya'at'eeh! How are you! Did you bring me my neck?" she called to her youngest brother, Jádí, teasing him with a mock scowl.

"Would I come home without it?" he called back, sliding from his horse and catching the reins of his brother's mount. "Who would dare risk such peril?"

In the laughter and shouts of welcome, the men handed their horses and their burdens to the slaves and walked across to Narbona's courtyard. With a quick tug of her hair, her youngest brother called back to her, "We had good fortune in the hunt. Think you'll have the same at Chuska Mountain, little sister?" He grinned and ducked as she pretended to stoop, pick up a rock, and throw it at his head.

*   *   *

That evening the tables were full of bounty, as platters of fresh venison, rabbit, and quail came in from the spits in a steady stream, each to the welcome shouts of pleasure from Narbona's clan. The slaves kept the wooden platters of warm mutton stew and cornmush full and the serving baskets of bread moving, heaping up beans and squash, corn and melons, and hands reached across the boards in happy confusion.

As each new platter was brought in from the roasting fires, Narbona nodded to Deezbaa, and she began a prayer of thanksgiving, thanking the Holy Ones for the animals and the men who had killed them. The songs and prayers only increased as bellies grew full, and finally Narbona put down his knife, signaling he was finished with the meal. He rose, still steady on his feet despite the Mexican tequila and the heavy meat, laid a gentle hand on Deezbaa's shoulder, and took his leave.

The men followed him then, as was the custom, out to the council fire to smoke and talk and let their bellies settle. The slaves cleared the platters, and the women began to herd the children toward their sleeping pallets. Pahe went to help one of her aunts with the children, for she had been ill for several days. Other relations would help her with her corn, her melons, and her pumpkins, for that was their way, to show feelings of kinship not with words but with action.

Narbona said often that what set the People apart from the Hopi and the Pueblo and the Ute and the Zuni, indeed from the Mexicans and the Spanish as well, was their responsibility for each other. Debts of one clansman was the debt of all; the wealth of one clansman was, also, the wealth of all. In that way, they would outlast the rocks themselves, Narbona said.

Indeed, it must be so, Pahe thought, for Narbona was a *rico*, the wealthy head of one of the largest and the richest clans in the land. She knew many young girls did not have their own horse until they were married; she had had her own horse since she was high enough to mount.

She thought then of her gentle mare and yearned to rest her cheek on her neck, to feel the soft tickle of her nose in her palm, before she went to her pallet. She hurried her small cousins to their beds and went outside the noisy hogan to the dark once more, back toward the hacienda.

Pahe inhaled the night air, closing her eyes in quiet joy. With the men back from the hunt, the hacienda had a whole different feel to it, a mood of busy, important work, a hum of strong voices and commands. Even the dogs were more obedient. When the men were gone, her grandfather's lands and hogans seemed only to be waiting quietly for them to return to bring it to life once more.

Her mother told her often enough how important it was to be a Navajo woman, a mother of the People. She reminded her that all of the sheep, the goats, every member of the flock which made them so rich belonged, in fact, to the women, not to the men. The hogans belonged to the women, the children belonged to the women, and even the future belonged to the women, for the Holy Ones found the female half of the world more precious than the male.

But so far as Pahe could see, the men were the lords of the earth, and the women were its handmaidens. She often wished she had been born another son to Manuelito instead of his only daughter. No matter how he singled her out for attention, bouncing her on his knee, making his embraces more frequent and tender than those he gave his boys, she still wished she could go with them on their adventures, their raiding parties, their hunts. It seemed to her that life stopped when they were gone and only resumed when their horses cantered back into the corral.

Deezbaa had known fifty-five winters, but she was in many ways older than Narbona. She was more cantankerous, that much was certain. He called her, sometimes, his "favorite mule," because of her stubborn disposition. But they were strong in their affection for one another, and Deezbaa had, in more treacherous times, held the clan together by the sheer strength of her will, or so the stories said.

Some of the men wanted to go to other places in *Dinétah*, the lands of the People, and move their flocks to different pastures. Some of them murmured that they wished to raid the Mexicans to the south and the Utes to the north for slaves. But Narbona wished war between the tribes to cease. He said that they must be strong to weather what was coming. No one knew what he meant, but Deezbaa insisted that her husband's will be followed, and she backed up Narbona's soft words with louder ones whenever the women said their men wished to move on.

Pahe heard the horses nicker in the far pasture, calling one to the other in the warm night air. As always, the sounds of the animals in the dark soothed her and made her feel smaller, held in the hand of something larger than herself. She would go to see her mare in a moment, but first she must attend to her own duties.

She went to the corral where her goats were confined to check that all of them were inside, as she did every evening. Her father's slaves had the duties of herding the goats, but the animals belonged to her. Whether they thrived or died, bred or were barren, they were her responsibility. Each one was ear-notched with her mark, two V-shaped cuts symbolizing ears for her name, and they had been gifts from her mother and grandmother each spring since she was born.

Now she had sixty-three goats, and she knew that this herd made her richer than some of the grown women in the clan. She had milked each one many times; she had nursed their kids and seen to their silly squabbles and salved the hoof-cuts they got in each rut, and they belonged to her as surely as she belonged to her mother and father. But she knew also that they belonged as well to the entire clan, and so she must take her turn providing a good suckling kid and plenty of fresh milk when guests came to feast.

She knew, also, that if famine or drought ever came to the clan, if real trouble were ever upon them, then she would be expected to share her goats with every member of the clan equally, keeping the People alive with her property. This was both the honor and duty of being a daughter of Manuelito.

The corral was dark, and as the moon rose higher, she could see the light-colored buck in the corner, standing alone as he usually did, away from the nannies. She had never seen a buck so uninterested in his women. Yet he was the best breeder she'd had, traded with her cousin for a surly buck and two kids. Pahe got the best of that bargain, she knew, for the buck she'd traded was mean as a gila lizard and tried to ram her each time she came to inspect her herd.

"I'm going to slit that one's throat," she had said angrily to her mother one day, coming back with her blanket skirt torn and filthy from the buck's attack. "He's too evil to live."

"Trade him instead," her mother said evenly, glancing up from her weaving. "Someone else may find your thorn easy enough to tread."

Pahe had turned to her mother with surprise. "You mean, to someone in our clan? That demon goat?"

Her mother shrugged. "If you can. You may wish to say nothing of his temper, of course."

"That does not seem honorable."

Her mother had smiled wryly. "A trade is a trade. It is not a marriage. If they find him as evil as you do, he won't last long anyway."

"Or they may trade him to someone else who has not heard of his horns."

Ayoi nodded. "Try not to give up more than one kid in the bargain."

Pahe smiled slowly. She could see then that there was a solution, that her mother was showing her that nothing must be endured forever. Someone, somewhere, would be willing to take on her burden if she was able to give them something they wanted in exchange. That was the way of the trade.

Not for nothing, she told herself, are the People known as wily traders among the tribes. Of course, she had had to give up two kids, but she was not sorry. She hoped that evil goat was riding someone's belly by now.

She climbed over the corral gates and spread her skirt, herding the goats toward one corner, trying to keep the older nannies away from the ones with kids tight to their sides. She took her long herding stick and swung it slowly over her head, hissing softly to the goats, her signal to them that it was she, Pahe, who came to count them every night, and they must not be afraid.

The goats clumped nervously in one corner and then divided as she approached. More clever than sheep, they were not really afraid of her, merely stubborn about being pushed where they suddenly did not wish to go. This was the game they played each night: they pretended to balk, she pretended to get angry. Then they rushed and divided, as though reluctantly, and she followed them about trying to see the kids, the nannies' bellies, their hooves and their teats for infection. She could spend a short while at the task or many hours, it did not matter. She loved being among her animals, loved the smell and jostle and bleat of them, and she felt very womanly and mature when she thought: these creatures are mine.

Red Horn was waiting for her, pretending not to see her approach. An elderly nanny past her prime, she had one red horn and one black horn, a clear sign of wisdom. Pahe had spared her numerous times from the feast knife for those horns, but now she had infected teats, a common problem in nannies with no sucklings. She was letting the kids suckle her for the pleasure of it, and her teats were getting sore and cracked, despite the salve Pahe applied each night. The sucklings were eager, Red Horn was complaisant, and, soon, if she did not kick them away, her bag would be infected as well. And then Pahe would have to cut her throat or separate her from the herd.

Might as well kill her as cut her off from the others, Pahe knew. She was just desperate for affection, and she would let the others take from her, aye, even if she was in pain with each suckling mouth which set upon her.

Pahe crooned low and soft to the old nanny, spreading her skirt wide and flicking it to keep her distracted. She circled the goat's neck with her arms and held her still, until she felt the nanny's heartbeat slow and calm. Then she bent and looked closely at the nanny's bag, feeling gently for the heat of infection. So far, the soreness had not spread. Perhaps she had learned some wisdom after all.

"You must not let them take from you what you do not have to give," Pahe told the old goat solemnly. "Let the young mothers do their duty. Yours is to watch over that old man over there," she added, gesturing to the buck. "He needs all the help he can get, I am thinking. He might be a good husband, but he seems a poor father. Look at him, standing all alone. How will the little bucks learn their duties? You must show him how to lead them, Red Horn."

The old goat listened intently, her eyes wide and dark and moist in the shadows, her tail switching back and forth in concentration. Pahe had no doubt that she understood some of the words said to her, and more of the tone.

"Now, keep away from those greedy mouths," Pahe said in a scolding tone. "Do your duty for your clan."

The old goat slipped away, glancing over her shoulder at Pahe and frisking her ears like a yearling.

Pahe counted quickly: ten kids still suckling, same as two nights before. It looked to her as though three nannies were carrying life in their bellies. That new buck was going to be a fine breeder for less trouble, well worth the two kids she had to give her cousin to make the swap. With a sudden leap, one of the breeders, her oldest, jumped past her skirt, and then she was swamped with ten of them following the willful goat's example. Goats were smart and stubborn, but she preferred them to sheep. She sensed they enjoyed the game each night as much as she did.

As she herded the goats away from the gate and went out, fastening it behind her, she wondered if she would be married within the year, as her mother said. She placed her herding stick on the latch, as she always did, glancing back inside the corral. Now the goats were bunched as before, as if to show her how little she mattered. Like the men did when she passed. They glanced, parted to let her through, and then clumped together again in their conversation as though she had not even been there at all.

Marriage seemed like the end of her life, Pahe thought. Such a prospect seemed unreal to her, even unwelcome. She thought of her mother, of her father's other wife, Juanita, and it seemed to her that, though they were well respected, they had lived out most of their lives already. She wished to be beautiful and desired, she wished the young men to ask for her, but she did not want to be married. Not yet. She did not want to belong to someone in that way, to give herself in the foolish, desperate way she saw other girls give their hearts. She wished no other man to command her—it was enough that she had to stand up to her brothers and heed the words of her father and grandfather.

I am more goat than sheep, she smiled to herself. I am not easily herded by fools.

She heard the horses in the near corral moving restlessly, and a dog barked in the shadows. She came out of the goat pen and walked toward the corral, peering into the darkness, wondering if a coyote had sneaked into the compound. From behind, a strong arm snatched her back into the deep shadows near the fence, and a rough palm came over her mouth before she could scream. She twisted and kicked, but she was swiftly picked up off her feet and covered with a heavy blanket, a shroud which muffled her cries and blocked her vision completely. She heard hurrying footsteps, was jostled roughly onto the bony back of a horse, and the wind was knocked out of her belly as swiftly as though she'd been punched.

The horse began to canter and then to gallop, and she heard the dogs barking, the shouts of the men and a wail from the women's quarters, and then all the noise was blocked out by the pounding of hooves beneath her as her abductor rode hard away.

*   *   *

They galloped in the darkness for what seemed to Pahe to be a painfully long time. Her belly was cramped and bruised and she was breathless when they finally stopped and again, she felt the rough hands, this time pulling her down off the horse and taking the blanket off her face.

In the dark, she could dimly see moving shapes around her, several horses, and the naked, painted bodies of the Ute war party which had kidnapped her from her home. The coarse, guttural Ute tongue was easy enough to recognize, even over the snorting and wheezing of the hard-run horses, and her captors made no effort to keep their voices from her, insolent in their belief they would not be followed.

Nota-a, the Utes, had been an ancient enemy of the People for so long that it was now accepted custom that all bad things came from the north, where they lived.

She snapped at the nearest man who tried to put his hand on her arm, wrenching her shoulder from his grasp. "My father will kill you for this!"

The men laughed derisively, obviously enjoying her discomfort. One Ute bent down from his horse and said to her, "By the time Manuelito gets home from his hunting party, even our tracks will be gone."

"And you will be safe in the bed of a Mexican *hombre*, picking the fleas off his testicles!" another offered.

She laughed suddenly, scornfully. "You are fools! The men came home this night! They are even now on your trail!"

In a flurry of curses and shouts, the men wheeled their horses for flight. Her kidnapper hurriedly bound her hands behind her, tied his headscarf round her mouth, and threw her onto the horse. They took off at a hard gallop, and it was all she could do to keep her seat, with her long skirt flapping in the night wind.

Pahe kept her head down, scolding herself harshly for her hasty words. If she had only kept still, kept her eyes down and her mouth shut as her mother often warned her to do, they would have thought themselves safe. They would not have hurried, and, likely, she would be on one of her brother's horses back home before the moon was much higher.

But, no, she had to taunt them, she had to speak what she knew, and now her spine would be bounced to jelly before they would stop again, if they stopped at all.

The Ute war party seemed to be slowing as they reached the hills, and Pahe could feel the horse beneath her moving upward, straining to keep up with the horses ahead. He was panting heavily, and she felt the warrior kick and urge him faster. They climbed in the darkness, and she sweated heavily beneath the blanket, with the hot withers of the horse working under her belly. Her head was pounding with the heat, the jostling of the horse, the hard beating of her heart, and she reared upward finally and tried to pull herself desperately off the horse, even if it meant she would fall, perhaps down a cliff, but the Ute shoved her back onto the horse's back, shouting out to his companions to slow down.

The horses turned and descended, and she felt the air cool suddenly: a canyon, likely one of the many near Narbona's lands. They stopped finally and she was once more pulled off the horse and the blind taken from her eyes.

The canyon was unfamiliar to her, one of the hundred or more that pleated the hills and low mountains around Narbona's valley. The night was particularly dark here, as though the light of the moon and the stars refused to enter. The air was cooler, though, and for that, she was grateful. She ran her hand over her brow and wiped the sweat from her eyes. They were watering with the salt, and she did not wish her captives to think her weeping. She stood silent and proud, watching them as they went about preparing camp.

There were seven Ute kidnappers. No, she would not call them warriors or men, not even in her mind. Kidnappers, slavers, carrion crows who stole women and children in the dark of night. She narrowed her eyes at one of them who was staring at her, raising her chin in mute defiance, refusing to avert her eyes, a normal Navajo courtesy. To her frustration, he only chuckled and continued to stare with insolence. Once the horses were hobbled and the firewood collected, the men gathered round to throw their blankets down and pull rations from their traveling sacks. One of them grunted at her, motioning her down by the fire. She sat slowly, keeping well away from all of them. Of course, they did not offer her food or drink. She had not expected them to; they were no better than scavenging wolves.

Raiding for slaves was something the Navajo did better than the Utes, the Zuni, or the Hopi; she knew it was true now that she was among these dog-eaters. Raiding was part hunting and part religion, but of course these Utes could never understand such power. When her brothers and the other men went raiding for slaves and horses, they would spend days in the sweat house purifying themselves, singing songs and praying to the Wind People and the Sun People. Then they put on their special magic shields made of three or four thicknesses of buckskin. They anointed their arrows with magic poison made of charcoal from a lightning-struck tree; they carried stone clubs and a leather shield bordered with eagle feathers. Over themselves they threw pinches of pollen which had been shaken off a live squirrel. In this way, they made themselves invisible to their enemies and sure of victory.

But these Utes scarcely had bothered to bathe before they stole her. They were dirty as goats. She would relish seeing them die under her brothers' arrows.

Ignoring her, they talked among themselves, evidently not realizing how much of their tongue she understood. After a few moments of bragging to each other about their thievery, one of them glanced in her direction and then rose to offer her the bota bag. She took it, glaring at him, and handled it for a moment, feeling the damp coolness of it. She would have liked to put it against her throbbing forehead, but she did not want to give them the satisfaction. She took a long drink from it and then set it beside her, as though it were now her own. Daring them to try to take it from her again. At least she did not intend to be thirsty through the night.

These Ute fools followed none of the rules of raiding. They cared not what words they spoke, what they ate or drank, and they knew no hunting magic, that much was certain. They had not painted their bodies with snakes or bear tracks for power and courage as her brothers did. Her brothers! It struck her that, likely, her brothers were searching for her, even now. But there were so many canyons to hide her abductors, so many places they could disappear within, that without light to see tracks, it would be nearly impossible to follow them on the hardened ground and rocks of the hills.

She sighed and made herself sink further into the comfort of the earth beneath her. She was going to be here for at least the night. She might as well rest herself as best she could.

She tried to assess her situation in a calm manner, something her grandmother had often told her to do. "Do not fly into a passion, giving up your head to your heart," Deezbaa had warned her. "That way lies madness."

Any woman taken for a slave was more valuable if she was delivered unharmed, intact, and without obvious damage. Even the Utes knew that much. And yet, Pahe knew enough about men to understand that they did not always act in their own interest. Perhaps they wished more to insult her clan than to gain profit from her sale. She closed her eyes and gathered her will to a point in her forehead, holding it there, shining and strong.

After a few moments, she opened her eyes. Her sense of calm was unwavering. Her instincts told her that she was in no real danger. There was nothing in the wind, the night, nothing coming from the earth or the rustling junipers that warned her of peril. Likely, she realized, these fools had no real plan save that of revenge on her kinsmen for Utes stolen in earlier raids. Her kinsmen were more important to them than she was. Therefore, she could take risks; they would not dare to harm her.

The men ignored her now, talking among themselves. She was thankful she had enough Ute slaves to understand their speech, and her ears came to full alertness when she heard them speak of the strangers coming. Pahe kept her face carefully stolid and bland, but every other part of her was open and listening.

"I have seen the long-whiskers," one of the Ute brutes was boasting. "You know I know what I know. I saw them, with my clan, when we traded in Pueblo. And I tell you, my brothers, that they are going to come to us. From below where the sun constantly rises, they are going to come to us. And they will bring their long guns and their horses. Their ears are wider than anything. They extend down to their ankles. And these people at night cover themselves with their ears for sleeping."

"This sounds like a tale for women and children, to keep them close to the fires at night," one of his comrades said jocularly. "Save your words for more foolish ears."

But the man shook his head. "I am telling you true. The white men are coming. Already, they are trapping beaver in the lands of the Green River, and soon they will come to these lands."

"And if they do," another man said wearily, "we will drive them forth as we will the Navajo." He glanced over to her and spat in the fire.

She snorted in clear disgust and turned away. But her ears were still keen for the men's voices.

"The long-whiskers are miraculous men," the first speaker was going on, ignoring the disdain of some of his comrades. "They can build fires on their knees and warm themselves upon the flames. They have weapons superior to the Spanish. Their horses are strong and fast."

To Pahe, this sounded like another of the tales about spirits and monsters that were told around the campfires. Yet the Ute said he had seen such people and even traded with them. Perhaps her grandfather or her father had heard such tales—or true reports, she could not know which they might be. She must remember everything this Ute fool said, in case it might be important for her father or grandfather to know. The men talked among themselves for a while about the coming strangers, and she listened hard, knowing that her father would wish to hear all.

At the thought of her father, she felt suddenly weary and anxious. Suppose she were not found quickly enough, and the Utes took her away to a far place where she could not be rescued? Suppose she never saw her mother or grandmother, her father and her brothers again? What would Narbona say when they discovered her missing? For all of his spirit, he was frail in the body, Deezbaa said often enough. Perhaps the news of her kidnapping would harm his heart, bend his spine, make him succumb to the despair of death . . .

One of the men rose then and came to where she was sitting. "It is time for sleeping," he said, half gesturing with his hands in case she did not understand him.

She ignored him, turning away.

He reached down and hauled her upright, pulling her by her

hair. Firmly, but without anger, he directed her to the center of the men who were arranging their sleeping blankets in a circle. She froze with sudden fear and rage. If these Utes dared to touch her, against all moral law and decency—

But he only shoved her gently down in the middle of the men, who seemed to care little for her presence. She had only a moment to see that someone had taken the bota bag back again, and she was now bereft even of its small comfort, before they threw a blanket over her head suddenly, and the men took ends of the blanket, tugging it low to the ground. Grunting to each other and arranging themselves with a minimum of speech and none whatsoever directed to her, they laid themselves down on the blanket at all of its corners. Pahe was now confined under a blanket with a Ute kidnapper lying on all edges.

She struggled for a moment, speaking sharply to them and protesting the smothering tightness of the blanket and the harsh dust in her nose, her inability to move or to raise her head above her ankles. But they ignored her as though she were nothing more than a captured mare to be hobbled at their convenience.

It was true what her brothers said about the Enemy, she told herself coldly. They deserved to die. But only after they had given up all their property to those who were strong enough to take it from them. She said loudly, "My father will take great pleasure in stringing your testicles from his war lance, when he comes for me."

In answer, the closest Ute kicked at her casually, knocking her over on her side. She lay there, breathless, waiting to be kicked or beaten, but they only pulled the blanket tighter and fell into silence.

Pahe lay stiff and desperate for what seemed to her to be many hours. She felt the ground beneath her warm and soften, as though to welcome her, but she took no comfort from the earth. The sounds of the sleeping Utes were like animal noises, so close that it seemed to her she must be sleeping in dens with packs of brutes rather than with human beings.

She dozed once, and then woke, catching herself into wakefulness with a start. Her father's voice whispered in her heart: Remember that the Enemy is less than you, my daughter. They cannot defeat you without your cooperation.

Well, and she did not intend to cooperate. She listened hard for the sounds of the night, trying to tell where they might be. But the sough of the wind and the silence of the darkness was all she could hear. Finally, as the night wore on, she began slowly to creep about to the edge of her blanket, testing each corner. She discovered that one Ute had rolled away, slightly off of the side of her blanket, and she carefully eased the wool cloth away from him, holding her breath and moving as slow as ice melting. Then she was able to get her head free. She moved back under the blanket and kept pulling, gently and quietly, until, with a grunt, the Ute eased over, no doubt dreaming of his fat wife. She slipped out from under the blanket and stood for a moment, surrounded by sleeping bodies. The fire was very low, nothing more than a few embers. Likely, there were many things here she should take with her for protection in the dark, but she could not afford the chance that someone might wake while she foraged through their sacks.

She reached down and slipped a knife from one of the enemy's belts, easing it out so carefully that she scarcely breathed. She bent and cut through her hobbles, keeping her eyes on the men and sawing with a frenzy. When she was free, she took a few paces away, almost dizzy with the rush of freedom. She put the knife in her girdle and picked up one of the horse blankets off the pile at the edge of camp, wrapping her head and shoulders.

Then she hurried away, in the opposite direction of the horses, for she knew that if they saw her, they would wicker and stomp, perhaps even call to her. Pahe found the trail out of the canyon and took it downhill, praying low in her throat to all of the Holy Ones that this one would take her out of the canyon, rather than further within it. When she was far enough away from the camp that she could no longer hear the horses mumbling, she stopped and gazed up at the sky. It was wide and black as a bowl, spangled with the familiar stars she had seen since she first looked up. The moon was half full, offering just enough light to see through the brush dimly. There was no time to wait for more light.

She tightened the blanket about her shoulders, touched her knife for courage, and bent down to pick up a pinyon stick. It would not protect her from animals, but it might help her keep her balance in the night and alert the scorpions before she trod on them. She started off, shuffling her feet to warn the sleeping snakes, moving always downhill.

*   *   *

A coyote stood silently and watched Pahe picking her way down the mountain. The coyote cocked her head this way and that, twitching and widening her large ears to pick up the smallest stumble of rock under the human's feet. She did not move, for she knew from long experience that the figure moving haltingly downwind could not sense her presence, would not chase her if she did not move. The human's eyes were not keen, its nose not strong enough to hunt her.

Indeed, Latra could tell that the figure was a young female, simply by her scent, and so she felt no fear. She hunkered down on her gray haunches and watched curiously. Rarely were the humans out in the desert alone at night. More often, she saw them round their dirt caves when she came down to kill their lambs. They hunted her then, but she eluded them easily. She did not understand why they chased her with such vigor after her kills. They had many lambs, and they themselves rarely complained, for they knew their part in the hunt, and she took only enough to keep herself sleek and healthy.

Most often, it was the female humans who tended the lambs, and so Latra had seen more females of this species than males. It was the females who threw rocks at her and hurled sticks and shouted when she came close to their herds, but they also rarely had weapons. And so she was not afraid.

This one had no lambs. No weapons, either, that Latra could smell. She moved in behind the human, padding after her silently, drawn to her by her curiosity and her instinct to follow whatever moved on the desert.

Latra was *Canis latrans*, a gray coyote with buff underparts, long yellowish legs, and a bushy tail with a black tip. Her ears were larger than her coyote cousins to the north, for like other desert species as the jackrabbit, the mule deer, and the kangaroo rat, she used her ears to help aerate her head in the hottest months. She was smaller, also, than others of her clan, only twenty inches at the shoulder and twenty pounds. She was one of the best runners in the desert, faster than the wolf, able to leap fourteen feet from a standstill and keep going for good distances at more than thirty miles an hour. She ran with her tail down, unlike the wolf, which kept its tail horizontal, and she swam better than most of her prey.

Lately, Latra had been learning to sing, choosing a high vantage point from which she could watch the moon and all that moved below. Many nights, she had been developing her song, a series of barks and yelps followed by a long howl, ending with five short, sharp yaps. The call was her own, and she was hoping for a chorus soon, for Latra was in season for the first time in her life. Though she did not understand the currents of restlessness that surged through her body, she was driven to travel more than three hundred miles across the desert, searching for something. The scent of the young female who walked before her fascinated her. She put her nose to the ground carefully, keeping her eyes riveted on the human.

The human turned as if sensing her presence, and Latra froze, half crouched on the ground, making herself as small as possible. Scarcely breathing, she watched as the human gazed right through her back up the mountain, ready to flee in an instant. But then she relaxed, for the human turned once more, set upon her course down the mountain.

In the distance, Latra saw a small herd of deer on the side of the lower hill moving out of the moonlight. She lifted her nose searching for their scent. The human did not even know they were there. Then Latra decided to ignore the deer. She was too small to take down such prey without a mate. For now, she must content herself with mice, ground squirrels, frogs, snakes, and whatever else she might catch and kill.

Last season, she had good fortune. An old female badger was worrying a ground squirrel compound, a series of tunnels and holes that sheltered more rodents than the badger could consume. As she dug at one end of a tunnel, Latra pounced on whatever came out the other end. She'd had good eating for a moon or more, for the nearsighted badger made slow work of those holes. But the badger had moved on, and now she must as well.

Suddenly, the female turned again and Latra froze. All at once, the human spoke to her, and the sound of the human voice lifted the hair on the back of Latra's neck and made her whine softly.

"*Ya'at'eeh, coyotl,*" the human said. "Hello. I know you are there."

Of course Latra could not understand the words, but she knew that she was discovered. Instead of turning to run, however, she lay down on her paws, panting with a mix of fear and uncertainty. She did not wish to leave the human, and she did not understand what held her.

"Walk beside me, *coyotl,*" the human beckoned, "and show me the way to my father's lambs. I know you know the trail." The human's hand moved slowly in a welcoming manner, urging Latra forward. The hand was empty, open, and beguiling.

Latra rose up slowly and went toward the human, her head low, her tongue lolling with fear. She could not bring herself to bolt away. The human's voice was so soft, so arresting. She had heard many human voices before, and all had made her as nervous as the buzz of a rattler hidden in the brush.

But this voice was different. This one carried no menace. She came so close that the human could have reached out and touched her. Then Latra whined louder and crouched on her belly as she might before a larger male.

"I will not hurt you," the human said, slowly opening her other hand so that Latra could see that both were empty.

She cringed but she did not run.

"Come. You must show me the way."

Latra came closer now as the human turned again down the path, a deer path only, blocked by juniper and sage as it twisted its way between boulders and deep cracks in the canyon wall. She moved slightly ahead of the human, glancing back to see that those empty hands had not picked up a stone. Then she started down the mountain, following the trail easily, her eyes shining in the moonlight, panting in excitement. She knew she could be seen easily, more easily than the narrow path that the human was trying to follow. She did not know where she was headed or why she listened to that voice, but she knew that the human did not belong on the mountain.

She looked back again. The human was following her now, more quickly. She began to trot, but not so quickly that the human could not keep up.

*   *   *

After several hours walking, Pahe felt the land begin to level off, and she could see, when she looked up into the night sky, how high the mountain was where it was black against the stars. She had come a long distance, but it was still too near to her captors. On horseback, they could find her fast.

To those who did not know the land, it looked an endless maze of canyons and mesas, a labyrinth of dead ends and rock walls that wound through the slickrock deserts. But Pahe knew many of the canyons, from her years herding the flocks, as did most of her People. The Utes would not know it so well, but they would likely know it well enough to find her.

Perhaps she should hide. She could squeeze into one of the cracks of the rocks, pull herself up with handholds and move upward until she was a long way from the desert floor. But then her own kinsmen would not be able to find her, either. She was grateful it was summer. In the winter season, the nights could well be too cold for escape.

She bent and picked up two stones, and she began to sing quietly.

> Placing rocks, Male One,
> Placing rocks, Female One,
> Everywhere I go, myself,
> May I have luck,
> Everywhere my relatives go,
> May they have luck.

It was a song she had heard her mother and grandmother sing whenever they were on a trail. It was a tradition of the People, her grandmother said, to sing a song for a safe journey. Indeed, by the side of all trails all over the *Dinétah* land, she had seen cairns of rocks three or four feet high made of stones, twigs, or bits of shell. Now there would be another sacred place, a place where Pahe had come and gone, she thought. She found two more stones and piled them one on another.

She saw that the coyote stopped and stared at her. She spoke softly to the beast several times, encouraging it to lead her down the trail, and she marveled that the animal had not fled. She knew better than to raise her voice, speak too often, or make any movement with her hand toward the creature, and she sent up a prayer to her mother's spirit partner, Spider Woman, that the coyote would not abandon her or, worse still, turn and attack her. She must look strong enough to discourage attack but not strong enough to seem a threat, and she also must keep moving, keep moving as fast as she was able. She knew that some of her People thought the coyote a bad omen. They called it *Ma'ii*, the Trickster, for coyotes always waited and their bellies were never full. But to Pahe, the beast seemed somehow a great comfort: a messenger of hope and courage and home.

She thought of the new hogan her brothers had built for her. They had placed the poles just so, with the doorway to the east, as was seemly, so that when the Holy Ones came out in the morning, they would see that they were welcome within. The walls were high and smooth. The hogan was for her prayer time and her learning time, to be used exclusively by Pahe for becoming a woman. She was very proud of it, and when her mother and grandmother came to dedicate the hogan, with ceremonies to name the east pole the Earth Woman, the south pole the Mountain Woman, the west pole the Water Woman, and the north pole the Corn Woman, she had felt for the first time a part of the sacred earth, in a way grown women were meant to be, and when it was time for her Becoming-A-Woman Ceremony, the *Kinaaldá*, her home was waiting for her.

Beneath her feet, she could feel the life in the earth as she walked, could sense its hidden spirits just beneath its tough hide. The sense of space around her was vast, even in the darkness. But it did not make her feel small. Pahe was used to this quiet, empty space, this largeness of the land. To her, it was an enormous comfort, and in her mind's eye, she could soar over it as the hawk soared, seeing the revealed spine and ribs of the land, its warps and wefts of rock and sky.

She concentrated on how it would be when she reached her hogan and sat outside in the shade of the cottonwoods, when the stillness would be broken only by the croak of a raven gliding above, the brittle rustle of dry grass in the wind, the distant bleats of the lambs in the far pen.

She began to speak to the coyote, using his Spanish name so that he would not be afraid, for the Mexicans were not the hunters that the People were. She sensed that her voice was both hypnotic to the animal and alarming; she hoped to hold the coyote to her by its mix of curiosity and fear. "I will tell you now about my people," she said to the animal casually, as though she were speaking to her mare. "This is the way it was told to me, by Deezbaa, wife to Narbona, mother to Ayoi, and grandmother to Pahe.

"Are you listening?" she asked the coyote. The animal's ears were cocked back to catch her voice on the night breeze, but its paws were still moving steadily forward.

"Good. They say this, that the First People came up through the Three Worlds and settled in the Fourth World. That is this one, *coyotl,* the one we walk this night. They had been driven out of all the worlds before this one because they had quarreled with one another and did bad things to the women." She took on the scolding tone of her mother. "Those who do bad things with women, who are perverse and immoral, will be driven out and must live alone and wander always with no one."

She sighed and resumed her own tone. "But then, you know that. Anyway, the First People never saw anyone like themselves in all the land, so they were lonely. Finally, they came upon the Pueblo clan. You know the Pueblos?"

The coyote glanced back at her curiously at the lift of the question in her voice and kept on moving.

"I see you know them well enough," Pahe said wryly. "Of course the Pueblo people were as slow then as they are now. And they listened no better, either. But at any rate, the First People were at their fires, wondering what to do in this Fourth World, when four gods walked in from the night. These were White Body, the god of this world, Blue Body, the sprinkler, Yellow Body, and Black Body, the god of fire. Don't ask me about Yellow Body yet, I will tell you in time."

The coyote's tail twitched and plumed back and forth with a slight wag like a dog. Pahe chuckled softly. "You are as impatient as I was when Deezbaa told me the tale. Now, listen with both ears. These gods tried to teach the stupid Pueblo, but they couldn't make them understand. They used signs and they shouted, and still the Pueblo could not understand. So, finally, Black Body lost all patience and spoke to them in their own language. He said, 'Stupid Ones, you do not know the simplest signs of the gods, so I must tell you in plain talk. We want you to make people who look more like us and less like you. You have bodies like ours, but your hands and feet look like the beasts and insects. The new humans will have feet and hands like ours. Also, you are unclean. You smell bad. Now, we will come back in twelve days. Be clean when we return.' And then they went away."

The coyote panted happily, moving a little faster. "Yes, I know." Pahe grinned. "The Pueblo haven't changed much since then. But they finally understood at least that much. So they washed themselves, and their women dried themselves with yellow cornmeal and the men dried themselves with white cornmeal, and they waited. When the gods appeared, Blue Body and Black Body each carried a sacred buckskin. They laid the buckskins on the ground and they put an ear of white corn on one and an ear of yellow corn on the other. Under the white corn ear, they put a feather from a white eagle, and under the yellow corn ear, they put a feather from a yellow eagle. Then they told the stupid Pueblo to stand back and let the wind enter."

The coyote whined anxiously, raising her nose to sniff the wind, slowing slightly.

"Don't worry," Pahe soothed the animal. "They knew what they were doing. Anyway, the wind was blowing, and then Yellow Body—see, Yellow Body could call the gods quicker than anyone else; remember I told you I'd explain about Yellow Body—anyway, Yellow Body called the Mirage People, the People of Magic, to come and walk around the buckskins four times, and when they had finished, the gods lifted up the buckskins and underneath them was the first man and the first woman." She used her hands for emphasis, just as her grandmother had done, bending her shoulders slightly as though she took on the spirit of the old woman. "And they looked about as they do today! Except that the woman was less beautiful, because she was not yet *Dinéh*. No silver or turquoise yet, also. But anyway, they were alive. It was the wind that gave them life, and it is the wind that comes out of our mouths now that gives us life. See, when that wind ceases to blow, then we die."

She nodded encouragement to the coyote who had turned back to glance at her again. "But then you knew that, too. So the First Man and First Woman built a little hut of juniper and pinyon—the gods had not yet made them Navajo, so they did not know how to make a hogan—and they lived together as husband and wife. And four days later, the Woman had twins, a boy and a girl. And they grew up in four days and they had twins, too, another boy and a girl. And so it went, until the land was filled with People. But still, they were not Navajo. Lots of mating, like the Pueblo, but still they were not People as we are today. And the stupid Pueblo thought they were like them, but, of course, they were not. So when the last children were born, the gods came again and took the People to the eastern mountains, the place of the Holy Ones, and the People stayed there for four days. There, they learned the secrets of the Holy Ones and they learned about the Blessingway and witchcraft and a hundred mysteries. And when they came back, they were the Navajo. And so, that is how the People came to be." She laughed softly. "And they never told the secrets to the stupid Pueblo."

The coyote did not turn around when her voice ceased. She thought this was a good sign. The animal was clearly thinking over what she had told and would show that it understood when it was ready.

Deezbaa often said that there was more wisdom in silence, but no one really wanted wisdom, what everyone really wanted was pleasure and company. So that was why the Holy Ones gave us mouths. She thought of her initiation rite many seasons past, on the last night of the Night Way. It was the time of *Ye'ii Bicheii*, the Ceremony of Coming Forth, when the boys and the girls were made Navajo, instead of just People. She had ten summers that year.

Her mother and father took her to a great fire in the middle of the ceremonial grounds, where a hundred boys and girls of the clans also waited. There, they were arranged in two crescent circles on each side of the fire, the boys on the north, the girls on the south. The mothers stayed off to the west, and the fathers to the east. They joked back and forth and teased the children so they would not be afraid, but when her mother put a blanket over her head and whispered, "Do not look at the Holy Ones, my daughter," Pahe had been very much afraid, no matter how many times she had been told to feel no fear.

But she was grateful she was not a boy. The boys wore only breechcloths, and they were more afraid and nervous, it seemed to her, feeling often for their penises to see if they were hanging properly and frowning, with their eyes on the ground.

The girls wore white blankets, with their hair unbound down their backs. Pahe could hear the scratch of the blanket on her thighs, the weight of its rough heaviness on her back even now, if she closed her eyes. It was a feeling of great comfort, of rootedness, and she suddenly missed her grandmother with a deep ache. But she pushed the ache away and concentrated on the memory again.

She had stood silently with the rest of the girls in her clan, stood until her legs began to feel as heavy as her head, when finally two medicine men came forth from the crowd, wearing masks. One of the chanters was covered with white clay on his body and he wore a white mask. He was the Female. The other one was covered with ash and wore a black mask. He was the Grandfather of Monsters. Pahe had peeped out from the edge of her blanket and then shut her eyes tight, afraid of being caught spying on the Holy Ones.

They brought forth the first boy, bound his eyes, and the singing began from the mothers and fathers. The god in the white mask made a mark on his shoulder with sacred cornmeal and the god in the black mask lightly struck the cornmeal marks with sacred reeds. Each time they did this with no warning, the boy jumped and flinched, and the fathers teased him. Someone, likely an uncle or a brother, shouted for harder strikes and his mother pleaded for lighter strikes, but the masked gods always did just the opposite of what had been asked for, so the boy never knew what to expect. After each boy had been marked and struck, then the gods moved to the girls.

Pahe had closed her eyes tightly, willing herself to stand tall and firm. She was selected not first, but second, which was, she told herself, the best luck of all, for she did not have to go first but got it over quickly. The hardest part was when they bound her eyes with the red sash. When it was her turn, she was marked first on the shoulder, then on the cheek, then on the hip, and she steeled herself not to flinch. She heard her father's shout of encouragement, dimly heard her mother's cry for mercy, but was so concentrating on the gods that both her parents seemed to be calling from a far distance. Then to her surprise, the white god only pressed an ear of corn wrapped in spruce twigs gently on each mark. She could feel the heavy corn, could smell the spruce, and a flood of relief and gratitude washed over her. While the other girls were initiated, she willed herself to calmness, understanding that somehow a great mystery had been passed to her.

When the chanters took off their masks, the parents began to shout directions then, for the boys and girls to throw the pollen on the masks and then throw some on each of the gods. With shouting whoops of glee and relief, they ran at the chanters, dusting them all over with pollen. Then the chanters put the black mask or the white mask on each of them and let them look out of the eye holes so that they could see what it was like to be a god, just for a blink. Pahe remembered this moment most of all.

The chanter had whispered to her, "Look up, daughter of Ayoi, born for Manuelito. Look to the stars and see the future. Listen in the wind for the songs of the Holy People. There is no fear here, only wisdom. Tell no one what you have seen; tell all what you have heard."

She knew those words were for her alone, and she had heard them again and again in her heart. Now she told herself once more that she must remember: she must live to tell what she had heard.

Finally, after what seemed half a night of walking, Pahe stopped, taking a chance that the coyote would leave her. She had to rest, she knew, or she would begin to see things in the darkness which were not there. She sat down on her heels, as her father had taught her, letting her head drop in silence. She watched the coyote out of the corner of her eye.

The creature sat down, cocking its head at her quizzically, panting as though it had run long miles.

Pahe sighed deeply and closed her eyes. "When the sun comes up," she said softly, "you can leave me then. I will find my way."

The coyote flinched at the sound of her voice, but it did not move. She realized that the animal was somehow bound to her will in a way she did not understand. It would not leave her until she was able to make it alone. That knowledge gave her new strength and she rose again, slowly so as not to startle the coyote. It rose as well and trotted out across the desert.

As Pahe walked, she thought of her mother, her grandmother, her father. They would have missed her very soon after she was taken, and likely, even now, her father and his men were searching the nearby canyons for her. But there were so many canyons and the Utes had run so far, he could search a moon before he found their trail. She knew that her mother would be wailing, her grandmother fierce with outrage, and even Narbona would turn from his talks with the headmen to worry for his granddaughter.

Her grandmother would likely be consulting with the Yeis, the Holy Ones, bartering for her safe deliverance. Deezbaa was well known for her ability to persuade the Yeis to look on her requests with favor, and, in fact, Pahe had grown up with the coming and going of women who came to beg her grandmother to help them with their husbands, their sons, their lovers. Deezbaa was not a chanter, but she was a good hand-trembler. She could pass her hand over a person's body, chanting to the Gila Monster spirit who knows and sees everthing, and when her hand trembled, she knew where the illness hid. She could tell if the illness came from within or when it came from outside, from a person's trespass of some law of nature or offense to the Holy Ones. And more, she knew how to make the Holy Ones heal and restore the stricken one to balance and wellness.

And so they came to her hogan, bringing lambs and silver and turquoise, that she might bring them *hozho* or harmony once more.

Her grandmother had taught her when she was very small that for every evil under the sun, there was a remedy. The spirits provided the plant, the part of an animal, the essence of the earth that would heal whatever was ill or in need of repair, whether a heart or a bone.

Deezbaa knew the old remedies, and so they came. If a ewe could not drop her lamb, if a goat gave milk runny with blood, if the rain would not come, or a child was born with a twisted limb, they came, usually with their men waiting outside while the women consulted with Deezbaa over the proper cure.

But other times, they came alone. And then Pahe knew the trouble was one of the heart. A woman had quarreled with her mate or could not abide her husband's bed or feared he favored another woman's more, and so she came alone to Deezbaa's dark hogan, where the earth floor was always swept and cool, even in the hottest days of July, and no breaking heart was ever turned away without hope.

Pahe had learned to despise those women who came, creeping in with their heads down and their hair askew, wishing they would not scuttle in and out of her grandmother's door. Many of them were sensible, strong women who had been turned to fools over love. She was ashamed for them, and turned her head away so that they would not be more shamed by her seeing them go inside Deezbaa's door. She sometimes wished, too, that her grandmother was more like other grandmothers, who contented themselves with weaving and the flocks and tormenting their husbands and their slaves.

But most of all, Pahe wished that she would never be one of those women, never have such a pain in her heart that she would seek out help, and so, early on, she had decided never to love a man like those women did. It was obviously more trouble than it was worth.

Deezbaa always moaned sympathetically when she saw one of these women arrive; whether she came by foot or on her pony, Deezbaa had but to glance out her door to see that she was in pain. She could read love's desperation a quarter mile in the distance, though she could scarcely see the goats if they got outside their pen.

These women would give up silver and turquoise, would give away their best ewe, their whole crop of spring lambs, if only Deezbaa would help them get back the love they had lost. They were as twisted as pig tails with desire, and Pahe wanted none of it. That way was madness, she was certain.

She stopped once more and looked slowly all around her. The coyote stopped, too, glancing back at her patiently. To her right was the high, stark spine of the Abajo Mountains. She knew if she kept them to her right, she must come out soon to the river. Once she came to the river, she was not far from home. It still was not light to the east, but she guessed that it must be halfway through the night at least.

Once the sun rose, she would be more certain of her surroundings. And less afraid of where she put her feet. She knew that in the darkness, the rattlesnakes, the spiders, the poison lizards, and the scorpions were more likely to be insulted by her intrusion. But she was determined to keep on. She pictured her father's face, handsome, concerned, and searching, and she kept on.

She imagined herself herding the flocks, so as to keep herself moving. When she was small, she had herded, as did most of the children. In the morning, she let the sheep out of the corral. She sang a song as she opened the gate, and when she was half finished with the song, the sheep were half out; when she was all finished with the song, the sheep were all out.

She hummed it to herself now, thinking of the quiet as the sheep ate the sparse grass all the day. She watched for loco weed, what the People called *ch'il'agháni*, for if the sheep ate it, they would run about and froth at the mouth and go mad. If they ate sagebrush, she could not let them have water or they would get blown up. If they got blown up, she had to punch them in the belly until they vomited up what they had eaten. If they would not throw it up, she would have to lead them back home, and her mother would take a needle and puncture their bellies to let the gas escape. But often, the sheep so treated would die, or flies would get into the wound and blow them up again. Also, they would get blown up if they ate milkweed in the spring, or they'd vomit and die if they ate owl-foot weed.

She sang all the songs for the protection and increase of the flock, but they were such stupid animals, it was hard to protect them from themselves. Goats were smarter but harder to herd, for they were stubborn creatures with wills as strong as her own. She was glad she was too old to herd the flocks anymore.

Pahe walked up a steep mesa, following the coyote at a slight distance now as she grew more weary, pretending she was herding her sheep again. The night seemed to go on forever. It was colder now, and she held her arms close to her side to save their heat.

She thought of her mother, how she brushed her long, black hair into such skillful coils and ropes, twisting them in designs that other women tried to imitate. She could hear her mother's hair moving when she wore it down, long over her back, could hear it whisper over her shoulders even before she heard her footsteps.

In the distance, Pahe now heard a faint howling, and she looked up anxiously at the coyote. The animal heard it, too, of course, and turned its head in that direction. But the coyote kept on going.

Pahe thought of how she had been named for her ears, named by her grandmother when she was not yet able to stand. Deezbaa had told the tale often. How Pahe, even as a baby, tilted her head and listened to the rain before it fell. How she pointed to the window of the hogan moments before a dragonfly appeared at that spot. How she looked to the door and smiled well before her mother's footsteps came up the dusty path.

"We will call her She-Who-Hears-The-Sun," Deezbaa had told Ayoi. "She will one day hear the very winds as they whisper."

And so only her family called her Pahe, Little Bird, if they said her name at all. To the People, a person's name had such power, such intimacy, that it should not be used idly. To the clansmen, to distant kin, and to strangers, she was known as At'ééd Jóhonaa'éí Yidiits'a'í, She-Who-Hears-The-Sun, but they called her Granddaughter to Narbona or Daughter of Manuelito, and they smiled at her oddly, as they did her grandmother, as though they were afraid not to.

Pahe knew that once she had found a husband, she would be looked upon as complete and whole. Even if she did not intend to love him with the same passion others allowed themselves, she still wished for that peaceful contentment that she saw in other wives' faces. One part of her heart wished never to marry; in another part, she wished for that part of her life to be decided once and forever.

Finally, it seemed to Pahe that it was growing lighter on the horizon behind her, and she knew that she had been walking west, toward the setting sun, in the right direction toward home. The mountains were still on her right side, the darkness behind was growing more gray than black, and she could begin to see small differences in the shadows on either side. She sat down again to rest, no longer afraid.

The ground beneath her feet had very little soil. It was mostly bare rock. And yet she knew that soon she would come to a canyon close to the river, and there she would find a grove of cottonwood and pockets of green grass, even in the summer.

Hidden ferns and small flowers would be peeping from grottos and seeps in the canyon walls.

She would not be alone. Indeed, she rarely felt alone in the desert. Often she came upon rocks covered with drawings and paintings of huge men more than twice her height, surrounded by pictures of antelopes and salamanders and snakes. She knew most of the places where the Old Ones had their abandoned hogans and towns, ruins of pueblos and kivas and sacred towers to their gods. Manuelito told her that they had lived in these places far before Narbona's father's father had been born. She had often picked up pieces of broken pottery and carried them about for pleasure. The spirits of these Old Ones were all around her. The desert was not a lonely place.

The coyote had stopped and was hunkered down patiently. The two regarded each other calmly, as though they had been companions for a season instead of a night.

"I am grateful," Pahe said softly to the creature, noticing now that it was lighter how very beautiful was its fur. "I know the way now."

The coyote stood and shook itself all over. It whined once and snapped at its flanks as though to dislodge something, and then turned without a backward glance and loped off across the mesa. Pahe watched as the animal picked up speed and finally disappeared over the rise of the hill.

It began to rain, a soft female rain. Pahe smelled the air, sniffing the welcome scents of good grazing and crops that Sky Father was bringing to Mother Earth. Her mother always wore her hair down her back when it rained, her black hair raining down in harmony with the earth. She sang a quiet chant: "When I cross a deep canyon, with nowhere for a belly and nothing for a heart, I seek my friend, Rainbow. I walk softly as a young deer, following Rainbow's rain-colored road." She turned and welcomed the rising sun with another prayer, and then started off in the direction of home.

*   *   *

Deezbaa and Ayoi sat silently in the weaving shelter, each one working at her tall loom. It was where they usually spent many pleasant hours of each day, fingers moving rapidly over the coarse woolen threads, pulling and combing and running the wooden shuttle through the wool to make the colorful blankets the men would wear at the next clan meeting. The slaves sheared, washed and carded the wool, making the saddle blankets and their own clothing, but the personal blankets of the men for honored occasions, those only Ayoi and Deezbaa would weave.

The women of Narbona were well respected for their loom work, and it was said that Spider Woman looked upon their weaving with more favor than most. They made their blankets in the traditional colors of creamy white, brown, red, yellow, and black, but they often carded two wools together, and so they got colors of more subtle shadings: grays, tans, and browns, which few of the other clans produced.

In the summer, they could most often be found in the weaving shed; in the winter months, they used the weaving hogan, the earthen house where the women went for tasks requiring concentration, away from the smoke and clamor of the central family hogan. Once there, they were free to speak their minds about any subject under the sun.

Usually, their mouths moved as rapidly as their fingers, laughing, complaining, teasing, and trading gossip. But today, they had little to say to one another, each one lost in her own thoughts. It had been three days since the men galloped off in search of Pahe, and still no news. Each day, they prayed that she was safe, that she was even, in that moment, astride Manuelito's mount, coming home to them. And each night, they were disappointed.

Ayoi murmured, for at least the third time, "I should have taken more care. She was of the age when a slave should have been with her at all times. But I still think of her as my child—"

"She is, of course," Deezbaa said shortly. They had had these words before, and she was impatient with her daughter's sadness. Sadness led to weakness, and neither of them could afford such weakness now. "Even had a slave been right beside her, they still would have stolen her, likely the slave as well. You are wasting your heart on such regrets."

To Deezbaa's surprise and concern, Ayoi suddenly bowed her head and began to weep softly, her hands dropping away from her loom and covering her face. Deezbaa rose and went to her daughter's side, moaning slightly with sadness. "You must be

strong with faith," she said to her gently, "and not give yourself
to despair. This daughter will come home safely—"

"How do you know such a thing?" Ayoi asked desperately.
"Daughters are stolen every season and most of them never
return!"

"Not Narbona's granddaughter," Deezbaa said firmly, gripping Ayoi's shoulder. "And Narbona's daughter must hold up
her head and let the slaves and her kinsmen see that she has the
courage to do what is difficult in life."

"What could be more difficult than losing a daughter?" Ayoi
moaned.

"Losing your heart. Losing your courage. Losing your own life
as well as the respect and dignity of your clansmen." She reached
down and took up a corner of the blanket Ayoi was weaving in
the colors of black, red, and green, Manuelito's colors. Ayoi was
one of the few women who knew how to blend the colors to such
brightness, using the minerals she dug from the earth as mordants
and mixing them with fermented urine she stored in her clay
pots.

Deezbaa wiped her daughter's cheeks, tucked back her hair,
and placed her hands once again on her loom. "You are Narbona's
daughter. You are wife to Manuelito. Your daughter is blessed
by the Holy Ones in ways you can scarcely know at her young
age. The Utes took her because they wished to weaken your
husband and your father. Your tears help them to do this."

Ayoi straightened her shoulders and took a breath, and at
that moment, a slave woman entered the weaving hut, glanced
timorously at the two women and asked, "Will you come and
take the meal?"

Deezbaa said, "Of course," speaking for them both and helping
her daughter to stand. "Go, and say we follow."

The slave went out again, fearful of their grief and obviously
anxious to be away from her mistresses. "Now, come," Deezbaa
said firmly, straightening Ayoi's hair and pulling her forward.
"The others will look to see if you smile so that they know all
will be well."

The two women went out into the blinding sunlight, shielding
themselves from the glare with their blankets. Deezbaa was heartened to see that Ayoi stood a little taller, held her head up, and

ignored the bows and compassionate murmurs of the slaves they passed, as was seemly. As they rounded the corner of the corral toward the hacienda, Ayoi suddenly stopped and cried out. Deezbaa took her arm to steady her, and Ayoi pulled away, pointing out to the mesa. "There! Something is out there!"

Deezbaa squinted against the sun, but her eyes were too feeble at distances to see anything at all. The dogs were not barking, so it could not be the hunting party. "What is it?"

But Ayoi had thrown off her arm and was running, her blanket loosened and dropping to the ground, toward some moving point in the distance that Deezbaa could not see. She turned and started to call out to a nearby slave for him to run and get his master, but then she thought better of it. She watched and waited, and as Ayoi grew smaller and the thing she was running toward grew larger, Deezbaa began to laugh, for she could tell by her daughter's body what it was she was running to embrace.

Now she called to a slave, "Run and tell your master that my granddaughter is returned to me!"

The slaves set up a clamor, some of them hurrying to see for themselves and peering around her, others racing to be the first to tell Narbona of the good news. Deezbaa chuckled and leaned against the corral fence, watching as now the two figures turned and came together back to the hacienda. "I said that she would escape the Ute dogs, for they are despised by all the Holy Ones," Deezbaa said loudly to the slaves. She did not miss an opportunity to let the slaves know that it was their own good fortune to be taken up by her clansmen, and that, indeed, it was better to be a slave within a Navajo clan than free within any other. "And so, here comes She-Who-Hears-The-Sun! I wonder how many of them she made foolish before she tricked them."

Now the two figures were coming closer, and Deezbaa walked with slow dignity to meet her granddaughter and daughter, noticing with great satisfaction that Pahe looked well, if tired, that she walked firmly on the earth, and that she was mindful enough of the slaves watching to keep her tears inside. Deezbaa embraced her granddaughter and murmured to her, "I told the Holy Ones to see you safely home, my little bird."

"She is safe," Ayoi said softly. "She escaped them and followed a spirit partner home to us."

"A spirit partner? Which one of my people came to help you, my granddaughter?" Deezbaa felt all of the Holy Ones belonged to her, personally.

"*Coyotl* came to me," Pahe said wearily.

"*Coyotl!*" cried Deezbaa. "The Trickster! But he is a messenger of great power! And what did he reveal to you?"

"The way home," Pahe said, her knees nearly buckling, now that she felt her mother's arms around her. "I am very tired."

"She is safe!" Ayoi cried happily, embracing her again. "They did not insult her."

Deezbaa laughed now with relish. "Of course they did, as they did all of our clan. But they did not put their dog-penises inside her, and when her father catches them, they will think of that, as it was the last chance they had to use those useless organs forever."

Pahe smiled faintly. "I am very hungry."

"She followed the river, down out of the mountains—"

"Let her tell the story once," Deezbaa said, then briskly to Ayoi, bundling her granddaughter in her bony arms, "Narbona waits."

The three women walked arm in arm down the length of the corral, acknowledging the greetings of the slaves, and when Pahe rounded the gated yard and saw that Narbona stood in the door of his hogan waiting for her, she realized that it was the first time in her memory that he had waited for a woman thus. She smiled then, more strongly, and lifted her arm to wave to him, resisting the urge to run to him like a child. She walked to him, tall and strong, as she thought a woman should walk.

*   *   *

There were many places in the Four Corners region that seemed uninhabitable. Places where there was almost no soil, and only a few tough, scabrous plants such as sagebrush, snakeweed, and saltbrush managed to survive on what appeared to be barren rock. And yet even places like these had their mysteries. Descend down into a rocky canyon, and one could find hidden groves of cottonwood trees and pockets of grass, supported by underground springs and tiny trickles of rock-cradled water. Sometimes the walls were covered with pictographs and petroglyphs of huge, faint giants with headdresses and kilts more than ten feet high, surrounded by drawings of bighorn sheep, antelopes, coyotes, snakes, and lizards, their colors of red and brown and yellow still perceptible within the protected canyon walls. Everywhere, even on the barest ground, were the remains of the peoples who had lived or simply passed the land, leaving the debris of their villages, their pueblos, their cooking fires. The dry desert air preserved it all, down to the charred kernels of corn, which were more than seven hundred years old but looked as though the ancient Anasazi just finished the meal a month before.

In one of these barren places, a small herd of antelope had found shelter from predators and a hidden pocket of food and water. They were *Antilocapra americana,* meaning "antelope goat," but the Pronghorns of the desert were neither goat nor antelope. In fact, they were not even closely related to either, but were instead a single species, the sole remnant of an ancient family dating back twenty million years and surviving only in this small region on a single continent.

Tilo, a buck of four years, stood guard at the rear of the herd, watching the six does which were under his protection. He was a medium-size animal, three feet high at the shoulder, weighing about one hundred twenty pounds, deerlike from a distance, with a pale tan upper body and a white chest, belly, and rump patch. The broken pattern of his coat made him harder to see from a distance, particularly in the heat mirages of the desert. He had two broad white blazes across his tan throat and a broad black band from his eyes down to his snout. His does had no such black blaze, but, more important, his does did not have his horns. Small horns, yes, but not horns of splendid size and shape as his own.

Tilo's horns, from whence he got his name, were unbranched, and they grew continually and would so long as he lived, which if he were lucky and could escape enemies, would be four or five more years. His horns shed their sheath of keratin each year, but their length only increased, lyre-shaped, curving back and tipped with a broad short prong which jutted up like a hooking finger.

Tilo kept his eyes constantly moving over the open ground and the upper rocks, his short mane erect and at attention. At the least suggestion of danger, he gave a warning snort, stamped his small heart-shaped hoof and erected his white mane and white rump hairs in a flashing signal, making his does startle and run.

Run, run, run—it was the beat of his heart and all that the herd lived for and by. Tilo had been born in these canyons, and he knew them well. His mother, like all does, had dropped him in May, after a breeding in September, half of twins, for he was her third breeding. He was born with an unspotted coat, weighing only about four pounds, with no odor at all and unable to run. His brother was identical, and they stayed hidden in the grass a good distance from their grazing mother, waiting for her to come back and nurse them several times a day. After five days, they joined the herd, and Tilo and his brother could, by then, outrun a man. But, unfortunately, Tilo's brother could not outrun the coyote pack which attacked that spring, and no matter how hard Tilo's mother fought them, threatening them with her hooves and horns, she could not protect both fawns.

Tilo learned then that only his speed could save him, for he ran from the terror of the coyotes, ran desperately with a pounding heart in horror, not even wasting breath with cries, until he stopped and looked and they were not there. Neither, however, was his brother. When his mother came to his side, he ran in circles around her, unable to stop running until the fear subsided and the scent of the death was no longer at his heels.

Now he was a full-grown buck of a species which was the fastest animal in the Western Hemisphere, among the fastest in the world, able to make twenty-foot bounds and run at seventy miles an hour for five minutes at a time with his mouth open, not from exhaustion, but to gasp extra oxygen. He could easily run at thirty miles an hour for more than fifteen miles, if he had to do so. His large, protruding eyes had a wide arc of vision and could detect movement four miles away. Coyotes did not frighten him anymore, but each time he saw one, he felt the rage of loss that he could not comprehend nor scarcely remember.

Now, Tilo began to move his does down the canyon, gently pushing them away from the grass and onto the open plain. Dusk was coming, and it was necessary to move away from the cover of the high canyon walls, for predators could more easily take them there. The breeding would be soon, he knew it. And then would begin the only time of the year when something mattered more than running. Then would begin the time of the rut, when he must battle other bucks to hold his does, staring down rivals, snorting, chasing them off, and using his splendid horns to fight them away. This season, he would have the largest bunch of does he had ever had, and he was fiercely proud of his prowess. Older bucks might have fifty or more does, but Tilo could not know this. To him, each season was the only season there was.

A sudden movement in a small copse of cottonwood caught his eye, and he snorted angrily. All six does instantly looked up from their feeding and then to where he stared. A patch of sunlight dappled with shade moved of its own accord, and then it was a puma, and then it was bolting from cover toward the nearest doe. Tilo snorted again and bounded from a standstill to a flanking movement behind the herd, trying to get between the does and the puma, and the doe chosen for attack bleated once, leaping high and wide away from the snatching claws. The puma raked her back legs, trying to trip her up, but she scrabbled away and bolted, bouncing ten feet in the air and away. In a second, the herd was in motion, running from the threat; in ten seconds, the herd had raced almost a quarter of a mile, leaving the threat behind.

Tilo circled them continuously, snorting and ruffling his mane, calming them down and bunching them close. Now they were out on the open ground, where he had wanted them to be anyway. The puma was not visible over the flat, open terrain, and he could detect no other danger near.

With small preamble, Tilo approached the largest, oldest doe, circled her quickly, sniffed her vaginal ruff, shouldered her roughly, and then mounted her. She walked away under him, forcing him to fall off. He came at her again, feeling that after such an escape, he was due his reward. But the doe flinched away and snorted, letting him know that she was unready for his attentions.

Tilo shook his head as though a swarm of flies had bothered him and stood staring out over the horizon. The does were unreliable. They would come and go, leaving their fawns and finally leaving him, though he could only vaguely sense that on an instinctive level. What mattered was the running.

Running was all that mattered, when it was all over.

Wisdom which his mother had passed to him with her milk, memories of her teachings came back to him now in small bits and starts, flashes of thoughts: the last hooves up in any chase will surely be the first to die, sniff the air and stamp the earth, for you must run soon past your birth. Run, for there's nothing fleeter, run where the grass is sweeter; run, for life is swift but death is slow, so run. Tilo saw that the sun was low now, and he bunched the does together, moving them away from all cover. Tomorrow, he would try to mount the doe again.

But today was the running.

*   *   *

The sun was going low on the horizon. Golden light began to move up the valley, filling the aspen with shimmering yellows and rustling whites. Inside her hogan, Deezbaa was preparing for the Blessingway Ceremony for Pahe, roasting the mutton ribs and making the corn mush. She looked out the door of her hogan again for the tenth time impatiently, and finally she saw the *Hataalii* approaching on his dark horse. She called out to Ayoi, "The chanter comes!" The *Hataalii* or chanter had been many miles away when Manuelito sent a runner for him, but finally he had come.

Pahe came out of her mother's hogan at Deezbaa's call, took a deep breath, and calmed herself. She reminded herself that this Blessingway Ceremony was for her, in her honor, and there was no shame in needing such a cleansing after all she had endured. Now she would be protected again by the Four Sacred Mountains. Now she would be supported once more in the right path, after coming back from the alien places and peoples who had stolen her.

The chanter leaned down and spoke to Deezbaa and then rode in the direction of Ayoi's hogan. Pahe stood quietly, watching him, though she had seen him many times before. He was an old man, and under his head scarf his hair was gray and wiry as a ram's tail. He wore a single silver necklace and double turquoise bracelets on both wrists.

As he came near he said, *"Ya'at'eeh,* daughter of Ayoi, born for Manuelito. Hello and good health."

"Ya'at'eeh, Hataalii," she said softly.

"It is a good night for the Blessingway. You are ready?"

"I am," she murmured. She knew that it was not usual for the chanter to speak so to her directly. Normally, he would speak to her father and her mother only. But she had gone to the edge of the world and returned, and so he was honoring her by treating her as a grown woman.

Ayoi came to the door then and said, "Manuelito waits, *Hataalii*. We will follow you."

Ayoi and Pahe walked then to Deezbaa's hogan and, together, the three women went to the hogan in the center of the hacienda used for the ceremonies of purification. Now the moon was rising, and Pahe could see its roundness moving swiftly into the dark sky. The Blessingway could only take place when the moon was full, and so they were bathed in light as they walked.

When Pahe reached the hogan, she saw that all was made ready for her. The hogan reflected the rising white light of the moon and stood silent and dark, as though it had been there for generations. Her clansmen and all of the headmen who had gathered with their families waited outside, talking quietly among themselves. The chanter was there, standing by Manuelito and Narbona. Juanita, her stepmother, smiled gently at her in encouragement. Her brothers were there as well, and she caught Jádí's smile as she walked past him, ducking her head so that her own smile would not be so obvious.

Pahe followed Ayoi and Deezbaa through the open doorway, and she sat to the left of the fire, her mother and grandmother and stepmother then proceeding around the rounded room after her in the sunwise direction, as was proper. The walls were covered with gray sheepskins, and the floor was bare except for the sheepskins for her to sit upon. It was cool inside the high, domed hogan, and Pahe pulled her blanket tightly around her shoulders. The chanter and her father and Narbona followed her inside now, and then other headmen and other clansmen and women, until the hogan was as full with the people as the space would allow. The others, she knew, would wait outside, taking pleasure from the nearness of the ceremony, even if they could not see every movement within.

The chanter man sat down by the door now and told a small story in low tones, a tale of a sheep sold to a Zuni headman, a sheep which was more trouble than a dozen goats. The men and women laughed appreciatively when he had finished, louder than was even necessary, and Pahe knew that he told the story both to make them happy and to wait until the moon was in the right position to begin.

Finally, the chanter took out a buckskin medicine bundle, and from his bundle he took a small pipe and filled it with tobacco made from the top of the *Azee'ntlini*, the red mallow flower. From another pouch, he took a bag of corn pollen and set it on the earth before him. Manuelito took a small stick and bent to the fire, letting it kindle and glow. He handed it carefully to the medicine man, who lit the pipe and puffed it into strength.

"Take off your moccasins," Ayoi whispered to Pahe.

Pahe took off her moccasins so that her bare feet rested on the soft sheepskin.

Now the chanter began to sing in an ancient falsetto nasal voice, and he took large puffs of smoke and blew first one upward, to Father Sky, then downward to Mother Earth. He blew smoke on his palms and rubbed his palms on his feet, his legs, and his chest and face, to give himself spiritual strength. He continued chanting, now passing the pipe to Manuelito, who took large inhalations, and passed it to Narbona. Each man then took the pipe, washing himself with the smoke and adding his voice to the chants, and the women, too, Ayoi and Deezbaa and Juanita, and all of the others, until all had smoked and all had washed themselves in the smoke, and all were chanting together.

Finally, the pipe was passed to Pahe. She wondered that there was any tobacco left at all within, but to her surprise, the smell and taste of the stuff was strong and bitter and cool, all at once. She took deep puffs, aware that all were watching her, and then she blew the smoke on her chest, her hands, her legs and feet, as the chanter sang about the Smoke of Life.

The singing went on for so long and the pipe kept passing around, and the chanter repeated the same rich deep sounds, with everyone all together, first his voice alone and then all of them repeating.

Pahe felt as though the top of her head was lifting slowly, gently, right off her skull and hovering above her body near the top of the hogan. She glanced at her grandmother, and Deezbaa smiled at her slowly, a private warm smile which made Pahe feel as though her grandmother was inside her as well as next to her.

The chanter finally retrieved the pipe and, as the singing continued, shook the ash from the pipe into a clay bowl of water. He
mixed the ash and the water and dipped his fingers in the liquid,
dabbing himself on the mouth, the forehead, the arms and legs,
and passed the bowl to Manuelito. From her father, the bowl
came to her mother and then to Pahe, and each did the same
thing with the liquid. Pahe passed the bowl to Deezbaa, and she
passed it to Narbona, and then to the other headmen, and finally
all had touched the ash and water mix and anointed themselves,
and, still, the chanting went on, slow and low and hypnotic. The
bowl was finally brought back to the chanter, and he handed it
to Pahe. There was only a small bit left of the liquid, and he
gestured to her that she should drink it.

She did so, without hesitation, and she was surprised once
more at how cool and comforting it felt going down her throat.

The chanting continued, and Pahe felt no weariness. She looked
around at the faces of her relations and her kinsmen, and she saw
no sleepiness, no fatigue, though many of them had come many
miles for the Blessingway.

The chanter took the corn pollen then and touched Pahe with
it, on the sole of her foot, on her knee, on her hip, her chest, her
shoulders, and her head. He then gently touched her jaw, and
she opened her mouth, closing her eyes. He put the smallest part
of corn pollen on her tongue, and the chanting rose higher and
higher around her like a benediction.

Somewhere in the night, before the dawn, Pahe was led out
of the hogan by her mother and her grandmother and behind the
hogan. Shielded by blankets held by Juanita and the other women
in her clan, she was cleansed and purified. Her hair was washed
with yucca roots and fresh water, her body was rubbed with white
corn meal. When she was cleansed and dressed once more, she
was brought back inside the hogan for the remaining chants, still
amazed that she felt no need for sleep.

When dawn came, the chanter led her out of the hogan and
to a small rise behind the hacienda, the rest of the people following
behind. As they walked, he reminded her that she carried the
continuity of life in her body, that all of her family, her clan, her
people, supported her in her walk back to beauty and wholeness
and balance. Pahe closed her eyes and felt the prayers flowing

through her still, all the voices giving her acceptance and taking strength from her courage. On the rise, he faced the rising sun and murmured to her how to take the sun's life into her body. She breathed and opened her arms as he told her, her eyes closed, facing the sun.

"May you walk always in beauty, daughter of Ayoi, born for Manuelito," said the chanter to her gently.

And then they walked slowly back to the hacienda, to share the feast prepared by the women.

Pahe was herself again. She was home.

*   *   *

Two days later, Pahe sat in a circle of headmen, relating again the story she had told three times since her safe arrival home. First, she had told her mother and grandmother. Then, Narbona had asked to hear the story from her own lips. When Manuelito arrived, summoned by the runners with the news that his daughter was safe, she told it again. And now, at the invitation of Narbona, six headmen sat silently, their pipes glowing in the shadows around her, as she related her capture by the Utes.

To her surprise, she was not afraid. She remembered what the chanter told her at the Ceremony of Coming Forth. Tell what you have heard, he said. And so she began.

"They said that the white men were coming from over the mountains," she said softly, "from where the sun rises. Within two seasons, perhaps three. They are bringing large guns, cannons they said, which will kill many warriors at once. And they are bringing their women and their horses."

The headmen looked grim and solemnly nodded. Several began to murmur together, and Narbona did not attempt to stop them. Pahe watched carefully, noticing that the old man allowed them to speak among themselves for several moments before he held up his hand requesting silence.

"Did they say why the whites were coming?"

"To make war on the Mexicans," Pahe said.

Now the murmurings grew louder. One headman said, "If the whites are coming with a large army to make war on the Mexicans, then perhaps our women and children will soon be returned to us."

The men were respectfully silent. The headman who spoke was from a clan who had lost four women and seven children to Mexican raids.

"Did the Utes say anything else?" Narbona asked quietly after long moments had passed.

"Think hard, Daughter," Manuelito said gently. "There were no other words?"

She shrugged lightly. "They said that the long-whiskers have ears long enough to cover themselves when they sleep. But I supposed this to be untrue."

"Leave it to us to suppose," Manuelito said. "Repeat all that you heard."

Pahe thought for a long moment. Narbona's eyes had drifted to the fire. She sensed that he would wait, would expect the others to wait, as long as it might take for her to remember.

"Only this," she finally said. "The Utes said that the long-whiskers were men of miracles, for they can build fires on their own legs for warmth."

The circle of men was struck silent at that. Pahe had half expected to hear scornful laughter, but no one laughed.

"There is more?" Narbona asked then.

"There is no more," she said softly.

"Thank you, Daughter," Manuelito said. "You may go to your mother now."

Pahe rose unsteadily and went out of the circle of men, infinitely relieved to be away from all those somber eyes. As she came out of the dark room, her mother and Deezbaa were waiting.

"What did they say?" Ayoi asked.

"That does not matter," Deezbaa said shortly. "What did Narbona say?"

"Nothing. He only listened. All of them listened. And then my father told me to go out."

Deezbaa raised her brows. "This means that what she told them was not known before. This means that they must speak of it together before they can decide what must be done."

"This means, then," Ayoi said kindly, "that you have done the People a great service by bringing this news. I am proud to have such a daughter, who is called to speak to the headmen of what she has heard."

Deezbaa turned her granddaughter to her so that she might look into her face more closely. "Is there anything else you need to say to us of this . . . incident?"

Pahe knew that her grandmother chose her words carefully. In the tradition of her people, she knew that so long as a woman did not consider herself degraded, she was not degraded. So long as she had not, in her own mind, been violated, she was not violated. Pahe knew that Deezbaa wished to keep her abduction as small as possible, a tiny corner of her mind that would not infect her heart, a place she would not need to inhabit very often in her life. "No, my grandmother," she said evenly. "There is nothing else."

Ayoi searched her face anxiously, and Pahe allowed herself a smile. "I think no matter how hard you look, you will see nothing here but me."

Ayoi laughed with relief and embraced her.

Deezbaa tugged gently at her long braid. "Come, Little Bird. We will speak of this no more. Let us go where the eyes of men cannot follow."

Pahe nodded wearily. "If I never have to be stared at again by such eyes, I will die happy."

"Oho!" chuckled Deezbaa. "You will change those words soon enough!"

"Not too soon," Ayoi said, embracing her daughter again and kissing her cheeks. "When you were taken, I thought my heart would break. I will not, so easily, give you up again."

"Neither will I," murmured Pahe.

*   *   *

The Utes may have been foolhardy dogs, as the People called them, but they were right about the coming of the white men. The American of the 1840's was energetic, restless, vigorous, and possessed of unwavering faith in his democratic institutions, so unwavering that his call for "Manifest Destiny" became a flag under which territorial expansion became a sacred religion.

At first, the United States offered to buy the territory that would one day become California, Nevada, Utah, Arizona, New Mexico, and parts of Wyoming and Colorado from Mexico for thirty million dollars. But when Mexico refused to negotiate, President Polk decided to take it. He ordered General Zachary Taylor to march into Mexican land and take "the whole hog, not just the trotters," declaring war with Mexico the minute Taylor's army was fired upon for trespassing.

Colonel Stephen Kearny was one of the first called to arms, and ordered to organize the Army of the West at Fort Levenworth, Kansas. He promptly set off for Santa Fe and reached Bent's Fort in Arkansas in the last week of July 1846. Not wishing to lose a man unnecessarily, Kearny sent a delegation to bribe the governor of Santa Fe to walk away from the fight for twenty-five thousand dollars in gold. Governor Manuel Armijo decided to "submit to fate," pocket the bribe, and leave Santa Fe to the Americans. Thus, Colonel Kearny marched into Santa Fe without firing a shot, raised a flag, and declared New Mexico a possession of the United States by right of conquest on August 22, 1846.

Having acquired the land, the first thing Kearny decided to do was set about to create a view. Recently promoted to Brigadier General, he felt he needed a commanding post worthy of his new position, and so he built Fort Marcy just northeast of the city on the highest peak he could find.

Next, he looked about and decided that his primary role should be that of protector to the New Mexicans under the American flag, so he issued a proclamation stating that since, "the Navajos come down from the mountains and carry off your sheep and your women whenever they please, my Government will correct all this. We will keep off the Indians and protect you in your persons and property."

Meanwhile, of course, the Navajo knew the Americans were coming before they crossed the borders of the Mexican Territory. No sooner had Kearny arrived in Santa Fe, but Navajo raiders noticed the superiority of U.S. Cavalry horses and stole a small herd belonging to the Army. This theft annoyed Kearny. It seemed to him that if the Mexicans could be so easily brought to heel, the Navajos should pose even less of an obstacle. He called on Narbona, then nearly eighty years of age, to come to Santa Fe to make peace terms for his people.

Narbona consulted with the rest of the headmen as to whether or not to accept the American invitation to a peace talk. Two recent Navajo peace parties on their way to Santa Fe had been ambushed, and Deezbaa insisted that the Holy Ones were warning him not to go. Narbona sent word to Kearny that he would talk peace, but only on his own territory. Kearny agreed and said he would send word about the meeting time and place.

Narbona then set out with a few close companions to see what manner of people these white men might be. He took a secret trail through the mountains of Santa Fe, coming upon the fort from the north, and observed the scene from a safe distance.

What he saw impressed him, and he went back to his home in the Tunicha Valley with recountings of regimental drills, parades, waving flags, and the sounds of thunderous cannon fire coming from the walls of Fort Marcy. After due deliberation, Narbona counseled the People to follow the peace trail with the Americans.

PART ONE

1847–1861

"Their skill in manufacturing and their excellence in some useful and ornamental arts show a decided superiority of genius over all the other tribes of the Western Continent. They have fine flocks of sheep, abundance of mules and herds of cattle of a superior kind. They have gardens and peach orchards. Several articles of their woolen manufacture equal the quality of ours."

—Samuel Patton, writing of the Navajo in
the Missouri *Intelligencer*, 1824

Narbona and Manuelito had been holding council since the morning meal. No one came or went from the men's hogan for many hours. Deezbaa, Ayoi, and Pahe sat at their weaving looms, their fingers moving the shuttles back and forth in what seemed to be concentrated work. In fact, Pahe knew that her grandmother scarcely saw the pattern she created. Her inner eye was focused on the conversation she imagined between her husband and her son-in-law.

Finally, Deezbaa said fretfully, "The young warriors all want war, that much is certain. The old man can scarcely close his ears to *all* of their voices."

"He can if he thinks they are fools," Ayoi said calmly. "And well he should."

"The only fools are those who think that by waiting, the white men will grow weaker," Deezbaa snapped. "Let the Utes and the Pueblos fawn at their feet, we are the People, and this is our land. The longer we wait, the more likely we lose. I say, we kill them all now while we can."

"Yet they come in peace," Ayoi said, still not raising her voice. "It is said that the Pueblos went in willingly to speak with the white headmen—"

"Of course they did," Deezbaa snorted. "It is only with the help of the whites that the Pueblo dogs could ever defeat us."

"The runners say they have great weapons." Ayoi glanced at

Pahe, who quickly dropped her head so that she might appear concentrated on her work.

"They have muskets. We have seen those before. Our men can shoot two arrows in the time it takes a white man to fire a musket. They also say the whites number only thirty," Deezbaa answered. "Do we wait until their nest grows, like that of the scorpion, to many times thirty before we strike? Kill them now in their ridiculous high-walled square hogan, and then the *chindi*, the spirits of the dead, will infect the whole place. They'll have to abandon it or risk ghost sickness."

Pahe listened intently. The arguments had been going on for ten days now, ever since Narbona had given his opinion that the Americans could be trusted. No two heads agreed, and most particularly did the young men wish to rush to war with these trespassing strangers. She could not tell her father's feelings in this matter, but her mother obviously did not relish sending her sons off to battle. Pahe wondered why this battle should be different. Always before, when the men went off to raid the Mexicans, the Utes, the Pueblos, the Zunis, her mother stood with the other women, waving them farewell, smiling with pride and pleasure.

"It is said that Sandoval leads them here," Ayoi added. "Even now, they have passed the mountains; the runners say it."

"All the more reason to kill them while we can. Sandoval is an enemy of the People."

"He is Navajo—"

"No more than the coyote who feeds off our lambs is Navajo," Deezbaa said.

Pahe knew that Sandoval, leader of what some called the Enemy Navajos, came from Cebolleta, the only Navajo hogans east of the mountains. It was said that Sandoval and his kin had joined the Spanish, worshiping their gods and guiding them across the desert to the strongholds of the People. They were called *Dinéh Ana'aii*, Navajo Who Are Enemy.

Manuelito stood outside the weaving shed suddenly, clearing his throat to announce his presence. Ayoi called him inside. He looked uncomfortable, but Deezbaa called out with annoyance, "I am not here, son-in-law! Come in and speak to your wife!"

It was an old custom, that a man did not speak to or acknowledge his mother-in-law, so as to allow for harmony in his wife's hogan. But Manuelito had long ago learned that Deezbaa would not tolerate such a custom, though she occasionally kept away from him when the other headmen came to see Narbona, for the sake of appearances. Usually, however, she merely said she was not there when she was there and was not listening, when, in fact, she was dominating the discussion.

"What says Narbona?" Deezbaa asked him, without preamble.

"He counsels peace." Manuelito smiled slightly and addressed himself to his wife, though he answered Deezbaa. It was safer that way. He was aware, as were all with ears in Narbona's compound, of Deezbaa's open scorn for any talk of trusting the white man.

"Well, and what *else* does he say?" his mother-in-law asked him again with increased exasperation.

"The Americans wish to meet with us. We will suggest a neutral ground. We will invite them to the Chuska Mountains—"

"To the dance?" Ayoi looked up, alarmed. "But that is not a time for meeting with enemies, that is a time for—"

All eyes turned then to Pahe, for, of course, the dance which was held each year in the Chuska Mountains was the primary place for young men and young women to meet with an eye to courtship.

"Yes, and what better time to see what the whites have in mind, when all of us are together in strength."

"The old man will not be there," Deezbaa said firmly.

"No," Manuelito agreed, to her surprise. "He sends me in his place. Since I will be there anyway." He smiled at Pahe.

Pahe flushed. Every time she thought of the upcoming gathering in the Chuska Mountains, she was caught between terror and yearning.

"That is enough for today, I think," Ayoi said abruptly, standing and nodding to Pahe. She yawned and stretched larger than she usually did. "My fingers ache."

Pahe followed her mother out, glancing back at Deezbaa who continued to throw her shuttle through the loom, as though to slap it into submission. Her grandmother was muttering to herself angrily, too low for Manuelito or Ayoi to hear. But Pahe heard. She knew that the discussion was not over, not so long as Deezbaa drew breath.

She walked behind her father, kicking restlessly at stones in her path. With the Americans present, all would be changed. She had never been to the Chuska Mountains before, yet she already resented their presence at a gathering that was so important to her future.

"I have had many meetings with the young warriors," Manuelito was saying rather loudly.

She saw that he still wore that smile on his mouth.

Ayoi looked up at him quizzically.

"And not all of them wish to speak only of war."

Pahe glanced sideways at her father, now having lengthened her strides so that she walked alongside him.

"One at least asks after a certain young woman when he is not speaking of the white man."

Ayoi grinned broadly. "Oho, my daughter!" She took her husband's arm. "Which young warrior is this?"

"Nataallith," he said calmly.

"The one the Mexicans call Zarcillas Largos, Long Earrings! He has asked after my daughter?" She smiled more broadly now. "But he is a headman of a great clan!" She turned to Pahe. "He shows you great honor, Little Bird. And what does this warrior wish to know?"

"Only if your daughter is of age to journey to the Chuskas," Manuelito said. "Of course, I told him that she was not."

"Father!" Pahe protested.

Manuelito chuckled softly and took his daughter's hand, putting it through his other arm. "I told him he might dance with my wife's mother instead, if she will have him."

"She will have him all right," Ayoi said wryly. "And there will be nothing left of him but crow meat."

"Very old crow meat," Pahe said with feigned disdain. She knew it was unseemly for her to express an interest in another man within her father's hearing. In truth, it was easy to be scornful, for in her heart, the thought of Long Earrings did not fill her with joy. If he was who she remembered, he was almost old enough to be her father himself.

Her mother seemed no longer interested in her words, however, and only asked Manuelito, "Did you make your fears known to my father, then?"

"I told him that for every warrior who was grooming his horse and decorating himself with his finest silver in anticipation of the arriving Americans, there was another who was sharpening his arrows."

"But," Ayoi persisted, "did you tell him that *you* question the wisdom of peace with the white men?"

Pahe looked up at her father's face with surprise. Until that moment, she had not known that he was, in fact, in agreement with Deezbaa.

Manuelito nodded.

"My mother says they cannot be trusted," Ayoi said sadly.

"I fear your mother is wiser than we know."

*   *   *

At the top of the mountain range which the Mexicans called the Chuskas and the People called the Goods of Value Mountains was a wide pasturage which had been grazed longer than any other lands in *Dinétah*. It was here, above the vast cornfields of the Tunicha Valley, which belonged to Narbona, that the People gathered toward the end of each summer harvest to celebrate. Unlike the many other ceremonies that livened the year, however, this one attracted every young woman for hundreds of miles with her kin, for it was at the Chuska Mountains that marriages were made.

Pahe was mounted on her father's finest horse, wearing her grandmother's silver, swathed in her mother's most intricately woven blanket. No one came to the Night Dance in anything but their finest garments, even if such finery must be borrowed, Ayoi told her. Pahe could hear the singing long before she saw the fires, and the sound of so many of her people all together made her heart swell and her eyes water. All the way up the mountain, riding behind her mother and father, her stepmother, and brothers, she had felt heavy. Heavy with silver, with blankets, heavy with hair, heavy even with duty that lay across her shoulders like a second blanket. But once she heard the singing, like a thousand birds calling from some secret canyon, she felt light, and she kicked her mare to urge her forward.

"Oho!" Jádí laughed at her. "Are you so eager then to beg some three-legs to dance with your two?"

Jádí, her youngest brother, was fleet of foot and sharp-tongued, named for the pronghorn when he was a baby. Pahe flushed hotly under her blanket, glancing at her father. But he looked ahead, ignoring her brother's jibe. She knew that only now, at the Night Dance, would he allow her brothers to tease her about things of men and women. She called back, "It will be well for my brother to see how men behave, indeed. Then when he is man enough to be invited by some woman, he will know what to do."

Ayoi smiled at her as her older brothers laughed at her wit. "The man who wins you must be quick on his feet, my daughter."

"And wear a shield on his head!" Jádí laughed.

They came to the top of the plateau, and Pahe was astonished to see so many horses hobbled in one place. Her own mare answered the call of another horse in the pasture, and she wondered if perhaps the animals also knew what the Night Dance was for.

Her father was greeted by many as they drew near to the fires. Hands reached up to touch his mount, and voices called out even to her brothers. She felt proud to be born for such a clan. She dismounted and stood behind her mother, waiting to be taken to the dancers.

Not far away, in two wide circles surrounded by singers and drummers, the dancers moved in opposite directions facing each other. She could see from where she stood that the women were gaily moving, free and wide with their arms and their smiles, and the men watched them carefully, mimicking their movements. The usual constraint between men and women was gone, and the women looked sleek and lovely and full of life, like prancing deer. To her surprise, her mother quickly drew her forward and pulled her in front of a waiting gaggle of young men.

Pahe shrank back, suddenly afraid and angry that her mother should so display her, but Ayoi only laughed and pushed her playfully. "Ask that one to dance," she said loudly. "His mother has five hundred sheep."

Pahe looked at her mother, amazed. Suddenly she had turned to Deezbaa before these men. Before she could protest, her mother pushed her again. "Go on, my daughter," she said more softly this time. "They are only men, after all."

Pahe shook off her hand angrily and pulled back, taking a deep breath. Nothing had prepared her for this moment, no matter how many times she had been told that at the Night Dance, women must ask the men to dance with them. She suddenly wished she were a child again, herding the flocks. She glanced up and saw that her father and brothers were watching her, even as they laughed and talked with other men. She closed her eyes and listened.

The drums came into her heart then, the pounding rhythms of the dance and the voices of the women singing, the deeper calls of the men following their steps, their cries. Like water pulsing into her, the music and the voices swept away her anger. She turned to the closest grouping of men and saw that they were watching her also. She felt suddenly full of power, magic, and beauty. She looked into their faces, one by one. When she found a face that seemed to her one of equal beauty, she said, "I would dance with you," and held out her hand.

She was not surprised when he took her hand and followed her to the dancing circles, she was not surprised that she knew the steps without thinking of them, she was not even surprised at the eyes of other men which followed her as she danced. She knew that she was a woman of strength and that in her power, she was lovely.

The drums beat insistently and the voices were louder and more urgent once she was among the singers. She felt her hair begin to fall down her neck. Wispy strands clung to her face as her skin grew warm and moist, and she could not keep from smiling widely at the man—a complete stranger—as he moved before her in the intricate steps of the Night Dance. To her left were scores of women, to her right were the same. All of them seemed more beautiful than she, but none of them, she knew, felt more powerful or moved with the drums so well.

The circles moved, and she danced before another stranger.

The drums beat a command again which the rattles echoed, the circles shifted, and, once more, she faced a gleaming, dark face. No one was familiar and yet no one was strange. All of them were somehow kinsmen, though she had never seen any of them before.

The drums beat faster and faster. She laughed aloud as her feet moved with them, and she put out her arms to keep herself from whirling into the man before her, only to see that the other women and most of the men had their arms out as well. Faster and faster, the night seemed as close as her blanket round her legs, and, finally, they ended abruptly. She stopped, swaying forward into the man nearest her and laughing with abandon.

"Daughter of Manuelito!" he saluted her, and the circles suddenly dissolved to women and men moving away from one another. He knows who I am, she thought in wonder. Do all of them know me? She turned and saw her mother watching her from a near distance, smiling and beckoning her to come. As she went forward, a man came close to her and said, "Perhaps you will ask me when the drums begin again."

She whirled around, startled, and she saw the man they called Long Earrings standing there grinning at her. He was taller than she remembered, taller, wider, and just as old. She was struck with mute astonishment that so large a man should concern himself with so small a girl. She smiled timidly at him, unsure what else to do and then hurried away to her mother's side.

"Nataallith spoke to you!" her mother said.

"I know," Pahe gasped. "He told me to come to him when the drums begin again."

From a group of headmen, her father came toward her, his arms out to embrace her. She went to him gratefully. "You were the most graceful of all of them," he said softly.

"No." She shook her head ruefully. "I never knew there were so many unmarried girls in all the world."

"For Long Earrings, there is only one," her mother crowed happily. "And when the drums begin, you must go to him unafraid. Show him you are your father's daughter."

"They all seem to know that well enough," Pahe said, glancing over her shoulder. "How is it that they know of me and I do not know them at all?"

Manuelito shrugged. "That is the way of things."

A noise from the far side of the pasture caused them all to turn, and the cry went up from the crowd, *"Bilagáana, Bilagáana!"* The Americans had arrived.

Pahe slid behind her father to watch as the crowd parted for the mounted soldiers. She counted thirty men on horseback, all of them armed with long muskets in view, all of them bearded with hats pulled low on their brown faces.

"Why, they are no whiter than we," she murmured to her mother.

"I have heard they are, beneath their garments."

Pahe turned and looked at her mother with astonishment. The headmen went forward to greet the newcomers, and Manuelito was at the front of the crowd. Pahe saw that her brothers were close behind him, their hands on their knives. The women drew back to the fringes of the crowd, and Ayoi asked, "What are they saying?"

Pahe listened hard, but she could not hear the words over the barking of the dogs and the stamping of the horses.

The soldiers began to dismount, and hands reached forward to take their horses. In the jumble of excitement, Pahe heard several warriors say, "The Americans are going to stay to dance! We shall feast them!"

The drums began once more, and the headman of the *Bilagáana* went with the headmen to the fires. The women began to scurry, and mutton roasts were taken off the spits and offered to the men. Soon, to Pahe's amazement, it was as if the whites had been taken into the clans. They ate the good mutton, wiping their hands on the dogs, just as the People did; they laughed and pushed one another in bewildering jokes, grabbing hold of the women as they passed, as though they had lived among them forever.

The women seemed unconcerned at their attentions, though Pahe noticed that most of the younger maidens like herself were not pushed forward to the front of the crowds. And when the drums and the rattles and the singing began, the white men joined the dancers eagerly, still holding their muskets and their half-eaten legs of mutton.

These were amazing newcomers, she quickly decided. They were brash and discourteous, ugly as armadillos, but obviously men of power. They took what they wanted almost before it was offered.

As she moved away from her mother slightly so that she could see the strangers more closely, a voice said close to her ear, "Some say we should kill them all now. While they are weak and well fed."

She flinched at Long Earrings's words, unwilling to turn to face him. Staring straight ahead, she murmured, "Some say this. Others say they come in peace."

He came before her so that she must face him. "I know the thoughts of your father. Do you share them?"

She dropped her head, thinking of her mother's warnings. No man would wish to have her if she were so outspoken. Even if she did not want this man, she knew it was important that he want her. "I am too young and unimportant to have any thoughts at all on such a subject," she said.

He frowned. "I had heard that the daughter of Manuelito has the wisdom of her father and the wit of her grandmother. Are they speaking of another daughter?"

She smiled, despite herself. "There is no other."

"No," he said then, gently. "There is no other."

She sensed that they had said more than she had intended. In confusion, she looked over his shoulder, suddenly desperate to be farther from this man's face.

He touched her arm. "Will you dance, then?"

She laughed lightly. "It is I who must ask, O Impatient One."

He dropped his head in mock humility, and she took sudden pity on him. "Come, then," she murmured. Without waiting for Nataallith's answer, she hurried to the circles and thought of losing herself in the dancers, but he was before her in a flash, moving to the drums and the voices, his body moving more confidently than her last partner's.

She glanced over to where she had last seen her mother. She was there, nodding and smiling in a dignified manner. Pahe knew that most who saw Ayoi would suppose that she was mildly amused by her daughter's choice of partner. Only Pahe knew that her mother was grinning inside as widely as a coyote.

The night went on until dawn, and the Americans feasted until the mutton was gone and the fires were low. Many times, Long

Earrings claimed her for the dances, and when she could, she also danced with others. But each time she danced away from him, she felt his eyes on her, felt his heat following her, more insistently than the drums.

The drums became her heartbeat, somewhere in the last dances, and her legs seemed to move of their own accord, pushed forward by the drums, her heart, the song which vibrated up through her ears to her head and enveloped her like the most beautiful, shining shawl. When he spoke to her, she threw back her hair as she had seen other, older, more lovely women move, and she laughed gaily, only partially pretending. She had never felt so womanly. And she knew, by the buzzing in her ears, that it was he who made her feel so. He and all the rest of the men, the ones who watched her, who grinned at her, even the ones who seemed to have eyes for other girls, even they added to her sense of power and joy.

By the end of the night, when her father helped her on her horse, the man they called Long Earrings seemed not so old after all.

*   *   *

They returned from the Chuskas to discover that runners had already been there with a request from the white headman, Reid, for a meeting of all the headmen of the People, and, most especially, Narbona.

Deezbaa said loudly and long that such a meeting was foolhardy, that to go to meet the whites on their own territory was madness. They could not be trusted, she said over and over, and Narbona was too old for such a journey.

Over the night meal, the discussions were of nothing but the white men, until Pahe grew sick of their name. The young warriors still were divided, some clamoring for war, others wishing to make peace with the strangers.

Narbona said, "The corn is not yet harvested. It would be well to keep peace, at least until we get in the winter supplies. Tell the whites to come closer still, and we will meet them." And then he smiled slightly. "Tell them I am an old man, and cannot journey far." He made a temple of his fingers when he said this, seated not far from the women's table. His fingernails, which he wore three inches long as did most of the elder headmen, clicked lightly together like rattles in the dance.

Deezbaa laughed wryly. "That much is true, at least."

"They say they are out of food," one of the visiting headmen protested. "They will turn around and leave, and make their treaties with the Hopi and the Utes."

"Then take them food," Deezbaa said, ladling more mutton stew out of the bowl onto her trencher. "Keep them waiting in the mountains until they freeze."

"They will not freeze," Manuelito said quietly. "They are not so weak as you suppose."

Narbona said, "She is right, you will take them provisions. And then invite them to our pastures. Tell them we will wait here for them and welcome."

The meal was over then and the headmen gathered outside to make the messages for the runners. Narbona stood slowly, his shoulders crippled with the stiffness that had plagued him since Pahe was a child. Deezbaa went to his side protectively. "Ah, old man," Pahe heard her say softly. "You are as foolish as the young jays. You do not need to meet with the white wolves. Let the other headmen go to them—"

Pahe was sitting by her mother among the other women, pretending to ignore their talk, but her ears were pricked like a jackrabbit's to catch every word—

"I wish to make peace with our old enemies before I die," Narbona was saying to Deezbaa, his hand on her shoulder for support. "That much I can leave my people. A quiet land. No more women and children taken as slaves by our enemies. A land of peace which we share with our neighbors. And with these new men, as well."

Deezbaa frowned and helped him from his seat, supporting him as he walked out the door.

It took only seven days for the clans to arrive; from all corners of *Dinétah* they came, more than two thousand of them, men and women on horseback, to meet with the white strangers. They came into Narbona's valley, tethered their horses on his rich pasture lands, set up their camps in clan circles, and put up shelters against the sun. Narbona went to each fire to greet them and learn their views of the whites.

He came back to Manuelito and said, "Many of them wish for peace."

Pahe saw her father drop his head silently.

Narbona sighed wearily. "And also many wish for war."

"So, then," Manuelito said quietly, "we must wait and see what the whites wish for, eh?"

"Many say they need not wait to know what the whites wish for, my brother. They wish for our land." Long Earrings had come behind Narbona and spoke up as he entered the hogan. Pahe glanced up at his voice. She was sitting behind her mother, tending the cook pots for the midday meal. Long Earrings's clan had been one of the first to arrive in Narbona's valley, and he had been in and out of her mother's hogan often since he arrived, speaking to her father each time he found him there with more and more easiness. Her mother kept her face from him and did not speak in his presence, as though she were already his mother-in-law.

Pahe said suddenly, "Well, and if we kill them now, they will only send more soldiers to avenge our betrayal—"

Her mother hissed sharply at her, glaring her to silence.

Manuelito only smiled without turning his head in her direction. "My daughter has been encouraged to speak her mind," he confided to Long Earrings as though she were not in the room. "You must excuse her interruption."

"There is nothing to excuse," Long Earrings said genially, smiling directly at her. "We will need all the minds of the People to keep the whites off our lands, those of our men and those of our women, alike."

Narbona said impatiently, "They are only a day's march away. What says your clan?"

Nataallith shrugged importantly. "Nothing with one voice. Like the others, they are divided."

"Then a peaceful welcome is our only choice for now," Narbona said firmly.

After the old man left, Long Earrings stood for a long moment, waiting to be invited to sit. Manuelito chuckled and gestured him over. "It may perhaps be your only quiet meal for a good while."

Pahe snorted softly and rolled her eyes.

"Or perhaps not," Long Earrings said, grinning. "Actually, I have eaten. May I walk your daughter to see some of the clans as they are arriving?"

"If she is willing," Manuelito said, glancing at her.

In answer, Pahe stood quickly, brushing off her blanket. She deliberately did not meet her father's eyes, did not look at her mother. She followed Long Earrings from the hogan, careful that her body did not brush against his in any way. Once outside, she lifted her face to the sky and took a deep breath.

"It is sometimes good to get away from even those who love you," Long Earrings said easily.

She said nothing still. She did not wish to make it easy for him, and yet she did not wish him to give up. Silence seemed the safest path.

They walked toward the makeshift camps, fires, and shelters which the People had erected in groupings around the vast pasture. To the unknowing eye, the clusterings seemed haphazard, but Pahe knew that each group had its own kinship, its own headman, its own set of marriages, births, and losses. Each fire had a woman with a strong tongue, a boy who held everyone's highest hopes, an aging warrior who alternately clamored for one last victory or death. It seemed to her if she listened closely, she could hear a low buzz coming from the shelters, the way the air hummed with insect life in the summer months.

Long Earrings stopped at several fires, speaking to kinsmen and acquaintances, encouraging her to speak to them as well. He was always welcomed, she noted, and many of the young women watched him carefully, appraising her to see why it was Nataallith had her with him. He called her "Daughter of Ayoi, born for Manuelito," including her clan names with great respect as he introduced her, and, to her surprise, most of those he spoke to knew who she was before he said her father's name.

They made the circle wider, taking in more and more welcomes, but she saw that he did not take her to his own fires. "Did your kinsmen not make the journey?" she finally asked lightly.

He laughed. "You know they did. And you know, also, that for me to take you to my fires is the same as assuming you have accepted me." He shook his head, his long shock of black hair falling over his headsash. "Don't play those games with me. With the others, perhaps, but not with me. I know you know more than you speak. You need not pretend to be deaf and blind with me."

Stung, she turned away in the direction of her father's hogan.

He took her arm carefully and turned her in another direction, toward the creek which meandered through the meadow. It was the thing of most value in all Narbona's land: water that stayed through the hottest months.

"I have only the finest regard for you, Little Bird."

"That is the name of my childhood." She slid her arm gently from his grasp.

"I find you lovely to look upon, Daughter of Ayoi," he said formally. "Would you consider my attentions to you unwelcome?"

Now that the question was before her, she felt completely bewildered. How had she come to this place so quickly? It seemed to her only a few months before that she had left off herding the flocks and put up her hair. She knew that her mother and father approved of the match, and she wanted to please them. But when she closed her eyes and tried to see herself lying alongside this man for the rest of her days, she felt like running into the hills and living with the wolves, free and unrepentant and wild.

But she knew he deserved an answer. When she looked up at him, she could not bring herself to be unkind. "No," she only murmured, sensing that this single word somehow unloosed an avalanche of stone that might either bury her or become her shelter.

He ran his hand slowly, lightly, up her arm, causing her skin to prickle. "It is well for a warrior to take a woman with the same spirit as his own. I find your spirit as beautiful as your face."

With those words of formal courtship, Pahe suddenly flushed and became confused, looking this way and that for an escape. He laughed again, looking now up at the sky as she did. "There is nothing up there worth searching for, warrior-woman. Everything which will bring you pleasure is right here before you."

Despite herself, she had to smile. He was suddenly as brash and young as Jádí. She tilted her head as she had seen Deezbaa do when she teased Narbona, with her chin in the air and her eyes still on the sky. "We will see," she said playfully, no longer bewildered. He was just a man, after all. "But do not call me 'Little Bird.' "

He nodded. "Little Wolf, then?"

She turned in astonishment. Had he heard her thoughts? "Daughter of Manuelito," she murmured. "That is my proper name."

"For now," he said.

A quick fire rose in her at his sudden familiarity. He seemed at once arrogant and assuming. Her voice turned more chill than she had planned. "Perhaps it is better you not call my name at all," she said, turning and walking away. She did not turn when he spoke, and she did not slow her steps.

*   *   *

The white men came at last to Narbona's pastures and made their camp a short distance from the clustered camps and shelters of the People. In a great show of trust, they turned over their horses to be grazed with the horses of the Navajo, even allowing the warriors to take their mounts out of sight and some distance from the camp. The murmurs went through the clans that these white men had either the trusting hearts of children or they were the greatest fools to ever come over the mountains.

And then the dancing and the games and the feasting began, the necessary diversions that must happen before any serious convening of council. The soldiers exchanged garments with some of the warriors, but since there were only thirty soldiers and more than a thousand warriors, the garments of the soldiers must be passed from hand to hand, placed onto any number of bodies, until most of the soldiers wore Navajo blankets for the duration of their visit, as their own clothing was in tatters.

Finally, when the feasting was over, Narbona was brought to the soldiers' camp on a litter of willow rods, accompanied by Deezbaa, his grown sons, and most of the important headmen. Manuelito stood near him, with Ayoi, Juanita, his sons, and Pahe clustered behind him, as was fitting.

The leader of the white men, Captain Reid, spoke long and well of their search for peace. Through the translator, he spoke of the high mountains they had crossed, the deep canyons they had climbed, and the steep paths they had managed to traverse with their horses. He spoke of the Utes, the Pueblo, and Zuni, and the Hopi, all the tribes who wished for peace. He called the People, "The Lords of the Soil," and made many words and gestures of respect. And then he said that Narbona and the headmen must come to Zuni lands to the large fort of the white men, there to meet with the white headmen to make lasting peace.

There was some murmur among the People, then, for it became clear to them that peace would not be made here, on Narbona's lands, but elsewhere, on lands that they did not control. This was not what they had been promised; this was not what they had expected.

Pahe instinctively moved closer to her father when she heard the murmurs of her clan, for she felt she could almost hear their heartbeats as one deep, aroused growl within her head. Trouble was coming, she saw that clearly now. If it would not be today, it would be soon. Already, there was a perverseness present. A twisting of words.

The white men were asking too much, always more and more, each time they came onto *Dinétah*. They would not be satisfied with any compromise; they would not take a fair share and leave the rest for others. This all seemed so clear to her, so loud in her heart, that she wondered others could not hear it as well.

Pahe gazed up at her father, who listened hard and watched the white men before him as though he expected to see the larger truths of his future there. It struck her with a shock that her father was not hearing the hearts of the people as she did. For the first time in her life, she felt that her father was not as wise, not as powerful and all-knowing as she had supposed. He was a young man, after all. The knowledge made her feel sick and weak and afraid.

She moved closer to her mother for comfort.

Ayoi said, "My father must go to the white men. He must see if they are the enemy for himself."

"But he is so old," Pahe murmured softly.

"It is his duty. He knows this. And the People will not follow another headman as they will follow him."

Pahe fell silent, watching her grandfather carefully. As from a high cloud, she saw him weary and prone on the ground, surrounded by the standing men of his clan, as though he were already buried beneath the earth. She saw him dead in that moment, and her breath stopped in her throat. When her grandfather was dead, who would lead the People? Would her father be then the voice they followed? Would someone older—perhaps even Long Earrings—be the headman they put in her grandfather's place in their hearts?

Or would the white men find them weak and without leaders? Would they, like wolves, be drawn to the People in their weakness, choosing to attack them rather than the Zuni and the Utes, who seemed more unified in their defiance?

It was the first time in her life she had considered such questions, the first time she had put herself in the minds of the headmen, in the hearts of men who had the responsibility for the clans. She felt stronger when she put herself in their hearts, no longer felt weak and small and afraid. She moved closer to her father then, next to her brothers.

Deezbaa had moved closer to the front of the council, and she pushed herself forward suddenly, her red-feathered hat bobbing low among the shoulders of the men like a moving bird on the wing.

She suddenly moved to the center and turned her back to Captain Reid, speaking to her people with her hands outstretched. At her first words, high and trembling with passion, the crowd grew still and watchful.

Most had heard her speak before, but for a woman, even Narbona's woman, to interrupt such a council was so contrary to custom that they were frozen in wary surprise.

"My people, you must listen to my words!" she cried loudly. "We cannot trust the *Bilagáana!* They are not men of honor. They are not men of peace! They are allies of our enemies, and we have nothing to gain by welcoming them to our lands. Have they come all this way to stop the stealing of our women and children by the Mexicans and the Utes? No, they have not! Have they come over our mountains to tell us that they will fight the Pueblos at our sides? No, they have not! They have not even come to our lands to make a peace but to demand that we follow them back to the lands of our enemies to make this peace. A peace they will not keep, on lands they have trespassed!" She shouted louder now, encouraged by the silence of the men around her. "Do you think that because they allow us to pasture their horses with ours, they wish to become our kinsmen? They do not! And if we send our headmen to their lands to make peace, they will murder them all! I say, my people, kill the *Bilagáana* now, while they are weak and we are many! We cannot trust the white man!"

The silence was shocking on all sides. Pahe cringed for her grandmother, and she saw how her hands shook, heard the tremble in her voice. She was at once proud of her courage and humiliated by her trespass. Pahe knew that all who listened would never forget Deezbaa's brashness, and many would never forgive it. Some of the women turned away, including Juanita, and averted their heads in humiliation at her outburst.

Deezbaa went on in this manner for long moments, but Pahe could see, as she looked around, that her words were having some effect. Many of the warriors were nodding in agreement, and some of the Old Ones, heads which yearned for peace, were looking now at the white soldiers with frowning faces of distrust. Her words were loud, yes, but they were also full of passion and beauty. Whatever else voices might say against Deezbaa, Pahe knew that no one could claim she did not believe them herself.

Several of the nearest warriors were murmuring at her words and reaching for their weapons, when Narbona suddenly tapped three times with his long fingernails on his pallet. Deezbaa was instantly silent. Narbona's eldest son leaned down to hear his words, then spoke quietly to the headman who stood next to him. Quickly, two men took Deezbaa on either side, pinioned her arms, and led her from the council meadow. She did not cry out as she was rushed away. Not a head turned to see her go nor did Narbona change his expression.

Pahe kept her face still, although her heart was weeping for her grandmother. She glanced at her mother. Ayoi did not meet her eyes. She kept her gaze ahead, silent and unmoving.

After a long moment of silence, Narbona spoke again to his headman, and the council began once more. Within a short time, it was agreed that the clans should travel to *Shash Bitoo'*, Bear Springs, the very edge of Navajo lands, to make a lasting peace with the white men. It was as if Deezbaa had never spoken a word.

The *Bilagáana* gathered their horses, packed up their camp, and turned to go back over the mountains. The People packed up their wagons and their mounts and drifted away back to their own homes. Deezbaa spoke barely a word all the long ride back to Narbona's hacienda. When they came to the ranch, she went into her hogan and let the blanket drop over her door.

Runners came and went with messages then, and Pahe heard that a runner had been sent to the white men on their trail to their own lands. The word was that they should guard their horses well: several of the warriors who had listened to Deezbaa had taken off after them, intent on stealing what mounts they could catch unguarded.

Despite Narbona's warning, the runner came back with news that many of the soldiers' horses had been driven off successfully. "After all," Manuelito said over the fire when he heard the news, "does peace with the white men mean that we give up our way of life? Let the old ones talk of peace. The young ones will not waste time with talking when there are horses to be taken."

And still Deezbaa did not emerge from her hogan. So far as Pahe could see, she had barely seen the sun since her shame at the council. The headmen muttered that she was weakening Narbona with her anger, separating his heart from his body, and worse—that she was deliberately inflicting him with doubt at a time when he needed to save as much of his strength as he could. Pahe heard the talk even among the slaves, that Deezbaa was using witchcraft to bend her husband to her will.

Finally, Ayoi and Pahe went to plead with Deezbaa to put aside her anger and emerge from the silence of her hogan.

"The old fool will use up the last of his life chasing after the lies of the white man," Deezbaa said to them. "But he will not go to his death with my smile in his mind's eye, I will see to that. If he goes, he goes knowing I despise him for going."

Ayoi said, "You are trying to cripple him, when he most needs to stand upright."

"I am trying to save his life," Deezbaa said shortly, standing up with the help of the walking stick she had carried ever since her great shame.

"But the white men say they wish only peace—"

"They lie! And if they are going to betray us with their lies, I don't wish your father's last act as headman of his people to be that he led them down that path of betrayal."

"It may not be his last act," Ayoi said. "His last act may be to put you aside as his wife."

"Let him do so," Deezbaa said. "At least I will have my say."

"When did you ever not have that?" Pahe asked quietly, almost to herself. She was sitting in the corner of her grandmother's hogan, a place she had sat in so many times in her life. Above her were her grandmother's herding sticks and cooking pots, hanging on rafters. To one side was the niche in the wall where she burned her mutton fat for light; to the other was her pallet where she lay herself down. Pahe had seen the possessions of her grandmother so many times, but now they seemed unfamiliar. Her pots of herbs and roots and salves; her combs and blankets and buckskins—all belonged to a woman she scarcely knew. Even the hogan no longer felt like a comfortable, warm place of safety. She wanted to be small again, but she knew that she could not go back to that time, even as she could not go back to that place.

Again, she felt afraid . . . afraid of the future, afraid of the strangers, afraid even of her grandmother. And she was already tired of feeling afraid.

"Oho!" Deezbaa laughed wryly. "Who is that speaking? The Little Bird who sits in Long Earrings's hand? The Little Bird who still has her maidenhead intact? This Little Bird is going to tell an old wife how to best deal with a foolish husband?"

"They say you are killing him with your anger," Pahe said, keeping her chin firm. Never had she disagreed with her grandmother about anything more important than the colors of her weavings, but she had felt ashamed when Deezbaa was dragged away from council before all eyes. She wanted to punish her for that humiliation.

"Better me than the whites," Deezbaa snorted. "The old turtle knows what to do if he wishes my anger to die. He can send the other headmen without him. It is not so hard to do."

"All of his life, he has been a leader of the People—" Ayoi protested.

"All of his life, he has had my respect. If he wants to keep it to his death, he knows what he must do."

Pahe stood then and went to the door, amazed in some small

place of her heart that she had stood up before her mother, that she was walking away from more than just her grandmother's hogan. She stopped and said, "Well, and you better use witchcraft, as they believe you are doing. Because only that will keep my grandfather from keeping his word to the *Bilagáana.*"

*   *   *

Four days later, Narbona and five hundred mounted warriors and headmen left for Bear Springs to meet with the headman of the whites, Colonel Doniphan, to sign the peace treaty. Deezbaa was not in the crowds which waved them farewell, but they had to ride right past her hogan, as they left the hacienda. From the door of her hogan, a white blanket hung low, completely covering the opening, keeping her invisible within, the sign of a death in the family. Several of the warriors shouted condemnations to her as they rode past, but Narbona never turned his head or acknowledged either the blanket, her hogan, or her absence.

*   *   *

As the horses rode by, kicking up clouds of dust and making a thunder on the ground, one creature was dislodged from his daytime burrow, forcing him to scurry for cover from the passing hooves. A rattler would have stood his ground, coiled and threatened, and likely been trampled for his trouble. But Chalco was smarter than a rattler in many ways, less stubborn, and far less willing to fight.

Chalco was a desert tarantula, *Aphonopelma chalcodes,* a young gray male nearly two inches wide with eight heavy gray and hairy legs and a brownish-black abdomen. After his last moult, his pedipalps, or leglike sperm carriers, finally emerged distinctive and long, and he was now ready to mate. He was eager to do so. Like every male tarantula in the desert, he was exquisitely aware of every female in his territory. What he could not know was that the females he intended to pursue not only could live twenty years to his few, but also considered him food.

All that concerned Chalco in the moment was finding the female he'd been tracking for several days. He was moving over familiar territory, following her scent trail, understanding in some dim way that she was attempting to evade him even as he sought her.

He frequently stopped and waved his seven-segmented legs in the air, as though feeling for her presence. When he did so, his fangs spasmodically moved out of his jaws, or *chelicerae*, as though he intended to bite his prey.

His venom would have been largely useless on the female, even if he intended such folly. Very effective against lizards, insects, and small moles and mice, Chalco's venom was much feared by men, but, in fact, was no more dangerous than that of a wasp or a bee sting. His prospective mate's venom was also largely ineffective against man—but extremely effective against Chalco. In fact, any male of his species took his life in his pedipalps each time he attempted to mate.

But that did not deter Chalco from the hunt. He stopped at a small burrow and felt with his sensitive feet pads over the rough terrain. Under the ground, he could sense vibrations, likely a nest of rodents. But he had fed recently, and rodents interested him less than the mating urge which drove him. He went on with his quest, over rocks and around small shrubs, following the trail of the female.

As he rounded a boulder, he suddenly froze. Another spider crouched in the shade of a juniper root, watching him. Chalco instantly reared up on his back legs, pawing the air like a stallion in challenge. It was another male in his territory, an intrusion that made him swell with anger. He rushed at the other male and then stopped several inches from his foe, waving his front legs anxiously. The scent of the female was strong on the ground between them, and this diverted him momentarily.

Suddenly, the other male rushed at him and attempted to push him backward with his front legs. Chalco stumbled, faltered, and finally rolled slightly to one side, dodging the intruder's blows. He then righted himself, raised up on his rear legs, and prepared for battle. Both males were poised, pushing at one another with all their strength, shifting their back legs for purchase on the rocks, their fangs moving audibly with fierce clicking. They would not bite; death was not the point of their battle, but supremacy. Chalco was slightly larger than the other male, but untested. He could smell the other male's anger and fear, but the scent of the female was urgent all around him, and he finally shoved backward with all his strength, toppling the other spider down.

The smaller male crouched, suddenly small and unassuming, backing away. Chalco let him go, immediately uninterested. He knew that the male would vacate the territory now, and all that mattered was the female.

Chalco hurried off down the rise of the sandy hill, rounded another juniper, and came face-to-face with his quarry. A large dark-brown female waited for him in the shade of a boulder. Still as stone, she sat, facing him and watching him warily with all eight eyes.

He began to sway gently, straightening his legs so that he looked as large as possible. Even with that effort, she was bigger than he was, darker, and somehow more formidable. He gradually moved closer, then closer still, until he was within a few inches of her, still swaying and moving with deliberate calm.

Suddenly, she reared back with her front legs up and her fangs exposed, ready to deliver his death. But before she could strike, he rushed forward, pushed her front legs up with his own, and caught her fangs with his spurs, forcing her upward. In that position, a furrow on her abdomen was exposed, the place he knew waited for him, despite her fangs. Quickly, he extended his palpi, deposited sperm in that furrow, and then waited for a moment to make sure that she was still off balance. With a final thrust, he pushed her over backward, scrambling out of her way lest she decide to give chase.

The female righted herself and ambled off, with never a backward glance at him. This time, he did not follow.

*   *   *

When Narbona and the council returned from *Shash Bitoo'*, the Bear Springs, they reported that this Colonel Doniphan wanted a peace "that would last so long as the mountains of the land stood where they stand."

"Nataallith brought much honor to his clan," Manuelito said to Pahe. He sat before Ayoi's fire, relating the journey and all he saw and heard to them.

Ayoi smiled at Pahe, nodding her approval. "Many say he will be another Narbona."

Manuelito had his hand on her bare leg, and he stroked it softly. "There will never be another Narbona," he said courteously, "but Nataallith is gaining no small attention from the headmen for his words."

"Did he speak to the whites?" Pahe asked, surprised.

Manuelito nodded. "He told them that when they asked for peace between the People and the Mexicans, they could not hope for success unless they understand the reasons for war."

"This makes sense," Ayoi murmured.

"He said that we have fought with the Mexicans for many years, with both sides taking captives, stealing horses, and killing warriors. Now, the *Bilagáana* have taken the land from the Mexicans, defeating them in battle. This, we understand. But when the whites come to us and say that we must stop fighting the Mexicans, because they are now 'new Mexicans,' and protected by the White Father in Washington, this we do not understand. Nataallith told the whites that this is our war. He said that we are being asked to stop doing something which the whites themselves are doing. He told them that we have more right to complain to the whites that they are interfering with our war than they have to quarrel with us for continuing a war we started long before they got here."

"Very good sense," Ayoi repeated.

"And did they listen?" Pahe asked, impressed that Long Earrings had the courage to speak so before the headmen and the white soldiers.

Manuelito shrugged. "We made a peace. We signed their papers, and we promised to keep from fighting the Mexicans. But I do not think the warriors will heed such a promise. And the first time that a Mexican takes a woman or child from us, then I will not heed it, either."

"And Nataallith signed the paper as well?" Pahe asked.

"He did, Little Bird. And the whites will remember his words, I think."

"He does you great honor, my daughter," Ayoi said.

"You have told me this so many times," Pahe said, suddenly annoyed, "that I feel I should beg him to let me air his blankets."

"Share them, perhaps, but I believe the slaves can do the airing," Ayoi said dryly.

"Oho!" Manuelito laughed, waving away the tension with his hand like so much smoke in the hogan. "Deezbaa lives in both your mouths. And speaking of this, Nataallith says that you have encouraged his interest. I would hear this from you, my daughter. Is this true?"

Pahe flushed and dropped her eyes, for her mother was staring at her so avidly that she felt no matter what she said, she would disappoint her. "I told him," she murmured, "that I did not consider his attentions unwelcome. Only that."

"It is often difficult for a young woman to know her own heart," her father said kindly and quickly, before Ayoi could speak. "This is why, more often, her family knows best which match might be most suitable."

"In just this way, my mother found your father for me," Ayoi said. "And her mother before her matched her with Narbona."

"Hardly a good argument for such arrangements," murmured Pahe.

"My mother has been a good wife to my father all of her days," Ayoi said stiffly. "You listen too much to evil talk."

"You told her yourself that she was going to kill him with her anger—!"

"Enough," Manuelito said firmly. "I do not need any more heat at this fire. Pahe, if you can accept Nataallith, I will tell him so. If you cannot, then I will discourage him. We need say no more of this—"

"I think we need say *much* more of this, if she turns such a man away—" Ayoi began.

"No, we do not," he said, calling her by a name which, in Navajo, meant "one who would advise a sheep which grass to eat." It was a name of affection he had given her many years before. "Deezbaa would not have married your father unwillingly, no, not if she were tied to him hand and foot, and if you had not wished to be my wife, ten Deezbaas could not have forced you. I will not force my daughter."

Ayoi snorted softly.

Manuelito gazed at his wife calmly, with scarcely a crease of his brow. Pahe sensed the warmth between them and more: for just a moment, she could almost hear the silent chuckle of agreeable adversaries, taking each other's measure and bowing in respect.

She could hear, briefly, the secret song of their union. Her mother smiled and rolled her eyes in mock defeat.

"Thank you, my father," Pahe said meekly.

"And so?"

She smiled shyly. "I do not hate his attentions."

He grinned. "Spoken like a woman. He will have to find his own way around that maze of canyon walls, then. I will tell him he may offer what he will."

"Perhaps silver," Ayoi said happily. "He is rich, despite his youth—"

"He is hardly young," Pahe said.

"He has a heart of great passion, Little Bird, of that I am certain." Her father patted her softly. "And that is surely more important than youth."

*   *   *

Later that evening, as though he knew of their conversation, Nataallith came to her mother's hogan and asked her father if he might walk with her out in the night. She did not hesitate. In fact, after watching her parents alternately spar and embrace, all with little words in a private dance of communion, she felt lonely for such a feeling of partnership. It seemed to her somehow wondrous and frustrating that despite sharing their lives and even their sleeping spaces for so many years, there were parts of themselves they held privately for each other which she did not know. Parts of her father he shared only with Ayoi, not Juanita, not his sons, not his own heart. She could catch snatches of their intimacy like a distant song barely heard, but most of it eluded her. She suddenly wanted to have someone sing such a song to her, alone.

And so, when Nataallith walked her away from the hogans, out under the new moon, and she heard the distant call of the coyotes and the night songs of the desert, she was ready for his words. When he asked her to become his wife, she said that she would as simply as though she accepted a plate when she was hungry or a step up onto her pony.

It seemed to her that it felt the same as if she were weaving a blanket, working hard on a new and beautiful design, and, all of a sudden, she needed more wool in a certain color to make it perfect: and she looked into her basket and there it was, waiting for her to weave it as she would.

He was already accepted by her clan, he already knew her heart and accepted her imperfections, and he was here, now, asking her to weave him into the new design she had envisioned.

She made him ask a second time, because she knew that many years hence, it would please them both to remember this moment. And then she told him simply that she would become his wife. He embraced her lightly, as though he were not at all astonished. Then he led her back to her mother's hogan, and the marriage was arranged.

Pahe reflected on her decision much more after she had agreed than before. Many times henceforth, she would recall that night and his words, and she could never quite remember what she was thinking or how she felt. She could only suppose that she was too impressed by Nataallith, too proud of what others thought of him, to think much past the moment of her decision. It took her many months to understand that she had given her life away on that night and many more years to be glad.

*   *   *

For the first few months after the peace treaty, the People did their best to keep the promises made by their leaders. But they soon saw that none of their women and children stolen into slavery were going to come home. The Americans had come to *Dinétah*, had signed some papers, and had gone back to their homes again, leaving little changed in their wake.

It took most of a year, but eventually the young warriors, those who admired the words of Manuelito and wished to prove themselves to their clans and their women, began raiding once more. At first, only small, elusive parties pestered the ranchos along the Rio Grande, driving sheep and horses back up the sand valley of the Rio Puerco and through the well-worn trails of the Zuni Mountains to their strongholds in the Tunicha Valley. And then, as no reprisals came from the whites, bolder, larger parties struck at the richer haciendas, the *ricos* who owned the finest cattle and horses, stealing whatever they could drive away.

One raiding party then deliberately targeted the hacienda of the rich Mexican rancher, Juan Cruz Pino, who held more than two dozen Navajo women in slavery. In the raid, the rancher's son was killed.

Pino demanded revenge, hounded a friend in Congress, and a detachment of soldiers was sent out for swift retribution. But when the soldiers reached the lands of *Dinétah*, they found fields ready to harvest, hogans deserted, and sheep trails empty, and the only Navajos they saw were always far in the distance.

By early 1849, the raiding bands were striking all along the Mexican frontier from Abiquiu to Socorro, and every pueblo and ranch had lost livestock. In retaliation, more Navajo women and children were stolen from hogans and haciendas, "baptized" as Catholic, then sold to rich ranchers and New Mexican settlers as slaves. Increasingly, the women who were with child were taken, as it was a convenient way for Mexican slavers to take two for the effort of one. When a woman with several small children was surprised, her older children were taken from her and scattered to be sold, and any infants were left to die in the desert or thrown over the mesas, for there was no market for Navajo weanlings among rich white buyers.

Since Pahe had birthed her first son that summer, she was much more aware of the kidnappings. She remembered as if it was only the season before her own abduction by the Utes, and she realized now how lucky she had been to escape at all.

"Lucky," her mother often reminded her, "and very brave for one so young. When I think that you walked the mountain alone, across the land with only a coyote for companion—!"

"The land was safer then," Pahe said sadly. "My son must be braver still. I fear he will know harder times than we can imagine."

Ayoi fell silent as she rocked the baby. It was she who had been with Pahe when she birthed him, she who had first held him, swaddled him, and though her son-in-law would never know it, she who had given him his first birth name, Wasek, or "Spring Caterpillar" which spits blue spittle, for his early habit of drooling on her until her back was completely wet. She tied a squirrel tail to his cradle so that he might be protected from a fall, and she sang him good-luck songs as she carried him about while Pahe rested or worked.

Indeed, in that first season of Wasek's life, it seemed to Pahe at times that the child belonged more to Ayoi than he did to her.

Deezbaa came to her hogan now, but only at dusk, when most other women were busy preparing the cooking fires, that she might not be seen. Even in the hottest months, she wore her blanket tight round her head like a widow.

Deezbaa took Wasek in her lap and fed him pollen, that he might be safe from demons, and she rubbed his fat brown limbs with more pollen, murmuring, "May I be lively. May I be healthy," half to herself, half to the child.

"A child born in the summer is the most useful," Deezbaa told Pahe one evening. "When the snow is deep, you can roll a summer child in the deepest drift, and it will melt away."

"That sounds like Zuni craziness," Pahe scoffed. Her grandmother seemed to be slipping further and further away these days in her mind. Her laugh had changed. Always it seemed to Pahe that she laughed with an edge of anger now, as though nothing really was amusing in the world after all.

Deezbaa shook her head, ignoring Pahe and chuckling to Wasek. "Tell She-Who-Will-Not-Hear that a child who gets too smart dies young. Tell her also that many years ago, before she acquired all her wisdom, when the deep snow was up to our waists and the sheep and horses died and we were very hungry, my sister took her child and rolled it in the snow. He was a summer child, just like you, Little Sun, and the snow round her hogan melted away."

"What says Narbona of the raids?" Ayoi asked. Each time she saw her mother, she made it a point to say her father's name, as though to remind Deezbaa of her responsibility to him.

Deezbaa shrugged, handing the baby carefully back to Pahe and standing up. "Who asks him?"

Pahe felt older and more sure of herself with Wasek in her arms. "Have you shared his bed even once since his return?"

Ayoi turned and gaped at her. And then she laughed aloud. "This one, who has been married for more seasons than the corn has tassels, knows just how important that bed is for happiness."

Pahe sensed her mother's embarrassment, but she did not drop her eyes when Deezbaa glared at her.

"I have scarcely shared his air," she said shortly. "And the old fool can sleep with the sheep, for all I care."

"It makes me sad," Pahe said mildly, "to see both of you alone in the last years of your lives."

"Save your sadness for yourself, Little Bird," Deezbaa said, suddenly serious. "For, if your grandfather continues to lead the People down this trail, following behind the white man's scat, you and your man and this small caterpillar," she added this last as she reached out and caressed the baby's tiny foot, "will have more trouble than Narbona ever dreamed in his worst visions."

Ayoi and Pahe glanced at each other. For all that they had been shamed by Deezbaa's behavior, there was no discounting her wisdoms. All of Pahe's life, she had been used to her grandmother's gift of divination, something she was known for throughout *Dinétah*. It was such a useful thing to have a relative who could listen to the *Yeis*, the Holy Ones, or the ghosts or the plants or the birds and know where property was that had been lost or stolen, who could find water by gazing up at the stars and listening to their secrets, who could run a hand over anyone's body and sense the sickness within and the cure that was needed. But it was also a risk. If Deezbaa was known as a witch, she could be killed by anyone who believed that she had directed evil at them or their clan. Witches and skinwalkers, evil people who could take the shape of dogs or wolves and move about in the night at will, would not long be tolerated in a people so beset by trouble.

Pahe thought of all the women who had come to find out whether their husbands had been faithful, if their kidnapped children were alive, if their sons would come back safe from raiding parties. Those same women now were afraid to come to Deezbaa's hogan, for their men would feel that any visit was a further insult to Narbona and thus to all men. But Pahe knew that the clan was poorer for Deezbaa's invisibility and silence, and that many women must yearn for her counsel in the privacy of their hearts.

"Have you seen something, my mother?" Ayoi asked finally.

"Did you note how your grandfather greeted the white wolves while lying on the ground?" Deezbaa asked softly. "The Holy Ones are offended by such humbleness before the stranger. His knees will not hold him, so long as he crawls to the *Bilagáana*. Soon, he will be on his belly like the snake."

"You always told me that it is a woman's duty to stand alongside her husband," Pahe said firmly. "Not behind him, not before him, but beside him."

"I cannot stand alongside a man who will not rise up from his knees," Deezbaa said sadly. And she pulled the blanket close around her head and went out the door.

*   *   *

That night, as she curled around Nataallith on their sleeping pallet, Pahe played her grandmother's words over and over in her head. The baby slept soundlessly nearby; her husband slept silently, the world itself seemed to be asleep. Pahe felt she was the only woman awake under the moon. It seemed to her that there was some large, vital lesson that the Holy Ones were trying to send her, a message she was to hear in Deezbaa's words, and she yearned to know it as true as she could. And as she thought, a vision of her grandmother hoeing the garden came to her, as she had seen her when a small child, on her knees next to the corn rows and the squash vines, humming quietly, feeling the warm, firm earth beneath her and her grandmother working nearby. She was safe and content and attached to the world so that she could never fall off. Now it seemed that the world had tilted and no place was safe, perhaps would never be safe again. And yet she knew the earth was the same, the seeds were still there, waiting to be sown and hoed and harvested.

As she saw her grandmother's garden in her mind's eye, the words came to her then, as though in a night chant: "It will bring forth, bring forth, bring forth or die. Planted or neglected, it will bring forth. It is to you to plant the seeds of value or let the weeds grow and propagate their kind." Where had she heard such words?

She moved closer to Nataallith, spooning her body to his and gently stroking him until he began to stir. He took her hand and brought it to his mouth, kissing it gently. "You cannot rest?" he murmured, low and sleepy.

"My grandmother said something today which keeps me awake," she whispered. "She said that the mind is like a garden. And that as one tends a garden, so one must tend the mind, allowing to take root only those thoughts which can nurture us."

He turned to her slightly, more awake now. "Your grand-mother said this?" he asked.

She smiled. "Well, not in just that manner. But I recall her words when I was small, something like this was said. And today, she told me that my grandfather's thoughts were keeping him beneath the white man. That his own mind was already defeated, and it is for this that she cannot forgive him."

He grinned, his teeth white in the darkness. "I did not think Deezbaa so eloquent, my heart."

"Well, and perhaps she is not," Pahe admitted. "But the truth is hers, no matter."

"No, the truth is yours," Nataallith said gently. "And it is a good truth to remember. Narbona is Narbona, and he has changed little in many years. There is nothing less in him to respect than there was before the white man, except as Deezbaa chooses to see less."

"And in the same way," she murmured, "we are safe so long as we feel we are safe. In truth, we are never safe and always safe, for that is the way of the world."

"Another wisdom." He turned again back to the arm which cradled his head as he slept. "And perhaps we can speak of it again in the light."

She chuckled softly. "I will likely think of more thoughts which tremble the stars with their wisdom. Shall I wake you for them?"

"Could you be stopped?"

She did not need to look to see that still he smiled, even as he fell back asleep.

*   *   *

In the councils held that summer, when the headmen gathered to discuss what next should be done with these "New Men," Nataallith was one of many who spoke loudly against signing more paper with the whites. This was a surprise to many, for Nataallith had often been a voice for peace. Pahe heard her hus-band say again and again that the Americans were not to be admired or feared any more than the Mexicans, whom they could not make obey their own treaties. But Narbona and many of the elders still believed that the People could never win against such a foe and so must make a peace.

It seemed that talk over the fires was of nothing that year but the whites and what the People must do about them. The healers and hand-tremblers were very busy, going from one hogan to another, attempting to work, with pollen and dry paintings and turquoise and shells, the demons of fear and anger from the clans. As though Deezbaa was herself a sickness, many hogans were divided, husband and wife, son and father, in their visions of what must be done. There were more sunderings of married people that year than in any Pahe could remember, and she was grateful that Nataallith did not demand that she agree with him, for she truly could not say in her heart what was the best trail to follow.

"The wisest among us cannot agree," he said to her sadly as they saw yet another bundle of a headman's belongings sitting forlornly outside a hogan, sure evidence that his wife had decided to take the opposite side of the argument, perhaps agreeing with her father or her brothers rather than her husband. In the way of the People, their union was declared over, for all the clan to see. "When the white men finally do come to do battle, they will find us weakened and divided."

"No, my heart," Pahe reassured him. "The first time the clans see the *Bilagáana* soldiers, they will suddenly be of one mind on the matter." But she wondered if her words were mere wishes.

Finally, Manuelito said that the whites had accomplished what several thousand years of history had not: the People were now divided into two camps, a war camp of Manuelito, Nataallith and their warriors, and a peace camp of Narbona and some of the elder headmen.

The women found themselves divided as well, not only from their male relatives but also from each other, even if they were married to the same man. Some chose to support their husbands; others could not. Those who could not were called by the others "Daughters of Deezbaa," and men who were not even their relations dared to speak rudely to them when they passed.

Ayoi and Pahe saw Deezbaa even less than they had before. Mostly, she kept to her own hogan, and the smell of burning herbs and roots was strong from her fire. Now it was more than simply the slaves who spoke of witchcraft. Mothers were beginning to warn their daughters of the danger of headstrong wills and bold tongues, using Deezbaa as an example of what could befall such a woman.

Other mothers boasted that they were no less warrior-women then Deezbaa and wondered aloud if they should not take up weapons and be ready to greet the white wolves, if their men were unwilling or too weak to do so.

Meanwhile, Pahe watched as Wasek grew and thrived, toddling in and out of the hogan into the sunshine, crowing with out-stretched hands at the ravens, calling boldly to his father when he saw him, and laughing at his mother's efforts to keep him in sight. She felt, by the time that he was two years old, that his true name was *Háájísh ííyá*, Where Did He Go, and she loved him with an aching fullness she had never known before.

*   *   *

In the hottest moon of 1850, runners brought word that the white man was once more on the move into *Dinétah*. An expedition of soldiers was coming from Fort Marcy to chase and subdue the People, it was told, led by a white man named Colonel Washington. The runners said there were 178 soldiers, 123 Mexicans, 60 Pueblo Indians, a pack train of mules, one six-pound field gun, three twelve-pound howitzers, wagons full of rations, and tents for the lot. The spies were so efficient that Manuelito knew the number of buttons on the colonel's marching jacket when the trespassers were still twenty miles away.

The white men were heading for the Canyon de Chelly, the runners warned, and so, of course, by the time the soldiers reached the stronghold, all of the People had fled, to watch from a distance as the soldiers burned their hogans and crops.

After two days of destruction, Narbona sent in his sons and their wives to meet with the whites and turn over to them fifteen mules and horses and fifty sheep, as a good-faith payment for the livestock taken in the Navajo raids. He sent also the message that he could not be responsible for all the warriors of the People, but that he himself wanted a lasting peace.

Colonel Washington accepted the animals, demanded that Narbona come himself to make a peace, and took possession of all the cornfields in the valley. Narbona then sent in more than a thousand sheep and some cattle, claiming that he was too old and ill to make the trip himself. The soldiers, meanwhile, continued to destroy the cornfields by letting their stock graze it freely.

A council of headmen was called quickly to discuss once more how this latest violation could be stopped.

Nataallith spoke passionately at the fires, calling on his people to at least drive the whites from their main source of food. Many of the elders wondered aloud exactly how such a thing was to be accomplished.

"We are not only women and children," Manuelito said mildly. "We have sufficient warriors to kill those who are here. And if they send more, we can kill those as well. They cannot send all of the white men in the world at once. At least the corn will be saved."

"And they will be back by the time the snow flies to avenge their brothers," one elder spoke up. "It is because of the raids of the warriors that they are here tormenting us now. Better we should gather what tribute we can for them, as many sheep as we can sacrifice, and then they will leave us in peace."

To Pahe's surprise, Juanita spoke from the far side of the circle. More than fifty men were grouped round the fires with their women, and there were few wives who would have had the courage to speak at such a gathering. But her words were clear enough to startle the council to silence.

"And if we give them ten thousand sheep, what then will sustain us through the coming seasons? Corn can be grown more easily than sheep."

Pahe heard another woman hiss softly, "Deezbaa's daughter!" just loud enough to be heard by those close to her, yet not so loudly as to invite censure from her man, who kept his eyes fixed stolidly on Narbona.

Nataallith said then, "Is there no end to the woe these whites bring to us? Even if we give them what they ask for now, is that assurance they will leave us in peace? Each season, they ask for more and more. They do not want peace. They want the land and all that is on it. Even if we give them our last mule, as many sheep as there are stars in the sky, even if we beggar ourselves so that the Utes and the Zunis can then drive us south into the arms of the Mexicans, can we trust that they will not follow? That they will not then take our children as well?"

At the mention of the children, the murmurs from the women rose high and fast round the circle like a flock of birds taking flight in alarm. One or two began to weep quietly, adding a disquieting chorus to the voices. Pahe felt as though she could hear not only their words and murmurs, but could hear the sounds of the splitting of their hearts in sorrow.

"My brothers," Nataallith added, "you know that I have spoken for peace up to now. I have prayed for peace, I have humiliated myself for peace. But now I speak with a different voice. I do not see that peace is possible. Now, while we are still strong, I speak for war. We may not have that choice after we have given them all they now demand."

There was silence as all eyes turned to Narbona. It was the custom of the People that they discussed and discussed, gravely hearing all opinions, until the decision could be unanimous. But when a headman spoke, he often persuaded others. Narbona more than most. No matter that he was old, weak, and almost blind in his years. No matter that he must be held up by his two sons to rise above the level of the ground to meet their eyes. No matter that his woman sat behind him with a face twisted by anger and stern disapproval. He was Narbona, and they would hear his words as they would no other.

"There are many voices this night of wisdom," the old man said tiredly. "I know that Nataallith speaks with a clear head and a strong heart. My son-in-law does no less. The warriors who would lead us to battle against the whites are men of courage and faith. But I say to you now that this is a war we cannot win. The white men are too strong and too many. I have seen them in their own lands, in their own camps, as many of you have not. These that we meet here on our own lands are but a handful, and the weapons they bring are as a child's play arrows against what they can bring, if they so choose."

He stopped for a moment, overcome by his efforts. And then he added quietly, "My people, it does not matter what we decide. We are like the ants, attempting to agree what to do about the prairie dog who digs up our nest. We cannot overcome them; they are too large and too many and they scarcely feel our bites. We will lose our struggle against the whites if we fight. If we choose peace, we at least have a chance of survival."

He sighed wearily and his sons laid him back down on his blanket. An equal weariness seemed to wash over the listeners then, as though they were somehow connected to Narbona's very body instead of only hearing his words in their heads.

There was more small discussion, but Pahe knew how it would end. She was not surprised when, once more, the decision was made to meet with the white men again. She was not surprised when Narbona said that he would go himself to talk peace with this new Colonel Washington, even though every man there doubted that he could survive such a journey. He had no choice.

The only real surprise was that Deezbaa had remained silent throughout. For that, at least, Pahe was grateful.

And so finally, on the hottest day of the hottest moon, when the deer gave birth, Narbona went to make the peace, leading a thousand warriors to meet the Americans. Deezbaa insisted on accompanying the women, and no amount of protest from them would dissuade her. She dressed in her brightest colors, with one of her son's war helmets on her head. Like a small brown beetle, she sat her horse, her eyes gleaming in anger, her mouth so hard and silent that Pahe wondered if she had stitched it shut.

Pahe rode on Nataallith's finest mare, dressed in a colorful blanket, leggings, moccasins, and a girdle woven in shades of red and orange, the colors of the sun. Nataallith had spoken sometimes for peace and sometimes for war, but now that the decision had been made, he was of one mind with that decision. Pahe knew that this was one of the marks of a leader, that he was able to take for his own the will of the People, even if that will was not his first choice. Out of respect for many headmen who clamored for war, however, he put on his war helmet festooned with hawk feathers and rode alongside her father.

They rode behind Narbona before one thousand head of horses, cattle, and sheep, presents to the white headman, to make up for all that had been stolen by the raiding bands of warriors. "I cannot keep the young men in check," Narbona said, "but I can give back what they have taken."

Deezbaa rode with Ayoi and Pahe, and little could make her speak. But she spoke to herself loud enough so that many could hear. "You give them back what the warriors have taken, but you do so from your own herds, old man. And there is no guarantee the whites will make the Mexicans keep the peace even after they take all this—" And she swept her hand over the herds behind them, which made such a roiling of dust with their hooves that they could scarcely be seen spreading over the distant flatlands.

"It will take us ten winters to make up what is given up here," Ayoi said. There was no anger in her voice, only a dignified sadness.

"He does not have ten winters," Deezbaa said shortly.

"Perhaps none of us do," Ayoi answered. "But that does not matter to my father. The horses mean little. What matters to him is the People and the land. We must keep the land. If we do not keep the peace, the land will be taken from us."

"It will be taken from us, no matter," Deezbaa said as though to no one, her head turned away from her daughter even as she spoke.

They came into the valley where the Americans were camped, and the following day, Narbona and the other headmen sat down in council with Colonel Washington and James Calhoun, the Indian agent for the territory.

Pahe sat behind Long Earrings with the other women, listening carefully to every word. To one side, she could see Deezbaa, standing apart from the clan as though she knew what they whispered about her. The man they called Colonel Washington spoke to the interpreter, who then recounted his words to the listening people.

The interpreter was a speaker from the clan of Sandoval, the Navajo Who are Enemy, and though few of the People wished to hear him, they had no choice but to accept his words. He wore a soldier's coat and a soldier's hat, and he stood straight with his chest out as the soldiers did. He spoke in Spanish, which the People could barely understand, and so they listened intently with frowning eyes.

"The white man wants a peace which will last!" he said loudly so that those gathered in the back of the seated clans could hear. "The white man says you are now under the laws of the United States! All the Navajo are to assemble in the Canyon de Chelly to make this peace. You will no longer fight with your neighbors but you will apply to the United States for justice. If you make this peace, then all of your friends will be friends of the United

States and all of your enemies will be enemies of the United States."

A short ripple of laughter went up then, as the People wryly saw that, indeed, one of their enemies, a speaker for the Enemy Navajo, was standing before them now as an obvious friend of the United States.

The interpreter went on as though he did not hear the laughter. "Are you willing to be at peace with the United States?"

Narbona said quietly from his blanket, "We are willing."

The interpreter said as much to the listening white men, and then he listened for a moment. He said then, "By the treaty you will make, all trade between you and other nations will be under the laws of the United States." He smiled hugely. "This is so you will not be imposed upon by bad men."

This time, the laughter was larger but more quickly silenced.

Narbona said quietly, "We understand and we are content."

The interpreter went on. "They say that if you make this peace, the United States will protect you against all others. And to do this thing, they will fix and mark the boundaries of your lands so that there will be no misunderstandings with your neighbors."

A murmur went through the People, which Pahe heard was generally approving. Narbona said, "Tell them we are very glad of this."

The interpreter turned and did so. And then he continued. "And the United States will build forts on your lands wherever they think it is necessary so that they might protect you better from your neighbors."

This time, no laughter rolled through the listeners. The shocked silence was so loud that Pahe thought her ears were ringing.

"And if you keep this peace, the United States will make presents to you from time to time of many axes, hoes, and blankets."

Pahe looked down at her own blanket in bewilderment. She knew, for her mother told her, that the blankets of the Navajo were more prized by the traders than all the blankets in the territory, including those of the Pueblo and the Hopi. Why would they wish presents of blankets from the white men? Why would men like her father give up their lands for gifts of metal tools?

To her amazement, however, Narbona only nodded and said to the interpreter, "These things we will need to discuss among ourselves. Say only that we will consider all proposals and have our answer for this colonel in due time. Tell them also that in future council, the younger headmen, Armijo and Pedro Jose and he whom is called Long Earrings, will act for myself and my son-in-law who is called Manuelito." He looked up and smiled wryly. "Tell them we are too old to make this journey again."

Pahe glanced quickly at Nataallith, but his face betrayed nothing. So it was decided. He would speak in the place of her father and her grandfather. She was filled with a pride that burned at her heart like a warmed rock.

The interpreter spoke quickly to the white men, and they listened intently, turning to speak among themselves. Then Sandoval rose and began to talk loudly to the gathered people, telling them what a fine and powerful ally the United States had been to his clan. She saw her mother and father and a few of the other headmen and their wives move to the rear of the crowd quietly, with no disturbance, as though they had other duties to attend. She turned back to watch the colonel, for she felt it was on his face that she could see the future of these words.

Suddenly, a soldier standing near the colonel shouted to the white men and pointed to one of the warriors mounted in the front of the crowd, close to where Deezbaa stood. He pointed to the warrior and then to the warrior's horse, obviously agitated.

The interpreter said nervously, "He says that horse is stolen. He claims it as his—"

Narbona rose wearily and glanced at the warrior, who did not move or change his expression. "Tell the colonel that we will make a gift of two horses to this man—"

Before he could finish, Colonel Washington said angrily, "Arrest that man! The stolen mount must be returned at once!"

When the white man pointed at the warrior, the warrior shouted to Narbona, "Yes, it is stolen! As the Mexicans steal horses, so do we! And it has changed hands many times since then! If the Mexican dog were not standing among soldiers with guns, he would not dare to claim it even now!"

The colonel ignored the interpreter's frantic speech and shouted again for his soldiers. The warrior then turned his horse in confusion, unsure what to do, and in that moment, Deezbaa reached up with her walking stick and struck his withers, sending him bolting away from the crowd.

Narbona called out plaintively, "We are here to make peace! I call upon the headmen to keep order!"

"Seize the horse!" the white colonel shouted. "Seize any horse!"

Pahe sensed the confusion rising in the People, and many of them were backing away from the front of the crowd, turning and speaking to each other in rising tones of concern and anger, and then the colonel shouted something else, and the soldiers raised their guns to their shoulders, pointing them into the crowd.

Nataallith grabbed her shoulder and pushed her backward, turning her and shoving her away from her grandfather and the other elders. A woman screamed in the crowd, and the People began to run, some on foot, some on horseback.

Pahe was running with Nataallith behind her, turning to shout for her grandfather, saw her grandmother run as fast as a deer away from the soldiers, when her husband pushed her down roughly and threw himself on her body, and she heard the blistering cracks of rifle fire. She screamed then, the pain and agony of sudden knowing ripping through her like a dozen knives. She screamed again and again, smothered by her husband's body, rolling under him in panic.

Around them, the dust rolled and billowed, the horses thundered, and she could hear the screams and shouts of the People, the soldiers, and the stupefying booming of the guns.

She heard plainly the voice of the colonel shouting out again, and the guns ceased. She looked into her husband's face. His eyes were closed, and she could see blood on his shoulder, oozing through his blanket.

She pushed him off and rolled him over, checking his wounds. Then in a fury of panic and rage, she took his arms and dragged him swiftly to the cover of juniper scrub. He was bleeding, but he was alive. She crouched down alongside him, watching the soldiers from a distance.

To her horror, she saw that where Narbona had stood was now a crumpled form on the ground, a heap of blanket and limbs, and next to him was another fallen headman. She counted seven men down, but six of them were still moving. She could see her grandmother noplace at all.

While she watched, frozen with amazement and terror, the soldiers gathered round her grandfather's body, kneeling and prodding at him with their boots as if he were a coyote carcass. She almost rose and shouted at them, but she knew that she must live to tell what she saw, repeat what she heard. She sank back against Nataallith's motionless form, unable to pull her eyes from the scene.

The soldiers finally left her grandfather's form, and after rummaging about with some of the other fallen warriors, they broke camp, formed into their long lines, and marched off toward the canyon, with their bugler sounding before them and their colonel riding in the lead.

Pahe waited until the dust settled and then she rose and ran to her grandfather's side. She screamed then, when she saw him, screamed again to the sky and beat at her breasts until she was bruised and exhausted. The white men had scalped him, leaving his poor, torn head pitiful and bloodied, his eyes open in surprise, as though, even as he met death, he could not believe he had been so betrayed. She staggered back to her husband who still lay motionless, and she curled next to him and hid her eyes, retching and weeping.

By sunset, many of the People had returned. Six other warriors had been wounded, and three of those had died.

Manuelito and Ayoi came and collected Pahe and Nataallith, carrying him to shelter where Ayoi bound his wounds and reassured Pahe that he would live. Narbona's sons had meanwhile wrapped Narbona in a burial robe and carried him to a high mesa, where they keened and wept over his body.

Deezbaa came then to join them, her hair loose and straggling down over her shoulders, her face hard with grief. She had taken the white blanket off her hogan and wrapped herself within it, in defiance of all custom, and she leaned on her sons, suddenly more frail and smaller than she had seemed before.

When Pahe saw her grandmother, she went to her and embraced her, resolving to say nothing about seeing her strike the blow that caused the horse to bolt. Perhaps the soldiers would have fired upon the council even if the horse had not run. Perhaps not. It scarcely mattered now.

When dawn came again, Narbona's sons carried his corpse

with his bow and arrows, carried his war helmet and his silver buckle to a deep crevice in the canyon. They dropped him within and built fires all around to keep off the wolves. Deezbaa sat with her sons, praying to the Holy Ones to let Narbona's spirit rest. They sat death vigil for four days, and the People came and wept and left again, to be replaced by more, until all the clans had come to say farewell to Narbona, though no one would say his name lest his ghost be called back from its journey. Through the four days, Pahe saw no one speak to Deezbaa or acknowledge her presence at the burial cavern.

But Pahe could give little thought to her grandmother, for Nataallith must be tended. She bathed and wrapped her husband's shoulder wound over and over, and when he finally woke, he wept for the death of Narbona and the death of peace. "The time for talking is past," he said. "Now we must fight."

The headmen convened quick council that night over the fires, and Nataallith declared that he would neither go to Canyon de Chelly to make the peace nor would he keep his warriors in check any longer. His voice was steady and strong when he said, "The white men are like wolves, but worse. They have no honor, and they are men of great perversion. We have been told this by our neighbors, and now we see that it is so. They have not kept their promises to free our women and children from the Mexicans, they have invaded our lands, turned their horses into our corn, and now they have murdered a man who is father to our People, father of *Dinétah*. I will not make the peace. I will make war on these wolves and kill them whenever I find them on our lands."

Pahe held her breath. Many men had lost their wives and children and still wanted peace with the white men, for they feared the strength of the *Bilagáana*. Would they now go to war because of the death of Narbona, when they would not war for the loss of their loved ones?

But the circle of warriors was without dissent. "None of us will make this peace," they agreed. "Let the soldiers wait for us at Canyon de Chelly. They can wait until the rocks melt in the sun."

And so the soldiers marched to the canyon, setting fire to hogans and cornfields as they went. When they reached the place where peace was to be made, they captured a small local headman and made him sign the papers that Narbona, Nataallith, and the other headmen were to sign. They then marched back to Santa Fe, unaware that, behind them, Manuelito was leading raids on every hacienda and ranch he could hit, killing Mexicans with impunity and capturing every horse, sheep, and all cattle he and his warriors could drive away.

There was no more talk of peace and no more messages from the white men.

*   *   *

Two years later, in the middle of some of the richest Navajo pasture land where a flowing stream kept the grasses green, a place the People considered not only beautiful but holy, the soldiers built an adobe fort and named it Fort Defiance.

*   *   *

It was a windy day, and the air was October chill with the coming snow. Rus was foraging far from his burrow, farther than he normally would have hunted for food, but he was driven by a hunger which was more than hunger, the need to put on a last bit of fat before the coming winter sleep. He had been drawn away by his discovery of a patch of gramagrass which was still green, despite the colder temperatures, and he was determined to eat what he could as fast as possible, taking pouchfuls back to the nesting burrow when his stomach was full.

Rus was a White-Tailed Prairie Dog, *Cynomys leucurus,* a two-year-old male in his prime, stocky, with a buff coat and a short white-tipped tail. He had dark patches above and below his eyes, a small yellow nose, and tiny ears which were much less sensitive than his sense of smell.

Rus lived, as did his relations, in a broad dog town of interconnecting burrows with more than twenty entrance and exit holes. Unlike his cousins, the Black-Tailed Prairie Dog, he and his kin lived in the higher, cooler elevations of mountain meadows and high pastures, and so they hibernated from the early snows of October until the first spring breezes of March.

He glanced back at the closest conical mound which led down into the earth more than fourteen feet to his nesting burrow. On top of the mound, one of his mates stood sentry duty. Rus had four mates who shared his burrow, connected to the rest of the coterie which had six other males and their mates, which was connected to other coteries, which were connected to another ward which had four more coteries—more than two hundred kin, all told, and Rus recognized each of them by their familiar scent and flavor, a contact he tested each time he greeted one of them in the "kiss" of dog town, a touching of incisors, mouth to mouth.

His mate watched the skies and the horizon silently, sitting up straight and tall on her haunches, her paws folded over her belly. Her posture alone told him that all was well. He listened for her warning yip, which would send him scurrying back to the safety of the burrow ahead of a hawk, a snake, or some other enemy. The wind moaned more loudly, and Rus rose up on his haunches to test it for the smell of snow. It was coming soon, and he thought of the nesting burrow, warm and padded with dry grasses. Next spring, all four of his mates would likely litter, filling the burrow with their offspring, twenty tiny blind and helpless dogs which would be his responsibility only until the coming of the cool weather once more, when they would be gone. He bent again to the grasses and ate as fast as he could.

Rus could not know it, but dog towns like his would soon be rare, threatened by more than just the coyotes, the snakes, and the hawks. Out on the Great Plains, the white men were killing off the buffalo and bringing in vast herds of cattle. Since the prairie dogs competed with the cattle for grass—two hundred and fifty dogs could eat as much grass each day as a cow—the cowboys and ranchers were killing them off as fast as they could be shot, poisoned, trapped, or flooded out.

Before the coming of the cattle and the ranchers, dog towns once spread over huge territories. The largest one recorded in the Texas Panhandle was more than two hundred and fifty miles long and one hundred miles wide, with more than five billion prairie dogs in residence.

It would take one hundred and twenty-five thousand men poisoning more than twenty million acres to clear off the Texas cattle ranges, and within fifty years, dog towns would be reduced by more than ninety percent.

But for now, Rus and his relations were thriving, and their

numbers almost doubled each breeding spring. His mates were fat and healthy; the pups would be numerous and noisy. The wind moaned around his ears, and a small noise nearby caused Rus to look up again to check his mate's posture, only to find his view blocked by a large gray coyote not ten feet away.

Rus dropped instantly to the dirt, flattened himself and held perfectly still. The coyote had ambled between Rus and his burrow, and the warning yip of his mate had been smothered by the sound of the wind. The grass in his mouth nearly choked him, but he did not swallow, did not chew, did not dare to make a sound. The coyote was searching the grass curiously, but had not yet picked up his scent. The nearby conical mounds of the burrows were suddenly deserted, and it seemed as though there were not a single prairie dog for miles.

Rus watched the coyote moving slightly away to one side, then nearer still, as it searched the grasses, panting eagerly. It was a young coyote, less skilled in the hunt than it would be in another season, and, in that, Rus sensed he might escape. He did not blink, only his nose moved imperceptibly, for he could not keep his whiskers from trembling with the scent of coyote so close, so close, right between himself and safety. Oh, his burrow! A great sense of longing surged through him for the safety of his burrow, the place he had dug with his kin, the place of his mates, his pups, the larder for his winter food, the shelter from all storms and the bitter cold—he needed it now as urgently as he had ever needed food.

Rus yanked himself back to alertness, for he felt his senses wander and a great numb sleepiness steal over him. He could not know that this was his specie's response to shock, the same numbness that came quickly over a squirrel taken by a hawk, the brief pause of sensation that buffered the last few moments of horror.

The coyote suddenly stopped and sniffed eagerly at a mound of dirt which Rus had vacated moments before, and as it bent its head, picking up Rus's scent, Rus bolted suddenly from his prone position, dashing around the coyote within inches of its flinching paws. The coyote leaped in the air, came down running after him, its snapping jaws inches from Rus as he dove for the safety of the mound, barely reaching it ahead of sure and clumsy death.

Now, above him, the young coyote whined and dug frantically at the mound, as Rus scampered down the burrow, covering ten feet in seconds, to the safety of the nest, where he was immediately covered by his four mates, licking and yipping and biting him urgently, pawing him all over in an ecstasy of reunion. He panted in exhaustion, lying down and letting them groom him all over, pulling his paws and nosing his ears with their small deft claws, for this was the way they reassured themselves and him of their bond.

After a moment or two, Rus leaped up again, chirring a command for them to stay below. He raced up another passageway that led to an escape mound some fifteen feet from the one which he had just left and poked his head out up top. The coyote was no longer digging. It was scratching a flea, sitting almost on top of the mound Rus had escaped into, panting in frustration.

Rus yipped at it mockingly, causing two dozen heads to pop up out of the burrows all around in a chorus of yips. The coyote lunged for the nearest burrow, and of course the dog within popped out of sight. After lunging at five burrows and missing all five inhabitants, the coyote finally trotted off, its tail down in defeat.

Rus watched it depart until it was well away from dog town, and then he gave a leap into the air, throwing up his forelimbs and his head way back, giving a whistling, wheezing yip. It was the all-clear signal, and all around him, his kin echoed the call until dozens of dogs were leaping and yipping together.

*　　*　　*

In 1851, James Calhoun was promoted from Indian agent to the first governor of New Mexico, and one of his first proclamations was to officially sanction Indian slavery and slave trading in the territory. In the few months following that proclamation, fifty-one Navajo women and children were stolen by the New Mexicans and sold south to Mexico, including two nephews of Nataallith who were taken when their father was killed and their mother watched from a hiding place.

Calhoun was sensitive to the fact that talk of slavery in Washington was focused on black men, not red, and was growing more clamorous as the seasons went on. President Zachary Taylor was a Southerner and a Whig. So was Calhoun. Since California had just been admitted as a free state, New Mexico must declare for slavery if the balance was to be maintained in the Senate. That meant the rebellious Navajo must be quelled and a fort—or better yet, several forts—must be built on their lands to guarantee the safety of new pro-slave settlers.

The Navajo were Calhoun's chief political embarrassment. He urged President Taylor to put them on a reservation, despite the new treaty they had just signed which guaranteed them permission to "freely visit all parts of the United States and New Mexico."

* * *

The construction of Fort Defiance only a few yards from the springs the People considered holy so angered them that some of the young warriors could not be restrained from attack. Again and again, they raided the supply wagons, and even Nataallith was persuaded once to join them.

In the spring of 1853, five warriors from Black Eagle's clan attacked a Mexican rancher and kidnapped his son, his nephew, and three shepherds. Nataallith tried to make the warriors release their captives, but they refused. "The Mexicans have stolen a paint horse and a mule," they told him. "When the Americans make them give back what they stole, we will let the boys go."

Colonel Sumner of Fort Defiance sent a message to Nataallith demanding the return of the boys and more: the five warriors must turn themselves in for punishment as well. He said he would lay waste to the country, kill every man he could find, destroy every field of grain, and take every stock animal he could catch. He added, "Say to Zarcillos Largos, the one they call Long Earrings, and the other chiefs, to some of whom I am personally known, that it will give me great pain to destroy their crops and to leave their women and children to starve, for it will be too late to plant again this year, but they must be made to know once and for all the difference between American and Mexican governments."

This message reached Nataallith and Pahe when she was giving birth to their second child. Wasek was now an active boy of four, and Pahe had stopped taking the herbs that kept her belly from conceiving. No sooner had she decided that she was ready to be filled with life again but it came. Now she labored in the women's hogan, while her husband held council over this most recent message from the white man.

"What do they say?" she asked her mother between panting gasps. Ayoi supported her two arms with the pulling strap, and her two sisters-in-law went to and fro with warm poultices, herbal drinks for strength, and news from the council fires.

Ayoi shrugged and wiped her sweating brow. It was hot in the hogan, and she was out of patience with men, their talk of war and peace, and children who would never come.

"It will help me to speak of it!" Pahe pleaded painfully, twisting under the birth pangs. This one was coming faster and harder than Wasek. She felt it would surely be another boy, a warrior in his own right.

"It will help no one to speak of it," Ayoi said, sounding more and more like Deezbaa every day. "All they *do* is speak of it. If we had a sheep for every word they have used on the white men, we would be so rich, we could drive them off the face of the earth altogether, let alone these lands."

"But this time, the message comes for my husband," Pahe moaned.

"And the last one came for your grandmother's husband. See where it got him."

"Aiii, will this boy never come forth!" Pahe cried out. She made one, two, and then three hard pushes, and she felt the child slip free of her. Weeping with the exertion, she bent to see what lay in her mother's hands, caught in the act of being born.

"Never come forth a boy, that much is certain." Ayoi laughed, refreshed now by the sight and sounds of the infant. "You have a daughter, my little bird! A woman-child this time."

Pahe laughed then, too, with delight and surprise. "Well, and I would have thought her a pack of boys, as much as she battled to stay where she was. This one will be a fighter!"

Ayoi was crooning to the baby and wiping her vigorously with the warm, wet birthing blanket. "You were the same when you came."

"Go and tell her father," Pahe said to her sister-in-law. "Tell him this voice, at least, is a warrior's."

*   *   *

Council finished and it was agreed. The captives would be returned along with the sheep, but Black Eagle refused to turn over the five warriors. Nataallith sent a message to the new colonel with his apologies: he was not a king. He did not have such control over other clans, he explained; this was not the way of the People, and to attempt to take the warriors from their clan would be to risk disaster. The People braced for war.

A runner came back with the message from Indian Agent Henry Dodge, the man the Navajo called "Red Sleeves" for the red shirt he wore. He had persuaded the colonel not to punish the Navajo; there would be no reprisal. The headmen did not know what to make of this, and the clans spoke of it for months. How could a leader make such a warning and then not carry out the threat? What did his own people think of such weakness? What were they to make of this?

Often, now, Pahe would find Nataallith brooding by the fire in the night, long after she had fallen asleep. She would wake and see his hunched shoulders, a shadowed sentry in the silence of the hogan, staring at the embers. She sometimes rose, pretending that she had to check on Dolii, Little Bluebird, but it was pretense. From the first, her daughter slept through the night silently, as though she knew somehow that she would need her strength for whatever came with the dawn. But she would bend over the sleeping infant, pull a blanket higher on Wasek's shoulder, and then Pahe would touch her husband's shoulder gently and peer into his face.

"You cannot rest?" she whispered.

He shrugged, reaching up to touch her hand with his to comfort her.

But she was not comforted. She sat down beside him, careful not to stare at him. Sometimes he spoke; more often, he did not.

Once he said, "There is much I do not understand in this life."

"You are not alone in this, my heart," she murmured.

"And yet I must act, regardless. I must make decisions as though I understand what will come of them."

"And you do not understand the white men," she said wearily. Of course that was the source of his worry. It was always so.

He smiled sadly. "Go to sleep, my love."

She shook her head. "You do not need to understand them to defeat them."

"I wish that were so," he said, and he looked up at the rafters of the hogan as though the answer were somehow above him in the night sky.

She rose and patted him softly. She went to their sleeping pallet and closed her eyes. No matter what they did or did not solve in the night, the children would rise with the dawn and need food, embraces, and smiling faces. It was ever so, she thought. The mothers knew that they did not need to understand the white men; neither did they need to understand their own men. They must, however, be there for the children. Their men could ponder the future and rage against bad luck, the strangers, the drought. But the mothers must rise with the light and begin each morning as though life would endure, whether or not they believed it in their hearts.

She suddenly remembered her wedding day, a memory she had pulled out and fondled lovingly in her heart many times. She could see, in her mind's eye, so clearly the hogan of her mother draped with beautiful blankets, the empty space in the middle waiting for her, surrounded by many kin. They had come great distances, their horses and wagons were crowded outside, and Nataallith was dressed in his finest silver and turquoise. He wore a red band round his forehead, tied at the side with a flourish. She was wearing her most colorful blanket skirt with a heavy silver belt and her grandmother's silver over the blanket on her breasts.

The hogan was packed with clan members, young and old, laughing and talking and waiting for them to arrive. The chanter or medicine man sat in the center, and Ayoi and Manuelito sat quietly at the side, unsmiling and dignified. She came through the doorway with Nataallith, and the laughing and talking died down. She walked ahead of Nataallith carrying her wedding basket, her head high, the bells on her ankles making a singing sound which rose up into her head and made her feel giddy and light. Nataallith took her hand and they sat together on the rugs before the chanter. She put her basket on the floor before them. It was a *ts'aa*, a wedding basket that Deezbaa had given her made of spliced sumac in shades of tan and orange and red, and filled with ground corn meal, the symbol of fertility. Pahe had cooked it herself, as was fitting.

The chanter had knelt before the wedding basket and drew his *jish*, his medicine pouch, from his pocket. Murmuring prayers, he sprinkled corn pollen over the basket and then made a cross in the dirt with the basket in the center. The cross, where all lines came together, was the symbol for the center of the earth. The chanter took more pollen and spilled it carefully in all four directions, calling the spirits of the east, the south, the west, and the north to bless the marriage. He took out his groaning stick, a forked piece of wood that had been struck by lightning. If he swung it around his head by the buckskin thong, he could make it groan or roar, according to the needs of the ceremony.

Then the chanter reached for his water basket. It was old and covered with pitch. He gave the basket to Nataallith, who suddenly turned to Pahe and smiled the warmest, most intimate smile, and Juanita caught the look and laughed, and the laughter spread to all, and Nataallith's smile widened and the laughter raced round the corner of the hogan at that smile and it took some moments to settle the clan down again. Nataallith had loved that moment, she could tell. In that moment, he affirmed his leadership. He took the basket and poured the water on her hands carefully, lovingly, washing them in the water of life, and then washed his own. After he washed their hands, he helped her to kneel again, and he took a bit of corn mush from her basket and ate of it, nodding approvingly. She did the same, unable to keep from smiling.

Then her parents came forward, and her stepmother and brothers, and members of his own clan, to eat of the corn mush she had prepared and to welcome them into the round of family and fertility and kinship. When all had eaten, Nataallith stood and said that he was making a gift to his bride's mother, since she had given him her daughter in this ceremony: two fine horses, eight sheep, and a silver belt and harness set. He added that there was not enough wealth in all *Dinétah* to make up for the loss of such a daughter, but he humbly hoped that Ayoi would accept his small token of gratitude.

The clan had beamed and laughed and nodded their approval. Nataallith then embraced her before all the People, and the laughter and talking began again. Manuelito stood and said that he was pleased to have such a fine son-in-law, and Nataallith's uncle stood and said that Pahe was a blessing to their clan, and other old ones came forward and spoke of marriage and children and how to grow old together with happiness. Some of the old men had several wives with them, and Pahe had blushed and ducked her head at their jokes which grew more ribald as the night went on.

The chanter then reminded them all that there was no word for wedding in the language of the People. "The Ancients called this the Planting Ceremony, *ki' dilye*, male and female, planting equal seeds," he said. "The wedding basket is to remind you of your part of the earth and the sky, the land and the water, the fertility of all growing things. May you each walk in beauty all your days. And may you take that walk together."

When she came out of the hogan with Nataallith, to receive the embraces and good wishes of the clan, the sun was going down behind the mountains. Behind the hogan, the women were preparing the mutton stew and the kneel-down bread for the wedding feast, and the air was turning cool. A golden light seemed to well up from the last gleamings of the sun and turned the hogan, the hills, the trees, and the air itself a shimmering yellow, and she knew that she would remember this for all the days of her life.

And she now could recall every detail, as though it happened only yesterday, despite two children who lay sleeping, the product of that wedding day. She opened her eyes and saw that Nataallith was still sitting by the fire, staring into the embers. He had changed much since that day they were married. But she could still remember that smile he gave her then, still could see the ghost of it sometimes play upon his face. She closed her eyes again and prayed silently, "Let us grow old together, O Holy Ones. Let us die within hours of one another. Let us walk in beauty, as we vowed to do on our wedding day."

The prayer did not bring her the comfort she had hoped to

feel. Still, her man sat and stared into the future or the past. She sighed and turned over. The children would wake soon, and she must be able to smile for them.

*   *   *

Two seasons passed and the new President Franklin Pierce replaced Governor Lane with Governor Meriwether. The clans continued to wonder and debate, and finally it was decided. They would go to see these white men for themselves. Nataallith said, "Perhaps if we see them in their own village, with their women and children about them, we will understand them more. To understand the enemy is to know their weaknesses as well as their strengths."

And so, on a cool day in 1854, a delegation of Navajo rode into Santa Fe behind Agent Henry Dodge, more than one hundred of them, including Nataallith, Manuelito, Ganada Mucho, Armijo, and all of the other important headmen. Many of them brought their wives; all of them rode their finest mounts and wore every bit of silver and turquoise they owned. They carried painted shields and feathered lances, and those with rifles had them tied openly across their saddles.

Pahe rode beside Nataallith on a beautiful white mare, with her indigo-and-red blanket belted at her waist with a heavy silver concho belt, her deerskin leggings tied and beaded with jangling silver bells, and her hair coils pierced with six small silver arrows. Her daughter was on her back and her son sat astride her mare before her, eager to see these white men. Juanita and her sons rode behind them, and Ayoi set astride a black mare which shone like obsidian in the sun. They rode into the capital, announced by only the barking dogs and the running children, right into the central plaza before the governor's palace.

Dodge said to them as they came into town, "Most of these folks have never seen a Navajo before. They're more scared of you than a hundred rattlers. They likely won't know what to make of this."

Manuelito gave a quick order, and all riders tightened their procession, sat up straight and tall, and kept a dignified silence as they rode up to the palace.

Women on both sides of the street screamed for their children, slammed their doors and shutters shut, and the men kept their distance in uneasy silence as the delegation rode in. They circled the plaza slowly and then stopped their horses in line. Dodge dismounted and went inside the palace. He returned shortly, and a man appeared at the upstairs window. He came out to the balcony and surveyed the scene below, waving confidently to the crowd. "This is the man they call Meriwether," Manuelito said. "The new headman of the *Bilagáana.*"

"We welcome this delegation of Navajo to Santa Fe!" Meriwether shouted to the onlookers. "We thank our good friend, Agent Dodge, for bringing these chiefs to us in peace! We hope that we may have talks which will extend this peace to future generations and end the warfare between our peoples and all the Indians of this land!"

There was a brief hesitation while the crowd tried to assimilate these words with the vision of the Indian warriors mounted around them on all sides. But suddenly, a brave huzzah went up, followed by another, and then another, until finally the crowd was generally cheering in good faith, while casting sideways glances at the savages surrounding them.

Pahe surveyed the white people all around her. The women were garbed in long skirts that hid their legs, but some of them had tucked up the skirts out of the muddy streets, high enough that she could see their boots. They looked no different in that respect from her people. On their heads they wore hats against the sun; this, too, was no different. Their skin was generally lighter, but certainly not white. In fact, many of them were almost as brown as the lightest women in her clan.

The similarities both reassured and perturbed her. She had expected to see such differences that would explain a people so perverse, yet there were none apparent. Their children ran and gawked and laughed and shouted much as hers would have if the *Bilagáana* had ridden into her husband's hacienda. The dogs barked and jostled round the horses' legs in the same way.

"My mother, how can they think with their hair cut so short? They are so ugly," her son murmured to her uneasily. Wasek was not accustomed to the presence of strangers; he had not yet learned, as his cousins and stepbrothers had, to keep his face impassive and his mouth silent. Pahe put a hand on his leg, a touch meant both to comfort and quiet. "Not so very, I think," she said gently. "They are not monsters, after all. And we shall see if they are as powerful as the headmen say, eh? You look and see all they do, and then later you will tell me what you see."

Pahe noticed then that a woman who stood close to her mare with her man had heard her speaking in Navajo to Wasek. She had not understood the words but had certainly known the tone, as any mother would. She smiled hesitantly up at Pahe.

Pahe felt a slow smile begin on her own mouth, and she ducked her head shyly. In that moment, she felt her own soul freeze like a startled doe. These were the people who had murdered her grandfather. This was the enemy who had made her husband nearly mad with despair for the clans. And yet, the woman smiled at her in attempted friendship. She felt a great confusion in her heart and wondered if Nataallith had been wise to suggest this visit after all. Surely it would be more difficult to kill these enemies now. She knew that she would never forget this moment or the white woman's smile, and part of her wished she had never seen it.

*   *   *

That night, the Navajo put on a dance in the plaza for the people of Santa Fe, and each member of the delegation behaved as though he were a guest in an enemy camp. In fact, the next morning when Meriwether met with the headmen of the People, he congratulated them on their "remarkable sobriety and general good behavior."

Most of them did not understand the compliment, but they listened well when this Meriwether went on to say what he would do.

"We will be listening to the complaints of the white man with one ear and the red man with the other," he said, "and we will weigh both and then give our decision with impartiality." When the interpreter had changed his words to Spanish and then Manuelito's interpreter had changed the words once more to Navajo, the headmen nodded in agreement.

"Our decision," Meriwether added, "is irrevocable and must be obeyed."

The headmen glanced at Manuelito, who showed no change of expression.

Then Meriwether smiled and nodded. "And to show that this peace is based on compromise, we are willing to extend our pardon for all past offenses, including the most recent and unfortunate killing of one of our most prominent citizens."

Manuelito nodded then, after a brief moment of silence. It was good. The peace talks continued into the afternoon, and that evening the whole town turned out to see the governor present medals to the headmen and designate Nataallith, now called by the white man Zarcillos Largos, as "head chief" of the Navajo Nation by giving to him a cane as staff of office.

Pahe was filled with pride and fear for him all at once. As she explained to Wasek the honor put upon his father, and therefore to all of their clan, her son thrust out his chest and cried boldly, "My father is the chief of all the People!"

She cuffed him quickly to silence. How had he even heard such a white man's word? "He is not such a thing at all, foolish mouth. He is a respected headman, and so are others. Just because the white man says a thing, that does not make it so."

Wasek glowered at her. "This is something that women cannot understand."

She laughed then, shaking his shoulder gently. "There speaks a man. There is nothing that women cannot understand, my son. Learn that lesson well and quickly, if you wish to have a peaceful life."

"I do not want a peaceful life!" her son protested. "I want to be a warrior."

"And you shall be," she said, attempting to take him in her arms; but he wiggled away and ran to watch the men smoking in the shade of the governor's palace.

That night, the People danced again for the townspeople, and some of the white men and women even joined into the dance clumsily, cheered on and welcomed by the Navajo dancers.

In one instant, Pahe found herself dancing opposite one of the white men, a creature with a matted beard and long, tangled red hair tied back of his head. She could smell him from several feet away, but she kept the grimace from her mouth and tried to smile cordially at him. He rolled his eyes at her like a breeding stallion, and she was struck by the truth of her son's remark: indeed, the *Bilagáana* were an ugly race.

*   *   *

Domy felt the sun leaving the desert rather than saw it, for, as usual, he had slept away most of the day in his burrow, an intricate labyrinth of tunnels, sleeping compartments, food storage areas, and waste bins. Dusk was coming; he sensed it as a cooling and an urging toward activity. Nightfall made him hungry and made him aware of his bladder. He rose, stretched, and scratched himself vigorously. With a final yawn, he went off to void himself in his waste burrow.

It was getting rank, he noticed, as he urinated on his favorite corner. Time to wall it in and dig another. He yawned once more and padded uphill the six feet of diggings to the entrance to his burrow. Just inside the three-inch hole, he stopped and smelled the air carefully. The sun was almost down. Night would come fast on this side of the mountain, but the ground was still warm and would remain so most of the night, in this summer season.

Domy listened carefully for any vibrations above him, his wide white whiskers quivering with alertness. He was buff-colored on his head and back, about nine inches long, about two ounces in size, and his tail was almost as long as his body. Domy was a *Dipodomys ordii,* an Ord's Kangaroo Rat, the most common kangaroo rat of the seven Kangaroo Rat species found on the American continent. He was actually neither rat nor mouse but more closely related to the ground squirrel. Like the ground squirrel, he needed very little water, and, in fact, Domy's small, efficient body could manufacture water from the seeds of the mesquite, tumbleweed, Russian thistle, and sandburs that he ate. If he needed to, he could go without water altogether, a feat unknown in any other species in this region.

But he could not go long without food. And that need was what drove him forth each night to forage. Domy crept carefully out the opening of his burrow and stopped once more, his whiskers quivering. He rarely went more than about thirty feet from an entrance hole, and he could reach the safety of his burrow with a few fast bounds. His hind legs were long and powerful, his tail helped him to balance, and he could jump more than nine feet when alarmed.

But he was not alarmed now. There was nothing in the cooling night air to suggest danger. He scratched his neck vigorously with his claws, checked the mound of sand at his burrow hole to be sure it was proper, and then set to work.

Domy's latest endeavor had been to move a large piece of tumbleweed to his widest entrance hole. It would make excellent storage fodder for the coming cold months, and he was determined to get the bulk of it maneuvered down his tunnel and safely cached away. He had dragged it and gnawed it and yanked it into position, and now he was prepared to begin taking it apart branch by branch and wrestling it down under the ground. He scurried eagerly toward where he had left the tumbleweed, stopping to eat a few sandburs on the way and rolled in the sand to keep his fur from matting up.

As he approached the tumbleweed, he heard the smallest scraping sound on the bare rock above him, and he froze. Coiled above him on a slight rocky ledge, taking the last heat of the day from the stone, was a large rattlesnake. One of his most feared enemies. Domy instinctively drummed with his hind foot, the standard alarm signal for all kangaroo rats, though he had not been part of a colony since last breeding season. That small movement and hesitation was his error.

The rattlesnake instantly raised its head, alerted now to Domy's presence by the vibration and his movement. Where it had been somnolent in the cooling breeze, now it was alert and testing the air with its black, forked tongue. Domy squeaked in fear, a sound like a bird's soft chirp, and whirled to run for his escape hole, jumping more than the length of a man with each leap.

When he reached the entrance hole, he dove for cover, and, behind him, he saw the snake coming on fast. Domy's greatest fear was that the snake would enter his burrow itself, blocking him from taking refuge there and leaving him vulnerable and exposed to the dangers of the night. Once the snake was inside, there would be little he could do to dislodge it and noplace to defend himself. So he turned and took a curious and courageous stance, leaped high, and chirped at the snake in challenge.

The snake coiled quickly into striking position, warily rattling a soft warning buzz at Domy's new stance. Unused to prey which turned and faced it, the rattler hesitated just a moment. Domy took his chance then and kicked at the piled sand outside his burrow hole with all his strength, aiming the sand right into the snake's eyes. He had piled the fine, loose sand within easy reach of his long hind feet for exactly this purpose, and he only hoped there was enough ammunition to keep his attacker at bay.

The snake dodged the sand and made a quick strike in the general direction of Domy's head, but Domy was no longer there. He kicked the sand again at the snake, showering the twisting rattler with it, chirping in excitement and fear. The snake finally moved backward, dipping its head and rubbing its nose on its body. Because the snake had no eyelids and could not blink, the shower of sand fell on its unprotected eyes and caused it confusion and discomfort. As it hesitated, Domy bounded away toward another escape hole, this one leading to a blind alley of tunnels with only one narrow exit. If the snake followed, he might be able to trap it inside or block himself in a compartment where the snake could not enter.

But he looked back to see the snake crawling away toward the shelter of the rock ledge. It was either not very hungry or a young snake, Domy sensed, and he had been fortunate to escape.

He went down into his burrow to his favorite sleeping cavity and washed himself all over with his small paws, clawing at his ears and his genitals in anxiety. He had escaped this time, but the snake might well be back. This night, he would have to block that entrance hole and dig another one, more hidden from exploring reptiles. He would not be so lucky another time.

Domy sneezed twice violently, shook himself all over, and ascended to get back to work.

*　　*　　*

Throughout the long winter of 1854, the People kept the peace, despite strict rationing of corn and meal made necessary by the devastation of the crop fields the summer before. But in the spring, the ranchers began to believe that their flocks and herds were now safe from Navajo attack, and they pushed their grazing sheep and cattle far into *Dinétah*, crowding Navajo flocks off the already overgrazed pastures. It was no longer possible to let the younger boys and girls herd the sheep, for they might be challenged at any time by whites on horseback pushing herds before them. Now the men must tend the flocks, and tempers were high as they were pulled from other duties to do what always before had been a job for the women and children.

*   *   *

That spring, again a delegation of People traveled to Santa Fe to complain about the white man's livestock on their land and to receive some promised hoes, shovels, picks, and seed to work their land. No tools were there for them, because the Senate had not sent the money to buy them. The governor again promised that he would do what he could to keep trespassing herds off Navajo lands.

And then that spring, a new trouble blossomed, one which Nataallith prophesied would bring long-term problems to the People. The Utes made an alliance with the Apache and they went on the warpath, attacking ranches all over New Mexico and into Arizona and Nevada. They sent runners to Nataallith, asking for a council. Headmen came from the four corners of Navajo lands to listen to what their traditional enemies, the Utes and their new allies, the Mescalero Apaches, had to say.

Pahe sat with the women at one end of the fires as the Apache and Ute warriors gathered all around them, their ponies milling noisily in the corral. The Apache and Utes did not normally allow women to attend council, and so she and the women were stared at fiercely as the men came forward and then were ignored.

Strutting with success and new riches, the Apache and Ute warriors danced and shouted war cries, boasting of their victories over the whites on their lands. With each telling, it became more obvious that they had also come to taunt the Navajo for not going to war.

Finally, a Ute headman stood before the gathered Navajo and said, "We do not understand why our Navajo brothers will continue to take the bones from the white man's feast. They have broken their promises and they have taken your lands. Are our brothers, the Navajo, like the Pueblo, that they will be happy to farm whatever small pieces of dirt the whites will leave for them?"

All eyes turned to Nataallith then, and Pahe held her breath for her husband's voice.

He spoke quietly, but his words had an undercurrent of anger few could miss. "We have made a treaty of peace with the whites. We are the People, and we do not break our word."

"They break their own treaty!" an Apache headman said, standing now in earnestness. "Do the Navajo also make treaties with the coyotes and the wolves, to leave their flocks alone? We know the whites for what they are. They are enemies to be driven from these lands. We ask our Navajo brothers to join us in this fight."

Nataallith listened to the murmurs round the fires and waited long moments before he spoke again. "A man does not always find it easy to keep his word. Neither does a people. But a man who breaks his word can no longer be trusted. This is true, also, of a nation. Have you not made a treaty with the whites as well?"

The Ute headman took his long knife and plunged it into the dirt at his feet. "This is my treaty with the whites. That I will kill each one I can find on my lands. There is no other treaty I will honor."

"And the people of the Apache?" Nataallith asked the other headmen politely. "Have you not also made a treaty with the whites?"

"We do not honor this treaty," the Apache headman said with dignity. "We do not honor a promise which has been broken by our enemy."

Nataallith shook his head slowly. "It is difficult to make an alliance with men who have decided not to keep their previous alliances with honor. How can we know that any treaty made by such men will be kept?"

These words, however mildly they were spoken, obviously angered the Utes and the Apache, and several of the warriors called out insults to the listening Navajo, but they were ignored.

"You cannot know such a thing of any people," the Apache headman said, still keeping his temper. "But if the Navajo keeps his word, then so will the people of the Apache."

"And who is to determine when a treaty is broken?" Nataallith asked calmly. "One man decides that he has been wronged, that the treaty has been broken, and so he takes action against his enemy in retribution. The treaty is surely broken then. Another man, perhaps one less courageous"—and here, Nataallith's smile revealed the irony of his words—"this man chooses to take the wrong done to him to those who have made the treaty so that the wrongs can be righted and the grievances can be heard. While he is waiting for justice, he keeps the treaty and his word. He does this because he gave his *word,* and this is a thing of some importance to him." Nataallith spread his hands out in what appeared to be genuine supplication. "I must ask, which man is the man of courage then? You must tell me, for I do not know."

The murmurs from the Navajos listening turned then to laughter, for they well understood the insult veiled in Nataallith's words.

So did the Utes and Apaches, however, and their silence was black and glowering. Finally, a Ute headman said, "We are wasting our breath. It is as the Apache said. The Navajo are content to be farmers of corn, living always in the shadow of the white man's protection. Protection!" He spat in the fire with sudden derision. "They cannot even protect their daughters," he laughed, cupping his genitals in a gesture meant to show he had taken his fill of those daughters, "much less their flocks. I have taken more from the whites in one moon than my clan could make by our own efforts in five seasons. I say," he added with a sneer, "that this is good hunting indeed."

"And I thought we had come to speak of honor," Nataallith said quietly. "I see I was mistaken. You have come to speak of women."

"We speak of your survival as a people," the Apache headman said. "They will take everything you have and then they will take your lives. When future generations speak of the Navajo, they will speak of a people as dead and disappeared as the Old Ones of the Pueblos. They will say, 'Once there were the Navajo. And they were called the Lords of the Soil. But they trusted the white man and they lost everything.'"

"Perhaps. And perhaps they will say that the Navajo were wise enough to recognize a stronger ally and keep a peace which allowed them to bend with the winds of change instead of being blown away to dust, like the Apache and the Utes." Nataallith was speaking more to his people than to the council, and Pahe knew that every ear was listening hard to his words. She felt pride, sadness, and a great yearning to be away from these fires and back in her own blanket with the arms of her man around her at last.

"You are cowards," said an angry warrior.

Nataallith smiled sadly. "And you, my friends, are great fools."

The Utes rose as one man then, and the Apache struggled up after them quickly. "If you are not with us, then you are against us," the Ute headman said angrily.

"So has said every man who has broken his word to every man he meets thereafter," Manuelito broke in. He had been strangely silent, letting Nataallith speak his mind. But now his voice rose in anger. "We will not join you in this war. We have made a peace with the whites. We will keep our word unless they attack us. And when they make grievances against us, we will bring those grievances to the headmen of the whites for justice. This is what we have promised; this is what we will do."

"This is what you will become, then," one Ute warrior said loudly, holding up a passer of scalps in the firelight for all to see. "I declare war on all Navajo from this moment forward!"

The women quickly rose and moved back from the fires, herding the children before them. In the confusion and the angry shouts that followed, Manuelito's warriors pushed the Utes and Apache onto their horses and ran them out of the camp, and both sides waved their lances and called insults to each other in the flurry of their departure.

Nataallith said then to the headmen of the clans who were gathered, "We are now at war with the Utes and the Apache, at their insistence. Expect them to bring this war to those clans closest to their lands."

"Yes," Manuelito added. "Warn your kinsmen to keep vigilant and increase your guards. Tell your women and children to stay close to the fires at night. I will take this new challenge to the *Bilagáana* and ask them to bring soldiers against our enemies as they have promised. Perhaps in time, the lands of the Utes and the Apache will be ours."

Pahe heard one of the warriors mutter, "Or our scalps will be theirs."

She glared at him, and he turned away unconcerned. The Peo-

ple went back to their own fires then, and the council was dis-
persed. Pahe knew that many were afraid. It was bad enough to
be at peace with the white man; little good had come of that so
far. It was worse to be also at war with two large and powerful
tribes. Where was the safe place to stand that Narbona had yearned
to win for his people?

*   *   *

That night in their blanket, Nataallith turned to her for comfort,
nuzzling her neck and sighing with weary concern. "I had hoped
that tonight would bring a reconciliation," he said, "but as soon
as they began to mock us, I knew that they had come for war or
nothing."

"Your words were heard," she said softly, "and they were
wise words indeed."

"They are words and nothing more," he answered sadly. "I
fear that there is no good trail to follow. No matter what we do,
we may not survive."

"We will survive, my heart," she said, holding him tightly.
"And so will our children." She gestured to the sleeping forms
at the other end of the hogan. When they traveled like this, the
children slept so close to them, it was one of the only pleasures
of council she still relished, hearing their soft breaths all the night
long, sensing their closeness as she slept. "They are the children
of Nataallith, the grandchildren of Manuelito, the great-grand-
children of Narbona. They will deal with the whites with great
wisdom and courage, whichever trail they choose."

"You are my strength," he murmured then in her neck, "and
dearer to me than my life."

She slid her hands down his chest, finding his erection there
and pulling it gently toward her. "Show me then," she whispered.
"Show me, my heart."

*   *   *

The Utes and the Apache wasted no time in making war on
the People. Within a few months, they had attacked several Navajo
ranchos, running off more than a hundred horses and capturing
a dozen women and children for slaves. In the years the Navajo

had given up their war raids and concentrated on farming, they had become disused to conflict. They no longer could defend themselves against the better weapons and warring nature of the Utes. The Utes lived by the chase; they now lived by the plow. Their farms and their flocks were as easy targets for the Utes and the Apache as the New Mexican ranches and herds had once been for them.

Meriwether proposed a new treaty to the Navajos that would designate boundary lines once and for all, he said, and keep the Utes and the white man's livestock off their lands. He traveled to Laguna Negra, twenty-five miles north of Fort Defiance, with his delegation to meet with more than two thousand Navajo and all of the headmen to present the new treaty and to explain the boundaries.

The headmen gathered more wearily this time at Nataallith's hacienda, and many said aloud that they wondered how many times this peace must be spoken of to keep it alive. Once again, they ringed the council fires; once again, they listened while another representative of the white man's nation told them what they must do to preserve their lands.

Juanita said to Pahe, as they sat quietly listening to the men discuss this new treaty, "It is a wonder these white men have time to make children at all, so busy are they making new papers and speeches. How can a people have grown so large? I would rather be wife to a coyote, I think."

Pahe chuckled wryly, nodding her head. One of the advantages of these many councils was that now, even the women and children had learned some of the more important white words and meanings. But they had also learned that the white man did not place the same importance on words and their meanings as the People did. They signed papers which made promises that were to last "for all time," only to discover that they lasted until a new white representative came to their lands. Pahe often wondered if there really was a "great white father," as the white agents claimed. It seemed to her that, in fact, the whites had no headman at all, or at least no one who knew what his clansmen were doing.

The man they called Meriwether talked long and explained the new boundaries carefully, drawing on a piece of paper with many colored lines which showed the mountains, the rivers, and the canyons. But Pahe could not understand his pictures on the paper, nor could she see how they resembled the land she knew. When she looked around the circle of listening faces, she knew that they understood no better than she did. Nataallith caught her eye and grimaced, shaking his head slightly. She settled back, wondering if he understood more than the others. She listened carefully and heard the murmurs around her. No one could see the mountains and the canyons, but everyone sensed that nothing good was going to come from this Meriwether's drawings of them.

Finally, the questions began, hesitatingly at first, and then in an outpouring of incredulous anger. Where was *Sis Naajinii*, what the white man called Mount Baldy in Colorado? It was not on the map. Where was *Soodzil*, what they called Mount Taylor? Where was *Dibé Nitsaa*, what they had named the San Juan Mountains? Fingers were pointing at the map, and voices got louder. And where was *Tó Bil Hask'idii*, the Place Where the Waters Crossed? And *Tsé lichíí' beehooghan*, the House Made of Red Rock, and *Tsil si'ntha*, Among Aromatic Sumac? None of these were included within the lines this Meriwether had drawn.

The news went quickly to the back of the crowd, and it seemed to Pahe suddenly that all of the voices, all two thousand of them, were speaking at once in a cacophony of dismay. Not only was the land far smaller than that they knew they owned, but it also left out three of their most holy mountains, the best grazing meadows, and many of their most sacred places.

The white man Meriwether stood firmly before them, his eyes not on the crowd but on his map, patiently waiting for their objections to cease. When the People finally stopped speaking, he said, "Your White Father in Washington understands your concerns. But he must also hear the claims of the Apache, the Zuni, the Ute, and the Pueblo. Many of these tribes claim the same lands. He must be fair to *all* of his red children. He has instructed me to show you these lines on this paper"—and once again, the man struck the map lightly with his sword, which he had been using to point out the various markings—"and say to you that this is to be your land. Once and for all, until the winds no longer blow, these lands will be *Dinétah*."

Pahe flinched at the sound of her language coming from this

white, bearded face. It was as if a wolf had suddenly begun to speak in her own tongue, fascinating and horrifying all at once.

"And you must know that the other tribes will be receiving far less lands than the Navajo. They will object strenuously. But if the People will agree, then the White Father will keep all others off these lands. If the People cannot agree, then you must fight off the other tribes with no assistance. Know this, also. If you agree to sign this treaty, the United States Government will pay the Navajo people ten thousand dollars in silver every year forever. Each year, as well, the Navajo people will be given many valuable farming tools and seed to help you bring your fields into plenty. These gifts will be made to every clan, but no one will receive anything unless all agree."

One headman asked loudly, "Ten thousand dollars a year in silver?"

Meriwether nodded. "To be paid every year to the tribe, as tribute for your land and your friendship. This will be promised and paid by the United States Government."

Nataallith waited for the speaking behind him to subside and then he said, "You have given us much to think on. Please give us leave to talk of this among ourselves. We will give you an answer by tomorrow's end."

Meriwether saluted Nataallith with grave courtesy and withdrew with his men to their camp at the edge of the pasture. The picture-map stood alone in a center of many hundreds of Navajo as a great white eye, glaring at them from the future.

Nataallith asked each of the headmen to withdraw with his clan to discuss the boundaries that had been proposed and the treaty they were to sign, and then come back that evening with any questions. "In that way," he said, "we can understand best what we are being asked to do. We will know the answer to each question before we agree to do anything at all. Then I will ask you each to go to your clans once more for their answer. And when we meet tomorrow when the sun is high, we will decide our answer together."

Pahe smiled at him shyly. He made her very proud when he showed the wisdom of leadership. She thought quickly of how old he had seemed to her when they courted and how she had sometimes winced at the thought of marrying one so aged. She laughed to herself. A young man would never have been able to keep her respect so well. This was her man. For her, there could have been no other.

* * *

The headmen came back that night and the talk went on before the fires as the moon rose high over them all. The questions were often the same, and once the boundaries were more or less understood, they knew at last what they were being asked to give up. Twelve thousand people, they knew they numbered. More than two hundred thousand sheep, ten thousand horses, and too many other livestock to count, they owned. They were lords of more than five thousand acres, by the white man's count, and by their own, they claimed even more. They made all their own clothing, their saddles, their blankets, their houses, and fed and cared for their young and their old with no help from anyone. They had run off all interlopers, kept the land for their own, and battled the elements and the beasts to grow to the largest and richest of all the tribes, and they remembered a time clearly when they could have driven the white man off their lands forever.

But now they could not survive such a battle. Not and remain the People. And so they came to make peace with the white man, on terms they despised.

But would this peace even last? Could the white man keep the Apache, the Utes, the Zunis in their place? Could they keep the white herds away from what was left of the lands? Would they build more forts? Bring more of their kind to trespass where now there were only a few? Would they keep this treaty any more than they kept the others? The questions narrowed down to the same ones, over and over. Again and again, the headmen discussed them, attempting to understand all together what the best trail might be.

Finally, Manuelito stood, and all eyes and ears were turned to him. "I have listened to voices of wisdom this night," he said, "and I am proud that we have so many to hear. We have heard the white man's proposal, and we have asked all the questions we can think to ask. But I have one final question which I will bring to this council: who are the *Bilagáana* to tell the People where they may and may not live?"

There was a silence round the fires now as the headmen gave one of their most respected warriors and leaders every chance to speak his heart.

"We ask every question but this one, my brothers. Why should the word of the white man mean any more to us than the word of the Mexican, the Apache, the Zuni, or the Ute?"

A silence rose thick and heavy among the listeners. Pahe sensed that many of those who heard her father's words felt them to be true, indeed, had asked themselves the same questions. Why, truly, should they trust the white man?

Manuelito went on to object to any treaty with the whites, reminding them how time and again, they had hoped for peace, only to have those hopes destroyed. "We are now weaker than we have ever been as a people. We have less land, and that land which we do have is being trespassed upon by our enemies. More and more of our children have been taken as slaves, and our warriors' arrows are blunted by disuse. Now, young men who should be taking spoils in raids against our enemies are hoeing the fields, work which the women once did! And men are guarding the flocks, work which was once done by our children. When did we last have our Blessingway Ceremony? A Life-way? An Enemy Way? We have been so busy worrying about the white man and his threats that we have not even cared for our daughters and sons as good parents. The land, itself, is displeased with us, my brothers. We have not shown it the respect and honor we once did, and the white men among us have poisoned our faith. I tell you, so long as we follow the trail of the *Bilagáana*, we shall grow weaker and weaker as people. Soon we will all be made slaves of the Utes and the Apaches, who know that the road of the warrior is the only way."

Manuelito's words were eloquent and powerful, and Pahe felt her eyes watering with pride and dismay at her father's pleas. Not for nothing had he been named *Haskéh Naabaah*, Angry Warrior. She knew that the People would never agree to join the Utes and Apaches; the enmities were too ancient and deep there. But many of the warriors who listened, those men who were weary of farming, and frustrated by the complaints of their women, were ready to hear one headman at least call for war.

The talks went on late into the evening, and much of the discussion finally seemed to come down to how the ten thousand dollars in silver might be fairly apportioned. Pahe knew then that despite Manuelito's persuasive words, the mood of the clans was to accept this treaty and trust the white man's promises one more time. By noon of the following day, it was decided.

And so they signed. All of the headmen except for Manuelito made a mark on the white man's new treaty papers. Manuelito and Ayoi and Juanita and her sons had left the fires late that evening, before Manuelito could be counted as absent. No one but the People noticed that he was gone, and in the long line of headmen at the table, he was not missed by Meriwether.

The white man's paper said it was July 18, 1855, Nataallith told her later. The middle of the year, by *Bilagáana* reckoning. "This is the first step," he said, "of making us smaller as a people. It is the first time we have ever agreed to sell our land."

"The People want the money," she said.

"They do. And they also wish to stop being afraid."

"You could have stopped them."

He shook his head. "It is not for me to stop them. I know we will be weaker. But perhaps also, it is the first step in our survival." He held her. "I know no other way."

And so the papers were signed, Meriwether took his soldiers and went back to Fort Defiance, and the People waited to see what changes the paper might make. For a year, they waited. No silver dollars ever came. No tools and no seeds were delivered. Worse, the Mexican and Anglo ranchers seemed to know nothing of the treaty, for they continued to graze their herds where they pleased. When a delegation of headmen went to Meriwether to protest, they were told that the United States Government had not yet signed the treaty, and so it was not yet law. He warned them, however, that they must keep the law as they had promised, or it would be a show of bad faith. And so they came back to counsel patience once more.

*   *   *

The winter of 1855–56 was unusually severe and early. By November, *Dinétah* was covered with snow. The Rio Grande was frozen so solidly at Albuquerque that a man could drive a horse and cart across it, and on Christmas Day at Fort Defiance, the thermometer was stuck at thirty-two below zero. Sheep froze where they stood and were lost in deep drifts; horses died by the thousands. Clans squeezed into communal hogans to save firewood, bringing their lambs and dogs in with them.

Nataallith's two divorced sisters and their children came for the winter, to share Pahe's hogan. For a few days, it was festive and cheerful, with four more children to play with Wasek and Dolii, but the novelty of the crowd quickly paled and, soon, so many bodies around the fire at once was simply one more aspect of the winter to be endured.

But in many ways, they were fortunate. Other families did not have enough to feed themselves, and their men made the long trek in deadly weather to Nataallith's hacienda, to try to get extra food for their children. He gave them what he could spare and turned away no one, even from other clans. Finally, he had slaughtered most of the lambs, something Pahe had never heard of happening in even her grandmother's time.

When spring came, they emerged into a world which was far less hospitable than before. Most of the horses had died, and the flocks were devastated. Many families had eaten their seed stock to stay alive.

With the coming of spring, the Utes began their attacks again, forcing more Navajo to camp outside Fort Defiance for protection. The Comanches and the Kiowas joined the Apaches and the Utes, and the People were quite outnumbered in their stance for peace. The Apaches dared to attack Manuelito's camp, stole his favorite horse, and wounded him badly. When he recovered, he vowed that he would no longer depend on the Americans for protection, and his warriors began raiding the New Mexican ranches once more.

Pahe took the wagon and the children to see her mother, and she was shocked at how aged she had become in her absence. "It was a hard winter," Ayoi said simply as she embraced the children. "We have lost more than livestock, I think."

But more shocking was the change in her father. He spent more time now in his own hogan, visiting neither wife so often. His rage and frustration had finally altered his mind and his heart, and his face was set in lines of bitterness and despair. He spoke of nothing but war, wished nothing more than to see his enemies destroyed, and barely had words for her. Only Wasek could make him smile.

"It is the pain of his wound," Ayoi said when they went from his hogan. "When he heals, he will be himself again."

As she drove the wagon homeward, Pahe wept quietly, keeping her tears from the children. Ayoi and Manuelito were still young in years, yet she could see the death of her parents now, something she could never have imagined in her mind before. She would have only her brothers left, and if war came, she might lose them as well. As it was, she never saw them, for it was too dangerous to travel long distances with the other tribes raiding and the soldiers hunting for all warriors, of whatever clan. A bitterness rose in her throat against all who had brought this destruction on her people, on her family. But most of all, she began to see the wisdom of her father's demand for war against the white man. It seemed to her that life had been so fine before they came to the land, that any challenges they faced as a people were good ones which strengthened them and made them truly lords of all they saw.

Struggles with the white man had made them weak. She could see no clear answer to their troubles, and she knew that her own children would never know the freedom and joy she had known as a child. She wiped her tears angrily and wished she were a warrior. She would kill every white man she could find on the land and drive them away or die in the attempt. Anything would be better than this slow death of the heart and courage.

That spring, a Mormon wagon train came through *Dinétah.* These white men and women seemed different from those who peopled the forts. They said they were on their way to their "Zion," running from perverse white men to the east of the mountains. They traded fine rifles to the People and told them that they were being fools to allow the "Gentiles" on their lands. It was now two years since the treaty had been signed and still the promised silver, supplies, and farming tools had not come from the Americans. New Mexicans still grazed their flocks on Navajo lands with impunity.

Many of the warriors took the rifles and hid them away carefully in the rafters of their hogans, understanding that someday soon, these weapons might be their salvation.

And then Henry Dodge was ambushed and killed by some Apache raiders. All of the People mourned the passing of "Red Sleeves" and knew that the peace would not last long without his influence.

That year, it seemed even the land had turned against the Navajo. Seed was scarce, rain was scanty, and the deer and other animals, starving after the hard winter, boldly ate anything that was not closely guarded.

The People called it the Fearing Time—*Na'ádzidgo*—when they were surrounded by enemies on all sides and a man might return home from hunting to find his wife and children stolen, his horses and sheep gone, and his hogan burned to the ground. His attackers might be Apache, Kiowa, Ute, New Mexican, Mexican, or rich Anglo ranchers. If he appealed to the United States Army for help in pursuing his tormentors, he was told he must keep the peace. If he went to the fort for promised supplies, he was told they were coming soon and sent away again. There was nothing to do but try to keep alive and hope that something would change soon.

Pahe knew that it would be important to teach her children about the crops, something she would not have done when her grandfather was alive, with his many slaves, or when her own father still had all his wealth. Now it would be vital that they learned to keep the fields. So she took them to the rows of corn, that they might watch her water and weed and dig. She told them that each row was precious, each ear of corn a blessing of life. She dug a hole and planted the seeds. Then as the seedlings emerged, she took them back again to water carefully the mound of green seedlings coming up in a circle. She kneeled down and put her ear to the earth and told them, "There is a great talking happening here. The Holy Ones and the Earth are planning the season, and the corn is listening well. Can you hear them whispering?"

Dolii and Wasek obediently kneeled on the ground and put their ears to the earth.

"I can hear it!" Wasek said boldly.

"I can't," murmured Dolii.

"Well, and you must learn to listen," Pahe said to them.

As they went to and fro from the fields, Pahe sang a song to them of the corn. She told them that every living thing has a song, a prayer. "The cornfield has a prayer," she said. "It wants sun and water and good soil and respect."

"Respect?" challenged Wasek. "Why does corn need respect?"

"To thrive. Everything needs to know its place in the plan of things. We offer pollen and good thoughts so that the crop will be good."

Wasek looked skeptically at the small seedlings. "Will the crop be good?"

Pahe sighed. "I do not know. Lately, the corn has not been so good and strong. The cornfield is worried. So are the Holy Ones. We must think good thoughts so that we will have a good harvest."

*   *   *

There were many places in *Dinétah* where the forests seemed to go on forever. Vast stretches of low pinyon and juniper which were no taller than twenty feet above a man's head, the trees were solitary, well spaced, and spire-shaped at the top. This shape looked to be an adaptation to heavy snows, for the branches shed snow like a steeply pitched roof, protecting the trees from breakage. But the pinyon was actually a tough desert tree, and its evergreen needles more an adaptation to heat rather than cold.

Below the trees were the desert plants of candelabra, prickly pear, thickets of rabbit brush, sagebrush, and four-wing saltbush. Each plant had an adaptation to dry conditions, and the waxy outer surface of the pinyon and juniper's leaves or needles, like cactus spines, helped reduce water loss. Other tough, dry shrubs like serviceberry, mountain mahogany, and cliff rose survived here, but the pinyon and juniper were the unchanging sentinels of the Four Corners region.

Pinyon-juniper forests were one of the most common forests in the American West, covering more than seventy-five thousand square miles, all the way from the Rocky Mountains in Colorado to the Sierras in California, from Canada to Mexico. Two species were intertwined and most dominant—*Pinus edulis,* the Colorado pinyon pine, and *Juniperus osteoperma,* the Utah juniper. The native peoples of the land had used them for centuries for rot-proof poles and the pinyon nut for food.

In the pinyon-juniper forest south of Zuni, all sorts of animals sheltered from the heat. Mule deer, whiptail lizards, and desert wood rats foraged in the shade; chickadees and nuthatches quarreled among the branches, and from the tallest spires, ravens scanned for movement on the desert floor below.

But one of the most raucous visitors to the pinyon forest was the pinyon jay. The forest was quiet until the last weeks of August, when the pinyon jay arrived in huge flocks to harvest the nuts, and then the trees were alive with battles and noise and furious feeding. The key to life on the mountain was the pinyon pine, and no animal knew this more keenly than the pinyon jay.

The pinyon pine only put out a crop of nuts every three years. If drought or a plague of insects hindered it, the pine would even skip a year or two. But over the forest, each stretch of trees bore at a different time, so somewhere, someplace, the nuts were usually available. And the jays, which could fly from stand to stand, were the most rapacious and clever of all the animals which needed the pinyon nut to survive. The trick was to get the nuts away from the squirrels, the chipmunks, the wood rats, and the other birds who combed the forest floor and the trees for fresh new cones laden with harvest.

And then there was Man. Since the early nomad peoples moved into the region, they had used the pinyon as food. Deposits of seed husks and charcoal from pinecones more than six thousand years old suggested that the Anasazi not only lived in the forests but traveled from pine stand to pine stand, collecting the nuts. The harvest was high in fat and protein, could be eaten raw, roasted, boiled, and even ground into flour. Out along the western edges of the Colorado Plateau and the Great Basin, the Paiute and Shoshone stored the nuts in clay jars. The Spanish and the Mexicans gathered the nuts for trade, and the Navajo depended upon the harvest, believing that the pinyon nut had been the first food of the gods. In a single year, a large clan could collect more than a thousand pounds of nuts from a single forest.

Yano was well aware that Man could eat more nuts than fifty squirrels, and it was his job to watch for his supreme enemy from the tallest tree. Yano was a pinyon jay, *Gymnorrhinus cyanocephalus*, a robin-size bird with a long slender bill, gray-blue on his back, dark blue on his head, with two white streaks down his throat. He had only the year before lost his yearling gray feathers and status, and he was puffed with pride and importance at being chosen for flock sentinel.

He sat now on the second tallest tree in the stand, while the members of his flock foraged for nuts below. Around him, six more sentinels stood guard on higher trees, watching for hawks and owls, and if one gave the warning, "Caaa! Caa! Haa-a-a-a!", the entire flock, more than a hundred birds, would be on alert. Then the soldiers would move from the trees to the air and any intruder would find itself suddenly mobbed by thirty or forty hard-billed and determined pecking males, who would drive out anything that threatened the flock.

Except for Man. If Man came to the stand, the flock must leave. For only Man would not be driven forth by the soldiers.

Yano was not afraid of Man. Indeed, he was not afraid of anything, except solitude. So long as he was in the flock, he was invulnerable. The flock was everything. The flock was life. Without the flock, no single bird could find food enough to sustain the hatchlings; without the flock, no single bird could defend himself and his mate from hawks.

He watched his mate below busily feeding, and he puffed himself larger still. It was his first breeding season, and he had been relatively uninterested in mating until the flock came to his pinyon mountain and he had seen the bright green glistening cones full of waiting nuts. There was something about those cones that made him excited about mating, and within one week, he had courted and won a female of his own. Soon she would build their nest and fill it with three or four greenish-white small eggs. He would then be a soldier, an even more important position within the flock.

Yano could not know that it was the pinyon pine itself that regulated the breeding habits of his kind. The jays bred easily when the cones were many and full, late when the crop was late, and sometimes not at all when drought made the crop less likely. Indeed, Yano also did not know how interwoven his life and the lives of his clan were with the life cycle of the pinyon pines on which they fed.

In August, as the nuts ripened and the seductively green cones began to open, the flock gathered together, flying from place to place to hunt. They descended on a stand of pinyons and broke open the still-green cones to get at the nuts inside. Yano found this particularly pleasurable, the breaking-open act, and he was well suited for it, as were all his kind. His nares, or external nostrils, had no feathers. Unlike many birds, he had a bill adapted to prodding the cones without getting his bill clogged by sticky sap. Even his name, *Gymnorrhina*, meant "naked nose."

As he ate, he went from cone to cone, carefully checking each seed. He could hold a seed in his bill and know right away if it was edible by its heft and color and softness. Those which were not ready to eat, he stored in his esophagus, as many as twenty at a time, and carried them away to be buried as a food cache for leaner times.

Yano knew to choose the southern side of the stand of trees, where the snow would melt soonest and the ground would be quickly warmed in the spring. He buried twenty times more than he ate, for he was a young male, and this was his duty to the flock.

What Yano did not know was that the pinyon pine needed him as much as he needed its nuts. In the desert, moist ground for seeds is critical for survival, and pine nuts that do not get buried will not germinate. In fact, a single flock could bury hundreds of thousands of seeds, ensuring that the pinyon pine would survive, something the nuthatch, the deer, and Man could not guarantee.

Although Yano had seen few men, his kind knew them well enough, and his small brain was encoded through generations of contact to recognize Man as his most powerful foe. And so, when the four horses approached up the mountain with Man and his mates astride, he set up a warning caw which was quickly taken up by the other sentinels, causing the whole flock to stop feeding and come to alert.

They watched as the horses came close and then flew from the stand, more than a hundred of them, cawing in protest as the Man and his women tied their animals and walked under the trees. They carried large sticks which terrified the jays, and the women flapped great blankets at them to move them off faster. From a distant, gnarled juniper, Yano watched them, with his mate sitting alongside him, still protesting their presence.

The Man and his mates spread the blankets on the ground under the trees, and then the Man went from tree to tree, beating them with his stick. Soon his mates were doing this as well, until the sound of their beating was louder even than the cawing of the jays. No matter how loudly they cried, however, the Man and his mates would not be chased off. Soon the blankets were full of green cones and ripening cones and branches and needles from the trees. The mates of the Man went from blanket to blanket, collecting the cones into other blankets and tying them to the horses. When they had finished, they mounted their animals and rode up the mountain.

Yano and his flock flew back to the stand to investigate their losses. At least half of the cones were gone now, taken by the Man and his sticks. The flock fed with a new urgency, but Yano knew, even though he was young and inexperienced, that they would have to find another ripening stand before long. There was no longer enough here to hold them.

*   *   *

The spring and summer of 1857 brought a drought as extreme as that of the winter of 1856. Crops failed all over the Navajo lands, and the winter that year brought more hunger, as stores were so low. The Mormons were selling guns and ammunition to all Indian tribes, hoping they would drive out the whites, and even the peaceful Pueblos began to raid the People and their herds, driven to extremes by hunger and fear.

And then, in July 1858, a Navajo clansman who had been turned away three times in his request for seed, rode into Fort Defiance and shot an arrow into the back of Major Brook's Negro slave, Jim. The major was enraged and demanded that Nataallith bring in the murderer.

Nataallith held council with the clan of the man so accused, and heard their frustration and anger. He sent a message to Major Brook, explaining that the clan would fight to the death to defend their kinsman rather than turn him over to the whites for killing a slave.

The message came back to Nataallith's hacienda that Major Brook was now prepared to declare a state of war between the People and the United States.

Nataallith said to Pahe, "You must take the children and go

to your mother's hogan. I believe this major will send the soldiers here first."

For the first time in their marriage, she put her hands over her ears and turned her back to him angrily. "I will not listen to such cowardice. Not from you, my heart."

"If they come, I cannot protect you!" he shouted at her. "Do as I tell you, and do not plague me with more worry than I already have!"

It was the first time they had used such voices with each other, the first time the children had ever heard them lash out with anger, and they sat, wide-eyed and silent and afraid.

Pahe glanced at her son and lowered her voice. "Do not send us away, my husband. We will be no safer with my father than we will be here with you. If the soldiers come, I would rather face them than the Apache."

Nataallith winced at the truth of her words and shook his head in exasperation. "There is no safe place anymore," he said, also lowering his voice.

Mindful of her daughter, Pahe said, "That is not true. So long as we are together, we will be safe."

He sighed and turned away from her in defeat. "It has come to a place where a man cannot protect his family from enemies on all sides."

"Here is that place," she said, taking his arm and pulling him toward her. She beckoned to her children who instantly came and ran to them, wrapping their arms and legs around them as though they were roots to their tree. The embrace felt reassuring, but she saw the fear and doubt in her son's eyes, and she once more hated the white man for putting it there.

And so they stayed, and when the soldiers came, the warriors fought hard against them while the women and children hid in the root hold with the tubers and onion bulbs, hearing the sounds of battle and running horses over their heads. Nataallith and his warriors managed to fight back the soldiers from the hogans, but they set fire to his cornfields, drove off his horses, and killed two of his clansmen.

When the women and children emerged from hiding, Pahe ran to her husband and saw the blood still running from a wound to his shoulder. She cried out, remembering instantly the wound he took before at the murder of her grandfather, and the children began to weep and call for him, but he came forward and embraced them with his strong arm. "It is nothing," he told them, his voice firm and loud. "I sent a runner to your father's hogan; the soldiers will attack there next, I am certain."

She began to weep then, thinking of her mother, but then she stopped her tears, for her heart was too hot with anger for sorrow. "How many of them did you kill?" she asked.

"None," he said. "But we wounded some, I know. They will be back."

The wails of the wives of the dead then distracted them from each other, and they went to help their clansmen wrap their wounds and bury those they had lost.

They later learned that Manuelito got their warning in time to escape with his kinsmen, but his fields and hogans were burned.

*   *   *

The Fearing Time went on, and Nataallith got word that some of the clans were talking of moving over the mountains to the west, away from the warring tribes and the whites, to look for new land they might call their own. He called for a council and waited until more than a hundred headmen had gathered.

That night, Pahe sat and listened, feeling that her husband was himself again for the first time in many moons. He strode before the council with the legs of a younger man, his voice as strong and firm as it had been many seasons before. He ignored his wound, which had healed his shoulder stiff and twisted in an unnatural position. He was Nataallith, and beside him sat his son; around him were his clansmen. He let his anger build into something holy and then his words rolled over their ears like thunder.

"We have signed their treaty," he said, "and we have kept their laws. And until the murder of the slave, we had hopes that they would keep them as well. But now they use this minor killing as an excuse to move their soldiers on us like wolves on starving sheep. We are no longer strong, my brothers! We have let them weaken us beyond endurance!"

The heads nodded in agreement, and a few of the women wept

loudly enough so that their men could hear them from the back rows.

"We need time to strengthen ourselves again, before we war against the white wolves and drive them off our land once and for all time. We cannot be victorious in our present condition. Neither can we stand against the Apaches and the Utes. We must have peace! And we must have peace long enough to become the People once more!"

"We should have killed them all when we were strong enough to do so!" a warrior shouted angrily.

Nataallith nodded. "You are right. I was wrong. I spoke once for peace, and I now regret my words. I wish now that we had listened to the voices of Manuelito and his warriors, and not Narbona. Indeed, my wife's grandmother does not look so foolish now, to my eyes!"

All heads turned to Pahe with those words, and she dropped her head in mixed shame and pride. It was the first time her grandmother's name had been mentioned at council or in any other place where the People gathered since her son had been born.

The talk went on into the night, and it was decided that Nataallith would lead a delegation to Fort Defiance to ask for peace. But this time, he would ask in a manner he believed the white man would hear. And as the council ended, Pahe understood that it had been no accident that her husband had brought up the name of her grandmother before all ears. It was not by chance that all eyes turned to Pahe that night.

She traveled with the delegation to Fort Defiance, and behind her rode her children, many other wives and their children, and finally a score of headmen bringing up the rear. As she approached the fort, she felt a sense of dread building like a pair of black wings over her heart. This was the place of the white man, and no good could come of this journey, she felt sure. But her husband could think of no other way to keep the soldiers from burning more hogans and crops, and so they had come. And she was to ride into the fort ahead of him, for the first time in her life.

Pahe carried a white flag of truce, and her hair flew round her face in the breeze, in a symbol of respect for those who had died defending her home. She felt like a widow, though her husband rode behind her, for she knew the soldiers who watched with pointed rifles from behind the fort walls could shoot Nataallith at any time.

But the gates opened for them, and the delegation went inside, still following behind Pahe and her children and the white flag. Once inside, Nataallith stepped forward and addressed the commander of Fort Defiance, Colonel Bonneville, asking for peace. He said that he asked for it for his wife and all the women of his nation. He gestured with both hands to the women behind him, to the children who followed them, and he dropped his head as though he were already a defeated warrior.

The soldiers stepped aside and let Nataallith go into where this Bonneville sat waiting. He was inside with his enemy a very long time, and the sun rose high and hot above the waiting delegation. But none of the women moved from their positions and none of the children whimpered to be let down. Finally, Nataallith came forth once more and led them back out of the walls of the fort.

"They will agree to only thirty days of peace," he said to the waiting delegation. "For thirty days, they will not attack our homes or fields. When the thirty days are up, we must deliver all the horses that the warriors have stolen and our kinsman who killed the slave. If we do not bring the horses and our kinsman, they will make war on us once more. And next time, they will hear no talk of peace."

Pahe bowed her head. This felt like a defeat, but her husband was speaking as though some small victory had been won. She straightened her spine and held the flag aloft once more. She kicked her mare and went to the head of the line of horses, glancing back to be sure that her daughter and son were following. Let the white soldiers see that they departed with the same dignity with which they came, she told herself, her chin high and firm. Let this be the last time they see our backs. Next time they see the People, it will be as we attack them in battle.

The People rode away with little of the usual conversation and jibes which normally might have enlivened any journey. There would be no more attacks on the hogans and ranches for thirty days. But what would happen then? They would have to give up so many sheep and horses that they would be even more impoverished. One of their clansmen would be delivered to the soldiers to meet almost certain death. And his women and children and kinsmen would likely fight to keep him. There was no joy in any of it.

In fact, Pahe realized angrily, there had been little joy in *Dinétah* since the white man had first crossed their mountains. Once more she thought of Deezbaa and her warning. Surely it would have been better if they had killed the first white men they saw. Nothing could be worse than this slow weakening, a sort of death of the will and spirit which was like starving before a table of plenty, dying of thirst when the river was right at hand.

*   *   *

In a month, a messenger came with a new treaty. The chief of the white men did not even bother to call for a council this time, he merely sent his paper and a translator. The boundary lines were to be pushed even farther west, eliminating from *Dinétah* almost all good farming fields and most of the best grazing lands. One headman must be appointed to speak for all the People, the paper demanded, and the clans must agree to allow the United States to build forts on their land at any time and place.

This new treaty was in punishment for the breaking of the old treaty, the translator said. But Pahe believed that it was because they had showed weakness. She remembered Manuelito's words: Once an enemy sees weakness, they want also to see blood.

The white man wanted now not only their lands but their hearts. She looked at her husband with new eyes, wondering if he had the strength to lead the People into the war which must surely follow. Her son spoke of nothing but war, as did all the young men. Only the old ones—and her husband—spoke still of peace.

The new treaty was dismissed by all the headmen, and not a single clan agreed to sign. The translator was allowed to go back to the fort with their answer: no new treaty would be signed by any headman. He left, relieved to be still alive.

They got the news from a runner within ten days. The blacksmith at the fort, a minor headman of the smallest, most impoverished clan, a clan that made their hogans in the shadows of the fort and begged for food from the soldiers, had been appointed the new "chief" of all the Navajo by the white men, made to sign the new paper, and given full authority over all the People. Herrero, the blacksmith, was now according to the *Bilagáana*, the *Naataanii*, chief, of the People. The paper he signed agreed to give up their grazing grounds, the fertile lands of Collitas, Bear Springs, Ojo Caliente, Laguna Negra, and the lands of Narbona and Manuelito at Chuska and Tunicha Valleys, as well as the sacred dancing place at Chuska Mountains.

The clans called for war and, almost to a man, the warriors said they would follow the old headmen no more if peace was all they could counsel.

After several days and nights of mediation, Nataallith called for a *Naachid* to be held at Chinle. The clans once more gathered, this time with a wary weariness Pahe found even more alarming than the warriors' angry demands and war dances. Nataallith asked the warriors to build a ceremonial hogan, and for eight days he chanted, instructing the young men and women in the ways of the *Naachid*, while the fires of a thousand families flickered around the council grounds. On the ninth day, after sunup, the war leaders and the peace leaders gathered in a clearing before a pile of rifles, shields, lances, and bows and arrows.

Pahe found her son in a gathering of young men, all of them painted for war. She scarcely recognized her boy of ten summers under the broad stripes of black and white on his cheeks, the red paint in his hair, the yellow menacing markings on his chest and back. Her daughter yelped when she saw her brother and ran back inside the hogan in fear. He only laughed and turned away, his eyes glittering with excitement. I have lost him, Pahe thought sadly, half afraid of her own son. She went back to comfort her daughter, who wept with fear and anger. We have not even begun the battle yet, and already he is gone.

Nataallith met with the headmen and the warriors and told them of his vision. "I have seen this. I do not want to think of it, but it comes to me," he said. "I have dreamed this thing, and I must tell it. In my dream, our sacred mountains were covered with black clouds, billowing so that not even the Holy Ones could see the peaks. Throughout our valleys and across our mesas not a breath stirred, not a person moved. All that broke the death silence from the tops of the mountains to the very bottom of the canyons was the howl of wolves and the wail of the black wind, death."

The warriors began to murmur and hum, and Pahe heard their anger begin to grow again. They were not come to hear old men speak of dreams. They were come to speak of war. Their ears would hear nothing else. Even her son looked away from his father when he spoke, attentive instead to the oldest warrior who sat at the edge of the circle, watching for a signal how he should act before such a grouping of men.

She glanced to Nataallith and saw that he, too, noticed his son turn away, and her heart ached for him. She pulled her daughter closer to her, shushing her protest. She was only six winters. She was still her father's child and she, at least, would not betray her father's pride.

As Nataallith sensed the restlessness growing around him, the indecision and the fear from the old ones, the anger from the young ones, he said, "I, too, have urged war sometimes. I, too, have lost much. I heard the Mexicans of the Rio Grande cry when we burned their homes. I saw the soldiers fall when we attacked their supply wagons to Fort Defiance. Blood revenge for the slaying of my nephews at Wide Reeds has never been taken, and their women and children still work in the homes of Mexicans weaving blankets as slaves. In the last ripening, I watched as soldiers burned my hogans and my fields. I took a bullet then, as you all know. But still I plead for peace! Look how quickly they defeat their enemies when they wish to do so! Look how fast they overcame the Mexicans. Those you see at Fort Defiance have tens of thousands of brothers in their home camps. They are a great and powerful nation. And this much I know—they are not going to go away."

"Neither are we!" called out one of the warriors. "I am weary of hearing how strong the white men are, Long Earrings! They will bleed and die just like any other men!"

There was a shocked silence from the circle of elder headmen. No one called Nataallith by his white name and had not done so for many years. For such words and that name to come from the mouth of a young warrior seemed more disrespect than any headman could be expected to tolerate.

But Nataallith answered him calmly, without rancor. "Yes, we are a large and powerful nation. But we are not as powerful as the white man and we shall never be. We do not have their land, their weapons, or their numbers. It is folly to suppose that we can possibly win any war we begin with such an enemy."

"Then we can become their slaves and hoe their fields," another warrior called out angrily. "Is that what you would have us do? I would rather die in battle with honor! At least my children will remember my name."

"Your children will be homeless and without a father or a people," Nataallith said firmly. "You must listen to me. My blood has not grown thin. No, I am not afraid to fight. But I have learned in these last years of something better than war. From our friend, Red Shirt, I learned of a better trail. You know that when he spoke it, it was in truth."

"Red Shirt is dead!" the warriors called.

"But his truth still lives!" Nataallith let some of his own anger show now. "He told us that the only way to keep our land was to share it. He showed us that the only way to live with the white man was to learn from him his ways, take what we can from him which will make our lives better, and move aside from those ways which would weaken us. We want his weapons, his tools, his hats," he said pointedly, glaring at a warrior who had made a war hat of a soldier's felt hat with a feather stuck in the brim, "but we do not want his presence. We cannot have both, my people! It is time to bend like the reed to a stronger wind. There is much we can take from the white man and still be the People. But we cannot remain the People if we are slaughtered in battle like so many sheep!"

There was silence now, and Nataallith lowered his voice to a more gentle, persuasive tone. "I ask you to think of the future. I ask you to think of your children and their children." He smiled wryly. "It is a privilege of grandfathers to speak of children, just as it is a privilege of young men to speak of war. But we are a nation of women and children, as well as warriors. Reluctantly, I ask you to consider still a lasting peace."

The People listened to Nataallith, but when Manuelito rose to speak, his anger made him more eloquent. "I have signed too many papers!" he began loudly, "and I have sat in too many councils! My legs are weak with sitting, and my hand is bewildered from making my mark on papers which fly before the wind like leaves in the autumn. My legs yearn to ride a war pony and my hands must hold my rifle once more. And if this is the last thing they ever hold again, then this is my fate!"

About half of the warriors instantly jumped to their feet screaming war cries and shouts of approval. Pahe looked over at the elder headmen and saw the way their shoulders slumped. It was as if they could already smell defeat. Nataallith did not meet her eyes, but he did not drop his gaze. He stared at Manuelito with respect and patience. Only once did he turn his head to gaze at his son, a long stare of resignation and sadness.

Pahe caught her breath in her throat, a strangled sob. She saw the look pass between father and son. She saw the one reach out a hand and the other turn away from that embrace, and she wanted to leap to her feet and scream at her father for silence in that moment, but she stayed where she sat, holding her daughter close.

Manuelito began to stride up and down before the fire, his voice rising and falling in a strong recital of all the insults and wrongs and trespasses they had endured at the hands of the white men. Pahe felt her spine slumping like that of the old ones. There would be no easy trail to follow from now forward, she knew that much.

For four days, Manuelito urged the younger men to join him on the war trail. They needed little urging. It was the rest of the council that could not bring themselves to agreement. Finally, the People were split in two. They left their *Naachid* with no unity and no decision. Nataallith was still determined to keep the peace, and many families followed him. As he kept saying, it was not that he wished so much for peace, but that he knew a war with the whites would be disastrous. Manuelito was determined to rid the land of the white man forever, however, and many warriors had joined him. The council at Chinle, *Tsin Sikaad*, Standing Tree, left the People more divided and weakened than ever.

After council, Pahe took her son and her daughter to visit Manuelito and Ayoi, for she wished them to see that the survival of the family was more important than any victory in war. She left her daughter in the weaving hogan with her mother and her son out in the corral with her father, and she traipsed over the sand bluffs to Deezbaa's isolated hogan, where she lived alone, away from the clan, at the edge of Narbona's old fields.

The fields were gone now, ruined by the white man's grazing herds and gone back to sage and saltgrass. There was no smoke coming from the fire-hole, though it was time for the midday meal. A buzzard wheeled slowly overhead and stayed aloft without ever seeming to stir its long black white-tipped wings, never in a hurry to get anywhere or do anything. Pahe tilted her head and watched it, her eyes watering with the sunlight. It was a sacred, contemplative bird, she thought. Rising slowly, slipping off, sailing high winds without lifting a feather, its eye missed nothing. Maybe the bird slept on the winds, dreaming of a previous life when its wings were but a dream. She lowered her head, feeling dazed, and walked slowly to Deezbaa's hogan. She scratched gently on the blanket covering the doorway, clearing her throat and waiting, as was the custom to respect privacy and modesty. After a long wait, when her grandmother did not come out, she called, "It is I, Little Bird, come to see you."

There was nothing but silence from within, but Pahe sensed that her grandmother was there in the darkness alone.

"Grandmother!" she called again. "I have come to see you."

A hoarse croak of a voice answered, "There is no grandmother here."

Pahe smiled. "Then who is speaking, if not my old, ugly grandmother?"

A long pause. Then the voice said, weaker now, "A *chindi*. A ghost, only."

Pahe pulled the blanket aside and stepped within, the dark cool of the hogan momentarily making her blind. And then her eyes adjusted and she saw Deezbaa lying on her cot in the corner, her bare feet pulled up to her body like a child.

"I am come," she said to her gently. "Are you ill?"

Deezbaa did not bother to sit up. "I am dead."

Pahe chuckled and moved closer, sitting a little off the cot. Her grandmother's skirt was dirty and unkempt, her hair tangled and matted. The smell from her cot was unclean, but Pahe kept the dismay from her face and her voice. "The dead do not speak, Grandmother."

"Oho!" groaned Deezbaa. "That is all you know. The dead

speak as much as the living, and usually with more wisdom. Your grandfather and I have more conversations now than we did in the last five years of his life." She sat up abruptly. "Did your mother send you to spy on me?"

Pahe shook her head. "Why would my mother send me for such a fool's errand? If she wanted to see what you were doing, she would come herself."

"Exactly," Deezbaa said ironically. "To her, I am dead."

"Well, and she told me that she was here only four days ago," Pahe said soothingly.

"She takes better care of her mare," Deezbaa said shortly.

Pahe had no argument for that and did not wish to start one. She was struck by the memory of her grandmother when she was younger, how tenderly she had held her, sung to her, and saved choice morsels from the feast table for her. How had they come so far to this place, where they seemed like angry strangers from different clans? "Sit up, Grandmother," Pahe said softly, "and I will comb out your hair. Your skirt is a mess."

Grumbling, Deezbaa allowed Pahe to brush out her hair and attempt to bind it up on her head.

"You need a good washing," Pahe scolded her. "You smell like a coyote."

"This is one of the curiosities of age," Deezbaa said with an ancient dignity. "I can no longer smell my food and I can no longer smell myself. And so, neither interests me anymore."

Pahe gave up and cajoled Deezbaa outside with a basin and some yucca soap. As she washed her hair, she said, "The People are divided, Grandmother. The warriors want to make war against the whites, and some of the old ones wish still for peace."

"And the grass still grows and the sheep still bleat," Deezbaa snorted. "You are telling me nothing has changed."

"What has changed is that I have never seen such confusion," Pahe said sadly. "They have much that we need—the rifles, the hoes, the seed, the tools, the silver and jewelry and cloth. The women want the red and blue dye; the men want the saddles—"

Deezbaa waved away her words. "Much that you want; nothing that you need."

"The clans are divided," Pahe replied. "One against another, and no one seems to speak with a voice strong enough to be heard above this confusion."

"Not even your husband?"

Pahe smiled. Deezbaa obviously knew much of what was happening with the People, despite her isolation. "They listen to him. But the young men do not respect his words anymore."

"And your own father wishes to lead the war parties."

Pahe sighed. "I am caught between two strong voices."

"Your ears must be weary," Deezbaa chuckled. "They have always been too large for your head. But your first loyalty must be to your husband."

"You tell me this!" Pahe cried.

Deezbaa shrugged. "You are not as strong as I was. You are not a speaker, you are a listener. You were born to follow, I think, not to lead."

Pahe frowned. "You did not tell me this when I was younger."

Deezbaa tossed her wet hair back from her face and pulled herself up and away from Pahe's hands. "You were different then. You are older now, and you have stood inside Nataallith's shadow so long, I doubt you can cast one of your own." She shrugged, gathering her skirt about her as though the blanket were a thing of beauty instead of a rag. "You are more your mother's daughter than your father's, I fear."

Pahe felt the insult keenly, though she knew that her grandmother was goading her. "That blanket is filthy. I would be ashamed to have it on my body. You are not so old, you cannot keep yourself clean."

Deezbaa laughed happily. "No, you would not have it, but I would not have your husband on my body, as that goes. You come to me for counsel? I gave my counsel years ago. Kill the whites. Likely it is too late now, for they are many more and stronger."

"And we are weaker."

"And no less stupid than you were when I first gave this counsel."

Stung, Pahe said, "You are still a member of this clan, Grandmother, stupid though we may be."

"Am I? Am I, indeed. That must be why the much-traveled

trails around my hogan lead in all directions back to my clansmen."

Pahe dropped her head. For, of course, the grass grew high round Deezbaa's hogan, and no trails led to anywhere at all.

"They still think you a witch," she said. "They still warn their daughters against becoming like you."

"They are fools," Deezbaa wheezed, making her way back toward the door of her hogan. "And though the whites are fools as well, they are now powerful fools." She waved Pahe away. "Go back to your husband, Little Bird, and keep to his side. That is all you can do now. Your father will lead the men into battle, and, very likely, they will fail. But men will do as they will do."

"I will come again soon," Pahe said.

Deezbaa chuckled wryly. "No, you won't."

Pahe began to protest—

"It was such a difficult place to find, you could not even risk your children on the journey. Fly away, Little Bird, fly away." And Deezbaa went inside and pulled the blanket down after her.

Pahe stood for a long moment, filled with sorrow and anger. Her grandmother had always been difficult; now she was impossible. It was small wonder that her mother came here only reluctantly. And then Pahe was struck by a strong wave of remorse. There was a time when Deezbaa was young and beautiful and strong, and Narbona was envied for having such a wife. Now she was an outcast, growing old and wizened as a solitary juniper, twisted by time and the winds of change. Surely there was an easier way to face death.

Pahe sighed with regret. She had been an undutiful grandchild. She had not cared for her grandmother in the way she had been cared for by her when she was young. She had not done her duty to her kinswoman. She had not shown gratitude for the memory of all her grandmother had once felt for her, done for her.

Pahe went to the door again and pulled the blanket aside. "You are old and mean as a rattlesnake, Grandmother, and there are other places I would rather spend the day. But I will come back again soon, and next time, I will bring my daughter and my son. You can insult them as you have me, and they will know what it is to have Narbona's blood in their hearts. And next time I come, I want to smell something in this hogan besides your hair."

She walked away and could hear Deezbaa's laughter as far as the next ridge.

*   *   *

The voices for war grew strong over the next few months, for the white ranchers ran their herds now anyplace they pleased. Finally, those who were most angered found the courage to attack Fort Defiance. Manuelito and Barboncito, *Hastiin Dághd*, the Bearded One, of the Coyote Pass people, led the attack in spring of 1860, with the help of Herrero, the Blacksmith, who lived inside the fort. With a thousand warriors, they moved in before dawn and surrounded three sides of the fort. Then, about an hour before sunrise, they fired shots at the three sentries at the southwest corner of the fort, attacked the eastern hill, and took possession of the garden where the woodpiles gave them protection.

They quickly took all the outer buildings, including the storehouse, before the soldiers organized, but when they opened fire on the soldiers, they forgot the position of the cannon that protected the fort from the eastern hill slope. Also, they did not suppose that the Navajo watchman would take the whites' side and give the alarm. So, the alarm was sounded, the cannon fired, and the attackers finally scattered after an hour of fighting during which time the soldiers were able to get stronger defensive positions. The only American casualty was one soldier with an arrow through his heart. The Navajo lost eight men and, worse, they lost the battle.

Runners came with the news to Nataallith's hacienda, and Pahe went immediately to her hogan and scattered sacred pollen in all four corners of the hogan to the Holy Ones so that her father would be kept safe. She wanted to go to her mother, but Nataallith said that it would be too risky to take the wagon out on the trails, with the soldiers likely hunting for any of the People they could find. She sat in the darkened gloom of her hogan, thinking of the last time she had seen her father.

He was out in the corral with her son, showing him how to gentle a pony. He spoke low to the horse, moving always from the same side, sliding his hands along the animal's flanks in a caress. Wasek sat on the upper rail of the corral, watching his grandfather carefully. There was now no man he respected more than Manuelito, for he heard how the other warriors spoke of him, with respect and even reverence. She knew that he thought his own father an old man, at least, or perhaps even a coward.

She saw her son speaking to his grandfather, and she sensed that he was not asking about the pony. No doubt, he was telling him about how many white men he wanted to kill when the raiding began.

And now war had started, and defeat was already upon them. Nataallith said that the soldiers would punish all the clans, whether or not they had been part of the attack on the fort. There would be those, she knew, who would criticize her father now for bringing the soldiers down upon them, forgetting that before the attack, they were already being worried and punished by soldiers at every turn.

A scratch came at her door, and she sat silent, letting whomever wished entrance take it upon himself to come in without a welcome. To her surprise, it was her daughter who came inside, ducking her head and blinking in the dark.

"Are you sad?" she asked anxiously, coming over to sit as close to her mother as she could. She peered up into Pahe's face, looking for signs of sorrow.

Pahe reached out and patted her daughter's hand. "You are good to worry for me, my heart. But you are too young to be a mother yet, most particularly to your own."

"Father says that Grandfather was not injured," Dolii said quickly, always happy to be the bearer of news of any sort, "but other warriors were killed. Wasek says that was because our grandfather made himself invisible to the soldiers. Is that true? Was Grandfather invisible?"

Pahe shook her head. "I do not know, little one. You must ask your grandfather yourself when you see him."

"Will that be soon?"

Pahe fell silent.

"Mother?"

"Please ask me no more questions," Pahe said suddenly, her voice low and impatient. "I do not know what is going to happen. I do not know when the soldiers will come. I do not know what your father or your grandfather will do next. Do not ask me!"

Stung, her daughter looked away in shame. "I am afraid," she whispered. "Wasek is not afraid. Father is not afraid. No one is afraid but me."

Pahe wondered with a feeling of rising panic how her daughter had come to this place. Where was her little warrior, who had fought to be born and was so strong and vital when she was an infant? Such courage she had then! Pahe grabbed her daughter and pulled her close. "That is not true, *Shiyasha*, little one. I am afraid, as well. Look at your fingertips. You can see the trail that the wind of life left on you when it breathed into you. Those marks are like mine. We are the same, you and I. I am afraid, but I am doing my best to hide it."

"Why?"

"Because I am Deezbaa's granddaughter and Ayoi's daughter, born for Manuelito. I have Narbona's blood in my heart, and so do you. The People look to see if we are afraid. And if we are afraid, then they know to be afraid as well. If they see that we do not fear, they face their own fear with more courage."

"And then they think they can attack the white man and defeat him," Dolii said wonderingly. "Mama, is Father afraid, as well?"

Pahe sighed. "I do not know, my daughter. I cannot see into your father's heart so easily these days."

Her daughter considered this for a moment. "Wasek says he is afraid. But Wasek is wrong. Father is not afraid. He would fight the white men if he thought it was good to do that."

"He has fought them for more years than Wasek has been alive," Pahe said slowly.

"Is he tired? Wasek says he is too old."

Pahe put her cheek down on her daughter's head. "He is not too old for peace, but he is too old for war. You are too young, and he is too old."

"Is Wasek too young?"

Pahe kept her head turned away so that her daughter would not see her tears.

*   *   *

The People expected the most brutal vengeance for Manuelito's attack on Fort Defiance, so the clans scattered in panic, driving their horses and flocks into the deepest canyons, watching from behind rocks expecting to see General Canby and his troops arriving to attack them in return.

When the soldiers came, they brought also the New Mexicans, the Utes, and any other volunteers from the Zunis and the Pueblos they could gather together, but they found very few Navajo waiting to be captured.

Many had fled into the canyons; more were hiding in the mountains. For almost a year, the Navajo were chased and harassed, but few were captured or killed. The year of war took its toll, however. The flocks were abandoned, the fields left to rot, and the hogans were deserted, leaving the People without food or shelter as they began the winter of 1861.

Nataallith took his family into the mountains, pulling the wagons up into the secret canyons as far as he could and then blocking the passageways with felled trees and shrubs. He posted guards at the entrance to the canyons and set up camp in the shelter of the pinyons. The children thought it a great adventure to be sleeping in lean-to shelters and cooking out in the open, but Pahe felt the loss of her home and her comforts keenly. It was more difficult to keep from breaking the *báhádzid*, the taboos given them by Changing Woman, when they were so many so close together. It was forbidden to step over the reclining body of another, but how could one keep from it, when they were packed together in the same sleeping shelter?

She knew her mother and father were safe, but she wondered if Deezbaa had refused to hide from the white men, if she were still huddled in her hogan, grumbling in the darkness and awaiting the battle. Pahe was tortured by violent dreams those nights, visions in which the white soldiers came down on them from above the canyons and from below like ants, running over the guards and surprising them in their sleep. She woke a dozen times a night to listen to the silence and the even breathing of her children. And she began to despise her husband and all headmen who had brought them to this place of being hunted like wolves and driven from their homes.

And then the message came, a runner from a clan to the east, that the soldiers had marched out of the fort in the direction of Albuquerque. It was 1861, and the People could not know that suddenly their rebellion was much less important than a larger rebellion to the east. The soldiers who might have destroyed them were called to march to a civil war that the Navajo knew nothing of and could scarcely fathom.

The People came down out of the hills and the canyons once more, but peace did not last long. Once the Zunis and the Utes understood that there was no ultimate power in Fort Defiance waiting to reward or punish them for good behavior, they began the raids again in earnest. The territory was truly in chaos, and, this time, all enemies were armed with rifles, were familiar with military maneuvers, and were frustrated with all avenues of peace.

It was in that time, the belly of the Fearing Time, when a party of Zuni hunters ambushed Nataallith. It was many months before Pahe finally found out the way of his death, and even then she knew that there were details which she would never know. Would not wish to know. Her husband had been trapped by the Zunis in a low box canyon and could not escape, so he defended himself with honor. He shot one Zuni in the breast, one in the throat, one in the mouth, and one in the ear, galloping away and firing over his shoulder, but his plunging horse careened off a tree and threw him. He crawled behind the horse, using it as cover under a rain of bullets and lay there shooting until he had used up his arrows. Then he stood up to receive a mortal bullet. The Zunis rode up and each threw a stone at him until his body was crushed, and then they broke his arms and legs lest he stand up again and fight them. They then scalped him and took the sinews of his limbs to make war medicine.

The last strong advocate for peace was dead.

Pahe's brothers went to find his body, brought him home, and made the death ceremony for him, but Pahe could not look at his torn face and limbs. She knew that she would carry the memory of that single view all of her days, and she preferred not to add that vision of Nataallith to the other nightmares which kept her from peace these nights. She mourned him hard, and she knew that she would never feel safe again.

She had prayed to the Holy Ones to grow old together, prayed that they might die within hours of each other, and the Holy Ones had betrayed her. She was right all along, she brooded bitterly, love led only to sorrow and emptiness, loneliness and weakness. She decided she would never love again.

*   *   *

She left her husband's hacienda and went to her father's lands, leaving the care of her children to her mother for a moon or more. When she finally emerged from her sorrow, coming up to the surface of her life once more, she saw that her son was grown and hardened by loss and grief, made bitter against all enemies, but most particularly against the Zuni tribe. And her daughter was a frightened, nervous child who spoke rarely and never smiled. She took them in hand then and returned to her husband's lands. There were still enough clansmen to work the fields sufficiently to feed them; still enough sheep to see them through the winter, if barely. And she could not abide losing her daughter's spirit, her son's heart, as well as her husband and companion.

On the day before she was to leave her father's hogan, she went once more to see Deezbaa. She had visited her twice since she had arrived, but each visit seemed to take more strength than she could muster. Finally, however, she knew that she must go and say farewell. She did not know if she would ever see the old woman again, the way the world was changing. She did not know if she cared.

As she climbed over the rise to Deezbaa's hogan, she stopped suddenly, frozen in her steps. A coyote was coming toward her, its nose up and scenting the wind. Pahe rose to her full height, breathing hard from her climb, watching the animal approach. Either it did not see her or did not care whether she was so near, for it came on with no fear, its long tail plumed behind its gray body, its face sharp and angular and searching. She saw then that the coyote was old, not like the young creature which had accompanied her so many years ago as she escaped the Ute abductors. This one was grizzled around the muzzle and trotted slowly, with some obvious discomfort in its stride.

Pahe felt fear prickle the hair on the back of her neck. The coyote meant death in the custom of the People, a harbinger of loss and grief. Although she had never taken that belief to heart, since she had known a coyote to be, instead, an ally, she was certainly aware that most of her clan would be horrified by the close approach of this animal.

She said, *"Ya'at'eeh, coyotl,* I go to see Deezbaa. You know my grandmother, wife to Narbona. She lives just there—" She pointed to the dip in the valley floor ahead where Deezbaa's hogan waited.

The coyote turned and looked at her calmly, panting in what seemed to be a grin.

Pahe was filled with a sudden anger and fear. She bent to pick up a rock and hurled it at the animal, over its head so as to scare it away without injuring it. "Go from here!" she shouted at the coyote.

Still panting, the coyote moved away from her unhurriedly, glancing back over its shoulder as though it understood her meaning but chose to ignore her.

Pahe hurried then down to Deezbaa's hogan, breathing heavily and running all the way. When she came near, she saw that there was no smoke, no smell of the midday meal cooking. She scratched at her grandmother's door and once more was greeted with silence. Typically, Deezbaa made her wait and call for several moments, never acknowledging a visitor. Pahe wondered how many clansmen had come this way to see her and gone away again, bewildered by her silence. She called out loudly, "Grandmother, I am come!" Still, there was no noise from within. Not even an answering snort of disdain.

Impatiently, she pulled aside the blanket from the doorway and went in, once more waiting for her eyes to adjust to the dusty gloom. She sensed instantly a difference. Her grandmother was lying on her cot, her bare feet pulled up to her body as usual, but she was not there. Pahe knew it before she even touched her. She had been dead for at least a day. The coyote was in no hurry, as death is in no hurry. Both had already done their work. Deezbaa's spirit did not hover about the rafters of the hogan; her ghost did not wait in the corner to be discovered. Deezbaa was gone.

Pahe sat tiredly down in the corner and looked at her grandmother with a grudging envy. She would no longer know fear or loss or pain or despair. She was now with the gods and the spirits, and had left nothing behind for the living at all, not so much as a whisper of herself. Her brow was smoothed; her hands were relaxed. Pahe waited for the tears to come, but her eyes were dry. She had used all the tears her body had on her husband and her children; she had none left. She wondered idly if her body would ever know a man again, if her heart would ever love again. She hoped not.

Her people were afraid of the dead, she knew. The dead must not be looked upon or touched, but wrapped in a blanket and buried as quickly as possible. Their hogan must be burned, and their footsteps must be brushed away, else they might wander as ghosts forever.

Curiously, she did not feel afraid. If her grandmother gave her ghost sickness, then she would have a Blessing Way and be healed. She went to her grandmother's side and smoothed her tangled hair. "You left at a good time," she murmured. "The times ahead will be hardest for the young and the old."

She sat on the ground next to her grandmother's cot and rested her head against the woman's knees. It seemed to her that a thousand years had passed since she had been a young girl, first worn her grandmother's silver necklace, and been scolded for her impertinence. And it seemed that a thousand more must pass before she would be able to rest as well as Deezbaa.

Finally, she rose wearily and went out to tell her mother that Deezbaa was gone. She hoped that her mother would be able to weep.

*   *   *

Now that the Bilagáana *had abandoned Fort Defiance, Manuelito could graze his horses within the very grounds of United States property. The People forgot that they once cursed him for bringing down the soldiers' vengeance on them and began to believe what the warriors said, that the whites had run away rather than fight the People again.*

Manuelito said that there would be no peace. Not now and perhaps not ever. He let it be known that for every attack by their enemies, he would lead the warriors to retribution. He said that if the whites dared to return, he would destroy them. For every moon they stayed away, he said, the People would grow stronger, and soon, they would be able to withstand any attack by any enemy at all.

Those who might speak for peace were either dead or had gone away. The People could not know that there was a larger war that called the attention of the white men, but once that war was either abandoned or finished, they would be back to Dinétah *to reclaim what they had declared theirs.*

PART TWO

1861–1864

"Each night I think of this as darkness moves in, casting shadows at first, then immersing us in the clean night air.
I think of this as the moon glides slowly from east to west among the distant stars.
Because of this, I understand that I am valued. Because of the years I have lived, I am valued.
Yes, I am pitied by the huge sky,
the bright moon, and glittering stars.
We consist of long, breathless songs of healing. We are made of prayers that have no end."

—Night Song of At'ééd Jóhonaa'éí Yidiits'a'í

Months went by, and the soldiers came and went. Manuelito heard that many of the People were becoming accustomed to going to the newly built Fort Wingate to trade and draw rations from the soldiers as they could. Sometimes, they would race their ponies against the horses of the soldiers, and often they would win.

In the season of the falling leaf, Manuelito said that they would go to this fort and see for themselves what sort of horses the new soldiers had. Ayoi snorted and shook her head. "He cannot rest while races are run without him," she said to Pahe. But Pahe could see that her mother was pleased that he cared to do something besides eat his liver over the loss of the land and the encroachment of the whites.

And so they made the journey to Fort Wingate. Pahe did not wish to go. Indeed, since the death of Nataallith, there was little that interested her in life at all. Except her children. She knew that Wasek, who was twelve that summer, and her smallest blossom, Dolii, who was eight, needed to think of something other than loss. It would do them good, she knew, to dress in their brightest blankets and ride their ponies to where the People gathered, even if the *Bilagáana* gathered there as well.

When they rode up to the fort, Pahe was surprised to see so many of the clans camped so close to the high walls. Manuelito approached one of the guards and had a conversation with him, and Pahe saw that there was friendship on the white man's face and guarded pleasure on her father's. When he came back to where they had set up shelter, he said, "I will race against this man's horse. When I beat him, I shall have his horse and silver besides."

"I will race, too!" Wasek shouted eagerly. He was angry at being kept back with the women while his grandfather went to speak to the *Bilagáana,* and his shout was at least as much defiance as hope.

"No, not yet," Manuelito said, dropping a hand over his shoulder. "But you will hold the white man's silver until I come to claim it. And you will help me get my pony ready to run like the wind."

"*Hao, Che!* Yes, Grandfather," Wasek replied.

To Pahe's chagrin he then went off happily with Manuelito to ready the horses, with no stubborn refusal or defiance at all. "Why does he do whatever my father wishes with a civil tongue, and nothing but a thorny mouth for me?" she asked her mother.

"He is a man," Ayoi shrugged. "Who can understand why they are as they are?"

"He is a boy." Pahe frowned, struggling with the tiedowns for their shelter. "And little good he is to us while he dogs my father's heels."

"That is the one you should worry about." Ayoi dropped her voice confidentially, gesturing with her chin toward Dolii. The girl was unpacking one of the ponies, her hands moving slowly, listlessly, her eyes downcast. "Except for her adornments, she might be taken for a slave instead of a headman's daughter."

Pahe looked toward Dolii with a sigh. It was true, what her mother said. Dolii wore what silver necklaces and heavy turquoise they had left, and her blanket-skirts were as gay as those of any *rico* in the encampment, yet her shoulders drooped and her face was turned inward as though she saw nothing outside herself at all. "She needs to grieve in her own way," Pahe said faintly. It was hard to see such sadness in her daughter and not feel her own.

"So she has," Ayoi said. "Now she has other duties to those who are still alive."

Pahe's answer was broken off by a large cheer which came from the fort and the thronging soldiers and Navajo who crowded around the open gates. They hurriedly finished securing the shelter and their packs, as Wasek came bounding back into the encampment like a deer. "It is starting! Hurry up! Hurry up!"

They followed him through the crowd, and Pahe saw that silver was changing hands all around them, as well as beads, blankets, livestock, and whatever else men could place as bets. The soldiers mingled among the People freely, and it seemed to her that there was much laughter and smiling faces, as though they had never been enemies.

Wasek dragged his grandmother, mother, and sister to the front of the crowd, saying, "They gave my grandfather the name of Pistol Bullet! And he will race against that red horse there!"

Pahe saw that her father was up on his pony's back already, readying his reins and glancing around him as kinsmen slapped his feet and shouted at him to win. Next to him, a soldier was mounted on a large red horse, handing his coat to another soldier and shouting something to his friends in laughter.

"He races that soldier." Wasek pointed. "The one with the hair on his chin. Delgadito bet four ewes that Grandfather would beat him!"

Delgadito was one of the headmen with something left from the harsh winter and following droughts. Pahe was impressed that he would wager so much on a single race. But around her, she saw men handing over blankets, silver necklaces, turquoise, betting heavily on the speed of Manuelito's favorite horse.

Both racers were up; both horses stepped nervously, sensing that soon the signal to run would come. There was a shout from a group of soldiers near the jump-off place, and Pahe saw that three judges came foward, soldiers with Navajo blankets around their shoulders as though they were headmen of both the *Bilagáana* and the People in one. She grimaced, pulling Dolii closer to her, but her daughter squirmed away so that she might see her grandfather more clearly. Pahe smiled at that; at least she was showing some interest in the living.

Another shout, and someone fired a pistol. The horses bolted at once, and the race was on. She saw her father lean forward on his pony, reaching for the reins, and she wondered in that moment why he had not been ready for the signal. And then she saw clearly that the reins were slapping his pony's neck, out of control, and in a moment, the confused, frightened animal ran off the track and into the crowd. The soldier's horse finished the race to the finish line. Kinsmen ran to Manuelito, and she heard the buzz of questions and anger, and the voices came back to her. Manuelito was off his mount now, shouting and gesturing to the judges. His reins had been cut, the voices called back through the crowd. Someone had tampered with his pony's reins so that he would lose the race.

The crowd surged toward the judges, and Pahe heard two headmen call for quiet. Meanwhile, the soldier who had raced Manuelito came trotting back toward the judges, waving his hat and shouting of his victory. The mood of the crowd quickly turned ugly, and Pahe pulled Dolii toward her. This time, her daughter did not resist. She tried to call her son to her, but he did not listen. He surged toward the soldiers with many of the People, shouting for a new race to be run.

Finally, Manuelito and two other headmen got the People to draw back, and they approached the judges, asking for a new race. She saw her father hold up the reins for all to see. But the judges and the soldiers shook their heads and began to walk back to the fort gates.

An ominous hum came from the crowd, a sound of rising, incredulous anger, and in the voices, she heard danger. Snatches of protest, shouts of defiance, refusals to leave the grounds, and it was clear to her—indeed, to everyone—that the reins of Manuelito's pony had been cut by a white hand. But in the midst of the moving, surging crowd, the soldiers were oblivious to the anger of the People, and as she watched in amazement, they were forming a victory parade for a march back into the fort to collect their bets.

Like a wave, the People followed the parade, pushing forward and shouting their protests, and then Manuelito was there, pulling his pony through the crowd toward them, and she knew that they must get away, get away, move back from the anger and the confusion or they would be caught within the wave and propelled into the fort. She took Dolii's arm and pulled her back, shouted for Wasek to follow her, but his face was stern and twisted with anger, and he shouted like the others, waving his fist over his head like a flag.

"Get them back!" shouted Manuelito, and Pahe turned and pulled Dolii away, hollering once more for her son. As the shoulders parted before her and hurried toward the gate, she saw her son turn and follow Manuelito's pony back to their encampment, and she quickly blessed the Holy Ones that they had turned him away. She felt a rising fever of fear in her belly, for the crowds were louder now, and there were answering shouts from the tops of the fort walls, as soldiers angrily ordered the Navajo away. Then there was a loud thudding noise, and she could see that the fort gates had been closed against the crowd, and those in the front were being pushed against the massive wooden gates, shoved by the weight of those still pushing for entrance from behind.

Manuelito was off his pony now, taking Ayoi by the arm and pulling Wasek to him quickly.

"There will be trouble—" Pahe said to him anxiously.

"There already is," he said shortly. "Ready the packs; Wasek, bring the horses round."

And in that moment, they heard the unmistakable sound of a rifle report. They whirled and saw that at the side of the gate, a few of the men had tried to climb up the gates and force entry. The sentry on top had shot one of them down.

Now chaos erupted, and the women and children tried to turn back from the fort, but the press of bodies was so hard that some of them were trapped. The screams came up from the crowd, and those at the back began to run in all directions. More shots came from the fort walls, and Pahe saw bodies falling. She pulled Dolii onto her pony and slapped his rump, scarcely giving her daughter time to gather her reins. Ayoi wheeled by on her horse, clinging to the animal's neck perilously. Pahe screamed for her son and threw herself onto her own mount, whipping it away from the sounds of the gunfire, the panic which pushed out from the fort like a blazing heat.

They cantered away as quickly as the crowds and confusion allowed, looking back over their shoulders, following Manuelito's pony over a low rise. From there, they jumped from their horses and crouched on the ground, watching the massacre below.

Soldiers were pouring out of the fort, slashing about them with bayonets, firing into the crowds which scattered all over the valley. In the distance, they could see a band of warriors attacking the post herd, but the soldiers fired upon them, too, driving them off. One troop of soldiers was pulling the large cannons out of the gates and setting them up to fire upon the crowd. Women and children were screaming for each other and their men, warriors threw half-packed bags onto the horses and spurred them away, their goods falling out onto the ground, and still the soldiers kept firing, dropping bodies all around the fort. From a distance, they looked much like the spilled clothing and other goods, rumpled and motionless on the valley floor.

They mounted again and galloped a good distance from the fort before Manuelito stopped them once more. Wasek was panting in anger and fear; Ayoi moaned as she slid down from her pony, holding her side. "The demons!" she cried. "They have no honor! No shame!"

"Are you wounded?" Manuelito went to her, feeling her body and searching for blood.

She shook her head, pushing him off. "I will never go to the white devils again! You should not have brought us to this place!"

Pahe saw her father look down with shame, one of the few times she had seen him crestfallen before her mother. "I am grateful you are not injured," he said to her, to each of them. "Wasek, take that pack from your sister and tie it more securely on your pony. We will not stop before nightfall."

"There are many behind us who are dying," Pahe said quietly.

"We must let their kinsmen rescue them," Manuelito said sorrowfully. "There are not enough of us to make a difference."

Pahe turned to him in shocked silence. She realized that he was speaking of more than the brutal scene they had just witnessed. "Do you mean to surrender, then?" she asked him.

"Never!" Wasek shouted angrily.

Manuelito smiled grimly, a ghost of the grins she had seen on his face when he was a younger man. "Never," he repeated softly.

"Well, then we had better ride farther than the hacienda," Ayoi said shortly. "For the soldiers will find us there."

"They can find us everywhere," Dolii murmured.

Pahe was startled to hear her daughter speak. She realized then that she had not heard her voice for many days. She went to her and embraced her. "That is what they would have you think, but they are not gods. They are not warriors. They are only soldiers, and they are poor ones, at that. They have been left behind to guard this miserable fort while the ones who are the true fighters have been sent off to do battle with their own kind. They are weak, and they are stupid."

Pahe remembered suddenly something that her father had told her: that the Enemy was less than she was, than all of the People were. The Enemy could not defeat them without their cooperation. She said to Dolii, "We made a blunder by coming close enough for them to attack us, and we will not make that mistake again."

Dolii put her arms around Pahe's waist and her cheek on her breasts. "I am not brave enough," she murmured, softly so that her grandmother, her grandfather, and her brother could not hear her.

"You are, my daughter," Pahe reassured her, smoothing her hair. She lowered her voice. "Now, get on your pony and show your brother that it takes patience as well as courage to beat the enemy."

Dolii looked up at her mother skeptically, but she went to her horse and mounted.

Pahe breathed a prayer of praise to the Holy Ones that she had one child, at least, who was obedient.

They then rode away from the distant fort and the cries of the dying. No one looked back.

*   *   *

Four days after they arrived back at Manuelito's hacienda, they received word that the commanding officer of the fort, in an endeavor to make peace once more, had sent a few of the favored women of the soldiers to speak to the headmen. These were Navajo women who had left their clans and gone to live with the soldiers. Three of the headmen listened gravely to the apology taught to them by the commander and then gave the order to have the women roundly flogged and sent back to their soldiers with their clothing in tatters and their bodies exposed.

*   *   *

For many months, none of the People ventured close enough to the *Bilagáana* to be within rifle fire. From a distance, they watched as an army of Graycoats marched along the Rio Grande and fought battles with the army of the Bluecoats. The leader of the Bluecoats was Kit Carson, whom the People named Rope Thrower, for his skill with the lariat.

That spring, the headmen came to sit by Manuelito's fire to discuss the movements of the white men and the wars they fought among each other. Pahe sat near the circle of men, with Dolii beside her. Now, as the daughter of Manuelito and the widow of Nataallith, she was expected to have an opinion and voice it, so long as she did not take more of the speaking space than the men considered proper. Although she knew that the headmen would have preferred no child sit at council, she kept Dolii near. Someday, she believed, her daughter might well need to do more than listen.

Pahe thought it amusing that Wasek, who had only thirteen winters, was welcome at council because he was a boy, while her daughter, who had the steadier heart, was merely tolerated. This will have to change, she realized, if we are to beat the white men, for we need every heart and head, male and female. And so she sat, and when Dolii's attention wavered from the words around her, Pahe gently shoved her in the ribs, to keep her mind at the business at hand.

"The raiding parties are worse this season than any I recall,"

Manuelito said to the gathered headmen. "The New Mexicans act as though no treaty exists. I know four clans to the south which have lost ten women and children."

"There are more lost than that," Barboncito replied. He was a headman gathering strength to the west. "The raiders have come farther north than before, and one clan alone has lost six women and eight children, taken right from their fires. They are bolder than ever."

"It is said that the whites pay four hundred dollars in silver for a slave now in Santa Fe," Delgadito added. He was a younger headman, a strong voice for war.

"Only in Santa Fe," Barboncito said. "I know of few Mexicans who do not own Navajo slaves, some of them four or five, and they paid only one hundred or one hundred and fifty dollars in silver for each. They trade our children as regularly as they trade pigs and sheep."

"How many of our children have they taken?" Pahe asked quietly.

Barboncito said soberly, "I do not know. I have heard that there are white men in Santa Fe who keep track of such things, and it is their job to write on papers back to the Chief of the Americans with their countings. They say that five thousand of our women and children have been taken as slaves since they began the counting."

"Five thousand! And they have been stolen many more seasons than they have been counting!" Pahe said. She glanced at Dolii, who met her eyes soberly. "It is a wonder we have any children left at all."

"They can count them, but they cannot save them," Delgadito said angrily. "Since the white men came with their treaties, we have lost more children, not less."

"The soldiers are too busy fighting each other to keep the Mexicans off us," Manuelito agreed.

"Can we hope they will weaken each other enough for us to defeat them?" Pahe asked.

Delgadito shook his head. "For every soldier killed, they send two more to take his place. I believe that when they have finished their battles, many will stay on the land. And we have seen that they have no hesitation to kill our women and children. Why should we suppose that they will fight the Mexicans to defend them?"

A despairing silence fell over the council, as each mind recalled the bloody massacre of Fort Wingate: fifteen women and children had been shot and bayoneted over a horserace.

"What do we know of this new Star Chief, Carl-tun?" Manuelito asked.

Pahe knew that her father referred to the Chief sent down to command the Rope Thrower in battle. Kit Carson was an Eagle Chief; Carl-tun was a Star Chief, named for the gold ornaments on his coat.

"We know that he lusts for our land," Delgadito said. "He believes we have gold hidden in the canyons."

Wasek spoke up. "I can tell you of this Carl-tun. He has many soldiers who have nothing to do all day but march in the sun and rattle their rifles. He sits in the shade and watches them march, smoking his cigar and making marks on his papers. He is a fool."

"And how do you know this?" Barboncito asked patiently. He had a son near Wasek's age, and he was more able than many of the headmen to tolerate a boy's pride.

"I have seen him often," Wasek said.

"And from these spyings, you think him a fool?" Delgadito asked dryly.

"My grandson and his comrades have been observing the soldiers with my blessings," Manuelito said calmly. "I would imagine that their eyes are as strong as any here."

Wasek ducked his head gratefully at his grandfather's words.

"Why do you think this Carl-tun a fool, my son?" Pahe asked.

"Because he does nothing but march his soldiers. As I said." Wasek answered her with a touch of impatience.

"Perhaps he plans new battles, and those marches are his way of making sure that his soldiers are ready," Barboncito said gently. "Indeed, I have found it is very difficult to judge the white man's foolishness, even with the best of eyes."

"A white chief who has many soldiers and no battles to fight is dangerous," Manuelito observed. "He will soon need to turn his men to something other than marching."

The men spoke into the darkness for several hours, and finally

Pahe rose from the fire and took Dolii to bed. The girl had long before fallen asleep against her shoulder. As Pahe helped her onto her pallet, Dolii murmured, "I am hungry," her voice small and plaintive as a child's.

Pahe no longer flinched when she heard those words. There was a time when she would have felt a great sense of failure and responsibility if one of her family had hunger and she did nothing to assuage it. But now, they were hungry often enough, and she could say only, "I know. So am I, my child."

It was not that they were starving, but that they had so much less food than they were accustomed to enjoying. Meat was scarce, and there were fewer men to hunt for it. Crops were lean and spare; flocks must be protected and lambs saved for breeding. Many nights, they had cornmeal and dried squash to eat, and that was all. Yet they knew that many clans had less than they.

When Pahe remembered the great feasts of Narbona's time, her mouth filled with water and her eyes closed to keep the memory fresh. At least she had the memory. Her children did not even have that for comfort.

Pahe sat for a long moment at Dolii's side, watching her sleep. She was more like Nataallith in the face and body than Wasek. Wasek looked like Manuelito, like her own side of the blanket. Dolii had the narrow, wizened intensity of her father. With some fattening, she would be a beautiful woman. If she could remember how she used to be happy.

For a moment, Pahe missed Nataallith so much that she was breathless with the pain. There was a hot, hard spot on her heart that burned as though a coal glowed there, and she wondered with one part of her mind if she would ever be light again, ever feel completely at peace and contented. It was one thing to be a woman without a man. It was a far greater torture to be a woman without a man, yet still have his children to raise. In every word, each gesture, she saw him in them, yet there was no one to turn to for help, no one to comfort her when she did not know how to comfort them. She felt that alone, she could survive anything, could walk a thousand miles out of the desert away from the white devils, could live on sparse rabbit grass and cactus flowers, could sleep in the open and wear the same blanket until she died—but her children could not. For the sake of her children, she must find enough, make enough, raise enough, gather enough, save enough. And there would never be enough, she knew that in her heart. They asked for little, and it killed her to realize that little was all she would ever be able to give them now. If Nataallith were still alive—

But that trail led to madness. She knew women who were grateful for their children, even when their men were gone. At least I have the children, they would say, obviously taking much comfort there. Pahe wondered sometimes if there was something wrong with her, if she loved her children less because she took scant comfort in their presence. She had always felt herself more wife than mother, more woman than mother, and without her man, she felt bereft. The children did not suffice. Ah, my husband, she cried to herself, life is so empty without you!

She shook herself free of her melancholy and stood up, shivering and reaching for the solid side of the hogan as though she were ill. She could not think of him so long. Not yet. Like very cold water or very hot food, she must take only a little of her memories at a time, else she make herself ill.

A scratch at the door, and Wasek came in. He saw that Dolii slept, and he gestured to her to come outside in the darkness. Pahe roughly wiped her eyes and straightened, that she might face her son calmly.

"I am going to sleep in my grandfather's hogan," Wasek said with no preamble.

Pahe paused, confused. "Do you mean this night only?"

Wasek shook his head. "I will get my things tomorrow. It is best that I stay with Grandfather now."

"Best for whom? Your sister and mother are to sleep alone?" She had not anticipated this, was not ready for her son to grow so far away so suddenly.

Wasek frowned, trying to keep his voice light. "Grandfather and I will be close enough. If he can watch Grandmother from his hogan, than I can watch over you and my sister from the same place. And, besides, Grandfather needs me now."

Pahe snorted angrily, unable to help herself. She saw instantly the way Wasek's mouth thinned to a hard line. "You are not a man yet, my son. You are too new at war to know what it is.

Your grandfather needs many things to fight the whites, but a boy of thirteen summers is not one of them."

Wasek drew himself up with dignity. "You are a woman. You do not understand. I am my grandfather's eyes and ears."

"Better you should use those ears to listen to your mother now!" she said angrily. "Your father has been dead only a year. Your sister is like a bird with a broken wing—"

"My sister will do better with the comfort of women. My grandfather needs the help of every man he can find."

To Pahe's dismay, her eyes filled. "You are not a man," she said miserably. "You will waste your life fighting the *Bilagáana*, and I am wasting my breath fighting with you. Go, then, if this is what you think you must do." She turned her back to him so that he would not see her despair.

He stood silently for a long moment, and then he reached out and touched her shoulder gently. "It is not so very far, after all. There will be no mountains between us, no canyons to cross. Just a short walk across level ground."

She nodded, but she would not turn back to him or embrace him. "I will not be a foolish old woman. I will not fight the white man and you, as well."

He hesitated and then kissed the back of her head. When she did not turn, he walked away into the night. Pahe turned then and watched him go until she could no longer see him in the darkness. It was the way of things, she knew. She remembered when her two oldest brothers left, Manuelito Segundo and Tiene-su-se, two boys she had known all her life by their childhood names and now grown into manhood and gone. They left Ayoi's hogan when they had eighteen summers, and she was still a child. Even then, it seemed far too soon for them to be on their own. Juanita's sons left in time, as well. She knew that both mothers must have wept, but they never let their sons see their tears.

But those were different times. The People were strong then; Manuelito had a voice of growing power, Narbona was still alive—the departure of two sons was as natural as the growth of the lambs. She had not seen them for many seasons. They had their own clans, their own families. If times were prosperous, they would have visited frequently, shared their fires at Blessingway ceremonies, danced at Chuska Mountain, and made trade trips together over the year. Now it was too difficult to make such journeys, and so the clans could take little comfort from their united strength. Her grandfather, her husband, her brothers, and now her son. So many of the men either dead or departed.

Well, the women are still here, she thought to herself as she went back inside her hogan. The women are still here and must keep life alive somehow. She pulled the blanket up around her daughter's chin and went to her own pallet, falling into it with some gratitude and a heavy fatigue. Tomorrow would bring more life, which must be somehow endured. She must be strong enough to accept what came.

*   *   *

General James H. Carleton had one consuming ambition: to find gold in New Mexico. His plan was simple. The Indians must be eliminated and the land opened to prospectors. If money could be made in California, he reasoned, fortunes could be made in his territory. Carleton soon convinced Governor Henry Connelly, Chief Justice Benedict, most of the more influential New Mexican families, and the two Indian agents, Albert Pfeiffer and Christopher Carson, that he was the deliverer of the Southwest, and the Indians must be herded to a reservation distant from the region where they could learn to become good Christians and farmers.

Carleton chose a strip of land about two hundred miles southeast of Santa Fe at a spot where the Rio Pecos meandered through a stand of cottonwood trees called Bosque Redondo for his reservation. The general wrote glowing reports of the area and convinced the Department of War and the Bureau of Indian Affairs that those "wolves of the mountains," the Navajos and Apaches, could be made to live there in harmony with the land and each other.

When a board of army officers went to inspect the Bosque, they vehemently disagreed with Carleton, pointing out that the water was scarcely fit to drink and scant at that, that the soil was alkaline, that the land was flat and subject to flooding, and that there was no forage and little firewood. They recommended instead a site near Las Vegas, New Mexico, where the grazing was good, the water was ample, and the timber was plentiful. But Carleton was more persuasive, particularly to minds already made up. The War Department gave him funds to build his fort at Bosque Redondo, which he named Fort Sumner, and

General Carleton quickly began the campaign to remove every Indian from the Southwest.

In September, 1862, Carleton sent out an order:

> *There is to be no council held with the Indians, nor any talks. The men are to be slain whenever and wherever they can be found. The women and children may be taken as prisoners, but of course, they are not to be killed.*

In the autumn of that year, five headmen of the Apache were murdered in their camp on their way to negotiate with Carleton for terms of surrender. Three other Mescalero chiefs, Cadette, Chato, and Estrella reached Santa Fe and said words to Carleton which reached the Navajo and were quoted from fire to fire:

> *You are stronger than we. We have fought you so long as we had rifles and powder, but your arms are better than ours. We are worn out; we have no more heart. We have no provisions, no means to live. Your troops are everywhere. Do with us as may seem good to you, but do not forget we are men and braves.*

Carleton told the Apache headmen that the only way they could live was to go to the Bosque Redondo. Outnumbered, unable to protect their women and children, and trusting in the goodwill of Rope Thrower Carson, the Mescalero chiefs took their people into imprisonment at Bosque Redondo.

*   *   *

General Carleton's attack on the Apache made the People even more nervous than before. The headmen knew that the Mescaleros were weaker and poorer than their own clans, and likely had not been able to commit all the raids and crimes they were accused of, yet they were being driven from the land even as they begged for peace. Barboncito sent a message to Manuelito that his spies had seen for themselves the Army's brutality. Barboncito's hunting party had watched from a ridge as an aged Mescalero chief journeyed with his small band to an army encampment to surrender. When they came into camp, they carried the white flag, as the Army had instructed them, but before they could dismount, the white men attacked them, shooting six men and one woman. As the others turned to run, the soldiers chased them down and killed five more.

Barboncito said, "Do not believe that surrender will save your people. I have seen otherwise with my own eyes."

Wasek and his band of comrades, six boys all his own age, had been sent to spy on the white men at Fort Wingate. He reported that four hundred Apache men, women, and children had been loaded into wagons and taken on the trail to the east. He followed them for a time and then turned back. "They did not appear to be mistreated," he told the headmen. "They had food and blankets and horses. They are going to have new land at *Hwééldi,* what the whites call the Bosque Redondo, they say."

Barboncito said, "They will find a new place to die, and that is all they will find. I will not leave my land. If I must die, it will be where I was born, where my people were born, and where my people are buried."

Manuelito said, "Perhaps once this Carl-tun moves the Apache, he will rest content."

Pahe knew even as her father said this, he did not believe it.

Barboncito laughed mirthlessly. "You would not say this if you had seen him, my brother."

Six months before, eighteen of the headmen including Delgadito and Barboncito had gone to Santa Fe to see the general. Manuelito had chosen not to accompany them. They told Carleton they represented peaceful farming Navajo and that they wanted no more war.

"The Star Chief has a hairy face and his eyes are fierce." Barboncito went on. "His mouth has no humor. He does not smile when he speaks. He told us that we would have no peace until we went the way of the Apache. He said he would believe none of our promises again."

"Perhaps it is time to consider moving to the west," Pahe suggested hesitantly. She and her father had often discussed such a choice, but no one knew about these lands, and Manuelito was always reluctant to consider such a drastic journey. "At least we could then pick our own lands, rather than be driven to those chosen by the white man."

"There are no open lands," Barboncito said. "Do you think the

Mexicans and the whites will simply let us move our people to their grazing pastures and rivers without protest? They will fight for their lands, as we would if another tribe trespassed upon us. It is too late. Many have moved, and some of them have returned because there is nothing for them to the west."

Pahe fell silent. It seemed to her that as fear grew larger, the ears of the men grew smaller, at least when it came to her words or thoughts. She rose from the council and went back to her hogan, and as she walked away, the voices of the men rose in dispute, once more angered at their own helplessness.

To her surprise, when she approached her door, she saw that a woman waited for her in the darkness, shawled in a blanket. "I am here," she said formally, since she did not recognize the blanket design as from her own clan.

The woman said, "I have come to see the granddaughter of Deezbaa." Her voice was low and nervous.

"You have found her," Pahe said. "Please come in out of the darkness." She led the woman inside and gestured to Dolii. "This is my daughter, Dolii, born for Nataallith."

"I am Nanibaa, from the *Bit'ahnii* clan. The women say that you are your grandmother's spirit."

"Do they?" asked Pahe, genuinely surprised. "Why do they say such a thing?"

Nanibaa shrugged. "You speak your mind at council. You live alone, with no man." She gestured impatiently. "But that is not important. I have come to ask for your help, in the healing ways. My man has the water sickness."

The water sickness was the old name for that condition which came to many men as they aged, when they felt the urge to urinate often, but could not make their water come as easily or copiously as they could when they were young. It was common enough, it did not take a hand-trembler to diagnose the difficulty, and most wives knew their husbands' symptoms before their husbands did.

Pahe knew that if such a condition continued, often the men could no longer satisfy their wives. They also suffered pain of the groin and weakness in the rest of their bodies. She remembered that Deezbaa had herbs and roots for this sickness, as she did for so many illnesses, and the women often came for them. But she had not paid sufficient attention as she became a young woman, to learn her grandmother's wisdoms. She took the woman's hand and pulled her gently down by the fire. "I would gladly help you if I could, but I do not know what my grandmother knew. I have no herbs to give you."

"I did not think you did," Nanibaa said quickly, "but I had hoped that you could remember which ones she used, that I might gather them myself." She looked down at her hands. "My man began with pain in the night. Now he has pain in the day as well. I fear he will soon lose hope of ever being without this pain again."

"When a man loses hope, he is nearly dead," Pahe murmured.

Nanibaa clutched her hand. "I knew you would understand. Can you help me?"

"There is no other wise one in your clan who knows the old ways? No chanter who can come and bring your man harmony?" Pahe asked. It was alarming to think that the clans were so scattered, so distracted by the *Bilagáana*, that the old healing ways were being lost along with the lands.

"There was one close who did the sings," she said sadly, "but he was killed in the massacre last year. The others will not travel so far."

Pahe's mouth twisted in anguish. An old man shot down or bayoneted by the white men, and with him went the chants, the songs, the power of the asking the Holy Ones to heal, wisdom that would have nurtured an entire clan. With him went the memories of generations. Her man needed a Mountaintop sing, but who would lead it? "You must let me think," she said to gain time. In fact, she did not remember the exact plant stuff that Deezbaa had used for this complaint, but she thought she might recall if she could rest her mind. But what about all the other illnesses? The other healings? Perhaps Ayoi might remember some of them . . .

"You must come to me again tomorrow," she said, "and I will try to have what you need to know. I will go and see my mother."

"Ah! Your mother is still alive!" Nanibaa said happily. "You are so fortunate! Surely, she will remember."

"Perhaps she may. But, of course, she will not have the herbs, either—"

"Oh, I know," Nanibaa said quickly. "I did not expect that she would. And I ask no one to gather them for me. With the slave raiders everywhere, it is too dangerous. But if you can tell me, I shall go myself and find them."

Pahe wondered sadly if she would next hear that this woman had also been stolen and sold to the New Mexicans for her trouble. All so that she could help her husband hold on to his hope. If she had come this far for help, she was certainly not going to let fear keep her from finding what she needed.

"Do you have someplace to rest tonight?"

"Your father has welcomed me to sleep in the women's hogan," she said.

Dolii asked suddenly, "Do you have a daughter?"

Nanibaa turned to her with surprise; clearly she had forgotten the girl was present. "Yes, I do. She has ten summers."

"I have nine." Dolii faintly smiled.

"There are few in our clan for her to befriend," Nanibaa said. "Many of her cousins have either left for other places or . . ." She hesitated, glancing to Pahe. "Or are gone. Perhaps if I come again, I shall bring her."

"I would like that," Dolii said.

Pahe's heart turned over. It had come to a sad place when young girls could not leave their hogans to visit and befriend each other, for fear of all that ran wild outside the narrow confines of their family lands. "Come to me tomorrow," she said again to Nanibaa, suddenly glad for the woman to be gone. "I will do what I can."

Nanibaa stood and dropped her head to her gratefully. "My man did not wish me to come," she confided. "He waits for me now, out by the men's fire. He said it was not seemly to bother the wife of Nataallith with such things. But your father made us welcome."

"You tell your man that I am honored at your visit. These days, if we can help one another, no matter who we were born for, we must do so. You tell him that pride is no longer a commodity we can afford."

She smiled. "I will tell him, Deezbaa's granddaughter. I imagine, you are very like her."

She went out, and Pahe sat down next to Dolii, pulling her closer. "You are lonely, my little bird. I have been so concerned with my own thoughts and grief that I have not seen it. You need to be with other women and other girls, yes? We must find some girls who are brave enough for friendship. We must tell the headmen that even if we are at war, we should find a place and time to have the Blessingway."

Dolii shook her head. "The soldiers will find us. And if they do not, then the slave raiders will follow us like coyotes, looking for someone to stray too far from the fires."

"Come with me to see your grandmother," Pahe said. "I believe she will remember what her mother used to cure the water sickness. And if she does not, well, we will gamble with her for her red beads. They would look far prettier around your neck than on hers."

"Tonight?"

"Tonight."

"Dare we go out in the darkness alone?"

"I would say a man's penis hangs in the balance." Pahe grinned, rolling her eyes for emphasis.

Dolii giggled, a rare liquid sound which was so welcome, it made Pahe's eyes water with gratitude. She took her daughter's hand and led her outside into the night.

Ayoi's hogan was on a slight rise overlooking the valley, a good distance from Juanita's, a place she had insisted upon after the departure of her sons. She said she wanted to see what was coming. It was a joke at the time, for everyone knew that her eyes were as bad as a badger's from all the years of weaving, but now it was not such a joke. For it did seem to Pahe that plenty of things were always coming these days, and it was essential to see them before being seen.

She had not been on the desert at night for too long. Walking with Dolii across the dry land, she could feel her feet touch the earth, and the rock and sand seemed to yield to her, welcome her, in a way that made her feel old and rooted, like a wizened juniper. These were her lands. This was where her grandfather was buried, and her husband, and where she had buried the umbilical cords of her children. She looked up at the stars and was filled with a sense of completion and wonder. The mountains rose to either side of the valley, dark and steepled against the sky, black as the grave and silent. They were sharply etched, as though no trees softened their contours, as if the *Yeis* had only just created them the night before, and the winds had not yet had time to wear them down.

Dolii hummed softly as they walked, a welcome sound in the night silence. Pahe found herself smiling for no reason at all. "I used to come out every night," she said. "It has been too long."

"Why did you come out every night?"

"To tend my goats. That was the reason all girls went out. At any rate, that was the reason we gave. But, of course, mostly we just liked to be away from the eyes of our mothers when we could, for other reasons. Tonight, I am reminded of those, I think."

"How many goats did you have?" Dolii asked wistfully.

Pahe felt a pang, for, of course, Dolii had no goats of her own. No animal of any kind. Flocks were too precious now and too small to be given to girls. Even dogs were scarce. And so, there was no opportunity for a young woman to feel rich in her own right. "Twenty-eight," she said. "And every night I went out to the pen to see to them. The nights are just as beautiful now." She looked around her. "The land is, too. All that has changed is the white men upon it."

Dolii said quietly, "Everything has changed."

"Not everything."

"Everything that matters. It is dangerous to be out here," she added, her voice suddenly turned anxious.

"We will not say those words again," Pahe said firmly. "We are on the lands of my father, the lands of my grandfather. If someone comes, we will hear them well before they see us. I will no longer be penned into my hogan every night like a goat! We should have come out long ago."

"Mother, I have such dreams . . ." Dolii began hesitantly. "They come so often." She sighed wearily. "I cannot sleep."

"Dreams of your father?"

"And of the soldiers and the bayonets and the cannons and the deaths." She began to walk faster as though to rid herself of her own words. "They will not leave me!" Her voice broke, and Pahe could tell that she was trying hard to keep from crying out.

Pahe realized then how her own dreams had changed as well. She, too, had been having poor rest because of fearsome visions and dreams, and there had been no one to tell them to, no one to help her translate them into something that was trivial in the daylight. That was one of the things she suddenly could put a name to, one of the ways she missed Nataallith most. There was no one to tell her dreams to anymore, no one who listened in the night, who laughed them away or argued with her or translated or gave back his own dreams, and with that loss went a loss of herself, as well.

She saw that she could be that someone for her daughter, at least for a while. And Dolii could be that mirrored translation for her also. "Tell me the worst one," she said quietly. "The one which comes most often."

Dolii began to tell a dream of her father, which was somehow also mixed up with a vision of ten soldiers with rifles bearing down on a river, and her brother and mother were there as well, and there was noise of battle and smoke and blood and screaming, and somehow in the middle of it all, her father was sliding from his horse into the current, struggling to stay afloat—

It was, as Dolii said, an awful dream. Pahe talked with her about it for a while as they walked, turning it over and over in their mouths as they would a piece of turquoise in their hands, to see where it had value or flaws. When she sensed that Dolii had talked of it enough, she said, "If that dream comes again, say aloud, 'I know this one well enough. I don't need to see it again.' Perhaps it will go away."

Dolii smiled in the shadows, turning her head so that Pahe could see the gleam of her teeth. "I will shout it away."

"That's right! You must take a big stick with you to bed and hold it over your head in the dream. When it comes for you, whack it hard and scare it off!"

They were almost to Ayoi's hogan now, and they spoke louder as they approached, that the old woman might hear them coming. She stuck her head out the door and said, "I am being attacked by crazy women! And to think I feared the *Bilagáana!*"

Laughing, they went inside, embraced each other, and then Ayoi said soberly, "Well, and what are you doing out in the night with no men to guard you? Do you wish to be sleeping with Mexicans by the next moon?"

"We have decided that such fear is foolishness," Pahe said

briskly. "It is enough that they try to steal our lands. I will not let them steal the nights from me as well."

"That may well be enough for you," Ayoi said, dropping her voice. "But Dolii is a valuable commodity on the slave market. To let her out after dark—"

"Is necessary, I think," Dolii finished her grandmother's sentence. "I am sick of being sorrowful and gazing at walls."

Ayoi smiled wryly. "Who is this come to see me? Did you barter your quiet dove for a bold jay when I was not looking?" She hugged her granddaughter heartily. "Well, if the slavers take you, at least you will make them sorry, eh?"

They sat by Ayoi's fire and shared her supper, and Pahe told her about Nanibaa's visit.

"I am surprised she came so far," Ayoi said wonderingly. "That there is no one closer to her, someone in her own clan, is a sorry thing, indeed."

"There must be many out there like her," Pahe agreed, "who can't find a chanter or a hand-trembler to bring them peace and harmony in their bodies. There is no one to pass down the old songs. And this is just one calamity that the whites have brought to us: that we are forgetting how to help one another with the simple aches and pains of living."

"I remember what my mother would give to the women for such troubles, but, of course, I do not have any about." She grinned slyly. "That is one piece of his body which has never failed your father."

"You are becoming more your mother every day," Pahe said dryly.

"I hope that is true," Ayoi said. "There was little she feared, no matter what else they said of her."

"I wish I could remember her," Dolii said.

"She is still here," Pahe said softly. "I feel her often. And especially tonight."

"Can we find the plant she used?" Dolii asked. "Does it still grow here?"

"Of course it does," Ayoi said. "And I know where."

"You do?" Dolii asked. "Can we go and gather it tonight?"

It was so good to hear excitement in her daughter's voice that

Pahe was almost persuaded to comply. "We had better wait until dawn. The land is not so easy to walk in the darkness."

"I remember well when you did it, Little Bird!" Ayoi laughed. "Have you never told her the story of your journey?"

"Of course I have." Pahe smiled.

"Tell it again," Dolii begged. "I need to hear the stories again, I think."

Pahe nodded, understanding what she meant. So she told once more the story of her long journey through the dark land, the nights she traveled behind Coyote, weaving the tale larger and larger, telling it and retelling it, for that was the Navajo way. In her words, she knew that her daughter would learn how to be cautious with night footfalls, how to keep her courage when surrounded by the enemy, and how to respect the past even as she walked the present. Dolii knew the story by heart, and that was the best way to know any story, but most particularly one about the courage of her mother.

After she finished telling the story, Ayoi began recounting her memories of her mother's herbs and roots. "One of her favorites was *Wóláchíí beeyigá*, Red-Ant-Killer. It is the purple-stemmed plant with little yellow flowers that appears in the late part of the hottest months—"

"I have seen that!" Dolii said happily.

Ayoi nodded. "It is very good for cuts, I know. If you take the gum and hold it over the place that bleeds, it will hold together the skin until the bleeding stops."

"Why is it called the Red-Ant-Killer?"

Ayoi laughed. "Because a man named it, I suppose. They always choose the least important part of a woman to name her, and they do the same with the flowers of the Holy Ones, as well. If you mix the gum with water and pour it down an anthill, one can wage war on the ants and be victorious. Obviously more important than binding wounds. There is another one, *Hazéí-yiltsee'í*, the plant with the chipmunk tail—"

"I know that one, too!" Dolii exclaimed. "Is that one good for a man's water?"

"Yes, and also for fevers and headaches—and saddle sores on horses. It is a life medicine . . . very important. The chanters use it in the Night Way and the Enemy Way Ceremony."

They fell silent then. It had been many years since Pahe had seen either ceremony, and Dolii had never seen them at all. This left them feeling bereft.

"It is time for sleep," Pahe said suddenly, to break the silence.

"I will tell you more, little one," Ayoi murmured to Dolii. "There is plenty of time."

That night, sleeping around Ayoi's fire, Pahe was more comfortable than she had been for many nights. It was good to sleep with women, she realized. Good that the generations of women closed ranks and protected each other.

*   *   *

In the morning, they went out to gather roots and herbs together, finding many that were useful and some which they believed might be helpful, if they could only recall how they were used. Pahe felt she walked where many generations of women had walked before, and she was comforted by that. She did not feel afraid for hours at a time. And when they came back to Ayoi's hogan to prepare the morning meal, she said, "You know that Wasek has gone to sleep in his grandfather's house."

Ayoi nodded. "It is time."

"How can you say that? He is just a boy."

"He must be a man quickly these days. He would not become so at your fire."

Pahe was quickly angered. "So, my son must be one more thing that we sacrifice to the white men?"

"No. One more thing sacrificed for the People. And in that, he is no different than his father, his grandfather, or his great-grandfather before him."

Pahe fell silent. "It is hard," she finally said.

"Yes," Ayoi replied, taking her hand. "And that is another reason I think you should come here and live with me."

Pahe laughed aloud with surprise. "You would drive us out like scorpions after seven days!"

Ayoi shook her head. "You are wrong. I would be grateful for your company." She spoke almost formally. "Times are changed. We must change with them, as we can. I think that two women in one hogan and one old woman alone in another is something we can change. We will be safer and more happy together. We will see our men more often, and we will take comfort from each other when we do not." She grinned. "I think we will laugh often and loud."

"I think it is a good plan," Dolii said.

Pahe raised her brows at that. "I wonder that you think you should have a voice in this, my daughter."

Dolii raised her brows as well. "I should have no voice in where I live?"

"Daughters too young for marriage generally do not."

"Daughters generally have their fathers and their brothers making that decision," Dolii replied a little tartly. "Times have changed, even Grandmother knows as much. I think it a good plan, and I think my voice should be heard as well as anyone else's here."

Ayoi laughed again, this time with a rich sound of delight. "There speaks Deezbaa, to be sure! The old woman is closer than we think!"

Pahe shook her head. "I never said that I did not think it a good plan. I am not yet ready, I suppose, to have one more child tell me how life will go."

Dolii embraced her firmly. "Just this once, I promise. Never again."

At that, Ayoi laughed again, this time so hard that she had to sit down. "Now you must move in with me. Because it will be so amusing to see you try to keep that promise, if you do not come to me, I must come to you."

"I would give all the silver in Barboncito's pack if she could keep it!" Pahe laughed in agreement.

"Has he so much, then?" Ayoi asked, instantly diverted.

And so they sat down once more to share gossip, and their voices carried outside the hogan and over the morning grasses like the sounds of desert birds.

*   *   *

In July of 1863, General Carleton gave the order to Kit Carson: "Every Navajo that is seen will be considered hostile and treated accordingly."

Carson set out with one thousand men to Dinétah to implement the government's plan. At first, the headmen were unimpressed. They had been given ultimatums before, and soldiers had been chasing them for

*years. Delgadito reminded them that they had ten times the warriors
that the Mescaleros had and ten times the land. Their stronghold, the
Canyon de Chelly, was more than three hundred miles of deep canyons,
steep-banked walls and mesas, narrowing in some places to fifty yards
and rising in others to more than a thousand feet. There, they had
successfully hidden their best flocks, the finest corn and melon patches,
and their peach orchards, carefully tended since the days of the Spanish.
Water flowed through the Canyon de Chelly in all seasons, and there
was enough timber for fuel. "If the Americans come for us, we will kill
them," Delgadito said. And he moved the women and children of his
clans to the farthest reaches of the canyon to await Carson's coming.*

*Carleton sent a message to the headmen: "Say to them, 'Go to the
Bosque Redondo or we will pursue and destroy you. We will not make
peace with you on any other terms. This war shall be pursued against
you if it takes years, until you cease to exist or move.' "*

*Carleton also wrote to the War Department for more soldiers, stating,
"Providence has indeed blessed us. The gold lies here at our feet to be
had by the mere picking of it up!"*

*By autumn, Carson had destroyed every corn, wheat field, melon or
pumpkin patch he could find between Fort Canby and Canyon de Chelly.
On October 17, Delgadito sent a delegation into Fort Canby under a
truce flag, representing his five hundred clan members. They said that
their food was gone, they were too fearful of soldiers to build fires for
warmth, and they wished to surrender.*

*Barboncito and Manuelito with their warriors watched from the
mountains as Delgadito and his people were escorted from the fort to
make the Long Walk into imprisonment. Despite his bold words two
seasons before, he could not feed his people from the canyon harvest
alone.*

*Carleton offered Delgadito a bargain: If he could convince Barboncito
and Manuelito that life at the Bosque was better than the hell to be
visited upon them by Kit Carson, he and his family could return to
Dinétah. Delgadito agreed.*

*   *   *

On a broad, flat rock which had absorbed winter sun, a large
lizard lay, somnolent and still. Seemingly without interest in anything that moved around him, the lizard looked as though it could
scarcely run fast enough to catch his prey, much less evade an

enemy. He was Loder, and his lazy look did not fool any creature within his territory. Each rodent and most other lizards within a half-mile all around him knew which rocks he frequented, which burrows he used to rest from the heat of the day, and which trails he took to travel his piece of the desert. Loder had killed often and well.

Loder was a Gila Monster, *Heloderma suspectum,* the only venomous lizard in America. He stretched nearly two feet from the end of his blunt, black nose to the tip of his squat, banded tail. Now, in the season of cold, his tail was thin, as his body used up his stored fat. A few months before, when he had eaten well all summer and fall, his tail was twenty percent wider and heavier. He was banded all over his pinkish body with black blotches and spots, as though his Creator had had a careless hand in his coloring. But the bars and blotches did much to break up his contour, making it easier for him to stay still and not be seen against the sandstone.

Loder was one of the largest, heaviest lizards in the desert, bigger than the chuckwalla, than all of the spiny lizards, the collared lizards, the night lizards, the whiptails, and most of the iguanas. There were a lot of lizards in the territory and he had eaten good samplings of most of them, as well as many of the small birds, their eggs, and any mice and shrews who were careless enough to come too close.

Loder was an irascible lizard, slow to move off and quick to take offense. Like the rattler, he considered all trails his own and feared little. But unlike the rattler, he could not be bluffed and he gave no warning. This morning, he was grumpier than usual, for the waning winter sun made him feel slow and stupid, a poor combination when there was little in his belly.

His mate of the last summer, a smaller female with an oranger body, had spent only a few hours with him, before she flared in anger, pushed him away, and ambled off to her own burrow. Somewhere in the arid, sandy soil, she had laid five eggs of that mating, but Loder neither knew of their existence nor did he care. Indeed, if one of his offspring should stumble upon him carelessly, he would eat it as eagerly as he would any other creature he could catch.

The hours dragged on, and Loder lost patience with his perch.

He slowly crawled down from the rock and began to hunt, dragging his long thick tongue across the ground, looking for scent. Loder's vision was poor, but his sense of smell was acute, mostly located in his tongue. More primitive than the vipers, he did not have their heat-sensing capacity, but he could store fat during lean times, and he was dogged in the hunt. And so, he was able to live, particularly in a place where lizards and rodents were plentiful.

As he moved slowly over the rocky ground, his belly dragged on the sand, for Loder's legs, short and squat, could hardly support his body. Any raptor might think him an easy victim, but Loder's bite had the same chemical composition of cobra venom, and though he did not have the cobra's efficient delivery system, he could make an enemy very sorry, indeed, that he had come close enough to have his nervous system painfully destroyed by the chewing, clamping bite of Loder.

He was following the dim trail of a kangaroo rat, and his small reptile brain told him that the rodent had come this way sometime in the night. Normally, he was nocturnal, most active in the darkness, but the cold slowed him markedly, and he had missed this catch. He twisted his head back and forth, trying to keep the scent fresh on his tongue, following it out onto the open ground recklessly, suddenly determined to find this invading rat and devour him. And then he stopped suddenly, lowered his head, and squatted his body down in a partial-defense, partial-attack position.

On a rock above him, a roadrunner stood watching him carefully, its beak open, its tail flicking jerkily in a movement that translated to excitement. Loder curled himself slightly, with his head to the center of his body, ready to bite. He knew that the roadrunner was as fierce a raptor for its size as any hawk or eagle in the desert. There was no way to run, no place to hide, and he knew that he could not move fast enough to outpace the bird. Loder felt a certain raw emptiness in his belly which he recognized as fear, and he swelled himself with air, to look as large and formidable as possible.

The roadrunner hopped down from the rock and walked toward him slowly, as though it knew it need not hurry. When the bird was a few feet from Loder, it cawed at him raucously, with a taunting cry somewhere between that of a crow and a magpie. Loder lifted his head slightly to watch the bird, and at that moment, the bird rushed him and struck him with its long, scissors bill, right at the place where Loder's neck would be, if he had a neck.

Loder writhed and gaped his mouth at the bird, ready to inflict the worst wound he could, if he could only get a mouthful of something other than feathers. Loder's strength was in his grip. Normally, he would not let go, not even if his head was severed from his body, and he chewed and bit with such stubborn ferocity, pressing the poison from glands in his cheek into the open wound, that his victim eventually succumbed.

But this roadrunner jumped over him easily, flapping his head with its wings and kicking sand into his eyes. The instant it landed, it turned and jabbed Loder again, this time wasting no time with a taunting cry.

Loder knew that he must move, and he uncurled himself, closed his mouth, lowered his head, and made for a crevice between two rocks, moving as fast as his clumsy body would allow. But the roadrunner would not allow his escape, and blocked his departure with another hop over his back, another painful jab to the same place behind his head.

Now Loder began to feel confused, and the pain in his head made him enraged. But he knew that he must keep moving, or the bird would wound him to the point of death. He had doggedly kept going to the crevice, almost could feel its cool depths calming him and refuging him, when the bird struck again, harder this time and with a certain twist to its bill that made Loder writhe in pain, reaching to bite the bird on the leg, the wing, anyplace he could reach. But the bird was so quick, so full of confident moves, that Loder felt he was sparring with the wind: it was here, it was there, it jarred him with its wings and sharp, curved claws, and then struck him again and again unerringly on the same wounded place. Loder was nearly to the crevice, could sense its welcoming darkness, when suddenly the roadrunner leaped again, this time bending low and pecking him hard on the leg, causing him to crumple to the ground, immobile and helpless.

He bent backward, trying desperately to bite the bird, who now took hold of his tail and was dragging him away from the safety he sought, away from the darkness, and he grappled and clawed at the rock, holding himself stubbornly in place, but the bird leaped again, clawed his back, and stabbed him hard, and he twisted loose, feeling himself dragged again. Finally, he lay still, dazed and exhausted, while the bird speared him again and again, now making victory cries as it beat the air above his head. His belly felt cold against the ground, and his eyes were closed. He knew he bled, but he could not say from where.

Before the lizard lost his sense of his surroundings and while he still had enough life to feel his death, the roadrunner ripped at his belly, raking his entrails open with great, spurred claws, pecking him again and again. Finally, the roadrunner dragged him to a hot, flat rock with no shade and left him there to dry and roast in the sun. Even the winter sun was hot enough to eventually kill the lizard, though it took him more than an afternoon to die.

*   *   *

Manuelito received word in the coldest month of 1863 that Colonel Kit Carson, the Rope Thrower, was readying a pack herd to carry supplies for the invasion of Canyon de Chelly. Barboncito sent a runner to ask that Manuelito join him in an attack on the pack train. Manuelito refused, saying that he had too few warriors to spare and that those he had left must be kept to defend their families and the flocks. Barboncito was ominously quiet, Pahe noticed, and no more runners came to Manuelito's hacienda.

A month later, they got the news that Barboncito's warriors had attacked the pack herd, running the mules off to one of his hidden canyons to be used as a winter meat supply. Carson sent soldiers after the warriors, but they escaped under cover of a snowstorm.

Kinsmen told Manuelito that not a scrap of the mules went to waste. Every bit of meat and intestines and every shred of skin and ligaments were used. Even the hooves were ground to powder and put into broth for the aged, that they might be able to walk farther.

Unfortunately, in the hunt for the stolen mules, the soldiers stumbled upon a small camp from a different clan, mostly women and children, who were unrelated to Barboncito's band. They captured the women and children and shot three of the men.

Pahe heard the murmuring then. Some of Manuelito's men heard complaints from their women: at least Barboncito had meat. What good did it do to keep the peace? Those who kept the peace were captured and killed; those who ran off the white man's mules had meat. The choice seemed clear enough to them.

"Until it is their own men who are shot," Ayoi said wryly. "Then they will say that Barboncito is a madman who risks lives for no good reason. There is no pleasing them now. Every headman will have to defend his decisions, no matter what they may be."

Finally, those clans who still sheltered in the Canyon de Chelly saw the Rope Thrower and his soldiers come to the mouth of their sanctuary. The snow was over the horses' knees, and the People thought the soldiers would surely turn back, but they came on relentlessly.

The half-starved People threw stones down on the heads of the soldiers, but the soldiers shot up into the canyon walls and killed fourteen men, captured nineteen women and children, and killed thirty sheep. Those on the upper mesas shouted curses down on them and called to the *Yeis* to destroy their enemy, but the soldiers methodically burned all the hogans, the fields, and even the peach orchards: five thousand trees which had been carefully tended by the People for more than two hundred years.

Runners told Manuelito that when some of the old ones saw the orchards burning, they sat where they were, refusing to move, until they froze to death on the mesa. Sixty ragged, freezing warriors finally surrendered to the Rope Thrower, and he marched them through the snow to Fort Wingate.

One headman who escaped came to council and told the others that he could no longer keep running, leaving behind his aged, his pregnant women, and his children. "I have seen my women, with babies at their breasts, smother them with their own hands because their hungry cries might call the soldiers or the slave raiders to the fires." He wept openly before the other headmen. "I will go to *Hwééldi* and live or die, but I will no longer run."

The seventy-six warriors and minor headmen who were left of Manuelito's clan sat in two circles around the fire in a light dusting of snow, watching their kinsman weep. It seemed to Pahe that no matter how many blankets she wrapped round her head, she could not get warm. She had more meat than most, she knew, and still she could not stay warm. Either the snow was colder and damper than she remembered, or she was weaker. She listened as the men recounted all the disasters they already knew well enough, and, finally, Manuelito raised his hand for silence, something he rarely did.

Pahe watched her father with sorrowful eyes. He had seen fifty-three winters now. This one already looked as though it would be the hardest so far. How long would the others follow him? How long could he continue to keep them safe?

"Many of the People have decided to surrender," Manuelito said quietly. "And for this, I cannot blame them. However, I will not surrender, and I will not give up our lands."

"We cannot stay here," one of the warriors said. "Carson knows you are here, and if we do not go to him, he will come to us."

"It is surprising he has not come already," said another kinsman.

"I agree," Manuelito said. "We must leave this place."

Pahe looked up in surprise. She saw that the others waited now, that Manuelito had their full attention and respect.

"We will go to the north, to the deepest canyons of the Colorado, and there we will wait until the white man gives up looking for us."

Pahe was astonished. The place Manuelito spoke of, the canyons of the Colorado and the Little Colorado, were the old places of the Anasazi, the Ancient Tribe, the Old Ones who first walked these lands. It was the land of the Hopi and farther north, their enemy, the Ute. So far as she knew, few of the People had ever been there.

"That is a long journey," one of the headmen said hesitantly. "But if we can get there safely, the *Bilagáana* surely will not be able to follow."

"And how will we survive in those haunted places?" another said. "The spirits of the Old Ones will not welcome us. If the Hopi and the Ute do not kill us, the Ancient Ones will."

"No," Pahe said softly, "they will not. The Ancient Ones know our clan well. I remember how Deezbaa used to call to them often, and they came to her fire and gave her secrets of healing. If the Hopi and the Pueblo people will let us sojourn among them, the Old Ones will be the least of our worries. In fact, if we can make it there safely, perhaps we can learn again some of Deezbaa's cures which my mother has now forgotten—"

"I do not need cures of Deezbaa for my well-being," grumbled one of the men. "Indeed, I wonder often if we would be in this peril if Narbona were still alive."

Manuelito kept his face still and his words courteous. "That is one thing we shall never know, eh? But I believe he would counsel that we take refuge wherever we think we can be hidden safely. And I know of no deeper canyon, no more difficult trail to follow than that which leads down to the bowels of the earth in that strange land."

"It is forbidden," another man said. "The Holy Ones said we were never to cross the three rivers—"

"We will ask for their protection," Manuelito said. "We can do little else."

"But the Hopi are so different from us," a headman said. "They are rule-bound, we are free—"

"The question is, will we be taken before we can reach that safety?" another asked.

"No more easily than we will be taken if we stay here. A people on the move is harder to track than those sitting in wait by their fires," Manuelito said. "I have been expecting the Rope Thrower with each new dawn. Not many will pass now, I think, before he comes for us."

Pahe saw suddenly what must be done. She must leave the graves of her grandparents, her husband, her lands, but it was a chance to survive free. Her father needed her support. She said quickly, "I think it is a good plan. I will be ready to move in two days." She stood as though the council were over. "I will ask for a blessing from the Holy Ones for this journey. Most likely, they will see us safely to refuge."

"Will Armijo and Barboncito join us?" one of the headmen asked.

"They are welcome," Manuelito said. "But I think they will choose to find other places. And that is well enough. The larger we are, the better reason to come and capture us. Let us keep small and out of sight. Let the white men think we are too few to trouble over, and we will make the journey unnoticed."

The men agreed, and the plans to move the clan commenced. Pahe listened until she saw that she was no longer heeded, and she went back to Ayoi's hogan to begin to prepare to leave it forever.

She was packing their belongings with Dolii's help, while Ayoi sat and rocked herself mournfully by the fire.

"Mother, do you wish to take this?" Pahe asked, holding up her silver mirror. She was hoping to divert Ayoi from the anxious rocking she had begun as soon as the decision was told round the fires. "Father can put it in his pack, I'm sure."

"What does it matter?" her mother moaned. "I will not live to use it."

"What are you talking about?" Dolii asked with some impatience. "You will ride all the way to the north, Grandfather has said it. The rest of us will have to walk most of the way, pushing the sheep before us."

"The great canyon goes to the belly of the earth," Ayoi said, "and even if we had mules, they would have to be as sure-footed as squirrels to make it down to the bottom. I will not make it alive, I know it. And if I do, the spirits of the Ancient Ones will come to me in the night and take me with them to the land of the dead."

Dolii laughed softly. "Old woman, you surprise me. I never knew you for a coward."

Pahe turned and appraised her daughter swiftly. She had never heard her speak in such a way; it was as though her mouth had aged five seasons in one. "Show respect for your grandmother," she said automatically, but she could not help but smile. "Yes or no, my mother." She held up the mirror again with some exasperation. "Perhaps you would like to see how you look one more time before the Ancient Ones take you off, eh?"

Ayoi grumbled and nodded, gathering her pots and baskets in one wide sweep of her arms. "You wait. The time will come when you say to Manuelito, 'We should have gone with the others!' "

"It's not too late," Manuelito said lightly, as he came into the hogan suddenly, startling them. Wasek was behind him, and the two of them instantly made the hogan seem small and cramped and insignificant as their concerns. "The runners say Delgadito has persuaded another seven hundred to surrender. Even now, they gather at the fort with their ragged blankets and their hands outstretched for food, begging from the white soldiers. If you wish to make the Long Walk to *Hwééldi,* I will take you there myself."

"Is Barboncito there?" Pahe asked.

"No. Neither is Armijo and his clan. But then"—he nodded cordially to his wife—"the other chiefs do not have my Tall One to do battle with, and so, of course, they are not used to war. Naturally, they would surrender."

Ayoi snorted with disdain, obviously quite pleased with herself. Pahe saw how her mother sought her father's eyes and attention after more than thirty-five winters of union. She sharply missed Nataallith in that moment.

Wasek spoke up, his eyes roving restlessly over the walls of the hogan as though to move what was left into packs by his own will. "You should take everything you think you will need. Probably, we won't be back."

"Is that true?" Dolii asked her grandfather.

Manuelito shrugged, patting her on the shoulder. "Who can say, my dove. If you want it, take it. We will find room for it somehow."

"Will we trade with the Hopi and the Pueblo?" Pahe asked.

"Likely," Manuelito said. "The rest of the clan will be packed before sunup. Juanita is not ready, either. Why are the hogans of my women the last to be ready to leave?"

"Because we are the women of Manuelito," Ayoi said with false sweetness, "the *rico* headman of the *Táchii'nii* clan, and so, of course, we have all of our silver and turquoise and treasure to pack."

Pahe laughed ruefully, for, of course, most of their silver and turquoise had been bartered long ago for food and seed. "We will be ready, my father," she reassured him. "Go and help the others. There are even older heads which must be pushed up the trail than this one—" She gestured to her mother.

Manuelito went out again, and Wasek stayed behind to tie the packs and move them outside to where the horses stood tethered.

Pahe asked her son quietly, "Are the others agreed to this decision?"

He nodded. "They fear the journey, only. Many think that the white men will not allow us to make it as far as the lands of the Hopi. They fear we will be taken someplace in the open, as we move."

"It is a real danger," Pahe said. "But if we are taken, we will join the others in surrender then. One walk can be no worse than another."

Wasek turned to her in amazement, his shoulders burdened with two packs. In that instant, he looked all of a man. "Surrender! We will never surrender. If we are attacked, we will fight to the death."

"With the women and children and old ones? That will be a short battle, surely," Pahe said shortly. "Courage is a fine thing, my son, but if we are surprised by the soldiers, we will have no choice. Surrender would be better than massacre."

"There will be no surrender," Wasek said with dignity. "Manuelito has said this."

Pahe reached up to touch her son's cheek. "You are so like your father in so many ways," she said softly, "but one. He was a man wise in the ways of compromise."

"A lesson the *Bilagáana* taught him," Wasek said. "That is one thing I do not intend to learn from them."

Pahe smiled sadly into his face, noticing again how far she had to look up to reach his eyes. "It is not the *Bilagáana* who taught your father but life itself. You will see, my son, and you will learn the same lesson. Or you will battle every day of your life—and it will be a short one, indeed."

Wasek shrugged and walked to the horses, clearly finished with the conversation. Dolii stuck her head out of the hogan. "Why do you let him speak to you that way?"

"Better that he speak his anger than fight," Pahe said. "He has had to be a man too soon."

"Not soon enough," Dolii sniffed. "I have finished, I think. Grandmother has stopped rocking."

Her voice carried out of the hogan to them. "Have the fools gone from here?"

"She would not dare to speak so if she did not know they had," Dolii laughed.

"Oh, yes, she would," Pahe said wryly. "In fact, it would pleasure her to say it to my father's face, and if his grandson could be insulted as well, she'd be more pleased still. She's more like Deezbaa every day."

"So are you." Dolii rolled her eyes. "I am surrounded by Deezbaas, indeed—"

"Let us hope it wards off the white men," Pahe said, and they went inside.

*   *   *

Manuelito's clan of one hundred and seventy-eight left their lands in the dark hours of dawn, walking behind the herds, riding what horses were left, spread out over the desert with sentries posted at high places along the trail. They moved as fast as the children and old ones could travel, certain that at any time, the soldiers would rush down on them and capture them all.

Their destination was the land of the Hopi and Pueblo, up the Little Colorado River to the depths of the Grand Canyon, where they believed they might be able to disappear and survive. It was a journey of more than a hundred miles across open desert, over mesas and the mountain passes, through smooth blankets of cold air and over frozen land, away from the places where they had walked in harmony and beauty for generations.

But they were a wandering people, and they were used to movement and the rhythms of walking after the flocks, and so they quickly grew content.

A day into the journey, Manuelito pointed to a place by the river where the sand was narrow and said, "There is a place where the earth will swallow a man. *Séí hasht'ishii*," he said, what the People called quicksand.

Wasek said, "It looks like any other sand."

"There are two things a man must know about this danger," Manuelito said. "First, where it is and, second, what it will do."

"Have you seen it swallow a man?" Wasek asked, his eyes large with fascination.

"Once I saw a whole family standing near it, just standing there and watching. I went to see what they watched and saw that their wagon was sinking down in the sand. They had unhitched the horse just in time. There was nothing I could do. Nothing anyone could do. They stood there for a long time, just looking down, even after the wagon was gone." He looked at Wasek. "They should have known where it was. They should have kept away."

Wasek rode next to Manuelito after that, and the old man talked to him for the long hours on the trail.

*   *   *

A few days into the journey, Pahe was walking behind Ayoi's horse, when she suddenly was struck with a wave of fear so powerful that it made her lose her footing and stumble slightly, putting her hand up on the horse's flank. She looked down and saw a lizard running to the north. Not a good omen. She glanced at her mother. Ayoi was sitting astride with her long back straight, as she always rode. On a horse, she looked half her age. She seemed lost in her thoughts, with the hood of her blanket almost covering her face.

Pahe looked for Dolii, who walked behind the flock, rhythmically tapping her stick on the ground to keep them moving forward. She, too, seemed unaware of any peril and relatively content. Pahe looked around for what might have caused her such a rush of fear. Even a moment later, her stomach felt hollowed by terror and her breathing was quick and shallow. Juanita was riding to the rear with a cousin; Manuelito was far ahead, riding with some of the warriors. Another band of warriors rode behind them for protection; there seemed nothing to fear.

Pahe looked up into the sky and there, overhead, she saw a wheeling raven, looking down on the traveling People. She gasped and pulled her hand away from her mother's horse as though it suddenly burned. The raven flew closer so that he was now almost directly over her head, and still no one else seemed to notice the creature observing them.

She moved away from her mother's horse as casually as she could so as not to draw attention, and she murmured, "O Raven, what is there here to fear?"

To her amazement, a voice came into her ears as clearly as though the bird sat on her shoulder. "I smell death among you,"

Raven answered her, in a voice that was more a man's than a bird's.

She glanced around quickly and saw that no one else heard what she heard, noticed what she noticed, or seemed to feel her fear. "You smell death?" she murmured aloud, keeping her head down. "From whence does it come?"

"From the People," Raven said. "And not only from the old ones. From the children, the mothers, and the young warriors."

To her amazement, she was somehow not surprised to hear Raven speak in her mind. A piece of her wondered, in fact, why the Holy Ones had taken so long to come to her at last. "Are we walking into Death?" she asked.

"Many are," he moaned, and she glanced up to see Raven wheeling slowly over her like a buzzard over a dead carcass. She shook her head from side to side, no, no, no, almost more a gesture of incomprehension than despair. "The soldiers are coming? The Hopi? Tell me, Raven!" she whispered urgently.

"Betrayal," Raven croaked, this time sounding as much bird as spirit. "Betrayal which will lead to Death. Listen, She-Who-Hears-The-Sun, listen and heed the warning." Raven wheeled again, dipped down close to the walking People, and then flapped his wings strongly, rising into the pale winter sun, and flew away in the direction of the northern mountains.

The fear left Pahe's heart as suddenly as it came. She looked around her in confusion, as though waking from a dream. All the while, her feet had kept moving steadily over the frozen ground as though they were separate from her mind. Raven was gone, and the People were moving, and, somehow, she must heed this warning and save them from this death, a death by betrayal.

But what did the words mean? Could she trust them? She did not ask herself if the words came from her own fear; she knew without question that the words and the warning came from outside herself. The Holy Ones had spoken to her. Just as they came to Deezbaa, they now came to her. She knew the truth of that as well as she knew the truth of her own life. She was born of Ayoi, named She-Who-Hears-The-Sun by her grandmother for a reason. And now, finally, she would know the meaning of her fate and the fate of her People.

But what should she do with this knowledge? She felt a sense of pride, but, more, a sense of fear and heavy duty. She glanced to her mother and saw that she was watching her now, her head turned toward Pahe as she rode. She lifted one hand and beckoned her nearer.

When Pahe moved to walk alongside her, Ayoi said, "Something is wrong?"

Pahe hesitated. "Why do you ask?"

"You seem in pain. Do you want to ride?"

Pahe shook her head. "I have been . . . hearing things." She immediately wished she could take back those words. There was nothing her mother could do, and causing her worry would only make the journey more difficult.

"What things?" Ayoi asked, pulling down her blanket so that she might see Pahe more clearly.

"Nothing, I suppose. It was only the wind."

Ayoi frowned quizzically. "There is no wind. What did you hear?"

"Ah, the cries of the sheep, the horses' hooves, the call of the birds—"

"Was there a voice speaking words in these things?"

Pahe glanced up at her mother searchingly. "Have you heard something as well?"

"No. But the Holy Ones will not come to me, my daughter. They will come to you."

"Why do you say this? They never have before."

"They will, if they have not. You are more Deezbaa's daughter than I ever was. Did Raven call to you?"

"You saw it, then."

Ayoi said, "I had a dream before we left our lands, and in my dream, Raven came and spoke to you, but you would not listen. You put your hands over your ears and walked away. When I saw the bird, I remembered my dream." She grinned. "I'm glad the Holy Ones think me of little use. I am too old for such trouble. What message did Raven bring?"

Pahe sighed wearily. "Nothing that we do not already know. That the way will be difficult and dangerous. That some of us will die. There is no great wisdom in this, I guess."

"I knew it," Ayoi groaned. "I will not make it to the lands of the Hopi. You will bury my bones in the deepest canyons, and my ghost will wander the places of the Old Ones forever."

Pahe's patience left her as quickly as her fatigue. "Oh, stop this bleating, Mother. You ride the best horse, you eat the best rations, you will be carried on your husband's shoulder until you are a withered crone. I have never seen a man love a woman more. Yet you croak worse than Raven. If anyone should fear death, it is Wasek and Dolii, for both of them have far more value to the slave traders. Wasek is determined to fight the soldiers, and Dolii is too young to travel so far on foot, pushing the sheep before her. Besides that, they have their whole lives before them, and I cannot see that they will ever feel the peace and freedom you and I have enjoyed."

"And I suppose my whole life is past, then!" Ayoi said indignantly.

"Not yet," Pahe answered shortly. "But if you keep complaining, others will certainly wish it so."

To her surprise, Ayoi chuckled and pulled the blanket up around her mouth again.

Pahe smiled wearily. "You were only trying to get my blood moving again, weren't you?"

"It worked. Now go back and tell the Holy Ones that Death can just wait for a while. The People are not ready for him, yet."

Pahe nodded resignedly. She suddenly recalled an old memory of her mother, when she was small. It was a hot windy day, and she was playing outside near her grandfather's hogan. The slaves were busy in the fields, and the dogs were sleeping in the dust. She remembered she was making a small hogan out of juniper twigs, humming to herself, when a movement drew her eye. There, across the desert, a huge whirlwind was coming quickly toward her, a high column of dark air and sand, swirling around and dancing along the baked earth. It was veering this way and that, picking up dirt and leaves, small branches, and throwing them high in the air. The dogs jumped up from their doze and barked at it fearfully, but Pahe had sat frozen, watching the whirlwind come upon her. She screamed out for her mother, and Ayoi's head was in the door of the hogan in a second. She looked in the direction Pahe was staring, saw the whirlwind, and stepped outside with her hands on her hips. As the whirlwind came near, she shouted out, *"Naadaaní!"* in a scolding voice, just as it came to Grandfather's hogan. The whirlwind suddenly twisted on itself, veering away from the hacienda out onto the open desert.

They had laughed about it later, how Ayoi had frightened away the whirlwind by shouting, "Your in-law!" at it. Because to the People, contact between a woman and her son-in-law is forbidden, family members warn them by saying, *"Naadaaní!"* if they are about to bump into each other. In that way, the son-in-law can leave the room before the custom is violated.

"It was clearly *Diné*," she said later of the whirlwind, "and a young warrior, at that."

Pahe supposed that if her mother could face down a whirlwind, Death might be considered simply another adversary to be defeated. They did not call her The Tall One simply for her ability to look over the heads of many of the men in the clan.

The way was long to the lands of the Hopi, and they stopped often for the old and young to rest. As they traveled to the north, the air became colder, and the flocks complained more, needing to be driven with sticks to keep them moving. Ahead, they could see the mountains looming, and Pahe knew that many were already regretting leaving their warm hogans, even if the soldiers were just now standing right outside their doors.

At night, the old ones told the old stories, and the young ones listened raptly, their faces lifted before the fire like shining cups. It was a great comfort for Pahe to hear the old stories as well, and she saw once again that more had been taken from the People than simply their land: they had been afraid to gather together to do what every people must do, speak of the past. Now, out in the open desert, they felt a freedom they had not felt for many seasons.

Often she walked with Dolii away from the fires, heedless of the risk of the slave raiders, for the sentries watched from all corners of the camp. They walked laughing, bumping lightly against each other, holding each other's arm or hand, and the stars glistened in the cold winter sky. Dolii liked to look up and turn slowly so that their bright beauty made her dizzy, and the mountain lay beneath them, dark and quiet, breathing its sacred wind. Pahe thought then that these might be the best days of her life, and her eyes watered with the pleasure of her daughter's laughter.

"When you were born," she told her, "you were so sweet that your father wanted to call you *Bithózhóhú*, She-Who-Brings-Happiness, because he could not hold you without feeling great joy."

"Really?" Dolii asked, pleased. "He held me often?"

"Each time he came into the hogan, he went first to your cradle. When he picked you up, you would nestle into his neck like a little bird, cheeping softly with joy. You knew who he was, even at your birth, I think. He would kiss your cheeks and your forehead and your little fat feet and say, 'She is so sweet.' And then he would sing to you, 'Hey na yah,' and you would hum like a small bee with pleasure."

Dolii laughed with delight.

Pahe nodded. "Your brother was always too full of fire and movement to hold him for long. He would struggle to get down to pick up this thing or that, to do battle with a small pebble he spied on the floor. But you, Little Bird, you were always glad to be held. I used to tease your father and tell him that you would be married by twelve winters and carrying a child by thirteen, he was getting you so accustomed to the arms of a man."

Dolii said wistfully, "And now I will be lucky to find a man at all. If the *Bilagáana* do not kill them all first."

"You will find a man soon enough," Pahe chuckled. "They are like the wind, the Holy Ones are always making more of them."

"Perhaps in the land of the Hopi," Dolii said thoughtfully.

"It is too soon to speak of that," Pahe soothed her. "Aye-ee! The air is so sweet and clear tonight."

Dolii nodded, looking up. "It is different than watching the clouds roll by Grandmother's fire hole. Are you glad we came?"

"I am," Pahe said. "Whatever comes, I think we are better for the journey. Stronger. We are not a people of place, like the Pueblo. We are a people of movement. It weakens us to sit and wait for the white man to decide our fate. Your grandfather was right."

And so they pushed on, through the pass and into the land of the Hopi. Of course, the Hopi, and their neighbors, the Pueblo, knew of their approach long before they reached the red rocks and desert expanses of their land, and even before they came to the Little Colorado, the Hopi sent out warriors to greet them and discover their intentions. Manuelito told them that they were merely wishing to cross Hopi lands in peace, on their way to find a refuge in the great canyon lands to the north.

The Hopi warriors invited them to sit at council with their headmen, and, of course, Manuelito agreed. They set up camp near the juncture of the Little Colorado and the Moenkopi rivers, and Manuelito, his wives, his headmen, his warriors, and a few of the women went to join the fires of the Hopi council. Pahe almost brought Dolii with her, but when she remembered her words about finding a husband among strangers, she thought better of it and left her behind at her grandmother's fire.

The Hopi welcomed them cordially, listening most carefully as Manuelito told of the events of the past seasons, most particularly the many betrayals by the white men. Pahe noticed that many of the Hopi women kept back from the fires, watching the Navajo men with hooded eyes. That was to be expected, she knew, since in times past, Navajo slave raiders had taken Hopi women and children as easily as they took Pueblo and Zuni. But now that the greater enemy was the white man, she hoped that they would forget all past trespasses and, indeed, it looked as though the men had done so.

One warrior, however, was more belligerent than the rest of his Hopi brothers. He said, "The *Bilagáana* will follow you here to our lands. You will be captured, just as you would have been if you had stayed on your own lands. But they will then attack us as well. You have done us no good by leading them here. I say," he added, looking round the council of headmen, "that we forbid them to cross our land. Force them to go back. So far, we have been little troubled by the white men. Why should we invite such a plague upon us? Particularly for an enemy?" This last, he said with a hard, dismissive gesture, scowling at Manuelito with impunity.

Manuelito studied the young man long and carefully, as though committing his face to memory. Then he said, "It is true, we have been your enemy. But not so much as others. It has been many seasons since we trespassed your land, and times have changed. We must now band together against a common foe, and that foe is the *Bilagáana*. If we are captured, you will stand alone against an enemy so powerful that you will be blown aside as a stalk of straw. If we stand beside you, they may think twice before they attack."

"We have heard that many of your people have surrendered rather than fight," an old Hopi leader said plaintively. "More than three thousand have gone to the white man, we are told."

There was a shocked silence from the People. They had not known that so many had surrendered. Pahe glanced at Manuelito and saw that he struggled to keep his face calm. "Some have surrendered. They have been persuaded, perhaps, that this is the best way," he said quietly. "But many more have not. It is not *our* way. We will fight before we surrender."

"We do not need Manuelito's advice or help to stand against the white men," another warrior said.

"Perhaps not," an older headman said calmly. "But if we are not prepared to go to war against our visitors, it may well be a wisdom to give them leave to cross our lands. Particularly"—the old one smiled—"when we have not yet heard the tribute they offer for this privilege."

Manuelito said, "I am no longer a *rico* headman. The white men have taken everything from us, otherwise we would not be making this journey in the first place."

"Let us discuss this tribute together," the chief of the Hopi said, gesturing dismissively to Manuelito. "We will tell you of our decision in the morning."

Manuelito glanced at his warriors who, to a man, glowered stubbornly at the Hopi warriors.

Pahe thought that the council had gone badly, and she was glad to get away from the Hopi fires.

Her father said only, "It is what I expected. The Hopi have always been a people of short vision. They cannot see that they will gain more from our friendship than they can ever gain from whatever tribute they demand. But let them ask what they may. If we must, we will go to the southwest until we are out of their territory, and then we will go where we will. If their demands are reasonable, we will pay them. But they will be sorry, I think, for their present stiff-backed greed."

Wasek said, "There are few warriors among them, for all their bold talk. Mostly old ones and women. We could fight them now and take their lands for our own."

"Do not be lulled by what you see," Manuelito warned him. "The Hopi have more warriors than we do. They are out on a hunting party, perhaps into the canyons where we are headed. No, it is in our best interest to keep the peace. We will know in the morning."

"Their women are uglier than most," Ayoi said gleefully. "Did you not think so? They are thin-shanked and brittle as sagebrush. As sharp-edged, too, I would suppose. No wonder the Hopi men are quick to offense. Their women offend them without let-up."

"I think that stores in the Hopi clans must be as low as those in our own," Manuelito agreed. "Which would explain why the warriors are like yellow jackets, disturbed by the walking stranger over their ground. If the white man does come here, he will have easy pickings."

They finished making their temporary camp a few miles outside the Hopi village, settling in with their cooking pots and their fires. The women spoke back and forth across the fires as they moved from shelter to shelter, and the men sat and smoked, speaking of the Hopi and the journey ahead. The children raced through camp, shouting and releasing the energy of the day, as though they had not walked many more miles than their legs should have traveled. One old man sat at a fire, telling stories and moving his fingers over a looped string he had woven of lamb's wool.

As he talked, little characters or land formations appeared and moved fluidly from one pose of his fingers to another, and the youngest children and the young dogs gathered around him close by the fire. He said, *"Shúúh sha atchíní,* Listen my children," and sang to them humorous songs about the donkey and the goat, or the lamb and the fox, and all the other animals, and his fingers made the string into the animals as his words hypnotized them into rapt silence. He imitated the animals' sounds until the children laughed so hard that they held their bellies, and the dogs jumped up and tried to lick their mouths eagerly.

Pahe and Ayoi were finishing cooking the meal, while Dolii was hunting something in the packs. Manuelito came over and took a plate, filling it with corn mush and the good mutton stew that Ayoi had prepared. He ate quickly, speaking all the while, something Narbona rarely did, Pahe noted. The old man had always said that food was meant to be enjoyed in its own time, without the distraction of talk or smoke. The stomach, he said, had no ears, only teeth.

"They are afraid," Manuelito was saying to Ayoi. And when Wasek came up, he spoke more to the boy than to his wife. "They are afraid, and they cover their fear with anger. They see what we have become, and they know in their hearts that if it can happen to the *Diné*, it will happen to them, only worse."

"What if they ask for a tribute we can't pay?" Wasek asked, picking up the bowl Ayoi handed him and sitting down next to his grandfather, imitating his stance and the jut of his elbows.

"Oh, we can pay it," Manuelito said. "There is nothing the Hopi can imagine that the People do not have. But the question is, will the clan agree to pay it? They may decide, instead, to take another route to refuge."

"Like right through the village of the Hopi," Wasek smirked. "Through the sleeping pallets of those with the biggest mouths."

"One would think," Ayoi said, "that they would see the wisdom of all of the tribes acting as one, now that the *Bilagáana* have set out to destroy all of us equally. Do they know of the Rope Thrower? Have they forgotten what happened to the Mescaleros? In their best times, the Hopi were never such warriors as the Apache, and yet the Apache now scratch in the dirt at the Bosque Redondo. The Hopi will soon scratch alongside them. My granddaughter!" she called. "Come and eat this before the men take it all for themselves!"

Dolii came from the tethered pack animals, stroking her hair absently with one hand. Pahe said, "My daughter, you look far away as Santa Fe. That is the second time your grandmother has called you."

Dolii smiled and ducked her chin. "A strange warrior is in camp," she murmured. "He spoke to me."

"A Hopi dog?" Wasek sneered. "It figures, he would prefer a child—"

"Enough," Pahe said mildly. "Your sister is quite worthy of attention from any warrior, Hopi or no. And in case you have not noticed, she is no longer a child. You must learn to halter your irritation, my son, or take it elsewhere. The camp is too small for such bad manners."

"He spoke to many of us," Dolii said casually, ignoring her brother. "I just happened to be standing nearby."

"I am sure that he is not blind," Manuelito said kindly, "even if he is Hopi." He stood and set down his bowl. "Come with me, my grandson, to Juanita's fire where there is only one woman. You are outnumbered and unwanted here."

Manuelito meant his words as a joke, she knew, but they hurt Pahe nonetheless. She wondered when it happened that she lost her son. She could not put her finger on the day or the sequence of events. Whenever she saw him, it seemed to her that he was angry or impatient or annoyed. Was it the sap of manhood rising in him with no outlet for his energy, or was he always going to be irascible as a rattler at any provocation? Perhaps he needed a woman. It might be as simple as that.

Or should be that simple, in ordinary times. By now, he would have been danced several times at Chuska Mountain and might even have chosen a girl. Or several. Instead, he followed the women and children and flocks across miles of open desert to a place in the belly of the earth, where they might hide a while longer from the white men. No wonder he was irritable. But there was nothing to be done but endure it, she sighed. Just as Dolii must take the passing glance of a Hopi fool and make of it what she could.

That night, the People were slow to take to their sleeping blankets, and many of them wandered from fire to fire, taking comfort in each other's nearness. At home, they might not have strayed from their hogan's even to speak to a neighbor on the other side of the pasture. Now, they moved restlessly among themselves, discussing what the Hopi might do, what the white men might do, what they might do when they reached the great canyon. It was all talk of the future, she noticed sadly. Few spoke of the past, as though it had been wiped away like footprints on the sand after a storm.

Finally, the camp was quiet, and even the dogs were silent, dark forms around the dwindling fires. Pahe had been asleep for long enough, so when she awoke, she felt as though she were underwater, heavy and groggy with dreams. She realized that the noise that woke her, which was dim and distant as she pulled herself from sleep, was now very near and much louder than she first thought. Her immediate fear was for Dolii.

A scream came from a clump of forms in the darkness, and there was the sound of rushing feet and pounding hooves. "Dolii!" Pahe called loudly, reaching for her daughter who was sleeping on the other side of the fire. "Mother! Wake up!" She stumbled onto her mother's sleeping robes, jostled her awake, and went instantly to Dolii, pulling her closer and looking wildly about in the darkness to see what the danger was and from which direction it came.

"Aye-ee!" another cry came, and Pahe knew then in a shivering flash of terror what Raven's warning of betrayal meant at last.

"Slave raiders!" she screamed, pulling Dolii to her feet, pushing Ayoi up roughly and hurrying them away from the fire. "We must hide!"

"Where!" Ayoi cried, fumbling with her robes. "My husband!"

From the other side of the encampment, they could hear the men fighting now, heard the sound of rifle fire and the shouts of their own warriors, but the darkness made it all confusing, and more frightening than any clear vision might have been. Pahe snatched Dolii's hand and pulled her away from the fire. The girl was weeping in fear and stumbling in half sleep, half terror. "Hush!" Pahe hissed at them both, yanking her mother closer. "Over that rise and behind those rocks, and do not cry out, not even if you are hit by rifle fire. We will not be taken by these Hopi dogs!"

They scrambled quickly over the rise, clutching at their blankets and sliding in the snow, Dolii moaning softly in fear as Pahe pulled her along, grim and silent. They fell over the side of a small embankment, sheltered by a short copse of juniper. Across the snow, they could see that the attack had come from the east, from the direction of the Hopi village, and the raiders had swept down upon the People so fast that already horsemen were rounding up hostages. The moonlight was bright enough on the gleaming ground to reveal that the People were being overwhelmed and the warriors were unable to defend them.

"I did not hear the sentries," Ayoi whispered. They were still too near some of the closest horsemen to speak aloud.

"Perhaps they killed them!" Dolii cried.

"No, they could not have killed them all," Pahe said bitterly. "We have been betrayed."

"The Hopi!" Ayoi moaned.

"Not only the Hopi," Pahe said. "By one of our own clan. There is no other way they could have taken us by surprise."

Dolii gasped in anguish. "Our own kinsman?"

"You do not know this," Ayoi said quickly. "Perhaps one of the sentries fell asleep. Why would one of our own warriors betray his clan?"

Pahe hesitated, her mind aswirl with Raven's words.

"You see enemies everywhere," Ayoi said. "That is yet another weakness the white man has brought to us. The Hopi have betrayed us, and that is all. I do not believe we were abandoned by one of our own."

The screams were dying now, and the horsemen were taking off across the frozen land with their captives. Many of the warriors lay on the ground in dark heaps, and the camp was emptied of movement. They waited until they saw the Hopi disappear over the mesa, and then they carefully made their way back down the rise toward the fallen men. As they came nearer, others came, too, until finally the weeping and cries began again, as those left alive discovered what they had lost.

Manuelito came with twenty warriors from behind the rocks, where they had been firing upon the enemy; other small bands came from other directions, other hiding places. Juanita came with her cousin; they had hidden themselves in the trees. They hurriedly started the fires, calling to one another in anguish, and the women fell upon the wounded and the dying and the dead, trying to ease their suffering or pull them back into life. In the confusion, Pahe could not see Wasek by Manuelito's side, and she called to her father, "Where is my son?"

"I saw him with his comrades," her father said over his shoulder, as he and two others were attempting to move an injured warrior closer to the light of the fire. Skradena, Corn Pollen, was wailing inconsolably. Her man was dead, and her daughter had been taken by the slave raiders, and together with the losses she had already borne, she was crippled by her anguish. Pahe went to her and embraced her, pulled her up off her knees and gently moved her to the fire, murmuring to her what comfort she could think of in the moment. "We will do what we can to get her back," she said, "and you must keep hope of that, my cousin. When your daughter returns, she must find a mother who has her mind still intact. Do not let them take that from you, as well."

She left Skradena rocking and weeping on a rock, and she went then from kin to kin, doing what she could to console and comfort, all the while looking for Wasek. She embraced Juanita and held her fast, taking comfort where she could. She knew finally, as she returned to Ayoi and Dolii, who were wrapping the wounds of three warriors, that she had lost her son. She went then quietly to Manuelito, unwilling for her mother and daughter to know until she was certain.

Manuelito was directing the men to bring the dead together in one place, that they might be buried properly. She was aghast as she counted twelve men and four women killed in the raid. She did not even know how many children were gone yet, but the wailing around her made her believe that many had been captured.

She stopped, almost reeling with the whole knowledge of the disaster. Manuelito was working quickly, calling calmly to the men and women who were helping him, keeping his voice clear of anguish and fury. She saw then what it was that made him so beloved and trusted, those things by which he was judged as a man. It was not his horses or the strength of his warriors or the width and breadth of his land. The People did not judge him powerful because of his wealth. He was admired and followed and heeded because of his hunting skills, his calmness in times of trouble, his ability to make decisions that would be good for most of the clan, and how abundantly he shared what wealth he had: how well he could care for how many.

It was this which made the People strong, she saw then in an instant, their leaders and their faith in their leaders. She waited for a moment, gathering herself for what she knew she must tell him and then acknowledge to herself. When he straightened his shoulders and put his hands to the small of his back for a moment to rest, she went to his side. "I cannot find my son," she said as calmly as she could. "I think he has been taken."

Manuelito whirled on her with a look of such pain that she

knew she must keep her own anguish controlled, lest the People lose him as well. "What of his comrades?" he asked.

"They are not here," she said, bowing her head. "Their mothers weep over there," she said, gesturing to a clump of women gathered together under the juniper trees. Now that it was becoming dawn, the details of their losses were not only apparent but somehow made real by the growing light.

Manuelito put his hands to his face. "It is my fault," he moaned. "The blame is mine, entirely. I should never have brought the clans to this place—"

She embraced him quickly, pulling him into her arms as she might have a child. "No, no, no, my father. You brought us here because we could no longer stay safely where we were. Can we go after the raiders? I think that my son and the others will try to escape at the first opportunity. We should ride after them."

"Who will go on such a rescue?" he asked desperately. "We are so weakened! The slavers would never have dared attack us in our former strength, but now we are prey to every roving band—"

"Then let us go to the Hopi village. Let us go and demand the return of our people."

"Yes." He nodded slowly. "We will do that. Of course, they will likely deny their betrayal, but at least they will know that we know them for the dogs they are."

"How many are dead?" she asked.

"I do not know yet," he said, shaking his head. "Three are badly wounded. They may not survive the day."

"And we must move," she said. "We cannot stay here in the open another night. You must speak to them, my father. You must call them together and tell them what to do. They wait to hear your words."

He straightened then and looked about him as though seeing the scattered camp and the huddled figures for the first time. "They took many of the horses," he said. "Now, all but the very old and the wounded must walk. Your mother is uninjured? And your daughter?"

"They are untouched."

"Do they know Wasek was taken?"

She shook her head. "We thought perhaps he and the others had ridden after the raiders."

"I will go with you to tell them," he said, his face suddenly older in the harsh morning light. "And then I will tell the People what must be done."

This is the hardest part, Pahe told herself as she walked with Manuelito back through the camp to where Dolii and Ayoi waited. Around her, women were weeping as they gathered their scattered belongings, weeping as they tended their men, while the children wailed and wandered from one set of arms to another, seeking solace.

The men were trying to collect the horses, help their wounded kin, and bury the dead. The snow was falling lightly, as though even the Holy Ones had turned from the People and were uninterested or unaware of their plight.

Ayoi saw Manuelito and knew at once what he came to say, since Wasek was not with him. "He is killed?" she asked, her voice high and weak.

Manuelito shook his head, wordless.

"He is taken, then?"

He nodded, still unable to speak, embracing her and hiding his face in her neck.

Dolii began to wail in protest, pushing herself out of Pahe's arms as her mother tried to embrace her. "My brother! My brother!" she cried desperately, and then turned on her grandfather with a fury. "You should have protected him! He believed in you!"

Manuelito's face went blank and smooth, and he closed his eyes in pain silently.

"That is unfair," Pahe said quickly, pulling Dolii into her arms. "Your grandfather did what he had to do, and your brother did what he thought he must do. It is no one's fault except the men who betrayed us. Save your anger for the Hopi raiders."

"He was just a boy," Dolii sobbed brokenly. "Grandfather told him he was a man, but he was not."

"Boy or man," Ayoi said, her throat thick with unshed tears, "they would have taken him. Perhaps if he had been more a man, he would be over there, instead of gone from us." She gestured to the small band of men who struggled with shovels and picks to break up the frozen ground, to the bodies which were carefully laid out, waiting their place in the earth.

Dolii shuddered, turning her eyes into Pahe's shoulder.

"We will do our best to find him," Manuelito said, going to her and touching her hair. "I am sorry I have broken your trust, Little Bird."

She turned then and went into his arms, weeping furiously and Pahe let her body sag, now that she no longer needed to hold her remaining child. She eased herself down to the stone by the guttering fire. The tears came then, and she let them flow down her cheeks unheeded, for her son was gone. In some quiet part of her heart, she was relieved that she could grieve for Wasek; it had been so long since she had wept for any reason at all. After the death of her husband, her grandmother, and so many other losses, she had wondered if her heart was as frozen as the top peaks of the highest mountains. She was grateful in that moment that Nataallith was not alive, for this loss would surely have broken him. But she must go on. She had to get Dolii to safety somehow. If she lost her entire family, then she would have nothing left of herself, nothing left of Nataallith, and no more reason to stay on the earth. Her tears came from some deep well within her, pure and painless and freely flowing as a spring freshet, and she felt that if she tried to stop them, she would die.

"I must go and help the others," Manuelito was saying. "We will call council when the sun is high so that we may decide what to do."

For hours then, they helped pull the people together, burying the dead, making the wounded as comfortable as they could, bringing kinsmen together to help one another with whatever they had left to share. And then, when they gathered before a single strong fire, Manuelito said, "We will decide with one voice what must now be done. I am certain that the raiders came from the Hopi village. I am certain, also, that they will attack again if we stay in this place. We can return to our homes, back the way we came. We can go to the Hopi village and claim vengeance for their betrayal. We can go on to the Colorado and heal ourselves there, in the protection of the canyons. What do you say, my kinsmen? What way would you follow?"

After Manuelito's words, a long silence ensued as the people looked around the fire and silently tallied themselves, taking stock once and for all who was gone and who had survived. Pahe counted fifty-four men left, with another ten or so too aged to be of any use in a battle. Of the fifty-four women, twelve were too old to work or walk very far. There were nineteen children left, including Dolii. Nineteen! They had lost six children, fourteen women, and twenty-two men to the raiders, more than half of their horses and about a third of their flock.

One hundred and thirty-six people left, of the strongest, most prosperous clan in *Dinétah*. And of those, many would need to be fed, carried, and cared for by the others.

But there was no weeping round the fire. No raging to the Holy Ones uselessly, no insults hurled at those who had the responsibility to guard them, and not a word of condemnation for their headmen or for Manuelito. Pahe sensed a deep weariness in the People, and that made her more afraid than any amount of anger or weeping would have done. They had taken their despair and turned it inside themselves, put it into their bellies, and it seemed to her that their spirits were sick with what they had eaten.

"Do we know for certain that it was the Hopi?" one woman asked plaintively. "Perhaps it was the Pueblos, from over the mountains. Perhaps the Hopis will shelter us, if we go to them for protection."

"It was the Hopi demons," Juanita said. "I recognized two of their horses."

Silence settled over them for a moment, while each person recalled the words spoken over the Hopi fires, the words of welcome and pledged support. Pahe felt a bitter taste of rage and fear in her mouth: Raven's warning was right. And if she had listened and believed, if she had warned Manuelito and the others, perhaps none of this disaster would have occurred. She glanced at Ayoi. Her mother returned her gaze and seemed to look inside her in that instant.

Ayoi slowly shook her head and murmured, "Do not go there, not even in the smallest place of your mind. Whatever warning you received from Raven was for your ears only."

"In your dream, I would not listen—" Pahe whispered. "Your dream has come true."

"It was *my* dream," Ayoi said, "and you do not know if the gods meant this warning or another one to come. Who knows what the Holy Ones mean when they speak? Certainly I never have. I do know, though, that no one would have listened even if you had screamed at them to go back, that certain death waited for them over the mountains. Even now, they will not go back."

Meanwhile, Manuelito was listening to the ideas from the headmen. Quickly they agreed that it would be useless to chase after the raiders, since the territory was so large and they had no idea what direction they were headed and few horses with which to follow them. They also, less quickly, agreed that to go to the Hopi village would get them no satisfaction and might even be dangerous.

"Let them think we are not sure that they are our enemy," Manuelito said. "Perhaps there are many in the Hopi village who know nothing of the raiders. There may be more who consider themselves our friends than our foes. At any rate, we are not strong enough to attack them successfully, and we would gain nothing from the effort. I say, we go on to the Colorado and once we are stronger, we consider then how to revenge ourselves against the Hopi."

"And I say, there are those here who will go no farther," Skradena said sadly. She glanced at her brother and jerked her chin, pushing him to speak.

Skradena's brother, Shida'í, spoke up then and said, "We will go to the Bosque Redondo. We would rather starve there than lose any more of our kin to the raiders."

A shocked silence greeted his brusque words, and Pahe heard the whistle of many sharp intakes of breath. All eyes turned to Manuelito then, and she saw sorrow and a great pity in his eyes. No one had ever formally discussed surrender to the *Bilagáana* in Manuelito's clan, at least within her hearing. Whatever misgivings or doubts the People may have had, they had never expressed them at council. For the first time, it seemed they might lose each other by choice.

"You would choose surrender?" Manuelito asked, using that hated word deliberately.

The man dropped his head but nodded. "We cannot ask our brothers to feed us through the winter." He looked up, his shame shining in his eyes. "I cannot feed my family and my sister's family alone."

"Of course you would not need to do so alone—" Juanita began gently.

"They are not the only ones who will choose that trail," another headman spoke up. "We also will go with the others to the place the white men have prepared for us. They say that the rations are good enough, and the soldiers protect the people from the raiders."

"How many will choose to surrender?" Manuelito asked then, abruptly.

Pahe saw that he would not soften his words, even to save their pride, for as they went, they weakened those who chose to remain. "We are so much stronger if we stay together," she said then, the words coming from her mouth almost unbidden. "Perhaps there is another way, one we have not seen yet—"

"We have decided," Skradena said firmly. "We will not bury more of our men and lose more of our children."

"How will you ensure that does not happen on the way to the white man?" another headman asked. "You will be vulnerable to attack no matter which trail you take."

"Yes," said Juanita, "you may bury more husbands and children between here and the white man than you will from here to the Colorado. And once you have surrendered to the *Bilagáana*, you will never see those graves again."

"We will travel fast and light," Shida'í answered, "and we will keep our night fires low and sheltered—"

"We are going," Skradena said again. "We would have . . ." Her voice broke with the agony of her decision. "We would have your blessing."

"Always, that goes with you," Manuelito said soothingly. "And as for the rest, what are your minds? Do we go on to the Colorado? I will not surrender, but I will not try to persuade anyone against this plan." He asked again, his voice steady. "How many will surrender?"

Now that they had heard the word enough, it was no longer so offensive. Skradena said, "Our clans," nodding to her brother, "and Chamisa and Tolani—"

The men spoke up then, unwilling to have a woman speak for

them so completely. When it was all done, Pahe counted eleven men, fourteen women, and thirteen old ones and children who wished to make the journey back across the frozen ground to the white man's fort, nearly a quarter of their clan gone to surrender. As many lost to Bosque Redondo, almost, as they lost to the raiders. The rest decided, some reluctantly, that their best choice was to go on to the Colorado, keeping to the original plan. Manuelito never wavered. There was never any question in anyone's mind what he would do: surrender was not a choice he would consider, not so long as he could walk away in the other direction.

And so, when dawn came once more, they said farewell to their people, only a day after they had buried so many others. There was not a face without tears, not a mouth that was not filled with bitterness at this fork in the trail. Once again, they were weakened, and this time, they were not sure who to blame.

Skradena took Pahe's hand as she was leaving, and her eyes were red and swollen from weeping. Pahe wondered if she would ever see her cousin again. So much loss the woman had endured! Pahe looked into her eyes and saw defeat there, and death. She shuddered and pulled Skradena close so that she would not have to look at her face. "We will see each other again," she said, though she did not believe it.

"Yes," Skradena said weakly.

"Make the white men understand that you are of Manuelito's clan," she said firmly, repeating her father's name aloud despite tradition. "You are to be treated with honor! Tell them that if you are well treated, you will help them persuade Manuelito and his clan to go to the Bosque as well. Make them believe that a word from you will convince him. And then they will give you the best rations and the finest garments."

"Yes, I will," Skradena said once more, her smile painful to see. "We will see each other again, and I will be the fat one then, with my belly full of mutton and my arms full of gifts for you and Dolii."

They turned away from each other then, no longer able to hear each other's lies. Dolii wept as she said good-bye to her kin, but Ayoi and Juanita managed to keep their heads high and their tears inside. "Good fortune on your journey," they repeated over and over to all who were going, keeping themselves a little apart from the sorrow of the separations.

Pahe understood then that Ayoi and Juanita must be always the wives of Manuelito. Whatever their truest fears might be, following his trail, the others would never see them. They would wish the others well, but they would never let the others see that they might wish to be going where they were going.

Those departing took their part of the flocks, their dogs, their horses, and their belongings, and they set out over the snowy ground, their breath billowing up around them like a cloud. The sheep were confused, wishing to stay with the rest of the flock, and the dogs had to work hard, barking and nipping, to get them to move away. The horses, too, whinnied back to their comrades, tossing their heads and fighting the halters, and the children wept, leaving beloved uncles, aunts, and cousins. The noise of their leaving would have made their departure seem quite an adventure, Pahe thought, if it were not for their ultimate destination. The grown men and women put their best faces on it, trying to appear sure of their decision; only the animals and the children let the truth show clearly. No one wished to be left behind; no one wished to be going.

Manuelito knew that as soon as they were well out of camp, it would be best to move the rest of the clan as well. So he gently encouraged each family to pack up, load the horses, and make their farewells to whatever graves they must visit one more time. By the time the sun was high, they were moving to the north once more, skirting well wide of the Hopi village, taking the more difficult route through the mountains where the pass was steeper, the climb more demanding.

When they were higher up the mountain, they stopped to rest, and far in the distance, they could just make out their kinsmen moving across the desert, small dark spots on the land.

"They will never make it to the *Bilagáana*," Ayoi said quietly to Pahe, when Dolii was out of hearing. "The raiders will take them before they get that far."

"It does no good to think of the worst that can happen," Pahe said wearily. Her feet were sore and her back was aching, making the steep climb. The wind was cold and the snow was wet. It would have been good to ride, but there were not enough mounts for even the aged and the injured, much less the fit. "You don't know. They may get there safely, find the white men fair masters, and be content with full bellies within one moon."

"And I may sprout wings and fly to the Colorado before the night fires are embers," Ayoi said sourly, "but I doubt it."

"So do I," Pahe murmured. "But I am sick of sorrow and fear. I cannot bear it anymore."

Ayoi sighed and fell silent. When Dolii came up to them carrying a skirtful of pinyon cones and pleased with herself, Ayoi smiled and tweaked her chin, called her a clever little bird, and positioned herself so that Dolii could not easily see around her to the moving dark spots on the desert far below them.

And so, they kept going.

*   *   *

After endless climbing and sliding and slipping, they reached the canyon of the Colorado, the largest canyon for many miles in a land full of canyons, some of which were deep and wide enough to hide whole armies and flocks to feed them.

Pahe noticed that in the rock there was order, a method at work of plan and perseverance. Each groove in the rock wall led to another groove, to a channel, and then to a ditch, a gulch, a ravine, and each place of small water led to a bigger water, down finally to the canyon below and the great river. She touched the rock often as she walked, trying to take strength from its mass.

Others were not so careful. On the way down, they lost two more who were injured in falls, and they buried them in canyon crevices, protected by rocks instead of earth, for their kin were too exhausted to dig proper graves. They left the dead behind in such silence, Pahe thought, with only the creak of a bird flying overhead and the breath of the wind for company. She was glad to leave no dead in such a place and eager to stop moving always up and down and to reach level ground.

The crossing of the Colorado claimed twelve sheep and a dog who swam against the current, trying to save the animals. Exhausted, the sheep were pulled down by the fast, deep river and they could not be recovered.

The river also claimed one more child, a little girl, fourth cousin to Dolii, At'ééd Abíní, named for the morning mist in the winters.

She had only five moons, and this was her first winter. Her mother tried to swim holding her, but she was swept away. Had her father been alive, he would have held her up above the waters, but he had been killed in the raid. Now, his daughter was another death caused by the Hopi, and the people tightened their mouths against their tears, letting their rage fill their arms and strengthen them instead. Sorrow made them weak, they had learned. Only rage could keep them moving.

Manuelito found the little body after they made camp on the other side, and he brought Abíní to her mother, who sat stunned and unbelieving by the meager fires they had hastened to build. Everyone was wet right to the heart, and some were ill with water they had swallowed.

Abíní's mother held her carefully, staring into her white, still face. Pahe went to her and sat beside her quietly. The mother unwrapped her little child and touched slowly, slowly, every part of her smooth body. "I want to remember everything," she said softly. She pulled the wet pollen pouch from her pack and put a pinch of it in her daughter's little hand. "I would have done this when I gave her her first lamb," she said, "so that she would be gentle and firm with her pets." She looked at Pahe, suddenly stricken. "I have nothing now."

Pahe put her arm around her shoulders. "I know it must seem so. But you have your life, and it will be a long one."

"I will not care," Abíní's mother whispered.

Pahe sat with her as long as she could, and when she began to shiver, she went to the fire Manuelito had built to see to her mother and stepmother and daughter. No one was speaking. It was as though they felt it would take all the strength they had simply to build the fires and set up a makeshift camp; they could ill afford to waste a single effort on speech.

Pahe embraced Dolii. "I think we are past the worst of it now. We will be safe here, at least, from the raiders."

"We will be safe here," Dolii echoed, nodding as though her head were on a string.

Pahe knew she was trying to convince herself even as she spoke.

Ayoi made no complaint about the wet, the wood, or the river crossing, and that omission was as worrisome as anything, Pahe thought. If her mother was not complaining, she was only partially alive.

In fact, as she looked about, it seemed to her that all of them were only barely hanging on to life. What had happened to the spirit that held them together and made them strong? What had happened to their peace? There was no time to spend mourning what was lost, she told herself, shivering as she pulled pieces of wood to the central fire area. They must get warm; they must have food. Then, perhaps, they could care about life once more.

*   *   *

The sun was out on the rocky slopes above the Colorado, and though the air was cold, it was warmer down in the lower elevations, almost like early spring. Orvis knew that the warmth was deceptive, and that there would still be more snow before the first green shoots of grass came out in the valleys. Orvis knew this because she had twelve summers. She was the oldest ewe in the herd, and the wisest creature on either side of the great canyon. And if a sprigling forgot, she was quick enough to remind him with a fast jolt by her blunt horns.

Orvis was a Bighorn Sheep, *Orvis canadensis,* a large, pale-brown creature who roamed the canyons and the valleys on both sides of the Colorado. She had a muscular body with a thick neck, a white belly, rump patch, muzzle, and eye patch, and a pair of short curled horns which she rarely had to use. Were she male, she would have larger, fully curled horns, she would be larger, and she would have used her horns against all rivals during rut, charging at other males at speeds more than twenty miles per hour, crashing her forehead against another with a crack that would be heard for more than a mile.

Fortunately, Orvis thought, she was not a male and therefore not prone to such stupidity. She had but to lead, and the others followed. For three years, she had been the leader of the largest herd of Bighorn in the canyons, twenty ewes, lambs, yearlings, and two-year-olds, and in the time of rut, when the rams also joined the herd, she might lead as many as one hundred animals to and from grass, water, and the bedding sites.

Orvis used the same bedding sites over and over, unlike the mountain goats and the deer. She saw no reason to change something once she found it satisfactory: let the goats and the deer waste their time finding new places each night to sleep. She liked things to stay the same.

But things were definitely not staying the same this morning. Orvis stood at the edge of the cliff, clinging to the sides of the canyon with remarkable balance, watching the movement of Man below her. Man had arrived in the valley a few nights before, and the smoke from Man's fires now rose into the air, causing her muzzle to wrinkle with distaste. Man was the only thing Orvis feared.

Each spring, of course, the lions and the eagles tried to take the lambs, but they dared not trouble the grown ewes or even the two-year-olds, and so she did not fear them. In fact, she had charged a cougar last year, who slunk too close to one of the bud-horns. The lesser enemies, the wolves, the coyotes, the bears, and the bobcats, they could easily evade. Only the very stupid or the very slow ever fell prey to those, and perhaps they deserved to die, if they could not get away from something so slow as a bear.

She stamped her forefoot now in anger, watching Man. Her hoofs were hard at the outer edge and spongy in the center, providing excellent traction on the sheer rock face. The spriglings were weaned now, so they could move quickly. She shook her head back and forth nervously, making a low grumble of complaint in her throat.

With Man now in the valley, she must move her herd, for Man was the only enemy she could not combat. She had seen Man often enough, seen their weapons and come across the males they had killed, carved up their bodies and cut off their horns. She did not need to wait to see what Man would do. They were all alike. They would kill what they could catch.

Without a sound, she set off for the higher elevations, only once looking behind her to be sure that the rest were following. Here they came in a line, the small ones complaining, the older ewes already aware of the danger below and eager to move out of range. She knew of a canyon to the west, deeper and more precipitous, more difficult for Man to climb. The rams would also find it difficult to follow them there, but she cared little for that. If there were fewer battles at rutting time, that would not displease her. She was getting impatient with their noise and blowing and charging.

Orvis led the herd around the edge of the canyon wall, keeping to the shadowed places, for she knew instinctively that their dark wool would show up against the white snow to any eyes that watched from below. As she rounded a turn in the trail, a small indentation in the rock face which widened enough for her to turn to see behind her, she saw with some satisfaction that the herd was following her in an orderly manner, with few complaints. Even the two-year-olds, usually the source of most of the grousing, were quietly traipsing along in each other's hoofsteps, content to leave sight and smell of the herd of Man below.

As she rounded another turn in the cliff, reaching for a higher plateau, she heard a small snarl above her. She looked up and saw a lynx crouched on an upper ledge, poised to leap, its eyes glinting in the sunlight. She bleated once in sharp warning, and the lynx jumped on a lamb several sheep back in the line, knocking it to its knees. She turned and lowered her head for battle, struggling to get back to the lamb, which was bleating hideously, with the lynx's fangs sunk in its neck. The lamb's mother was bleating uselessly, confused and panicked, and Orvis butted her roughly aside, nearly toppling her off the cliff as she rushed to rescue the lamb. When she reached the lamb, she pushed it against the wall of the cliff with her shoulder, and attempted to crush the cat with her horns against the rock. The lynx snarled at her fiercely, but it did not let loose of the lamb. Again, Orvis pushed the lamb, not caring now if the lamb was crushed, knowing that if she did not injure or kill the lynx, it would prey on her herd again. This time, she managed to pin the lynx's paw between the rock and her horn, and she ground her horn into the rock as hard as she could, pushing all her weight against the cliff and scrambling with her back hooves to keep on the pressure. The cat squalled and released the lamb, rising above its body just enough so that Orvis could butt it again, knocking it off completely. The cat leaped for the higher precipice, but it was off balance, lost its clawhold, and tumbled down the rock face with a loud screech.

Orvis stood and looked down to where the cat had disappeared in the rocks below, snorting and stamping angrily. She did not see the enemy emerge from the boulders. It was either dead or too wounded to move. She turned back to the lamb, which was kneeling against the cliff face, bleeding badly, its eyes closed, its head nodding low.

She smelled death about the lamb, and she wanted the herd gone from this place as swiftly as she could move them. She turned to the lamb's dam and pushed her in the flanks, urging her forward. She protested, trying to stay with her lamb. Orvis butted her again roughly, shouldered past her, and continued up the rock face. Without question, the rest of the herd moved around the ewe like water around a boulder, and followed her up the trail, scarcely pausing at the dying lamb. Finally, bleating plaintively, the ewe followed, leaving her lamb behind.

Orvis knew that the ewe was more important to the health of the herd than the lamb. From the ewe would come other lambs; from the lamb would come only food for enemies now, and those enemies would come swiftly as the wind carried the scent of death. Also she knew that the herd was more important than anything else. She killed for the sake of the lamb, yes, but more for the sake of the herd. The herd must come first.

Orvis did not look back. To look back would cause the others to hesitate. She looked only ahead and upward, toward safety. And the others followed.

*   *   *

The People did their best to make camp comfortably in the valley beneath the high sheer walls of the canyon, venturing up and down the river for food and wood. The snow was light, and it was warmer in the valley, but they missed the sense of space and freedom that the open desert gave them, and some of the old men complained that if they must be buried beneath all this rock and dirt, they would rather be buried in their own lands, where at least they could see the sky wide and white above them.

At first, they built only brush shelters made by dragging big branches together in a circle. They left the door open to the east, of course, as was proper, but many of the shelters had no roofs, just open fires in the middle. With blankets and goat and sheep skins, they kept warm enough. But then, the fact that they were actually going to stay seeped into the old ones, and they began to badger the young men to put roofs on the shelters, and before long, they had built something that was half brush shelter, half hogan, and they called them hogans because they wished them to be.

Manuelito and all of his women shared a hogan now for the first time, and Manuelito was gone from camp many hours to find food enough for all of them in the long winter months. Fish were plentiful in the Colorado, but the People had never eaten them before. It was *báhádzid,* forbidden by the ways of the Holy Ones to eat such things. Pahe wished that the bellies of humans would go to sleep in the winter months, like the bellies of the squirrels, the fish, and the frogs. She knew it was worse on the top of the canyon, and she could only hope that the Hopi were starving, slowly and painfully.

Manuelito sat by the fire for the long hours of the winter darkness, and often he would not speak. Juanita could not get him to talk. Even when Ayoi goaded him or Dolii teased him, he would respond with merely a few words, perhaps a smile, and then slip back into silence. Pahe knew that her father was thinking of all those who were gone, that his spirit left his body and journeyed with them to the Bosque and it was difficult for him to pull it back again.

"Barboncito and Armijo are still hiding in the mountains," Manuelito said. "I wonder how they are feeding their people."

"Not so well as you are," Pahe said. "At least here, we need not worry about the raiders. At least the snow here is not so deep. We have the river and we have the valley. In the spring, we will plant again, and we will grow stronger."

"In the spring, we will be gone," Manuelito said to her quietly. "I do not think we can stay here long. The Hopi will not allow it. The raiders will not leave us be. Once the spring thaws the passes, they will hunt us down."

"How will they come across the river?"

"They will not. They will come on us from the north rim of the canyon. Once the ice melts, it will be easy enough to reach us." He shook his head. "By spring, we must be strong enough to move once more."

Pahe fell into dismayed silence. She had supposed that he meant to keep them there, that they would build a village, plant their crops, and graze their flocks. But now she understood that the valley of the canyon was only a winter camp. They must move again, must keep moving, until they were either captured or they surrendered. Could the People survive such migration? It had been many generations since they had been nomads, and not in anyone's memory had they moved even once. Now they faced a future of rootlessness. Many of the old ones would likely prefer death to constant motion. And the young ones? She sighed deeply.

Dolii would never find a husband if she escaped the raiders long enough to reach the age of marriage. The People were accustomed to traveling long distances to gather food, to attend the Blessingway ceremonies and the dances, and to visit with kinsmen. But always, they had one place that was their home, and there they always returned.

There was still no word about Wasek and the other captives. Manuelito had sent three warriors to spy on the Hopi village, and they went to the Pueblos, asking for information, but no one seemed to know where the raiders went after their attack. Most believed that the captives were now slaves in Mexican haciendas. But Pahe could not believe that Wasek was so far away. He felt closer to her heart, somehow, as though he were only just over the mountains. She believed that if he were dead, she would know it. If he were far from her, she would not feel his heart beating within her own. He was somewhere out there, waiting to return to her.

A month went by, and then two months, and finally the first signs of spring began to show in the valley. The Colorado was still murky with ice in the shallows, but there were small patches of green poking through the snow in places, and the birds were more active in the trees. It was time, Manuelito said, to send a message to the *Bilagáana* and ask for peace once more.

"What makes you think they will listen this time?" asked a headman at the council fire. "So many have already surrendered, why should they grant peace to a few?"

"Because we are of no threat to them anymore," Manuelito said. "We will ask only to be allowed to plant our crops and graze our sheep. We will promise to stay close enough to the fort so that they need not search for us. That way, they will not have to care for us with the others; they will not need to feed us and shelter us as they do those who have surrendered. Peace will be good for the white man, too. Surely they will allow this—"

"It is what Barboncito asked for, and he was refused," a warrior said.

"We are fewer than Barboncito. We will ask again. Surely they will listen," Manuelito said doggedly.

"And if they do not?" asked one of the women.

Manuelito bowed his head. "I do not have an answer for this now. When we need an answer, we will find it together."

There was stark silence around the circle. Even Pahe was shocked. She had never heard her father speak in such a way, admit that he did not have an idea for any possibility and, in fact, could not think of an answer when asked. "You are certain that we will not be safe here?" she asked finally.

"I am certain of nothing," Manuelito smiled wryly. "But my head tells me that when the spring winds thaw the passes, the north side of the canyon is easy enough to traverse. If I were looking for slaves, I would lead my raiders down into this canyon and walk back out everyone I could catch. After all"—he gestured around to the small camp area—"there are few places to run. This valley can be as much a trap as a refuge."

"And there is not enough grazing land here for the flocks," Juanita reminded them.

"We can go back to our lands," one of the old ones said.

Manuelito nodded. "We can. But we will not get there without being attacked, I fear. And once we get there, the soldiers will find us once more. I believe that we must go to the white men, for at least there, we are safe from the raiders."

"After the lambing," Juanita said.

More and more women sat at council now, Pahe saw, and many of them spoke out loud their fears and questions. This was good, she knew. Different from the past, but good. There were too few of the People now to ignore the wishes and ideas of half of them.

"We cannot afford to lose a single sheep," Juanita added. "We must get them to good pastures before their ribs stick out like handles to be hefted."

Everyone nodded in agreement. The winter had only been tolerable because of the flocks. Some nights, they had only goat milk and cornbread to eat, but no one had complained. Many of the old ones said that they could barely chew anything tougher anyway, for their teeth were loose in their heads. They boiled the milk, added the stale cornbread—stale because there was little fat to make it moist—and made a mush which filled their bellies.

The children had learned to hunt the little chipmunks which lived in the rocks all round the base of the valley. They had been breeding there, undisturbed, for so many generations that they crowded the rocks like prairie dogs, chirping and whistling brazenly at the children when they tried to catch them. And then the children discovered that with old blankets and pieces of wool, the chipmunks could be lured out of their burrows. There were so many of them that the males fought over any nesting materials they could find, and so they were more hungry for wool than for corn, and they'd venture out to where the older boys could catch them and club them. The pots were always full of chipmunks and, sometimes, they would also catch the small gray squirrels with the long, strange ears that slept in holes in the trees.

But Pahe knew that many felt as she did: they were not at home here in the valley of the great canyon, even if they were safe for the moment. The Holy Ones had forbidden them to cross any of the three rivers: the San Juan, the Colorado, or the Rio Grande. And now they had done so, and none felt easy in this place. On their own lands, they woke each morning and thought: Here I am where I ought to be. No amount of safety could take the place of that feeling, and she knew she would never feel that at the bottom of the canyon, like a frog living at the bottom of a well. There was not enough sky-space around them to breathe properly.

They had disobeyed the Holy Ones, and yet, Pahe felt their presence with her often as she moved about the canyon floor. The land and stone at this level of the earth's belly was like the talking papers that the white man used, telling about the rocks and the earth itself. She was hunting for firewood with Dolii one day, far up the canyon where the snow was lighter, and they came upon a small cave left behind when the Colorado shrank its waters down. They went inside, surprised to discover that the air was warmer within the cave than outside by the river.

Dolii ran her hand lightly over red marks on the walls, old

words and pictures left there by the Ancients. "Here are their stories," she whispered.

Pahe nodded. "A wise person should be able to look at stones and mountains and read stories older than the first man who walked on the earth."

"I found a large bone once," Dolii said, "of a giant animal. It must have walked the earth before the People were here. And I have seen the footprints of plants in the rock, plants which do not grow in that place anymore. Probably they died before the first people lived."

"But the land remembers them," Pahe said. "Look, here." She pointed to a small handprint in dark-brown stain. "It is a woman's sign."

"I wonder how old she was?" Dolii said, putting her own hand gently within the printed one on the wall.

"Perhaps only a little older than you."

"I wonder if she had a husband and children," Dolii said wistfully.

Pahe turned and began to gather the small pieces of wood that the river had pushed into the mouth of the cave. "Do you fear you will never know these things?"

Dolii thought for a moment. "No. I do not think of things like that. I am too young still for such thinking. I think of other things, but I do not think of husbands and children."

She spoke so formally that Pahe was confused. "What do you think of?"

She shrugged. "I think of my brother," she said softly. "I think of the turquoise bracelet I used to have. I think of how long the days were once and how short the nights." She picked up another bundle of wood and began to tie it with short, quick yanks on the cording. "I think of how I never feared the coming of a stranger. But I do not think about husbands and children."

Pahe felt the sadness flood into her heart, and she knelt to help Dolii tie the bundle of wood. She touched her daughter's hand. A small hand. She was not as tall as she should have been, for the lack of good food. "We will go to the fort, and your grandfather will persuade the white men to leave us in peace. And then, perhaps, we will have the ceremonies and the dances again. Life will begin again for us as it should. Perhaps, even, your brother will find his way back to us once more." She brightened. "Perhaps the soldiers will rescue those taken by the raiders. They did promise that once, I remember."

Dolii looked at her mother quizzically, as though she had suddenly changed in some fundamental way. "Yes," she said finally. "I remember, too. You are right, my mother. Things will be better soon."

Pahe realized that Dolii was only humoring her, as she might humor Ayoi, and she was abashed. She turned her head away and her hands to the bundling of more wood. Her daughter thought her foolish and naive. It was the first time in her twelve winters, but it would not be the last.

* * *

In the month when the lambs were strong enough to travel far and the grass was high enough to feed them, the clan set out for the white man's fort, to ask the *Bilagáana* once more for peace. They went to the north, past the place where the Colorado split off from the San Juan, so that the sheep might cross the river easier. They skirted wide of the Hopi lands, traveling as invisibly as possible until they descended south into their own lands. Everyone noticed how few signs of the People they saw, even as they neared those places where they should have seen their own. The nights were still cold, but the days were growing warmer, and they began to talk among themselves of the plantings to come.

"This will be a good year for rain," Ayoi said. "It was dry last year, and so this year will be wet. We will plant more squash than we did last year, and melons."

They were walking steadily south and east, resting the horses as they went. The flocks were pushing ahead of them, scenting water in the valley below them. It would be a good place to camp for the night. A thunder roll rumbled across the sky in the distance, and Pahe looked up, smiling.

"It was a long thunder," she said. "It will be a long rain tonight."

"Good for the grass," her father said, coming up behind her. Manuelito walked first with one clan and then another, falling behind and speeding up as necessary. "What do your spirit voices say to you about this journey, my daughter?" he asked cheerfully.

She looked at him with surprise. "My mother has been sharing secrets in the blankets."

He grinned. "Occasionally she does speak of more than her complaints. Have you heard anything you might tell me?"

She frowned. "Once I thought Raven spoke to me." She shook her head. "No, that is not the truth. I *know* he spoke to me. But he has not spoken again." She dropped her voice confidentially. "I have asked for guidance and wisdom, but my prayers are not heard."

"Oh, they are heard," Manuelito said. "Never believe they aren't heard. We are alive. We are together—"

"Some of us," Pahe said sadly.

"And we are not yet penned in a corral like so many goats under the white man's dogs. For that, I would say a blessing prayer, if for nothing else."

She walked silently on. It was surprising to her to see how well her body obeyed her mind and kept on walking, walking, even when she felt she might lay herself down on the ground and never move again. It was as though her feet obeyed her mind without her heart's consent.

"I think we will have a Blessingway ceremony when we get closer to the fort," Manuelito said. "Will you consider leading the women?"

"This is a new thing," she said wonderingly. "Since when do women lead women?"

"Since we have lost so many warriors and husbands, I am thinking," her father said. "Of course, I know how it is when a new thing enters the hogan. The old men mutter, the women walk away, and the young warriors start sharpening their knives. But I have also seen that when their children are hungry, the women are more likely to sit and listen to a new thing than either the old men or the young men." He paused for a moment. "And it seems to me that the daughter of Manuelito may be one they will hear. So will you lead them?"

She smiled. "If they will be led. I notice they are more and more outspoken these days. I do not envy their husbands."

"Once we are settled again, and they have their crops planted and their flocks grazing good pasture, they will quiet down,"

Manuelito said. "The Blessingway will remind them of how important they are to the harmony of the clan."

*   *   *

After days of walking, they finally arrived within two days walk of the fort, and they set up camp in a canyon where the springs were good and the forage would do for a time. Once they had the fires started and the shelters up, a runner came in from the north. He was from one of the other headmen, Armijo, one of the last remaining chiefs who had not surrendered. The runner said that they had seen Manuelito and his band crossing the desert from their outpost on a northern mesa, and they wished to have council. Manuelito sent the runner back to Armijo with one of their precious horses, so as to welcome and hasten the headman's arrival.

That night, Armijo and his headmen sat round the fire with Manuelito and all who were strong enough to sit up and listen. Armijo said, "We have heard many stories of the long walk our people made, since they left the white man's fort. The *Bilagáana* gave them thirty wagons and some horses, but it was not enough. One in ten died, from the cold or empty bellies or sickness of the bowels. All of them wept as they walked, and it was said that some of the old ones who died, perished of broken hearts and a starving for the land they left behind. Some of the children were stolen by the Mexicans, even as the soldiers stood guard. And yet," he added finally, "many say they are better off at the reservation than they would be, starving in the mountains. Some have escaped and come back to tell us these things. Others prefer to stay, for at least they are fed at the Bosque."

"Do you plan to surrender?" Manuelito asked Armijo. He had known the old headman for many years, and though they did not share kinship lines, he had respect for Armijo as a leader of his people.

Armijo hesitated for a long moment before he spoke, and when he did, half of the listeners round the fire took in their breath. "Yes," he said finally. "I believe it is the best trail to follow."

"And yet you see that others who have surrendered have escaped, rather than stay where the white man orders them to stay." Manuelito's voice was very gentle, as though he spoke to a woman.

"I see this," Armijo said, a little louder. "But I can no longer feed my people if I keep pushing them from one hideout to another. We cannot stay in one place long enough to plant a crop or birth a child." His voice roughened. "Always, I have taken a great pleasure from my life, as the Holy Ones told us to do. Since the coming of the *Bilagáana*, my life is a stone I carry in my belly instead of a star. I am weary of the burden. But I will not lay it down until my people are safe."

Manuelito looked past Armijo's shoulder, to give him a chance to recover himself.

The old headman went on. "We cannot graze behind our sheep from mountain to mountain, for fear of the whites. I think that if we go to the Bosque as the white man asks, and we are many rather than few, he will be forced to provide what he has promised. I ask you, Manuelito, to bring your people and join mine. I believe that with many, we will make the journey more safely, and the *Bilagáana* will give us more wagons, more horses, and more rations." He leaned forward toward the fire and stared into Manuelito's eyes intently. "You will have to surrender eventually. You cannot keep your people alive through another winter, and the white man will not let you alone. Why not surrender now with me, and our peoples will make such a tribe as must needs be accompanied by an army of soldiers, with all that they must bring to that effort. To me, this seems the way of wisdom." He looked around the fire meaningfully. "To me, this seems the way of a man who walks the best trail."

"Easiest, perhaps, but not necessarily the best," Manuelito said mildly. "You speak well, Armijo, and I know that you have spoken from your heart. But I have made a different decision and mean to walk a different trail. We will come with you to the white men, or at least close enough that we may council with them safely. But we do not intend to surrender."

"Why come at all, then?"

"We will ask once more for peace. We will ask that we be allowed to live near enough to the *Bilagáana* that they may see we are keeping that peace. And we will plant our crops and tend our herds and harm no one."

Armijo smiled sadly. "I think they will tell you that you no longer have that choice."

Manuelito shrugged. "Then we will consider your trail, my friend. Or perhaps we will think of something else in the waiting. But we have done nothing to make them hate us. We have kept the peace we promised the white headman, Canby."

"They hate you because you sit on land which they covet," Armijo said. "They will not care about your offer of peace, nor will they care whether you kept your promise. We have already seen that they are a people who care little for promises."

"Perhaps you are right, old friend," Manuelito said. "And if you are, then we may have to join you in the walk to the east. But for now, this is our decision."

Pahe felt the pride well in her chest at her father's words. He was still a strong leader, still the voice of the clan. His words sounded even and firm, like the steps of a young, healthy warrior on the earth.

Armijo said, "Shall we go together then to the *Bilagáana?*"

Manuelito agreed, and four days later, Armijo came back to their camp with the rest of his band, more than four hundred men, women, old ones, and children, with a thousand sheep and two hundred horses. Pahe was shocked to see that her clan was not the largest or the strongest anymore. In fact, with so many together, she wondered why surrender should be necessary at all.

It was so good to be together, to have so many familiar or almost-familiar faces and names about once more, that they put off riding to the fort for two nights, so they might have dancing and singing and visiting from one fire to another. Pahe sensed quickly as she spoke to women, moving from clan to clan, that although they were strong in number, the people of Armijo's clan were not strong in spirit. The soldiers had chased them and harried them from waterhole to refuge until they were exhausted and bitter and sick at heart. Some of the old mothers came to Juanita's fire to talk.

"We never sleep anymore, not really," one said to Juanita. "We close our eyes and rest, but we do not sleep. At any time, we fear the soldiers will come again, and so most of us cannot sleep deep enough to dream." She sighed wearily. "It has been two moons since I have dreamed. I feel as though my spirit will leave my body and go searching for dreams, so hungry am I for them again."

"And we cannot care for our bodies," another woman said with disgust. "We cannot bathe, we cannot wash our hair or our garments. There is no time and we cannot go near the larger rivers. Even if we can wet ourselves, we cannot sit for long hours by the fires, drying our hair or our blankets. And so, we are tormented by fleas and all manner of creeping, biting things, and we take no pleasure in our men, for we smell like animals."

"Our children cannot play," added another. "They cannot stray far from camp, and they cannot shout and holler and run, for fear they will be taken by raiders or found by the soldiers. And they are too weary to play anyway. They have only enough to eat to keep them alive, but not enough to keep them fat and healthy. And if we cannot plant a crop this spring, many of them will fail."

Pahe embraced many of the women and wept with a few of them, feeling better than she had felt in many months. With them, she was able to weep out loud for Wasek, and with them, she was able to lament Dolii's loneliness and narrowed hopes for a future. With them, she did not need to stay always strong, always the daughter of Manuelito, and she could be simply one of so many who had come to this place on the land, weary and emptied of will.

But then the morning came when it was time to travel the few miles to Fort Canby, and she tucked her sorrow and fear back inside her heart again, that she might once more be strong for her people.

Armijo went ahead with his people, for there were too many to travel together. The flocks could not be kept separate, and the forage was too sparse. Manuelito told him to go to the post commander and tell him that his band would come along in several days. "Tell him that I would council with him," Manuelito told Armijo. "No. Ask him if I may come to discuss the terms of peace."

Pahe was standing alongside her father, and she saw Armijo grimace again hopelessly. When he left, she asked her father, "Will he say the words as you want them said?" It would never have occurred to her to question the loyalty of one headman to another in years past, but now, she wondered.

Manuelito shrugged. "I believe he will. I will know when I get there."

Her father had decided that the majority of the clan should stay behind when he went to speak to the commander of the white men at the fort. But he wished several of the women, old and young, to accompany him, together with the children. He told Pahe, "The soldiers will wish to take me. But they really want the warriors, too. The warriors will stay and watch over the flocks and the old ones and the rest of the women. The white men will not wish to take on the care of the women and the children without the men, I think. And if I ride into the fort with women and children, they cannot say that I came for any other reason than peace."

And so it was that Pahe rode alongside her father, with her daughter behind her on their single horse, accompanied by his wives and ten other women and their children. They made an impressive display as they came near Fort Canby, for the women wore whatever good garments they still had left, and they were rested and sat their horses well. "It is not good to negotiate with the enemy from a place of weakness," Pahe told them. "Neither do we wish to look as though we have anything left for them to take."

The soldiers rode out to greet them and flanked them on all sides as they rode into the high walls of the fort. It had been a long while since Pahe had been within the places of the white man, and she felt a high, hard nervousness in her chest. "Are you afraid?" she asked Dolii quietly as they came up to the high gates.

Dolii whispered, "Yes. I had forgotten how noisy they are."

Pahe smiled wryly. After months on the desert and in the great canyon, her daughter was used to the silence of the land. Even when Armijo's four hundred had joined them, they did not make such a noise on the land as these white men, with their clanking spurs, their jingling harnesses, and their shouted orders.

"They are so many," Dolii murmured softly. "And they are larger than I remember."

"They only seem so," Pahe said to her. "The darkness of their costumes make them seem larger. But they can be killed as easily as any man."

Dolii did not look convinced. In fact, Pahe had to confess as she gazed about the inside of the fort, while seeming to keep her eyes straight ahead, that there were many more white men and women here than she had imagined. Obviously, they were moving to these lands in large numbers, and the removal of the People had been something that gave them the feeling they could do so safely. They were bundled in many cloaks and hats and capes, and it was difficult to see which of them were women and which were men, but they paid little attention to the Navajo as they rode quietly through them, as though the arrival of more Indians was nothing new or startling anymore.

The soldiers escorted them to a separate building within the walls, the place of the post commander, and Manuelito dismounted slowly, giving the headman of the whites plenty of time to come out to greet him properly. Finally, a small white man did come forth, bundled in a heavy coat with a hat all but obscuring his face.

"You are Manuelito?" he asked him shortly.

"I am," Manuelito replied mildly. He looked around for the translator. Usually, one was present at all councils with the white men. But no soldier or scout came forward.

"I am Captain Carey," the white man said then. "You wished to speak with me?"

"You are headman of these soldiers?" Manuelito asked in his careful English. He could understand more of the talk of the *Bilagáana* than most of the headmen, Pahe knew, but he had rarely spoken directly with them, except through an interpreter. She felt the fear rise higher in her chest. She wondered that he could appear so calm. Then it occurred to her. Always before, the discussions had never gone in their favor. Perhaps this time, with no interpreter, they might be better understood. She tried to keep her hope strong, sending out that strength to her father.

"I am temporary commanding officer," the white man said, "and you can tell me anything you want General Canby to know."

Manuelito waited to be asked to come inside the building, but the man made no gesture of welcome. After a few moments, when it was clear that any conversation they might have would take place out in the open, within the hearing of the soldiers and the women and children, Manuelito said, "I have brought a council of peace, Care-rey," and he gestured to the women and children behind him.

"Where are your warriors?" the white man asked.

"Nearby, guarding the rest of my people and the animals," Manuelito said slowly, searching for the white words. "They fear the slave raiders."

"As well they might," the man said shortly. "Bring them in, and we will protect them all from your enemies."

"I will do this," Manuelito said. "We wish to make camp near this fort. We will plant our fields. We will graze our sheep. You can see that we keep this peace."

"Good," the captain said, "and when you are assembled, we will escort you to Fort Sumner at the Bosque." He made as though to turn away.

"We do not wish to leave these lands," Manuelito said firmly. "We will stay close to the soldiers. You will see that we keep this peace. But we will not surrender."

The captain turned back again with some exasperation. "You will not surrender? Then what did you come for?"

"To ask you to allow us to keep this peace."

"The only place for you to keep the peace is at Fort Sumner. Go to the Bosque."

"Why must we go there?" Manuelito asked, his arms outstretched and empty. "We have kept our promises to the White Father in Washington. We have kept the peace. We have been attacked by enemies who have stolen our women and children, and still we did not fight. We have stolen nothing and we have killed no one."

"Since when?" the captain asked shortly. "You may have kept the peace for a few months, but before that, you raided haciendas north and south, and you have murdered those who resisted you. You have not kept the peace. You have only kept the peace when you became too weak to fight."

Manuelito dropped his head. "We are too weak to fight now. We will keep the peace. We will keep our promise."

Captain Carey dismissed Manuelito's words with a rude sweeping gesture. "Your promises mean nothing to me. They mean nothing to General Canby, and they mean nothing to the Great White Father in Washington. You must surrender or be killed. That is your choice. And there is nothing more that I will say."

Manuelito said, "Many of my people fear that once they surrender, they will be shot down. The soldiers will shoot them, as they did three summers past."

"The incident at Fort Fauntleroy was unfortunate," Captain Carey said, more patiently now. "Those responsible have been punished. You have my word that if you bring your people in to surrender, they will be protected. They will be taken to the Bosque and given food and clothing and shelter. They will plant their crops and live in peace with the many hundreds who have gone before them." He opened his hands wide around him. "Look around you, Manuelito. All are gone save you. Those few left will surrender before the year is out, I promise you that, or be captured and killed. Tell your people that the only safety for them is at the Bosque. Tell them that they must surrender or die." Captain Carey turned to speak to one of the soldiers who sat his horse close to Manuelito, and Pahe saw instantly the fear in her father's face and body. They might be captured right here, if they were not very quick and very wise.

Manuelito said, "I have considered your words carefully. I believe that you speak the truth. I will surrender my people, but first, I must speak with some who have seen the Bosque and returned. I must be able to say to my people what they say to me of this place. Otherwise, my warriors will not follow my commands."

Pahe smiled to herself within the covering of her cloak. The warriors would have smiled also if they heard Manuelito speak of commands, for no headman used such words.

"There is no one for you to speak with," Captain Carey said quickly. "You will see for yourself when you go to the Bosque."

"Herrero Grande has been there," Manuelito said. "He has been to the Bosque and returned. They say he is at Fort Wingate. I will travel there, and when I have spoken with him, I will bring my warriors in to surrender."

Captain Carey's face grew more angry.

"I will speak with General Carl-tun," Manuelito added quietly. "He has promised us fair dealing."

Pahe saw what her father was trying to do. Captain Carey did not want Manuelito to leave the fort; neither did he want him to go to the Star Chief Carl-tun with his requests. Either would make him look as though he could not control the Navajo and could not do his duty.

"You wish to speak to Herrero Grande?" the captain asked finally. "And then you will surrender your people?"

"If he tells me that the Bosque is a place where they can live, I will bring them," Manuelito said.

"I should simply arrest you now," the captain said disgustedly, "and send out my troops to capture the rest and bring them in."

Manuelito smiled. "You may do so, of course, but you will never find them. When they do not see me and their women leave the fort, they will scatter to the canyons, and my warriors will make war on the fort until I am released or each one is dead." He moved to his horse. "Perhaps it would be well if you kept the peace, as I keep the peace. In this way, we may perhaps each win what we most desire." Manuelito mounted his horse easily, keeping his back to the soldiers.

Captain Carey glared at Manuelito silently, and Pahe felt the tension move through the soldiers. They were ready to move instantly to either capture her father or escort him out to freedom. She glanced at Dolii. Her daughter did not move or slump or twist on her blanket; in no way did she reveal her fear. The other women listened quietly, and only the small cry of a nursing babe under a blanket broke the silence.

"I will report to General Carleton that you are ready to surrender if you are allowed to speak to another chief who has been to the Bosque," the captain finally said. "And if you do not keep *this* promise, I will lead my soldiers out myself to bring you in."

Manuelito nodded politely and turned his horse away. Pahe followed him, and behind her, Ayoi, Juanita, and the other women rode closely together, no one saying a word. The soldiers came behind them, and they were well away from the post commander's hogan when one of the women asked Pahe, "Will we surrender, then? Is that what has been promised?"

Pahe realized that few of the women understood as much of

the council as she had, and she was struck then by their courage. They sat and watched, knowing little except the tone of the voices, trying to understand by the movement of the men's bodies, and still they kept silent and still, waiting to comprehend their fate. She wondered if men would have been able to be so calm. She thought, with some wonder, that her father was very wise to bring women and children to the fort, instead of his warriors.

They rode out of the walls of the fort, all of them looking straight ahead, and, finally, as they went up the hill to the south, the soldiers fell away, letting them ride alone.

"I thought perhaps they meant to capture us," Dolii said with relief as they turned back to the fort.

"Your grandfather said they would not," Pahe said cheerfully. "He was right again." It was a pleasure to speak out loud, to speak in their own tongue, to hear neither the noises of the white men around them or their ugly, clumsy speech.

Manuelito turned his horse and waited until the women were all around him. "You were very brave," he told them. "Each of you helped today to prove to the *Bilagáana* that we are of a single mind. I am very glad that you accompanied me. Your men will be proud!"

The women laughed then, and the children drummed their heels on the horses and crowed. Many of the women had no men, of course, but they believed that Manuelito's words were true. Their men would know, somehow, of their courage, even if they no longer walked among the living.

They rode back to the springs at Quelitas where the rest of the clan was waiting, and round the fires that night, the women talked long and cheerfully about the white men and the fort, and all they saw and heard. It was as though they had been to battle and returned triumphant, Pahe thought. They needed this victory to keep going.

After several days rest, as they were preparing to move once more, a runner came with the message that General Carleton was sending several Navajo headmen to speak to Manuelito. All four had been to the Bosque, and they were coming to fulfill Manuelito's demand that he be allowed to hear for himself the conditions there from those who had seen the place with their own eyes.

"This is good," Pahe told Ayoi and Dolii. "While we are waiting for them, we are safe from capture. While they are here, we are likely safe, as well. When the white men are talking, they are not shooting, at least."

The sense of safety, however illusory, seemed to infect the whole clan, and small gaggles of women roamed away from the fires to search for herbs and roots in the early spring thaws, reveling in the new green things of the earth and laughing among themselves. The men heard their laughter blowing on the breeze like birdsong, and they began to pick up the spirit of the women, brushing the horses and repairing harnesses and joking back and forth among themselves. Most especially did the children feel the spring thaw, and they ran through the camp like rabbits, throwing sticks and shouting and imitating the white men with insulting gestures and rude postures, falling all over themselves with giddy games.

Four old headmen came riding into camp, accompanied by a troop of a dozen soldiers. Manuelito immediately greeted them with all the ritual and welcome that the small camp could provide, deliberately ignoring the soldiers as though they were only extra pack animals brought by the visitors. The soldiers withdrew to their own fires, and Manuelito had to tell the young children to stay away, for they were eager to spy on the soldiers and perhaps do them some mischief, so bold had they become with only a few days of feeling safe.

And then the entire camp gathered to hear the words of those men who had seen the Bosque for themselves. Pahe noticed the way the visitors ate eagerly and reached often for the platters offered them, and she felt she hardly needed to know more than what her eyes told her: these men had not seen the foods they most desired for a long while. That alone, she thought, should warn her father of what lay ahead for them at the Bosque. Even if the white men were feeding them, they were not filling their bellies.

"It is a wretched land . . ." One of the old ones began to speak as soon as he had fed. "The soldiers herd us like goats, sometimes prodding us with their swords to move to where they wish us to go."

"Where can they wish you to go?" asked a warrior. "You are already where they wish you to go."

"They make us assemble into fenced pens to be counted. They are forever making marks in their little books to make sure that we are all there," the old headman replied wearily. "Many have run away, and others are seeking escape when they can. The soldiers count us every day, and if the count is wrong, they count us again."

"And they keep counting until the count is right or someone tells them who is missing." Another headman spoke up then. "Sometimes we will stand in the corral for many hours, as the heat of the day makes us weak and thirsty. When the women and the children weep, they are told that they may leave when they tell the soldiers who is missing."

"And do they tell them?" Manuelito asked.

The old man shrugged. "Eventually. They cannot wait as long as the soldiers."

"What of the food?" Pahe asked them. "We see that you enjoy what we can offer you here. Is the white man's food not to your liking?"

The third old chief grimaced wryly. "We would eat whatever they gave us, but they give us little. The dark beans, our women boil and boil, and still they are too hard to eat. They give us the white flour and fat, but little meat."

"Why do you not hunt?"

"The game has been driven away. There are too many people and not enough forage, and the game left the land for other places where we cannot follow them. All the cottonwood and mesquite has been cut, and only the roots are left in the ground. The women dig them for firewood."

"And the blankets and the tools they have promised?" Juanita asked him pointedly. "Did you get none of these?"

"They have given many blankets and tools," the fourth old chief answered gravely, "and they are very welcome. But the water there is not good, and the crops will not thrive. We dig and dig, and we carry the water to the seed, but it does not grow."

"That is a truth!" the first old man barked angrily. "We live like prairie dogs. Because there is no wood, we must dig holes in the ground to sleep inside, and the women make mats of the dried grass to keep the dirt from falling upon us as we sleep."

"It sounds like a bad place," Manuelito said soberly.

"The Holy Ones do not live there," one of the old chiefs answered him. "However, you do your people no good by refusing to go. If you come to the Bosque, we can perhaps persuade Star Chief Carl-tun to give us better rations and something with which we can build our houses. We need more sheep and horses. We need medicine for our sick."

"There is sickness there?" asked a woman fearfully.

The old chiefs looked at each other, and one of them sighed regretfully. "There is some. But nothing which we could not cure if we could take care of our own. If you come," he said to Manuelito, "things will be better. And your own clan will not be hunted until the death."

"They will not let you stay on the land," the first old man said firmly. "They will hunt you down. You should think of your people and surrender. We will all be better if we are together once more."

"And yet, many have escaped," Manuelito said. "Many more try to escape each night, you say."

"That is true." They nodded. "We cannot tell you that the Bosque is a good place. It is not. But it is better than being shot by the soldiers. And at least the People will be together once more."

The old man's last words were his most powerful. There was not a woman or a man who listened who had not lost a kinsman or kinswoman to the soldiers, one way or another. Many felt that they could not be whole again until they were reunited, even if that meant coming together under the eyes and the guns of the white men. Pahe glanced at the listeners, watching the way their mouths turned down, the way their eyes filled with frustration and tears of regret. They had been happy, however briefly, and now they were reminded of so many who were gone.

"We will speak of this," Manuelito said, ever the diplomat. "We thank you for coming all this way to tell us your truths."

"You will not come," one of the old headmen murmured softly, almost to himself.

"Come with us," Manuelito said to him gently. "We will hide you."

He shook his head. "There is no hiding from these *Bilagáana*. It is like trying to hide from the wind. You can keep from them for a while, but sooner or later, they will hunt you down. And when they do, they are merciless."

"We will speak no more of this now," Manuelito said, glancing at the soldiers' fire in the distance. "Stay with us and eat your fill, warm your bodies at the fire and we will sing the old songs and dance. That much, at least, we can do."

And so the women brought more food, and the men began to laugh again, and no one said more about the soldiers or the Bosque or those who had been lost forever. The old men slept by the fire, and in the morning when the soldiers came to collect them, Manuelito lied to them and said that as soon as they could collect their flocks, they would follow them back to the fort. Once the soldiers were gone, the band quietly slipped to the north once more to hide among the great canyons of the Colorado.

* * *

Hemi had been hunting her prey for many hours, she knew, for the sun had moved from its position over the mountain to directly overhead. She darted from the shade of one rock to another, her dark wings flicking nervously. The scent of her prey was stronger and stronger; she sensed that it was near now, and she slowed her running stance, moving her antennae cautiously to pick up any sense of the spider.

Hemi was a Tarantula Hawk, *Hemipepsis pompilidae,* a short black spider wasp with orange wings. She was a female with a mission that so possessed her, she was unable to think of anything else but accomplishing her task, even if it meant going without precious nourishment herself until she did so.

She was tracking a tarantula, a spider many times her size and potentially lethal if she did not move faster, if she were not more clever than her prey. And if she died in the attempt, she would lose more than just her life. Hemi was ripe with eggs from her most recent mating, and this mating would likely be her last. She was many summers old, and she sensed her own death approaching. Consequently, she would risk much to see the spider die before she did.

Hemi could tell by the scent of the trail she followed that the tarantula was young and a male; in the same way that another spider could sense these things, she knew. And this was perfect:

a young male would likely be inexperienced. Quick to battle, he might be slow to defend himself, and thus more easily defeated. If it were a female spider she stalked, perhaps even pregnant like herself, Hemi would have been more afraid. The female tarantula was larger, faster, and carried more venom for her size than a wasp. No, Hemi was very glad this track belonged to a male.

She rounded another boulder and quivered with expectancy. There before her was the spider, himself laying in wait for a meal to pass by, and completely exposed to her attack. She buzzed lightly, letting her wings flutter, attracting his attention.

The spider instantly rose to his full height and faced her, bent slightly forward on his front legs, ready to run if necessary. Hemi wasted no time. She ran forward on the ground, and when he crouched to spring, she took to the air, buzzing fiercely over his head, flying tight circles to confuse him. He reached up toward her, and Hemi took her chance, darting between his legs and stinging him once, viciously, in the soft tissue there.

The spider turned to run, trying to take refuge in the fissures between two rocks, but Hemi stung him again, this time where his leg met his body, and he stopped instantly, trembling slightly and weaving. In a second, he was collapsed on the ground, numbed and paralyzed by her stings. His legs stopped moving in the air, his body was stiff and still.

Hemi watched him for a moment on the ground, waiting to be sure that he could not injure her with a sudden bite. She then moved to the spider and took him by one leg and pulled him in small, desperate jerks to a depression of earth overshadowed by the rocks. When she had him there, she did not stop to rest but began to dig furiously, using her mouth parts and her feet to burrow down in the light soil, creating a tunnel just large enough to accommodate the spider. The tunnel took her a good while to dig, and she came up often to check to be sure that the spider was still there, immobilized and safe. It had happened before that just as she had finished digging, she had emerged to discover her prey taken from her, by a bird or a squirrel.

But finally, she was finished, and she enlarged the end of the tunnel to make a terminal chamber in which to bury the spider, kicking out the dirt and turning without pause to the next task ahead.

Now Hemi began to pull and push the spider once more, satisfied with his stiffness that he was still paralyzed, and understanding by his smell that he was still alive. She pushed the spider down the tunnel, shoving him now with all her strength, bracing her back feet and pushing with remarkable fierceness, for if she failed at this juncture, all would be lost. Finally, finally, she got the spider down the tunnel and into the chamber, and only then did she pause for a moment to rest, her wings trembling with fatigue, her legs quivering.

Hemi then climbed on the spider and laid a single egg on the center of his paralyzed abdomen. After examining the egg one final time, she retreated back up out of the chamber, out of the tunnel, into the open air. She then hurriedly buried the entrance to the tunnel, dragging over small pebbles to obscure the site of the digging as best she could.

She felt a sudden weakness overtake her after her arduous task, and she hesitated in the shade of the boulder, her legs bent, her wings quivering slightly. Her egg was safe; she knew that on a deep, cellular level. The egg would hatch, her larva would feed on the spider, first nonessential tissues to keep the prey alive, and then as it grew, it would eat indiscriminately, killing the spider eventually. But not before it was grown to the stage where it would pupate. It would do so on the remains of its host and finally, finally, her offspring would emerge from the tomb she had prepared for it in the next hot season, fully winged and ready to fly.

For that was the way of things. And Hemi knew, also, that the way of things was soon ending for her. This would be her last season. She was slow now as she took to the air, slow and heavy and exhausted. She must be very careful, else she would become prey herself.

*   *   *

There were countless places in the canyons of the Colorado for water to seep and trickle and hide, countless more where once water did flow and now did no more. In these places, the old ones had lived, Pahe knew, for she often found remnants of their lives, their tools, and their bones. The canyons drew her for some inexplicable reason, and she often left the camp and climbed for hours, exploring open caves and small escarpments where old fires had once warmed people now long gone.

Sometimes she carried her small loom with her, for it pleased her to do her weaving in the presence of the spirits. For Pahe, weaving was not a chore, but a rhythm of her days that reminded her who she was. She would carry her lightweight loom on her back up the rocks, her bundles of wool tucked under her bodice. She set it up where she could look down on the mesas and canyons and river below, as though she were a mountain goat, picking her way from perch to perch. Her loom, like most of the women's, was simply built in a vertical stretch of rawhide thongs and smooth branches. It was as familiar to her as her own hair, as comforting as the blanket she wrapped herself in at night, somehow tied to the past and the future in a way she did not quite understand. Her loom was like the land—filled with ancient myths and the silent voices of all who had been there before.

One day, as she sat weaving in an open space of sunlight, sheltered by a rock overhang, high above the canyon below, she thought of one of the first things she remembered seeing as a girl. Within the Canyon de Chelly rose a huge tower of rock which the People called Spider Rock. Her mother had shown it to her as they passed, she riding behind her mother with her bare feet bouncing on the horse's flanks. It rose as high as a mountain upward from the canyon floor with double towers, as though it had been carved by a giant hand from the sandstone around it.

Ayoi said, "That is the home of Spider Woman," pointing to the spire as they rode.

Pahe recalled looking straight up the tower until her neck ached and her eyes were watering from the sun. The memory was so vivid that she could still smell the horse's sweat, still hear the faint howl of the wind on the high mesa, though it was breathless and still there at the bottom of the canyon. Spider Woman, she knew, was the Holy One who taught weaving to the People. Deezbaa had told her.

She remembered standing next to her grandmother's loom, watching her indoors in winter, outdoors on the shaded porch of the weaving hogan in summer, following the tapestry of colors as they rose from the bottom up, bringing to life a design that Deezbaa had in her mind's eye.

She divided the warp evenly by a quick glide of her right hand; with a swishing sound, she lifted her heddle rod, thrust a batten through the warp to hold it open, inserted a strand of red yarn, then beat the wool down on the warp with a boomp, boomp, boomph. While she wove, she sang the rug song softly.

Pahe watched and said, *"Nizhóní."* It is beautiful.

"Aoo', nizhóní," her grandmother murmured. Yes, it is beautiful.

It was exciting to see the wool make the pattern. "You left out a bit there," Pahe had told her grandmother then, pointing to a place where the black border did not quite meet the other border.

"That is for Spider Woman," Deezbaa had told her. "If you do not leave a place for her to come in and out, your next blanket will be poor indeed."

Deezbaa was an expert weaver; so was Ayoi. From them both, Pahe had learned to shear her sheep, selecting the best strands of wool for her loom. She learned how to clean the wool, card it out fine, spin it, and, finally, how to weave it. It seemed to her when she looked back over the years, that the first ten years of her life had been taken up mostly with weaving.

And her first blanket was carried to her father by her mother proudly, for his praise. The blanket was Pahe's property, hers to trade or give away or keep. She remembered that first blanket clearly and every blanket thereafter. She had given it to her grandfather, Narbona. The old man ran his gnarled fingers over the woven wool, searched out the design flaws with a critical eye, and said gravely, "It is well enough. Your next blanket will be better still. And that is important, that you be good, for the others will watch to see what you do."

At that moment, Pahe realized that she would never be allowed to be merely average at anything. She must be better than that, for she was the granddaughter of Narbona, born for Manuelito.

She smiled to herself as she wove the strands now in the sunlight. It seemed to her that Deezbaa was close to her when she wove, that Narbona also stood behind her, nodding silently as she made the colors into the old design he used to favor.

She straightened the crick in her back and paused her work to rest her eyes on the walls of stone around her. It was so still. Somewhere above her, she could hear the brittle rustle of dry grass, the clatter of loose stones kicked up by a bighorn. No other sounds.

The towering slopes of the canyon held her like cupped hands. The old ones had painted the walls, as they had so many of the caves and canyons along the river, with their handprints, their depictions of their hunts, their crops, their marriages and deaths, and the smoke stains from their fires. It seemed to Pahe that they had only been gone from these places a season or two, so vivid were their markings. She felt their spirits close to her, and she felt comforted. She knew that many of the People were afraid of the dead, frightened by the thought that a spirit might hover close to those still alive, but Pahe found it strangely reassuring to feel that many who had once walked these lands had stayed behind to watch over those who came after.

Suddenly, a raven wheeled into her view, first from below and then rising sharply on the thermal breeze, following it in a spiral all the way up to where she watched. She held her breath. The raven went past her, on up into the white sky, and then fell again, as though the breath she held was somehow part of the breeze he rode. He cawed at her loudly three times, and she fell still, listening as hard as she was able, her hands dropping down to her sides as though she slept.

"Betrayal, betrayal, betrayal!" he called to her, his voice wavering first strong and then faint, as he spiraled above her.

She felt a shimmer of fear and then she shook it off. She lifted one hand and beckoned to the bird in slow, waving circles. "Come and speak to me, then," she said as calmly as she could. "I cannot hear you."

"You hear me well," Raven answered, and his bill was open as he passed, she could see him that closely.

"Speak, then," she said, trying to keep her fear behind her, tucked into her skirt. "I listen. Is Death coming once more?"

"Death is always coming." Raven chuckled suddenly, surprising her. "And never when it is convenient. But the white man does not bring it this time. He brings betrayal."

"Well, and that is nothing new," she said wryly, attempting to match Raven's humor. She suspected that the gods liked to laugh even more than they liked to play with people. "Tell me something I do not know, O Raven. Tell me what I must do."

"You must be strong," Raven said. "You must surrender."

"Surrender! To the white man? What has this to do with being strong?" Pahe asked, astounded. She looked about as if to see someone or something listening. "Who are you? Why should I listen to your warning?"

Raven croaked gleefully. "Do not listen then, O She-Who-Hears-The-Sun. I shall go and tell my tale to the wind instead."

"I am sorry," Pahe said, hanging her head in what she hoped was her most humble display. "Please tell me what I must do."

Raven wheeled away, riding the thermals downward again. "I have said it. Surrender."

"And be betrayed."

"Awwrk-wwrk!" he cried, dipping one wing down and staring right at her. "Surrender and save your life!"

"And what of my daughter?"

"She will live, if you are strong." Raven was almost out of sight.

"Wait!" she called out frantically, angry at herself for having driven him away with disrespect. How did she dare to question the Holy Ones?

But Raven was gone as quickly as he had come.

She sighed and gathered up her weaving and her loom, packing it carefully on her back. Now what had been a place full of sun and peace was thronged with worry and doubt. Betrayal. He spoke of this once before, and it was true. She had told no one but her mother, and they had been attacked. Now she must tell Manuelito, for surely Raven had come to her for a reason. It was too much to carry that knowledge alone.

When she returned to the camp, she found Ayoi and Manuelito at opposite sides of the fire, bickering as usual. In a rare display of anger, her father strode off across the camp, throwing back over his shoulder, "I will not be back tonight!"

"I will give thanks to all the gods!" Ayoi called back to him harshly.

Pahe sat down next to her mother silently. After a long moment, she murmured, "You two have shared a blanket too long to be so hateful to one another."

"Sometimes that's the *best* reason to hate each other," Ayoi retorted shortly. "He can be such a fool, that man."

"And you can be so forgiving," Pahe said. "Perhaps it is good to remember that none of us has exactly what we would wish right now. But if we do not stand together, we will not survive."

"With any luck, I will be standing far longer than your father," Ayoi said. "And a goodly distance from where I last saw him. Let Juanita have him, the old lizard."

Pahe could not help smiling ruefully. Her mother's anger often made her laugh. "So, how has he offended you this time?"

"By being stupid. A runner came with a message," she said.

Pahe looked up with surprise. "Here? A runner came to this canyon?"

"Yes, and they were *Dinéh*," she said, using the word for the People. "The message was from the Star Chief."

"All the way from Fort Wingate? How did they get here?"

"The same way we did. Only our own could have found us."

"What did they say?" She rose to go after her father, for this was large news indeed.

"There is no reason to rush to hear these words," Ayoi said dryly. "Indeed, they will likely outlive us all. They say that the Star Chief sends his warning. He will hunt us down to the death unless we surrender before the grass is green."

"Surrender," Pahe murmured, reeling with the word. "Raven told me as much."

Ayoi glanced at her sharply. "Raven has come to you again? What did he tell you?"

"Where is Dolii?" Pahe asked, suddenly anxious, half rising from her seat.

"She is fine; she is at the fire of Juanita. What did Raven say?"

"He said that we must surrender."

"How did he come to you this time?"

"While I was weaving. Up the canyon—" She pointed dazedly up the steep walls.

"Perhaps it was Spider Woman, since you were weaving—"

"What does it matter," sighed Pahe. "We will not surrender. And we will be betrayed, even if we do."

"He said this as well?"

"Just as he did before."

"Before the attack by the Hopi dogs," Ayoi murmured thoughtfully. "Surrender. This was the word of the runners."

"And what did my father say to them?"

Ayoi shrugged. "What he always says. He told them that he does no harm to any man. That he is an honest farmer."

Pahe shook her head. "Why should they believe him when he says this? The white men surely have memories better than this. Of course, he has broken the promise of peace. So have they. That is not the point. He should promise to keep the peace in the future and not bring up the past. They will never believe him otherwise."

"It does not matter," Ayoi said disgustedly. "You and your father, you are all windy talk. He told them to tell the Star Chief that he will not leave his land. He told them he intends to die here." She jabbed her stick into the fire to make the embers glow. "He will do that, and sooner than he thinks."

"You think we should surrender?" Pahe asked her.

"I think if we do not, they will come and shoot us down, as they have so many others."

"What else did he say?"

"That is all. He agreed to talk again with the other headmen, some of those who have been to the lands to the east and who can tell us what we will find there. But what does that matter? They have already told us. We still must go. Whatever is there, it cannot be as bad as death. At least when we are all together, like Armijo told us, we will be stronger."

"And so they are coming?"

"They are out of patience." Ayoi shook her head. "The soldiers will simply come and kill us all."

"And so, you told my father that he was a fool." Pahe took the stick from her mother's hand and knocked her shoulder with it gently. "You are your mother's daughter."

"So are you," Ayoi said shortly. "None of us can escape that."

Pahe went after her father and found him at the fire of Juanita also. He looked more sad than angry. She sat beside him and gently touched his arm, looking into his face. He smiled wanly at her. "It seems we have not run so far after all," he said.

"Only our own people could have found us," she reassured him. She glanced at Dolii, who was working with Juanita over a basket, watching her weave the split sumac into a pattern. Their heads were bent together, and they were murmuring, absorbed in their work. She lowered her voice. "Raven has come to me, Father, and he has given me a warning from the Holy Ones."

"Today? This has happened this morning?" He did not look as surprised as she had thought he would.

"Yes, as I was weaving. He said that we must surrender."

Manuelito chuckled bitterly. "He must have visited with your mother before he visited with you."

"He spoke, too, of betrayal."

"If we do not surrender?"

"After we surrender. But we must surrender to save our lives."

Manuelito sighed and shook his head slightly. "I am well known among these hills, these canyons, these rocks. Here is *nihzhónígo*, where we walk in beauty. There is noplace but here. We cannot leave this land."

"We have already left our land," Pahe pointed out gently. "We have crossed the Colorado, we have crossed the San Juan, we have left our pastures and our springs. We are sojourners now in a strange place. What does it matter where we are strangers?"

"You say to me that we should surrender?" he asked. "My daughter, wife to Nataallith, granddaughter of Narbona, you say this to me?"

She shook her head. "I tell you only what Raven said to me. I do not know what is best. You are headman. You must tell the People."

He gazed into the fire. "I told the runners to say to the soldiers that I will meet again with those who have seen the Bosque for themselves. But not with headmen who have few kinsmen there. I will meet only with Herrero Grande at the Zuni trading post. I will hear him only tell of the place. I will decide what to do then."

"We have already done this. We try their patience, my father. They will capture us or shoot us when they find us."

"Then they will do what they will do. I have told them I will talk about this place one more time. The people murmur more and more, and I must do something. Perhaps they need to hear about the Bosque again—"

She sat down heavily and leaned on his shoulder, suddenly exhausted. "They are weary. It is hard enough to be away from their homes, but to be apart from the rest of the People, that is most difficult of all."

"Most difficult of all is death," Manuelito said, his voice rough and graveled. "Anything else is bearable."

For you, Father, Pahe thought silently. For the warriors, perhaps. But for the women, the children, the old ones, there might be worse tortures than death.

To Pahe's surprise, however, the runners brought word that once more there would be council.

And so, once more, they traveled to the south, past their old lands this time and then to the Zuni trading post, where they made camp in a hidden canyon several miles from the meeting place. Manuelito then went to the post to meet with Herrero Grande and five other headmen who had been to the Bosque and back again. He embraced them and led them back, with the soldiers who were guarding them, to the canyon camp.

The wind was cold, and all the people were wearing whatever blankets they had, and still Pahe could see that the headmen were thin and worn, their bodies without the flesh and muscle that men should have. They sat at Manuelito's fire and said again what all already knew: that the Bosque was a bad place. But, they said, it could be better if leaders like Manuelito would come; it could be better than being hunted down like wolves by the Star Chief.

All the while they talked, the soldiers stayed mounted, their horses blowing white steam clouds and stamping their hooves in the light snow.

Manuelito gestured to the men and women and children who sat and listened to the talk. "Here is all I have in the world," he said. "We have few sheep and fewer horses. We are poor. My children are eating palmilla roots. We threaten no one. We wish only to be left alone."

Herrero Grande said, "They will not suffer you to stay on the land, my friend. Not when they have captured so many."

"But we are peaceful."

"They do not care for peace," Herrero Grande said. "They want the land."

Manuelito said defiantly, "Well, and they can take it. But they cannot take us, as well."

For hours, the men talked back and forth. At first, Manuelito said he would surrender, for the sake of the women and children and old ones. Then he said that he would need until spring to get the horses ready to make the journey. And finally, he refused once more.

"I cannot surrender. Tell them this for me. My gods and my people live in these lands, and I will not leave them. The winds will not speak to me there. The Holy Ones will not know us there. The Holy Ones said that we should never cross the three rivers— yet we have done so. Perhaps it has only made us weaker. I will cross them no more. I will not leave the Chuska Mountains. I was born there and I shall remain there. *Shikéyah,* my land is my home. Let them come and kill me. I will not surrender. If they kill me, a peaceful man, they will shed innocent blood. Tell them that."

Herrero Grande stood and shook his head gently. The other headmen stood as well. "I have done all I can for you, old friend. I give you good advice. I leave you now, as though your grave is already made."

Pahe looked and saw that the soldiers had moved closer to the fire, still mounted and alert to any movements of the People. Clearly, they had been told to make sure that Herrero Grande and the other headmen did not escape with Manuelito's band. She stood and went to where Ayoi and Dolii sat, just back from the talkers. "They have little meat on their bones," she said to Ayoi, gesturing to the headmen who were slowly mounting the horses held for them by the soldiers. She saw that some of them suffered from the swollen lips and fingers of frostbite.

"We have less," Ayoi said. "But at least we are starving in freedom." She said that last with some disgust.

"You weaken my father with your words," Pahe said shortly to her mother. "He cannot fight all of the white men and you as well. Dolii, come back away from the soldiers," she said to her daughter, pulling her up to her feet. Dolii had turned to watch the soldiers and the headmen as they were leaving, and Pahe felt a sudden gust of fear blow through her heart. Betrayal. On which wind would it come?

The next morning, twenty-six more of the People announced that they would follow the soldiers across the Zuni lands to the fort to surrender. They did not wish to walk back to the deep canyon hideouts of the Colorado; neither did they wish to cross the river one more time.

Manuelito did not attempt to dissuade them. He wished them well and then went inside the shelter with his back to the door. As those who were leaving gathered to embrace their kinsmen in farewell, Ayoi said suddenly, "I will go with them to the Bosque."

"You cannot mean it!" Pahe said angrily.

Ayoi said, "I am too weary to go all the way back to a place I do not wish to be. Your father can hold out to the death if he wishes. I am going to surrender."

"You will not!" Pahe said, trying to pull her mother back to the shelter.

Ayoi shook off her hand. "Look at us, my daughter! We are being winnowed down to nothing! Come with me and bring Dolii, and at least we will be with the rest of our people. She can find a husband; she will have the babies she was meant to have in this life. If we go, then he will follow." She dropped her voice as she firmly pulled her arm from Pahe's grip. "The Holy Ones have told you what you must do. Will you be deaf to their words as well as all reason? No matter how hard it is at the Bosque, it cannot be worse than spending another winter in the wastelands of the Colorado. Come with me. Your father will do what he has to do."

"You have lost your mind," Pahe said. "You cannot do this to him."

Ayoi smiled grimly. "I may be saving his life. If there are no more of us to protect, perhaps he will surrender before they shoot him down."

Pahe looked at Dolii, who watched them both with wide eyes and open mouth of amazement. "Do you wish to do this thing also, my daughter?"

Dolii slowly nodded, as though only realizing it for the first time. "I would not have thought of it, but if the others are going—"

"Only some of them," Pahe said.

"More will follow," Ayoi said, "if they know that the wife of Manuelito goes also. He will follow also, I know it."

Pahe went then to her father. He looked up wearily. She saw that he knew everything. Before she could speak, he said, "Do what you think best, my daughter. The white men have sworn to kill me. I have no doubt that they will keep that word, at least. It may be for the best if I do not have to watch my people die as well."

"You tell me to surrender?" she asked, her words faint and harsh in her throat.

"I tell you to care for your mother," he said. "That is your duty."

She felt a great numbness steal over her. "Will it be easier for you if we go?"

"Nothing is easy for me. But at least I will not have to see your mother suffer." He turned his back to her and waved her away silently.

Pahe stumbled from the shelter, her eyes bright with tears and her heart pounding. Dolii met her and embraced her. Over her daughter's shoulder, Pahe saw that Ayoi was already gathering her bundles and saying her farewells. "If we are to do this," Pahe murmured to Dolii, "let us do it quickly. I cannot stand it otherwise."

In a daze, Pahe collected what small things she had left, Dolii bundled them on to a horse, and they went to Juanita to embrace her and say farewell. She did not weep, but only turned her head away as though in shame. They then went back to Manuelito to say good-bye. He stood and embraced Dolii, saying, "Walk in beauty always, my granddaughter. We will likely meet again before the green months are over."

To Pahe, he murmured, "Make your mother ride. She will wish to walk, to show that she can, but make her take the horse. When you get to the Bosque, go to Armijo and tell him I will come soon."

"And will you?" she asked.

He shrugged. "Perhaps. Let him think so, regardless. Be well, my daughter."

Her throat burned with unshed tears. "Be well, my father."

They were a mile away from the camp, following the others through the snow back to the Zuni trading post when the numb, dazed state that had enveloped her slipped away, and she suddenly began to weep. Her tears came so hard and fast that they did not freeze but fell upon her blanket and blurred her eyes and made her stumble. Dolii took her arm and they walked together then, weeping, their hands around each other for strength. Ayoi rode ahead on the brown mare. She did not look back.

PART THREE

1865–1868

"All is beautiful where I dream.
All is beautiful where I dream.
I dream amid the Dawn and all is beautiful
I dream amid the White Corn and all is beautiful
I dream amid the Beautiful Goods and all is beautiful
I dream amid the Mixed Waters and all is beautiful
I dream amid all the Pollens and all is beautiful
I am the Most-High-Power-Whose-Ways-Are-Beautiful
And I dream that all is beautiful."

—A Mountain Chant as sung by At'ééd
Jóhonaa'éí Yidiits'a'í

It took six days of walking to reach the Zuni trading post, for
they moved slowly, burdened with grief and fear, pushing the
sheep ahead of them. Each day, they ended in the canyons, where
there was just enough forage to keep the sheep from collapse,
just enough water to keep them going a few more miles. Ayoi
had more sheep than anyone, yet even her herd was only a fraction
of what it had been before. Dolii was able to herd them easily,
with just one dog. It was just as well. It would have been too
hard to see them die of starvation before their eyes.

New snow fell on the third day, and three of the old ones sat
down on their haunches, refusing to budge: an ancient grandmother and two aged grandfathers, all from the same clan.

"Leave us," the old woman said bitterly. "One place to die is
as good as another." She began to chant her Death Song.

Pahe sat down beside the three old ones and pleaded with
them to come a few miles farther, into the shelter of a nearby
canyon. She was surprised that their own children seemed not to
have the strength or will to argue them back into life.

Ayoi handed her horse's reins to Dolii and urged her to mount.
She came to where the three old ones were huddled and called
out, "Ayii, Grandparents! You have come this far just to give
up?"

None of them met her eyes. The two old men seemed too weary
to even raise their heads.

"Me, I would not wish to die out in the open where the wolves might disturb my bones," she added, almost casually. "Then I would be a ghost and wander all these lands in solitude." She spat on the frozen ground. "Me, I would rather die close to the white fort or perhaps even within their walls. Then I could give them all the ghost sickness and take my revenge on them for generations."

The old grandmother looked up at Ayoi skeptically, but Ayoi was looking to the east now, as though she might see the fort walls themselves.

The old woman closed her eyes and sighed wearily. Finally, when she saw that Ayoi was not going to leave her in peace, she grunted heavily and struggled to rise. Pahe helped her up. She kicked angrily at her spouse, shoving him against the other old grandfather. "Get up," she said to them imperiously. "There are better places to die."

Without a word the old men struggled to their feet also, and the long caravan of weary travelers went forward once more.

Pahe said to Ayoi as they walked alongside the horse, beating their herding sticks rhythmically on the frozen ground, "Someone will have to lead them. They are accustomed to having a headman suggest what must be done—"

"Your father will come soon enough," Ayoi said stubbornly. "He will not let me go to the whites alone."

Pahe glanced up at Dolii, who nodded in silent agreement. So they both believed that salvation would come at any time, as it always had, in the figure of Manuelito. Pahe closed her eyes in weary sorrow. Neither of them had lost a husband; neither had lost a son. Both of them still thought that, somehow, the men around them would never be defeated; indeed, would live forever. Pahe could not bring herself to tell them how futile she thought such a wait for deliverance might be.

They walked for many days, expecting at any time to be attacked by slave raiders, almost hoping to see soldiers over every rise. Finally, they made it to the Zuni trading post, and the soldiers there immediately herded them into a small encampment with the other refugees. They added their small flocks to the pitiful herds already corralled and joined the lines of waiting people outside the high fort walls.

Pahe waited with Dolii, for Ayoi was too weary to come with them. Ahead of her, the line seemed to stretch on forever, and she wondered that the People would wait so patiently, like so many sheep. How had they come to such a place?

Slowly the line moved forward, the People huddled together against the cold wind. As she neared the front, Pahe could hear the words of those who were ahead. There was not enough, the words came back quickly through the line. All of the food had been given out. All of the blankets were gone. And some of the men stepped forward in weak anger. But the soldiers said that provisions were coming in a few days from Fort Wingate, together with wagons to take them to the Bosque Redondo. In the meantime, the soldiers said, they would simply have to share what was available as best they could. Those in the back turned to those in the front who were walking away with their hands outstretched, calling to kinsmen to share what little was in their hands.

Dolii and Pahe and Ayoi were among the fortunate, for many of the People recognized them instantly as wives and daughters of important headmen. They were taken in by distant kin from the Red-Earth Streaked clan, given what food could be spared and dry blankets.

"These are thin as Hopi hearts," Ayoi grumbled, pulling the ragged piece of cloth about her shoulders.

"Better than nothing," Dolii sighed.

"Barely," Pahe said, huddling as close to her mother and daughter as she could. "If this is what the whites think are blankets, I fear to see what they think is food."

"How soon before the wagons come?" Ayoi asked.

Pahe shrugged. "As slowly as the *Bilagáana* do these things, it would not surprise me if we spent the winter here—"

"The longer they take, the better. When your father comes, he will make them give us better food and more horses," Ayoi said staunchly.

"Yes," Pahe agreed, unwilling to add her own doubts to their discomfort.

"How many are we?" Dolii asked.

"I cannot tell. More than I thought. But they say many have died since they came."

Ayoi snorted bitterly. "From the poison white dust, no doubt, and the black beans. If this is what the whites eat, then it is no wonder we are beaten. They are already ghosts."

The white dust, white wheat flour, and the black beans, coffee beans, were the staples given to the People once they gathered for the journey to the Bosque. When the women tried to make a gruel from the flour, as they would their own cornmeal, the unpalatable mess gave those who ate it sickness and cramps. No matter how many times the women boiled the dark beans, they could not make them into a stew or a paste like the Spanish beans. The coffee beans remained hard and inedible, and they threw out the black water they produced, for no one told them to drink it. And so, the soldiers kept bringing the food, and the People remained hungry, parceling out what small stores they had with them, trading what they could for foodstuffs they recognized, and killing their dogs and their goats to stay alive.

Meanwhile, the coyotes had gathered around the walls of the fort, and they boldly followed anyone on foot who went for wood or water. The hawks and the crows circled constantly overhead, looking for a stray animal or a human being who did not move.

Each morning, the bugle blew, and the People lined up to receive their food, something white and something black, and sometimes a tough-rinded slab of bacon. "There is more food at the Bosque," the soldiers told them as they walked away, trying to lick the white flour from their hands.

The white sentries passed around the encampment every hour, speaking only to each other, and when the headmen attempted to ask for council, they were turned away. The women walked as far as they could to find wood for cooking, but there was not enough to spare for shelter. Instead, they made what shelter they could from mounded earth, digging deeply in the hard ground and piling the soil high in frozen bricks that they might be protected from the wind.

Finally, the wagons arrived, and, with them, more food and blankets. The People began to believe that, indeed, the wagons had come from a place of plenty, a place they should get to as soon as they could. And so when, at the end of March, the month when the animals give birth and the fields are blessed before planting, nearly a thousand refugees began the Long Walk to the Bosque Redondo, they had some hope. Pahe and Ayoi and Dolii walked among them, herding their small flock as best they could.

The People quickly fell into the routine of travel, although they were not strong, well fed, or rested. They walked with the children and the old ones in the middle, talking quietly and weeping sometimes. They told themselves often why they had come. Pahe heard a man say, "Our family, we talked it over and we decided to go to this place. At least we will be safe from the gunfire and we will be together. They killed our sheep right before our eyes. They were like our children and the women wept. I cannot listen to the weeping anymore."

The soldiers followed on all sides so that no one would wander away or fall behind. Twenty-three wagons carried the sick, the aged, or the very young. Everyone else walked, pushing the animals ahead of them.

After the third day of travel, more than fifteen miles each day, the weakest horses began to stumble. When one fell, a soldier sentry immediately shot it dead. The clan who had owned the unfortunate animal hastily slaughtered it, divided up what meat they could carry, and kept on. The next day, three more horses fell and were killed.

From then on, the coyotes followed the lone line of wagons and walkers, marching a few abreast in family clans, just like the People themselves. Overhead, the crows and the buzzards circled, moving as the wagons moved.

On the sixth day, a late snowstorm roared down upon the wagons, and the walkers, some of them nearly naked, stumbled hunched over and huddled together, trying to keep warm. Four more horses were lost, and those clans who lost the horses tried to squeeze their aged or lame into the wagons. Finally, there was not another inch of space, and some of the old ones had to be left behind. Their relations gave them some food and left them on the side of the trail, walking on, openly weeping. When they were out of sight, a soldier left the wagons and rode back. They heard the gunshots behind them.

Ayoi led her mare herself, unwilling to have a soldier touch her horse, even to tie it to a wagon.

"You should ride," Pahe told her. "Your small body can scarcely make a difference to her, and you cannot walk all the way—"

"I certainly can," Ayoi said stubbornly. "When I get to the Bosque, I will ride up to the hogans with my back straight and a healthy horse under me. That is worth a walk, I am thinking."

"And I am thinking, better a healthy grandmother than a healthy horse," Dolii said, coming up behind them. She had her blanket hooded over her face so that she was scarcely visible beneath its folds.

"The horse will be worth more than a dozen grandmothers when we get to the Bosque," Ayoi said.

Pahe silently scanned the skies above her, as she had been doing ever since she left her father. So long as her daughter and her mother were talking, she knew they were surviving well enough. She felt that the Holy Ones would send her another message soon; she had been expecting to see Raven on each new wind. With every step she took farther from her father, she felt she took a step closer to peril, and yet her mind told her heart again and again that if Manuelito were with them, there would be nothing he could do to protect them, nothing more than what the other headmen were able to do to protect their families.

"Your neck is going to freeze in that position," Ayoi said to her quietly, when Dolii had moved off a few yards. "If Raven comes again, believe me, he will be sure to get your attention."

Pahe laughed ruefully. "You are probably right." She glanced at her mother who kept her head up, her eyes straight ahead, as though she walked in the body of a younger woman. "Do you think he will be there when we arrive?"

"Your father? Perhaps. Or perhaps he will fight to the death and we will be telling tales of his courage to your grandchildren."

She said this so calmly that Pahe was immediately affronted. She snorted indignantly. "Grandchildren! One must first have a son-in-law, even in times such as these. And one must have a daughter who wishes to live long enough to think of such things."

To her surprise, Ayoi laughed loudly, causing Dolii to glance back at them curiously and two soldiers to look in their direction. "And you think she does not? I will make you a wager, She-Who-Expects-Misfortune. Our little bluebird will be a married woman within a season, once we reach the white man's paradise."

Pahe shook her head in disbelief. "You had better get up on that horse, old woman. You're going to have to live a long time to see either grandchildren or paradise."

The sentries suddenly stopped the column and blew the bugle, as they did when the sun was high every day.

"They are such fools," Ayoi said, shaking her head. "Every day, it is the same."

Pahe nodded. "I do not understand this, either. Why stop the journey when the sun is high in a place with no shelter? The sun reaches the middle of the sky and the bugle blows, just as though the sun itself is making the decision. When we travel, we move with the sheep, from shade to water, and the hour of the day does not matter. But the *Bilagáana* do all things by the movement of the sun."

"And so," Ayoi grumbled, "we must take our midday meal when the sun says so, no matter that there is no shade and no water. How did they ever get to be such a large tribe?"

The sheep and goats spread out over the spaces around the wagons, searching out the small patches of brush and nibbling at shrubs which were largely bare of foliage. Pahe knew that by nightfall, they would be so hungry that they would be difficult to keep herded together.

Dolii and Ayoi sat together huddled under their blankets, eating the mutton jerky Pahe had prepared before they left. She walked over to where the sheep were grazing and watched them, counting them again. Twenty-eight sheep and goats, most of them belonging to Ayoi, were all they owned in the world. Last season, between her own flocks, Ayoi's, and those which belonged to Dolii, they had more than three hundred animals. And the year before that, twice that many. And they were wealthy women, compared to most! She shook her head in silent disbelief. Of course, this is what Narbona said: that what made the People the People was their willingness to take responsibility for each other, and so the flocks had gone to feed others of the clan who had lost more. Nearly a thousand people they were when they left Fort Canby. Now, they had lost two score. How many more would never see the Bosque alive?

Two nights before, a pregnant woman of a distant clan who kept falling behind was taken behind the rocks by the soldiers and shot before her kinsmen could intervene. She did not make a sound. And still, they kept telling themselves that they would be safe if they stayed together.

One of the largest ewes came toward her and planted herself right before Pahe, bleating impatiently.

"I know, Mother," Pahe soothed her. "There will be more to eat by nightfall." In the distance, she could see the band of coyotes which had been following them, watching silently from the rise of the hills. Despite the soldiers and their guns, they were much bolder than she recalled.

They smell Death among us, she thought. And they are right enough, as always.

She pulled the mutton jerky from her blanket and chewed it thoughtfully. For some reason, she was rarely hungry on this journey. As though her whole body was only feet and legs, her stomach seemed asleep. She peered down at her moccasins. They were already worn through. Soon, they would have to slaughter another goat, just to have something to wrap around their feet. Many of the People were walking barefooted over the ground, and she knew that some would never be able to make it to the Bosque without some sort of protection. The soldiers rarely let them stop to rest, and they said it was three hundred miles to travel.

Pahe did not know what three hundred miles was, but the way they pushed them, it must be a far distance indeed.

A movement in the distance caught her eye. She narrowed her eyes against the sun and saw that the coyote band was moving closer to the flock. She watched them, waiting to see what they would do. They approached nearer and then stopped, the rest of the band waiting while one lone, large male trotted confidently toward her. He was watching her as he came, and she knew instantly that something was suddenly changed.

She walked to the far edge of the flock, putting herself between the oncoming coyote and the sheep. She glanced back once at Dolii and Ayoi, but no one was watching her except the soldier sentry.

When the coyote was close enough so that she could see his teeth clearly when he panted, she sat on the ground and faced him. She was not surprised when he sat, as well, facing her, not at all intimidated by her nearness.

"O Holy One," she called to the animal. "I have been expecting you."

The coyote glanced at the far sentry, revealing his only caution, and then he growled slightly, letting his tongue loll out as he panted. A voice came to Pahe's mind then, as clearly as though it came from the coyote's mouth, though she could not see his grin change in any way.

"*Ya'at'eeh*," the coyote said to her, "Hello, At'ééd Jóhonaa'éí Yidiits'a'í. You are far from your lands."

"I am always far from my lands these days, I'm afraid," she sighed aloud. "We have surrendered to the *Bilagáana*. Many have died."

"Many more will follow that path," the coyote said.

"Will my father come?" she asked, surprised even in her own heart that her mind thought to ask this question first.

"In time. But this is what you must know. You must listen well, O She-Who-Hears-The-Sun, and you must tell the People what you hear. It will be hard for them to hear the old songs, the old laws in the place of the white man. You must be their ears."

"This is all you can tell me? That I must listen well? But I am not a Singer. Why have you come to me? Will you come again, O Holy One? Once we have reached the—"

"You are speaking. You are not listening," the coyote said in her mind, yawning hugely.

She could see his canines clearly at that distance. She dropped her head in humility.

"The People will come back to their lands," he said slowly, "but only if they keep to the old ways and the old laws. You must tell them."

"We will come back to *Dinétah!*" she gasped, unbelieving. "We will defeat the *Bilagáana?*"

The coyote rose suddenly with a quick expression of disgust, as though he had suddenly smelled something bad on the wind. She instantly dropped her head again in shame. "I am speaking again," she said humbly. "I am sorry, Holy One."

The coyote settled himself down again wearily. "You will not defeat the *Bilagáana*. The land will defeat the *Bilagáana*. You must survive until they are defeated. You will only survive in the old ways, and the People will listen to you as they will not to the old ones, for you and your clan are the future. And now, you may ask one question, She-Who-Hears-The-Sun, and it will be answered."

She thought quickly, trying to decide what was the one thing her heart most needed to know. "Will my daughter live to have daughters of her own?"

The coyote's grin widened and he panted harder, as he rose to trot off. He threw back over his shoulder, "That is three questions, to these ears. Will she live? Will she live long enough to have children? Will they be daughters?"

The laughter rang in her ears, not a sound of maliciousness, simply amusement at her attempt to wrest more from his offer than he was prepared to give.

"I will answer one of these three, Daughter of Manuelito. She will live." The words slid out of her head as soon as they were inside, for the coyote was now out of hearing, and only the sound of the breeze blew back to her from where he joined his comrades and they trotted away.

Pahe turned, dazed, and walked back to the wagons. To her

mind, it seemed as though many hours had passed, yet she could see by the way Dolii and Ayoi were still in their places that scarcely moments had gone by. She noted with some curiosity that the sheep and goats made wide berths around her, as though she still had something of the coyote inside her.

She hunkered down next to Dolii and Ayoi. Dolii handed her the army canteen, but she shook her head. She was trying to accustom herself to little water during the day, saving her thirst for the water they would reach with each sundown. Anyway, the water from the white man's canteen tasted horrible in her mouth, no matter how much sage she chewed after she drank.

"They will blow the wretched bugle soon," Ayoi grumbled.

"The Holy Ones have finally come again," Pahe said quickly, forgetting that Dolii had not known of their other appearances.

"What do you mean?" her daughter asked.

"Your mother has had Raven appear and speak to her two different times," Ayoi provided casually. "Each time, the Holy Ones warned her of a betrayal."

Dolii's eyes widened. "But you have never told me of this!"

"I did not wish to alarm you," Pahe said quietly. "And as it happened, there was little they told me that I could do anything about."

"I did not see Raven," Ayoi said.

Pahe could tell by her tone that Ayoi enjoyed sounding as though she knew as much about the visitations as Pahe did. "Raven did not speak to me this time. Coyote came and told me."

Dolii turned and stared out past the wagons to where the coyotes had lingered. They were no longer there. "A coyote talked to you?" Her eyes were wider still and full of fear now.

Pahe laughed lightly. "Do not worry, little bluebird, your mother is not losing her mind. Sometimes, when we get older, we hear voices many places."

"Not all of us," Ayoi said. "But She-Who-Hears-The-Sun hears more than most. It is a thing to be proud of, that your mother speaks to the Holy Ones!"

"Actually," Pahe sighed, "I do little speaking. Each time, I am told to listen more and speak less."

Ayoi laughed at that.

The bugle blew then and the three women automatically rose to take their place alongside the wagon, that the soldiers might count them before moving forward. Dolii said, "Did Grandfather know that the Holy Ones come to you?"

Pahe nodded. "And it does not happen often. Only twice before."

"Like Deezbaa," Dolii murmured.

"I suppose."

"Well, and what did they say to you this time?" Ayoi asked impatiently. "Yet another warning of betrayal? We've already surrendered. What else can happen?"

"We could die," Dolii said softly.

"No, we will not," Pahe said firmly. "And even more, we will one day return to these lands."

"Us? Or the children of our grandchildren?" Ayoi asked.

"The coyote told me that we would be returning to these lands." Pahe smiled. "That is something good at least."

"But that is wonderful news!" Dolii gasped. "How soon?"

"What was the bad news?" Ayoi asked, ever vigilant.

Pahe realized that the more she spoke of the words of the Holy One, the more she would likely reveal that she had asked only of the fate of her daughter—not her mother. One of the sentries moved down the line of wagons then and shouted at them to bunch up, and she took that opportunity to turn the subject away from herself. "Come on," she said, taking Dolii's arm. "We better not waste our breath on any more of this. There really was nothing bad in the message, only that we must listen to the old songs and the old laws when we are at the new place. And I must help the People hear. That was all."

"But, Mother, we are going home! They promised."

Pahe saw that in a moment, Dolii was able to believe. So long as the news was good, she was willing to accept that a coyote spoke with her mother and foretold the future. "The Holy One said so. They never promise, I think. They merely say what is so."

Dolii closed her eyes in happiness, gripping her mother's hand.

"We can stand anything, then. If we know we are going home again soon."

Ayoi peered at Pahe skeptically, but at her warning frown, she did not ask again.

*   *   *

It seemed to Pahe, after a full moon of walking, that she had never done anything but make this journey across the desert, following the wagons. She no longer wondered how much farther they must go; she somehow expected that she would simply keep moving all of the days of her life.

Ayoi was riding the horse now, for she was unable to walk the miles that the wagons went every day. The soldiers were weary of leaving so many alongside the trail, and they slowed the wagons, hoping that more could keep up. They even took a day occasionally and did not move at all, using the time to rest and to let the sheep graze.

When they reached rivers, they lost more people, for they did not know how to swim, and some were swept away by the current. They screamed, and only an arm, a leg, a strand of floating hair could be seen of them as they disappeared.

Finally, they crossed the Rio Grande, and the People knew then that they had completely left their lands, could not even see them anymore in the distance when they looked backward. They had crossed the great river which their Holy Ones had told them must never be crossed, and a certain resignation fell upon the travelers then, and they no longer seemed to care whether they went forward or stayed where they were. The soldiers had to shout at them angrily to get them to get back in the wagons, and even the arrival of more provisions from fresh wagons did little to raise their spirits.

When they reached Los Piños, below Albuquerque, other soldiers came and took away all of the wagons, forcing them to unload all of their belongings onto the open ground. The soldiers said that they would camp there until the wagons were returned. In the week they waited, four children were kidnapped by the New Mexican slave raiders when they wandered away from the fires in daylight. One of the mothers could not be consoled, and she cut her neck with a knife so badly that she bled to death before the soldiers could be called. Finally, the wagons were returned, and they traveled on.

Every night, Dolii examined her grandmother's feet, rubbing mutton fat into her heels and looking for thorns or tiny cuts. Ayoi walked little of the miles now, for her feet were weak, and within a short time, she was limping too badly to keep up. Each night, she insisted that their fire be high and bright, however, so that Manuelito might find them more easily in the darkness of the desert.

They had better food out of Albuquerque, but it seemed to come too late. By the time they reached Puerto de Luna, the Door to the Moon, a little village just to the north of the Bosque, more than a hundred had died, the coyotes had carried off a third of the flocks, and every family had either buried a loved one or left one along the trail to wait for death alone.

The land was different now, completely barren with only a few tufts of coarse salt grass or dry spikes of yucca sticking up into the endless white sky. Pahe had never seen a land so desolate, without even a rock or a tree to break up the vast expanse of flatness. Surely, she told herself, it could not be so at the new land, else everyone there would be dead.

Day after day they traveled over the flatness, and every night the bugle called them to line up for the black beans and the white meal and strips of hard meat, what the whites called bacon. By now, they had learned to boil the beans to make a black drink, but they could not get used to the bitter taste. They lay down in their blankets with the babies crying from hunger and the old ones fretting over the emptiness of the land. They saw no fields; they saw no mountains.

And every morning the bugle blew again, and they set forward once more. They turned to the south, following the Rio Pecos, and the People had their first taste of the water they would have to drink for the rest of their days.

"It tastes of salt," Ayoi said, grimacing, as she came from the shallow river.

"But at least it flows all the seasons," Pahe said.

"It tastes of the white man," Dolii murmured, shaking off her hands after she had wet them.

The People drank the water and shook their heads. They knew

that crops would not thrive with such water; they had seen alkali springs before on their own lands. Corn would grow, with sufficient rain, but the young seedlings would have to be coddled like premature lambs, to get the plants to live.

"No doubt it is better to the south," they told themselves. And they went on.

Finally, they reached a small plateau above the valley of the Pecos and looked down upon the place of the Bosque, where the white man had brought them. Pahe was surprised at how large it looked and was instantly heartened. In all directions the People had made their shelters, and she could see them moving about the little settlement, working in the distant fields, and she was suddenly eager to be among them, desperate to stop moving and find a place with kin.

The ground looked hard and level; the river flowed wide and shallow. There were few trees, but perhaps there were sources of wood over that small rise, where she could not see. She could see herds of horses, cattle, and flocks of sheep and goats: not enough for so many, but at least more than they had with them now.

"There are so many," Dolii affirmed, standing next to her. "I did not know that there were this many People alive in the world."

"These and more," Pahe said cheerfully. "You have simply never lived among so many."

It was May, the month of planting, when the young birds begin to fly. At home, they would have been putting seed into the earth, watching for the early rains and gathering the first blossoms. Here, in the arid country of the *Bilagáana*, they were exhausted, dazed, and uncertain what they should do away from their sacred mountains and the Holy Ones.

But the soldiers were not uncertain. The wagons were no sooner unloaded than they herded the newcomers into a small corral beside a shed where another group of soldiers sat at a table in the shade. No one was excused; even the lame, the sick, and the aged must be brought to them for counting and naming.

When Ayoi saw that one of the People sat on the ground alongside the soldier's table as a translator for them, she shouted to him, "I am the wife of Manuelito! Where is the hogan of Manuelito?"

"Manuelito has come and gone away again," the translator called out to her. "You are too late."

Pahe heard his words and saw the look of disbelief and horror on her mother's face. "Stay here," she said to her firmly. "Stay here in this shade and do not move. I will see what this fool means by such words." She approached the translator with an eye to the soldiers watching nearby and she said quietly, "I am the daughter of Manuelito. Please tell me of my father."

The translator shook his head. "You do not need to keep your voice low, She-Who-Hears-The-Sun. The whites cannot understand you."

"My father has been here?"

"And gone again. He did not like what he saw."

"Where did he go?"

The translator shrugged. "Back in hiding, I suppose. If he is even alive. The soldiers are chasing him even now."

"He would not surrender—" she murmured in wonder. "He came all of this way and would not surrender—"

"Barboncito also has come and gone away again. Ganado Mucho took some of his kin and escaped. The soldiers will kill him the next time they catch him."

"How long did my father stay in this place?"

The translator thought for a moment. "Five days. Perhaps six. I do not know, truly. He came and he went again, that is all that I know."

"And are you a headman? What is your clan?"

He smiled grimly. "The whites think that I am. They think that anyone who speaks for others is a chief. I am of the Black Earth clan, and I have been here from the first. Before the Mescaleros went away."

Pahe's eyes widened in surprise. "The Apache have escaped as well?"

A soldier suddenly spoke to the translator loudly, and he nodded, ignoring her once more. He listened to the soldier and then called out to the People to come forward and give their names. He said to her quickly, "Do not tell them you are Manuelito's daughter. They will not treat you better for it."

She went hurriedly back to the corner of the corral where Dolii and Ayoi were leaning on one another, their eyes closed in weariness. Ayoi said, "What was that fool saying about your father?"

Pahe put her hand on her mother's shoulder. "That he has come and gone. He came to see if we were here, likely, and he did not want to be captured, so he left again."

Ayoi opened her eyes, her face drawn and still.

In that moment, Pahe knew that her mother had aged more in the last year than the last five years before. "He will come back, I am certain. Probably he searches for us on the trail, even now."

"No," Ayoi said simply. "If the coyotes and the ravens could follow us, certainly Manuelito could." She turned her head away and buried her eyes in Dolii's hair. "It is over between him and me."

"No, it is not," Pahe said firmly. "Get up now, both of you. The sooner we get counted by the soldiers, the sooner we are set loose."

"To do what?" Ayoi murmured. "To go where?"

Pahe ignored her and pulled Dolii up. "Come on. We'll need to find shelter before it is dark."

They stood in line before the table where the soldiers sat, and as each person came forward and spoke his name and clan aloud, the translator turned and gave a name to the soldier who was making marks on the paper. Pahe heard the names and she heard what the translator told the soldier, sometimes understanding that the names given were far from the names these people owned. As each person was given a new name, he or she was also given a small packet of food, another blanket, and an army canteen. When it was her turn to speak, Pahe knew that she must set the example for her daughter and her mother, and she spoke up loudly. "I am At'ééd Jóhonaa'éí Yidiits'a'í, born for Manuelito."

The translator turned to the soldier and said, "This one's name is She-Who-Hears-The-Sun."

The soldier shook his head. "That's a mouthful, ain't it? Sunny will do, I reckon."

And in that way, Pahe was called Sunny, Dolii was called Dolly, and Ayoi, the Tall One, was named Tess.

They left the corral then, and the soldiers took them down to the place where the people were working. Everyone looked up from their labor as they were herded into their midst, and many came forward to embrace relations or welcome kinsmen. Pahe saw that no one was fat, and few wore enough clothing to cover themselves from the sun and the rain. Men were digging irrigation ditches for the fields, and the women were working the fields. The flocks were grazing at a distance, but she could see that they were frighteningly few, for so many people.

A headman came to them and welcomed them, saying many good words about Manuelito and Narbona, but Pahe was too dazed to thank him properly. She was appalled by the shelters she saw, if that was what they were. No proper hogans, scarcely shelters as good and strong as one would have expected in a summer sheep camp. Many families were living in holes they had dug in the dirt embankments; others had erected crooked poles and covered them with sheepskins. Many more were sleeping outside in the open, and Pahe saw their cold firepits dotting the desert all around her like lion ant craters.

Ayoi's sheep and goats had been added to the other flocks, and Pahe could see that the children were all put to work to keep them moved from sparse grazing in one field to no grazing in another. This land did not look to her as though it could support much more than the small flocks which were on it now. How could they expect to feed themselves in the winter?

They were welcomed to join their clansmen on the edge of the eastern fields, and before nightfall, Dolii and Ayoi were as comfortable as possible in a mean shelter with a fire and a cook pot between them. Pahe went out walking over the land.

The crops were barely up out of the ground, but she could see corn, some melons and squash, and a good deal of early wheat. This was odd, since the People did not eat wheat much, certainly not like the whites did.

She walked along the Rio Pecos, the little stream that cut through the Bosque. There were no trees along the river, merely stumps of cottonwood and small brush. She bent and dipped her hand to the water, grimacing when she tasted the alkali. This was why the People said the water was poison. It was not poison, but it would not set well on the stomachs of the young and the elderly. Probably not the sheep, either.

She sighed deeply and turned back to the settlement, already weary with disappointment. Here, there would be no *ricos*, no slaves, and no one to do the tedious chores of everyday life. Here, the rich would live alongside the poorest kin, in the same holes in the ground, working the same fields, digging the same ditches, and herding the same flocks. That sameness was so starkly different from what the People had known that it would likely cause bitterness and quarrels among them, if all else were well enough.

And what could she say to her mother? Manuelito had come and gone again, not waiting for them to arrive. He surely had known their route and could have joined them if he chose to do so. For that matter, he could have gone ahead, seen what a bad place this was, and come back and rescued them from the soldiers. Instead, he had acted as though he had no relations, the worst thing she could think of to say about anyone.

Worse still, he acted as though he no longer cared about his wife.

When Pahe came back to the mean shelter where Dolii and Ayoi were cooking some corn gruel, she saw instantly that something had changed. Ayoi was not speaking; indeed, she was doing nothing but sitting, staring out at the distant horizon, while Dolii stirred the pot and saw to the meal.

"We will have to boil the water," Pahe said. "At least until we are used to it. I fear it is too salty to drink as it is."

Neither of them responded.

"I think it would be better to build a shelter in the side of the cliff, as others have done. Unless we slaughter all the sheep you've got, my mother, we won't have enough skins for a proper shelter and clothing, besides."

Ayoi lay down then without a word and closed her eyes, as though shutting Pahe's words out.

"She is weary," Dolii said softly. "We should talk of all this tomorrow. We will be stronger then."

Pahe nodded and sat, supping at the gruel Dolii offered her. "I know how she feels," she murmured. She half expected that Ayoi would rise to the bait and respond, but she did not.

They made a sad and uncomfortable night of it, trying to find places on the ground where they might rest, with only a blanket apiece for warmth and padding. Somewhere in the night, Dolii moved close to Pahe and nestled against her, weeping softly. Pahe said nothing, only pulled her close and held her as tightly as she could. She could think of nothing to say that would change where they were, and so she kept silent.

*   *   *

The next morning, she woke to see that Ayoi was gone. Her blanket was empty, crumpled on a heap on the ground. "I will find her," she reassured Dolii. "Perhaps she has only gone to see to the sheep."

But Pahe grew more afraid with each step she took about the settlement, asking after her mother and searching for her. Finally, she reached a small foothill where she could look down upon the settlement, the river, and the herds bunched to the west. There was no sign of Ayoi, and the People were moving about now, toward the fields and the irrigation ditches for the work of the day. She must get back to Dolii.

As she came down from the hill, she came to a place in the river where the water was shallow and fast, near a cluster of cottonwood stumps. There, she saw a disturbance in the water. She drew nearer and saw that a body blocked the flow of water.

It was Ayoi, she knew as much before she was close enough to see her clearly. She began to weep before she even touched her mother, bending to pull her from the shallow water and up onto the bank. The water was scarcely deep enough to cover her head.

Pahe sat with her mother's head in her lap, looking in her face. "You must have tried very hard to die, old one," she sobbed. "And now you have left me here to do all of this alone."

Her mother's face was still and pale, almost yellow in the morning sun. She looked suddenly like Deezbaa, and Pahe pushed her off her lap and rose to her feet unsteadily. Weeping hard, she walked away. Let the *Bilagáana* bury her, she told herself. That is something they are good at. I have enough to attend to the living.

*   *   *

Aura was one of the first to know of Ayoi's death. She had been scouting the camp, as she did every day, for Death was common among the humans below. Even if they did not die themselves, they often killed other creatures, and Aura knew enough about the men with the guns to know that where they went, Death followed.

Aura was a Turkey Vulture, *Cathartes aura*, the largest bird in these lands. At six years old, her wingspan was more than five feet. Only the Brown Eagle was larger, but the eagles kept from the humans as much as possible, preferring the canyons to the open desert.

Of all the birds of these lands, only Aura and her kin knew the humans so well and still were not afraid to come near them. In fact, Aura had some of her best hunting around their flocks, their camps, and the remains of their fires.

Now, she flew in tight circles around the body which lay just out of the river, knowing she must move quickly. From miles away, her kin would see her circles tighten and know that such a signal meant a large kill. They would come in moments, many of them, and then she would need to share her meal.

Aura flew lower still, suddenly suspicious of the body left so alone. Humans did not leave their dead alone for long. If Ayoi could have looked up, she would have seen a brown-black body with an unfeathered red head peering down at her calmly. Aura's wings appeared two-toned from below, and, unlike the eagle, she held her wings at a slight dihedral angle with her primaries separated, the better to ride the wind currents with the least effort.

With a sudden decisive dip, Aura flew down to the ground to investigate from a safe distance. She hopped in an ungainly fashion on her yellow feet, ready to take off again if the human made the slightest movement. She cocked her head and gave a soft hiss of apprehension.

Aura was more hungry than usual, but also more cautious. On a nearby cliff, her three eggs, white blotched with brown, had hatched, and she had three hungry young to feed. Carrion in the spring was ample, for the young were born and, always, some of them did not stay alive for long.

But the coyotes had been unusually bold this season, stealing her finds before she could gulp them down. It seemed to Aura that she had never seen so many coyotes in other times.

It also seemed to Aura that, though Death was common as ever, the food that such deaths provided was more scarce. She was hungry often, and in this time of plenty, that itself was unusual.

284 ▼ ▲ ▼ *Pamela Jekel*

She hopped closer to the human body, watching for a movement, listening for a sound of life. Just as she was deciding to peck at the softest parts of the face, another human came hurrying toward her, waving its hands and making a fierce noise. Aura took off immediately into the sky, reaching a safe altitude in seconds. From there, she circled again, waiting to see what would happen below.

As she expected, her kin had already gathered. Now they soared in numbers, gliding in short circles, watching the humans move about beneath them. Aura soon tired of them, for they had picked up the body and carried it off, within a place where she could not see or sense the Death.

Aura soared higher and off to the west, where the herds of the humans were grazing. Often from these herds, some Death came, and it was worth a look before she went out to inspect the open desert once more. She flew in circles over the herd, watching the old and the young ones carefully for any signs of distress or weakness. Of course, she could not kill such prey; Aura rarely killed at all. But when others killed, she was quick to take her place at the carcass. As she watched, she saw that the sheep moved in stupid, slow, single file over the rocky ledge to a dry area of patchy grass at the crest of a hill. The goats led them, as always. At a certain spot on the ledge, she noticed that the sheep shied off the trail, and the goats looked back to see that they followed.

Aura dropped lower to confirm her guess. A Death was there, and the sheep and the goats went around it with distrust. She waited until the herds had passed, and then she dropped closer, closer still, until she saw that a large lizard lay still in the rocks. She landed and hopped to it, glancing around to see if she was observed. The lizard was mottled and gray, large and bleeding from several wounds. No doubt, one of the lead goats had trampled it in anger, as it refused to move from their path. Aura had learned that these goats of the humans did not suffer trespassers easily, and they were quick to kick or stomp intruders rather than alter their path.

Aura came closer and held the lizard down with one clawed foot, while she bent and pecked at it tentatively. When it did not move, she put the other foot on it and took a hold of its head, pulling sharply up with her beak, while twisting hard, her usual method for severing softer tissue from spine. She swallowed the head convulsively and then looked up to see her kin gathering.

Without hesitation, Aura snatched the lizard by the middle, gripping it tightly with both feet, and flew up and away from the gathering vultures toward her hidden young. She was heavy with the body of the Death and groaning with effort, for she normally did not take carrion from where it lay. The way of her kind was to gorge at the place of Death and then regurgitate what was needed for the chicks—but Aura knew that such a small meal would scarcely feed herself and her young. There was none to share with kin.

Aura reached the canyon ledge where her chicks waited, silent until they heard her approach. They then set up a clamor of hunger, and she landed on a rock near where they lay and dropped the lizard to the ground. Her chicks called for her frantically, leaning and hopping about each other, for, like most of her kind, Aura had not built them a nest, but only found a small depression on the ground for them to fledge. Ignoring them, she quickly bolted the lizard, ripping the hide in several places so that the meat of the creature would be well torn. Only after she had eaten all of it did she take off again to the sky, and her chicks once again fell silent.

She circled for a time, waiting for her gorge to do its work, and then she dropped once more to her young. This time, she came to them without hesitation, and when they called for food, the largest of them pecking at her beak insistently, she disgorged the lizard in a form they could easily bolt down. Coughing and bobbing her head, she emptied herself, and the chicks quickly ate all she dropped for them, pulling at the tougher fibers of the meat and shoving each other aside for more.

Once they had fed, Aura took to the air again, higher now and back in the direction of the human camp. Except for an occasional kill elsewhere, she had found that they provided the most dependable source of Death.

*   *   *

Pahe could not even get as far as the camp before she suddenly turned and ran back to her mother's body. Every instinct, all her youthful training, told her to keep away, for the customs of the

People warned of the dangers of ghost sickness and contagion from despair. But just as she had with her grandmother, she could not bring herself to leave her mother alone in death. She also did not want Dolii to see her; better that her daughter's memories of her grandmother be those which would not haunt her all her life.

Pahe went to the fire of a headman and, within hours, her mother was wrapped in a blanket, then wrapped again in the white man's cloth and buried on a sloping hill overlooking the river, together with the others who had died once they reached the Bosque.

Dolii stood next to Pahe, weeping on her shoulder. "She was so strong," she protested. "Why would she take her life? Why would she leave us alone here?"

Pahe's eyes were blurred, but she did her best to keep her tears subdued for Dolii's sake. "She was waiting for her husband. When she knew he would not come, she did not want to be here without him."

"But he will return!" Dolii sobbed. "He will not leave us here without him!"

"I believe you are right, little one," Pahe said, her voice trembling with the effort to keep her daughter hopeful. "But she did not believe. We cannot know what she felt. We cannot know what happened between them in their beds and their hearts."

Dolii put her hands to her face and turned away, and her sobs had as much of anger to them as sorrow. "I hate this place, and I hate what she did! I hate Manuelito for leaving us here!"

Pahe covered her daughter with the blanket and pulled her closer, walking her away from the grave, silently weeping into the cloth, stumbling back to the settlement. All she could do now was try to keep them both alive.

The differences between their own lands and those of the whites became more clear to Pahe now. With such a death at home, there would have been four days of food and drink and kinship and good thoughts and good deeds, where each member of the clan tried to do everything to ensure that the deceased would make a swift and safe journey. There would be sweatbaths and sings to bring them back to themselves and help them heal from the grief. Though there would be little mention of the dead, the presence of so many related, loving hearts would bring comfort and peace and a quick return to the concerns of the living.

Here in the lands of the whites, the Holy Ones would not come when bidden, and the ceremonies were without power or meaning. They were all alone with grief and loss and death, and there were no hearts at the Bosque who had not suffered as much or more, so compassion was stretched and thin.

*   *   *

After a month at the Bosque, Pahe began to understand just how much they had lost by surrender. Even in the months of plenty, there was never enough to eat. The men worked to dig the irrigation ditches so that the fields might be brought to bear, but the water was bad and the soil was worse, and none of the crops were as fruitful as they should have been, especially considering that they had more hands tending them than usual.

The sheep were not thriving; the grazing was poor and they moaned and bleated at the water, drinking only when they were forced in up to their knees. The lambs were weak and not a single ewe had twins, something Pahe had never seen in all her years.

And every day, the counting happened, no matter what the weather or whatever important task had to be accomplished, every morning, they were called by the bugles to be counted in the corral, and every night again. The soldiers watched them from horseback, riding among the camps and standing sentry on the hills, so Pahe could never forget that she was imprisoned. Despite the counting and the guards, however, each week a few escaped into the hills, and the soldiers took off after them, only to return with no captives.

"I wonder how far we would get," Dolii said one night. She was attempting to weave by firelight with a small loom Pahe had managed to make from sticks and rope. There was not enough timber in the camp to make traditional looms, but at least they had wool. Dolii was determined to make something of it of value, even if only to trade to the soldiers for food.

"Not far, I fear," Pahe said. "At least here, we don't have to worry about the slave traders, and the flocks are safe. There's food, even if it's scant, and there's water, even if it's bad."

"We settle for so little these days," Dolii murmured.

"Not for always," Pahe said firmly. "I know my father will come back here for us soon. If we can just make it until then, we will be home once more. The Holy Ones promised me."

Dolii sighed. Often enough, she had asked Pahe to tell her once more the words of Coyote, and, over and over, Pahe had recited them to her. Still, Dolii could hardly hold on to her hope. "Why would the Holy Ones keep their promises to us now? Why should they look with favor on people who have given themselves up to the whites to live like prairie dogs in holes in the ground?"

Pahe smiled as she had a picture of them popping up out of holes to check for coyotes, as the prairie dogs did. Her smile led to a chuckle, and soon she was laughing and rocking herself, despite Dolii's wry smile and arched brows.

Finally, she finished, gasping, and Dolii said, "Well, and I am glad you can still find such amusement in our plight."

"So am I," Pahe said lightly. "I refuse to give up. I refuse to let *you* give up. To give up is worse than surrender; to give up is to die."

A soft cough came then from the darkness, and both of the women turned to see who came upon their camp. Pahe did not recognize the young man who walked into the light, but when she glanced at her daughter, she saw that Dolii did.

Dolii blushed slightly and turned her attention urgently to her makeshift loom.

Pahe nodded to the young man with some diffidence, but, inside, her heart was suddenly alive with joy. *"Ya'at'eeh,"* she said to the young man. "Welcome to our fire."

"Thank you, wife of Nataallith. I am Honágháahnii, come from the clan of Clumped Trees, born for Mariano."

"I know your mother," Pahe said gently. "And you have two sisters."

He smiled. "Everyone knows my sisters."

"It is a small place." Pahe shrugged. In fact, this young man's sisters were well known to all in the settlement for their chattering speech and their quick feet. No doubt he was used to the noise of women in his ears. That was good. She glanced at Dolii, who still had not looked up.

"My daughter is quiet tonight," Pahe said, half apologetically.

She could not remember how the mother of a daughter was supposed to behave when a guest came to the fire.

"Quiet is good," Honá replied quickly.

At that, Dolii glanced up for the first time, met the man's eyes, and smiled briefly.

Pahe's smile widened. "We have little to offer in the way of a decent meal, of course," she said, "but we would be pleased to share with you what we have."

"I have already eaten," he said.

Of course, that would be the new courtesy in this place, she realized. The old custom, that a man would never refuse food at the risk of offending, now was replaced by a custom that dictated a man would not accept food, for fear of taking what little was available. Pahe decided in that moment that many of the old customs would no longer work here in the place of the white man, and she abruptly rose with a feigned casualness she did not feel. "I am very tired this night."

The young man began to rise, glancing at Dolii uncertainly.

"You need not leave." Pahe shook her head, reassuring him. "I will simply rest a bit before I go to see to the flocks."

He sat back down again, and Dolii gaped at her wonderingly. As little as she knew of the ways of a man with a woman, she knew that mothers did not leave their daughters alone at the fire with a visitor.

Pahe resolutely went within the tiny shelter as though it were a large and private hogan, lay down upon her blanket, and turned her back to the two of them. She grinned in the darkness, imagining their glances, one to the other. If she had reached out, she could have touched her daughter's foot, but she lay still, willing them to forget her presence.

And so, in a few moments, they seemed to do so. First, the young man asked, "Should I have stayed away?" His voice was low, as though he believed he might not be heard.

Dolii said nothing.

Pahe closed her eyes in pleasure, laughing to herself.

"I do not wish to make a fool of myself," he said, sounding a little wounded. "If my visit is not welcome—"

"Your visit is not unwelcome," she said softly.

Pahe did not need to see his smile; she could feel it from a few feet away. And where did Dolii learn such ambivalence and its power?

"I have heard your father's name many times," the man began on a new tack. "He was a warrior of great honor."

Dolii once more said nothing.

Pahe suddenly could not stand it anymore. This was not the way it was supposed to be when a young man came to visit the fire of a young woman. Like everything else, this simple pleasure, too, was being ruined by the whites. She sat up and said, "Daughter, I have decided that I am too tired to see to the herd. Will you please go and do so?"

Dolii nodded uncertainly.

"And take Honá with you, for the night is dark."

Dolii almost gasped aloud, but the young man rose before she could protest. "Your mother is right; two are safer than one."

Dolii rose then and followed him away from the fire, throwing back a single glance of amazement at her mother. Pahe smiled and nodded at her in encouragement. And then she watched as they walked out of sight.

To allow her daughter such freedom was unknown in the old days, but these were not those days, and this was not a place to linger in the past. She sighed, happier in this moment than she had been for a while. Despite their hardships and losses, the young would find a way to each other, like the river found its way up out of the dry, caked soil and across the land, following its own secret fate. Another mother might have been horrified that Pahe let her daughter go with a stranger, but another mother would not have known what Pahe knew: someday they would be going home again. And when they did, Dolii would have a life, a husband, and children of her own. What did it matter how such things happened, so long as they came about in their own time?

She smiled to herself. It was a joy to see her show an interest in this man. The Bosque was so crowded with the People that they would have a hard time finding as much privacy as they would in a large hogan. It was good to see the color come up in her face; it was joy to see her smile. Right now, Pahe asked for nothing else than to see her daughter happy again, if only for a few moments.

Pahe sat for a while, watching the fire and listening to the sounds of the night. To her ears, they were clear and unique, as individual as the voices of the settlement. She could hear a distant hoot of an owl, the weary stamp of horses' hooves, the call of a coyote, and the tinkle of a goat's bell. She could feel, as well as hear, the movement of the wind from the river, cool and seductive, smelling green in the darkness.

If she closed her eyes, she could hear her mother's voice and her grandmother's voice as well. They were separate and distinct in her mind, though they often chorused the same opinion. This night, they were arguing with her about Dolii's absence from the fire.

"She will be with child before the year is out, if you're not careful," Ayoi warned. "And that's just what you need right now—another mouth to feed. The water alone would kill it, if the poor food did not."

"And by a Pueblo fool!" Deezbaa added. "The boy is half Pueblo at least. You can tell by looking at him well enough. Is that what you want? A Pueblo grandson? They are people of place; we are people of movement. How can they walk the harmony road together? I'd rather she marry a Mexican. They're the only ones left with anything to hold on to—some of them are *ricos* now, and the whites won't be stealing *their* land, at any rate."

Pahe smiled to herself, murmuring to them in her head. "I knew you would both be pleased. Wasn't it pretty when she answered him. 'Your visit is not unwelcome'? Where did she get such cleverness?"

"From me, of course," Ayoi grumbled. "The winter lambs are always stronger and more clever than those raised in the summer. I told you she would be married within a season, and I was right. I know of these things."

"Ah, yes, you were so clever with your man," Deezbaa taunted her. "I think it is clear enough where my granddaughter gets her wit. Not for nothing did they call me a witch."

"They called you a witch because they feared your power," Pahe said, suddenly sobered. "And I fear they will say the same of me."

"Have the Holy Ones been to see you again?" Ayoi asked.

"I would think you would know such things from where you sit," Pahe said to her.

"She sees as little around her now as she did when she walked your world." Deezbaa laughed. "Just because we are ghosts does not mean we know everything—"

"Then what's the point of death?" Pahe asked, half in jest and half serious.

"We would have to die more than once, I am thinking, to understand it," Ayoi said. "So if the Holy Ones are not pestering you, why do you fear others saying you are a witch?"

"Because I must do what Coyote told me to do. I must tell the People to sing the old songs and remember the old ways—"

"And they will surely heed the words of a mother who has let her only daughter go off in the dark with a Pueblo fool—" Deezbaa snorted.

"Hush, old woman!" Ayoi said. "That alone will not cause them to say you are a witch. Besides, the People need to hear a voice of leadership now. Until Manuelito comes, you must speak as he would speak."

Before she could reply, she heard the approaching footsteps of Dolii and her visitor. She turned slightly away from the fire so that her face was in shadow, lest her daughter see her amusement.

"I am come back," Dolii said. There was a lilt in her voice and a quickness to her step.

"The herds are well enough," Honá added, as if that message was the reason for his return.

"Thank you for accompanying my daughter," Pahe said formally, now holding her head away from him as though she were already his mother-in-law. "You are welcome at our fire."

The young man took the hint and said something softly to Dolii which Pahe ignored.

After he left, she said, "Where did you meet this man?"

"He was moving his mother's sheep to the river."

"His sisters could not do that task?"

Dolii shrugged. "I did not ask him."

"He is not of the People altogether, I know. He is also of the Pueblo."

Dolii nodded. "So he told me. Does that matter?"

"That depends, my little bird. Do you desire him as a friend?" Pahe smiled. "As a suitor? As a husband?"

Dolii rolled her eyes in feigned scorn. "What makes you think I desire him at all?"

"The look on your pretty face when you imply that you do not." Pahe laughed again. It seemed to her that she had not enjoyed herself so much in many moons. "What did he say to you once away from our fire?"

"We spoke of the settlement. Of the journey here. Of how many suffered. His people have even less than we do."

Pahe said mildly, "That is no longer a reason to reject a suitor."

"Stop calling him a suitor." Dolii grimaced. "It is a word from the old ways."

"What, then?"

She smiled coyly. "A friend. Perhaps." She ducked her head. "It would be nice to have a friend, I think."

Pahe's heart stung at that. It had been so long since her daughter had played with others her age, had been teased, chased, and annoyed, in the way all young things should be. Never had she known the freedom of running with a pack of healthy children like herself, running wild over the land like a herd of colts. It had been a long time since she had even cared if someone spoke to her at all. "Yes," she murmured gladly. "A friend is something you should have. He makes a nice appearance."

Dolii smiled a little wider at that and turned away.

Pahe knew she need say no more. If it was the wish of the Holy Ones that Dolii find a husband, even if he be of the Pueblo people, she would have nothing but joy in her heart. If not, well, and at least it was a beginning.

When they lay down beside each other under the blanket, Pahe pulled her daughter close, spooning her knees into Dolii's knees and wrapping her arms around her chest. "Tonight," she whispered, "I remembered how I felt when your father first came to my mother's fire. How she brightened when she saw him! It was as though he came to court her, not me. I remembered how it felt the first time he said my name. The first time he touched me. And I was happy for you, my little bird, that you will soon know these things."

Dolii snuggled against her.

"It has been too long since you have known pleasure," Pahe added. "A man can bring that to you."

"Were you happy with my father?" Dolii asked wistfully. "Even when you disagreed?"

Pahe chuckled. "Especially when we disagreed. For even when we argued, I knew that he loved me and respected my wishes. And I knew the wisdom of his arguments, even if I did not agree with his thoughts. Our arguments made me feel truly married to your father." She tickled Dolii as she squeezed her. "And our lovemaking made me feel alive."

Dolii squirmed and jabbed her with her elbow as best she could, giggling in embarrassment.

"Sleep, then, daughter," Pahe finally whispered when they had settled down once more. "And in the morning, I will tell you how to turn a friend into a husband."

*   *   *

In the days that followed, Pahe could see Dolii turning toward Honá like a flower long in shade turns to the sun. But Pahe's pleasure in that process was distracted by the arrival of a man who was second only to her own father in his ability to escape the white soldiers. Barboncito came to the Bosque Redondo with eighteen half-starved warriors, all that was left of his clan.

He was surprised to discover that Manuelito was not among the People, and he came to her fire as soon as he had talked with the headmen, who gathered to hear him. Pahe was appalled at his appearance, for she remembered the proud warrior who had spoken for war and eluded the whites for so long.

Barboncito sat by her fire on his blanket, his eyes weary and watery with phlegm. He did not look at her when he spoke. His hand hung limply over his knees. "We could no longer hide from the soldiers and still stay alive. It is better to be with our kinsmen than to wander alone."

"You need not tell me this," Pahe said quietly. "I know full well the reasons"—she hesitated, not wishing to use the word "surrender" to such a warrior—"for such a decision."

"I know of your mother's death," he said then baldly, against all custom. The People rarely spoke of the dead, but death had become so commonplace that it no longer held much horror. "You have suffered a hard loss."

"Most here have," she murmured.

"Your father was alive when I left him last."

"How long ago?" she asked, leaning forward with eagerness.

"Not a moon. He will follow me, he said."

Pahe thought for a moment. "How many warriors did he have with him?"

Barboncito smiled tautly. "Not so many as me. Only twelve."

"Twelve! So many have died, then!"

"Or been captured. Or surrendered. Or escaped. We are winnowed to the bone now."

She said sadly, "You two are the last, then."

"He is the last."

"He will enjoy that."

Barboncito sighed and closed his eyes. "There is nothing to enjoy in any of this. I thought that when most of us were together, it would be better. But it is not. I will not stay."

She looked up in surprise. "But what will you do? Where will you go?"

He chuckled. "I knew you would ask me that, daughter of Manuelito. Ever the one who must hear the answers. Alone, I can keep from the soldiers. Alone, I can survive. But I cannot keep my warriors alive, and they cannot wander the lands like solitary wolves. They need their families."

"And you do not?" Somewhere, she was surprised that she asked him such a question, and yet she knew he would tell her the truth.

"I do not expect to live a long life," he said quietly. "But I will not live the rest of my days in this place."

"Neither will I," Pahe said firmly. "And neither will the rest of the People. The Holy Ones have promised me this. We will return to our lands, and we will prosper there once more."

He sat up a little more straight, and his eyes took on the shine of small interest. "The Holy Ones have come to you in a dream?"

"Not a dream," Pahe insisted. "Many times, in the brightness of day. Sometimes as Raven; sometimes as Coyote. As they did to my grandmother before me, they come and they give me warnings. The last time, they gave me hope."

"Well, and your words give me hope as well," he said thoughtfully. "Who have you told of these visits?"

"Only my family," Pahe said. "But I know it is time for me to

speak to the rest of the People. The Holy Ones said that I must."
She dropped her head. "I have felt afraid."

"Of what?"

"They will call me a witch. Here, they speak of skinwalkers,
the wolves that walk on two legs. They fear the corpse sickness,
and it seems they speak of such things more than I remember.
Perhaps because they live with fear and they feel helpless. I have
seen what such fear can do," she murmured.

He laughed gently. "Daughter of Deezbaa, eh? I think they
will listen well enough. The call of the bugle twice each day makes
them yearn to hear something else, I am thinking."

"I am tired of feeling afraid," she said suddenly.

"Then do something to feel brave," he said dismissively.
"Courage is easy when it is the only choice. What message do
you have for them?"

"That we must sing the old songs and keep to the old ways.
And if we do this, we will be set free to return to our lands. We
will survive as a people."

"And if they will not heed you?"

She shook her head. "I do not know. But I cannot imagine a
people lasting long without their beliefs to protect them. The
whites must have powerful gods indeed to have defeated us. We
must have the support of our own gods even to survive."

Barboncito stared at her thoughtfully as she spoke. In fact, his
gaze was so intense that she finally stopped speaking in confusion,
looking down at her hands. "You are a woman of great spirit,"
he said finally. "This does not surprise me, given your clan and
the blood in your heart. But it is surprising to hear a woman
speak so. If you tell them, I imagine they will believe you."

"They must," she said quietly.

He thought for a moment. Suddenly, he said, "We will call a
council. It is time for the People to have whatever hope they can
hold on to, and you must give it to them. The Holy Ones do not
come to many—"

"They came to my grandmother."

"And they drove her mad," Barboncito said abruptly. "But
these are mad times. Perhaps they will drive us all to a new place
of reason." He gazed down at the ground for a few moments.

Pahe felt an admiration for him wash over her. This warrior, a leader of his clan, had given up his own life and his own comfort to keep his kinsmen alive and free as long as he could. And when he could no longer keep them alive, he gave up his own freedom rather than have them starve. No matter what he said, she realized, he would not leave them now. He would live or die at the Bosque, but he would not leave them.

"My wives are all gone," he said sadly. "One by one, I lost them to the journey. Even the youngest, the strongest, could not withstand the hardships of being always hounded by the soldiers."

"You are still young," she said. "I have seen love find a place in the most hardened heart, just as water will wear away a stone." She smiled gently. "My daughter seems to have found it here among our enemy. I am grateful to the Holy Ones that she is able to find that joy. If the young ones can do this, there is hope for all of us."

"You have never taken another husband, since your own was killed," he said.

"No," she admitted.

"Do you think of it ever?"

She glanced up in surprise. It suddenly seemed to her that the conversation had taken a subtly different turn, although his voice betrayed nothing new. "No," she murmured. "Not yet."

"Perhaps now that your mother is gone and your daughter seeks her own way, you may think of it more."

"Perhaps," she heard herself agreeing. Now she was afraid to meet his eyes, and she was simultaneously annoyed with herself for feeling afraid. How had she come to be such a timorous woman? Was this something else she could lay at the feet of the whites? She suddenly decided that she was, after all, the daughter of Ayoi, the granddaughter of Deezbaa, and the daughter of Manuelito, and this was her fire and her shelter.

"Call a council," she said then, decided. "I will speak of my message from the Holy Ones. And those who will listen will hear it. Those whose ears are already dead will not. But I know that I will be going back to the lands of my grandfather, and my daughter will be coming with me, husband or no."

He smiled slowly. "I will call them, then." He rose to take his leave, bending slightly at the waist as though to touch her shoulder, but he thought better of it. "I think that when Manuelito comes, he will find you well enough."

"Yes," she said firmly. "And when he comes, I will tell him all that has come about in his absence."

"And what should be done about it. I have no doubt of that," Barboncito chuckled half to himself, half aloud.

When he had left her fire, Pahe found herself grinning privately. She was not so old, she told herself, that she could not sense the small heat coming from a man in her direction. This Barboncito might be near death from his journey, but he was alive enough to know a woman of worth when he was near one. Not that she cared one whit one way or the other, but it was amusing to see what one could make of it.

*   *   *

Barboncito called council, as he had promised he would, and Pahe found herself before the gathered heads of the clans. Dolii sat behind her, and Pahe kept her hands folded inside her blanket so that no one could see them shake. It had been many seasons since she had spoken before council. It seemed a lifetime ago, when her father was beside her, her husband alive or his memory so fresh that she was embraced and included in that, in each heart which listened.

Now she was only a woman without a man; a daughter without a father, and she knew that her people had known too much suffering and were struggling too hard to have patience with anything that seemed more trouble. She remembered her grandmother's words: she was born to follow, not to lead.

But she said, "I am here at council to speak with the words of the Holy Ones. They have come to me, not in dreams, but in the starkness of day."

She waited while the listeners settled themselves. It was against all tradition to interrupt a speaker, but the People had ways of showing that what was being said was disturbing. The restless shifting of the bodies and the clearing of the throats said more than any interruption would have. Pahe knew that Barboncito was watching her closely, however, and she was determined to say what she had come to say. "Once, Raven came to me and warned me of betrayal. We were then attacked by the Hopi raiders, and I lost my son."

Now she could see that she had the full attention of every mother's ears.

"Again, Raven came to me and warned me of betrayal. He said that we must surrender or die. He said we would be betrayed by the white man after our surrender, but if we did not surrender, we would not survive. My father would not heed his words. My mother and my daughter and many of the People came with me to this place, and now I see that the warning of betrayal was true. I also believe that if we had not surrendered, we would be dead."

"We wonder if we are dead anyway," murmured a man close to her.

Pahe looked at him and gripped her hands harder. She must tell them everything. Then, if they would not listen, at least she had fulfilled her responsibility. "We are not dead. But many who did not surrender are."

"And some who surrendered are dead anyway," a woman said pointedly.

Pahe dropped her head, for a moment speechless. Of course, no one would speak Ayoi's name, but all thought of her. She knew that whenever a woman took her own life, those left behind were often blamed. Perhaps they had not taken proper care of her; perhaps she had felt unloved or unwanted. She could do nothing with that shame and guilt but live with it. She had Dolii to think of now. She went on blindly. "Yes, all that is true. But again and once more, the Holy Ones came to me," she said, "on the trail to this place. This time, it was Coyote who spoke to me. This time, there were words of hope. I tell them to you now."

The circle was silent, waiting. Pahe was acutely aware of every breath around her, every stare, every shift of the bodies which made up her people, as though they were somehow inside her, as children inside a mother's womb. "We will live, my people. We will live to return to our lands." Her voice was stronger, more powerful. "We will be free once more. Coyote promised me this. But we must keep to the old ways and sing the old songs. If we do not, we will perish as a people, and the winds will blow away these shelters, cover our bones with dust, and we will be as the Ancient Ones, gone from these lands forever." She took a deep breath, suddenly light and filled with a quiet joy. She had told them all at last. What would come of this would come, but she had told them her truth. "I was told by the Holy Ones that this is so. And for me and my clan, I will obey."

There was a great hissing silence around the council circle now, as though each man and woman who listened was sifting her words through their teeth. Pahe heard every breath and sensed each of their fears. There was no fear she had not shared but now, miraculously, all her fear was gone.

"So," said one headman slowly, "we are to sing the old songs and have the Blessingway and the Enemyway and the Lifeway, and the soldiers will let us leave this place. We will go back to our lands, and we will be free once more. Is that what you are saying?"

When he put her beliefs into words, they seemed at once impossibly hopeful and naive. "It is not what I am saying," she said. "It is what the Holy Ones have told me. Each time they came to me before, their warnings were true. I believe that their promises are true as well."

A woman asked, "When is this to happen, daughter of Manuelito? How long must we endure this place of poison and death if your words are true?"

Pahe hesitated. She did not wish to speak of Dolii, and yet if she did not give the People hope that they could believe in, it was worse than no hope at all. Many would die, she knew, before the promises of the Holy Ones could come about. Yet even those who might not make it back to the lands of the People must help keep the old ways, if any of them were to survive. She sensed that half measures would not be enough. "Within three years," she said firmly, understanding what a dangerous turn she had taken. A lie could be repeated three times, according to the traditions of the People. With the fourth repetition, it locked the teller into the deceit. How many times would she have to repeat this lie?

The council broke into murmurs of surprise and growing excitement. Voices rose in the closest thing to joy that Pahe had heard since she arrived in this place.

"Three years! Perhaps shorter? Three years and we will be back on our own lands and free of the whites?" One of the headmen rose to his feet in his eagerness to hope that what she said was true. "This is what was told to you by the Holy Ones?"

"That is what I heard," she said, blurring the line between truths. She knew that they would not notice the difference between what he asked and what she answered. "But all of us must be of one mind and heart. We must keep the old ways. Coyote was very clear about this. We must not succumb to the ways of the whites, we must not give up our ways to them. Only in that way can we remain the People. Only in that way will the Holy Ones help us get back what is ours."

"And are you to lead us in this?" another woman asked. "Granddaughter of Deezbaa, daughter of Ayoi, you are not a singer, you are not a hand-trembler or a medicine woman."

A man added, "We have so few left to lead us in the old ways, so few have the heart to sing the old songs. We will die here, abandoned by the Holy Ones."

Suddenly, a voice came from behind her, and Dolii said softly, "If we cannot remember ourselves, then we deserve to die here, forgotten and betrayed."

Pahe turned around, astonished that Dolii could find the courage to speak so at council. In her memory, she could not recall ever hearing a young woman speak before the headmen— But wait. Yes, she smiled quietly to herself. Yes, she could remember. She recalled quite vividly that she herself had spoken before just such an assembly when she was just Dolii's age: to warn them of the coming of the white man, as she had heard it from the Ute dogs. Her head whirled with the sudden weight of all that had come since, all that had happened in all of their lives since that long-ago time.

Dolii added, "Have we forgotten so much so soon? Is there no one here who can believe? We do not need leaders to tell us how to live. We know how to live. And if we should have forgotten the words and the smallest details of the old ways, well, and then, there will be those who can lead us. My mother is one of those."

The rest of the council was obviously as shocked by Dolii's sudden interruption as Pahe herself. Eyes shifted back and forth, frowns met each other, and several of the headmen crossed their arms before their chests as though to defend themselves against such outspoken offense.

Pahe said softly, "My daughter is impatient with weakness and saddened by loss, as are all of our young."

"The young are not alone in this," one mother said staunchly.

Pahe knew then that she had one supporter, at least.

The headmen looked at one another silently, as though communing in a private language. Finally, one of them said, "We have nothing to lose by keeping to our ways, whether the Holy Ones have spoken to the daughter of Manuelito or not. We have lost our strength as a people, and we are now in danger of losing our spirit as well."

Several of them nodded in agreement.

Another headman added, "If the words of At'ééd Jóhonaa'éí Yidiits'a'í can lead us back to ourselves, then my ears are willing to listen."

Others murmured, "I, too," and "Yes, we will listen."

Pahe looked around the faces of her people and she saw there no suspicion or fear. Amazingly, no one had called her a witch or a liar. It was an indication, she realized, of how badly her people were splintered and defeated, that they did not question her words or her right to express them. More amazing still that they did not firmly, quickly, silence Dolii and ask Pahe to take her from council.

She remembered her grandmother and how she had suffered isolation and rejection for her words of warning, for her pleas to the People to keep from the white man, to kill them all while they still could, to reject their treaties, their papers, and their ways. For her trouble, she died alone in a hogan apart from all she loved, called a witch by even the meanest slave.

Anger rose in Pahe then, but it was a cool anger, distant and firm and righteous. "I come from a clan of women," she said slowly, "who have not been afraid to speak their minds. Indeed, if some of these women had been heeded, we might not be where we are today. I will not die with truths unspoken. I will tell what I have heard, as I have been commanded to do since the day I became a woman. Each will have to decide whether or not to listen. And that is all I have come to say." She fought down the sudden flood of tears that came into her throat, willing herself to show no weakness.

In that moment, she felt intensely proud to be a woman. She

could recall a time when she had wished she was born a man—never again would she wish to be so diminished in her power.

Barboncito cleared his throat then and shifted his body to draw attention to him and away from her. "Let us speak to our kinsmen of the words of the Holy Ones. Let us talk among ourselves and come to agreement. To my mind, we have nothing to lose by accepting the truth of this woman's words. She comes from a clan known for courage, strength, and leadership. Though we have not often known of a woman who is a singer or a shaman, still we have also not known ourselves to be in such a place before, surrendered to such a people. This is a time and a place for new solutions, I am thinking. The Holy Ones have not abandoned us, as we feared. They have only chosen to speak into new ears." He looked around the circle with a challenge in his eyes. "I am ready to listen to the old ways from a new source."

Pahe blinked away tears of gratitude, unwilling to meet his eyes lest she lose control.

The council broke then, and Dolii and Pahe walked back to their shelter, aware that eyes followed them now from all corners of the settlement, and mouths spoke their names as they passed. "I was proud when you spoke at council," Pahe said simply. She was too full of emotion to say more. "I was, too." Dolii grinned suddenly. "Would that Deezbaa was here to see us both!"

"She was, my daughter, she was."

*   *   *

There was a clan which lived within the confines of the Bosque which cared little for the white sentries and nothing at all for their fences. A mother, a father, and four daughters, they lived at the edge of the makeshift shelters, earth dwellings, and cave holes of the People, moving about them at night and causing them no small amount of annoyance.

The herders complained that they dug so many holes that the horses stumbled into them and the sheep broke their legs. Besides, it was grumbled, they were a strange and ugly clan with no use at all.

In fact, the first charge was true, but the second was quite unfairly false. They were *Dasypus novemcinctus*, Nine-banded armadillos, one of the only two armored mammals in North America—the other being the porcupine.

Dasy was the mother of the clan, far more adventurous and aggressive than her lazy mate, and the leader of the nocturnal digs which brought down so much annoyance on their collective heads. But Dasy was as supremely oblivious to the damage she might cause to the herds as she was to the movement of the stars. Her job was to dig, and to teach her daughters to dig, and she did it with an alacrity that made her mate weary just to watch.

Dasy had a small head with soft upright ears and soft underparts and a sparsely haired tan body. She could be slow to move from danger and understand what was right before her long, probing snout, but she had one enormous advantage in life: her heavy, bony plates of armor and her ability to curl quickly within them to keep her softest parts safe. That armor was as hard as a human toenail and made of the same substance, but most impressive were the nine flexible bands of armor on her belly, which contracted like an accordian to let her roll into a defensive ball. Like a small armored pig, she had evolved to be stubborn, persistent, and single-minded.

Dasy and her clan were more than examples of good engineering; they were actually examples of living art, for the armor they carried was made of perfect hexagons and pentagons arranged in a specific pattern for no reason other than to be attractive to each other. They had been on the land well before man and they would likely outlive him, mute evidence of a time when large reptiles walked the earth and volcanoes pushed the mountains to their present height. They were survivors.

Dasy's mother had taught her at her infancy, "Curl first and look last," and she learned the lesson well enough to survive to the age where she could teach the same lesson to her second brood of pups, all daughters this time. Curiously, like the rest of her clan, Dasy would never have both males and females in a single litter. She mated each fall; there was a single embryo implanted in her uterine wall from that mating, and that single egg divided into four identical quadruplets, never more, rarely less.

Dasy's senses told her that these daughters were more important even than the sons which had been born last year and long since departed to far corners of the desert. These daughters were the beginnings of a legacy, and she would train them with more attention than anything she had done before.

Dasy had the armament and also the digging tools to make any manner of archaeologist envious. The summer sun bothered her not at all, and her two forefeet with four three-inch claws and two hind feet with five shovels of claws made it possible for her to dig with a speed that rivaled any four prairie dogs. When Dasy was in the mood and the fever to dig was upon her, she could throw the dirt behind her more than five feet with a ferocious joy and a constant grunting noise that she displayed at few other times.

Her daughters were exactly like her, in miniature. They combed the dirt and their holes for every manner of beetle, ant, and spider, darting out their six-inch tongues, which were sticky and swift, consuming more than a pound of bugs a night between them with a cacophony of grunts. Dasy's mate brought up the rear, poking about in the holes they'd already abandoned, content to take their leavings and then scatter back to their home burrow at the slightest hint of danger.

When Dasy wished, she could swim the Pecos by gulping air, inflating her intestines, and floating across. Consequently, both sides of the river were her digging grounds, but she much preferred the softer earth and disturbed areas where the herds had gone before, for their droppings attracted the insects and their hooves made the ground easier to move.

And this preference would prove to be disastrous.

One night, Dasy led her daughters to a place where the herds had been the day before, hoping for a newly churned patch of ground and fresh manure with the inevitable insects. She waddled quickly up over a rise and smelled something she had smelled before but not in this place. It was fresh carrion, a delectable prize she rarely found in these dry, crowded places where the humans crowded together.

Dasy was not above eating carrion, fledgling birds, eggs, or small reptiles if she could get them. In fact, they packed enough protein to fill her gut admirably well—but she was not often able to get them so easily. Now it looked to her as though she had stumbled upon an amazing piece of luck. Directly ahead, if her snout was any barometer, was a pile of carrion with no other predator about, simply waiting to be enjoyed.

Dasy did not even stop to sniff the air for foe, and even if she had, it was unlikely that any scent could have pushed out the stronger, more alluring smell of decay. She hurried to the carcass with her daughters shoving behind her, and she stuck her snout into the soft parts of a dead lamb. Eagerly, she grunted to her daughters to hurry, though they did not need to be urged.

A nattering of anxiety rolled about Dasy's small mind all the while she rooted and grunted and gobbled, for it was so unusual to find such a carcass unclaimed that she was put on her guard. She was therefore scarcely startled when she heard something approaching from the rear and turned to see her worst enemy approaching.

It was two humans, the female sort, carring sticks of fire in the darkness. Dasy froze for an instant, grunting a loud warning to her daughters. She knew they had been seen, but she could only imagine that the humans wanted the carcass, not them. She backed off, reluctant to leave the find, and then turned with her daughters behind her and moved away from the lamb. She did not run as fast as she would have if the intruders had been coyotes or foxes, for all her experience told her that humans rarely chased her kind. The humans made their strange guttural sounds and, to her alarm, passed the carcass of the lamb and came fast upon them instead.

Dasy turned and bolted for the river, squealing in fright, her daughters racing behind her. Their noises attracted the attention of her mate who had been coming to join them in the feast, and he fell in behind them, grunting in fear. Dasy was faster than she looked, and she darted here and there, trying to stay out of the light of the pursuing fire-sticks, but the humans were quick, and they separated, so that the light seemed to come from all sides. Dasy felt confused and her terror made her careless, but she knew that if she could get to the river, she would likely escape. She turned abruptly, screeching for her daughters to follow, and she could hear her mate's answering grunt falling behind.

She knew that he could not keep up with them, for he was slow and unused to hard work. She went over the last small hill, raced down the riverbank, and began gulping air as she ran, hoping that her daughters would follow her example. The humans were closer now, and as she splashed into the river, she heard behind her the squeal and sudden silence that meant her mate had been taken. One human had him in its hands, and he was rolled tightly in a defensive ball, high off the ground.

Dasy walked right down to the bottom of the river on her short, stubby legs and trotted along the rocky base, holding her breath. Behind her, she knew her daughters had followed her, breathing the air they had gulped right before they plunged into the water. The river was narrow, she knew, with an easy current, and shallow. The humans could catch them easily if they floated on the surface. By staying under water, they might escape.

She was grateful that this river was not more treacherous; with a wider, deeper, faster river, they would not have been able to stay on the bottom. Finally, however, she reached the other side, pulled herself out of the water onto the bank, and gasped for breath. Behind her, her daughters followed her, shaking like dogs and panting heavily. She grunted in weary relief.

The humans were moving away from the river, and she could see the lights of their fire-sticks going back to where they lived altogether. Her mate was nowhere to be seen.

Dasy waited for a long while until the darkness was quiet again. Her daughters snuffled around the roots of the stumps by the river. There were no more trees; the humans had captured those as well. Dasy considered crossing the river once more to see what had become of her mate, to go back to their home burrow. But she decided against that plan.

There were too many humans in this place. Always before, her kind had lived close to the humans with little fear. The humans rarely hunted them and, except for their dogs, seemed not to notice their presence. These humans were different. Something had changed. She sensed that she would likely not see her mate alive again. She felt no sense of grief or loss, merely a vague prickle that danger lived here now, where none had lived before. Her daughters must survive to have daughters of their own.

She turned away from the river and led them up into the sandy foothills, under the strange rows of trees that the humans used to keep their herds in place, and out onto the open desert.

Once away from the lights and the smells of the humans, Dasy stopped and pointed her long snout up into the night air, searching for a reason to turn one way or another. In the distance, she could smell the night blossoms of the yucca, and she knew that near them, the insects would gather.

Grunting a refrain of part comfort, part command, she led her daughters away from the place of the humans, over the rise, and into the darkness.

* * *

Pahe sat happily, lining the armadillo shell with the traditional designs for the marriage ceremony. It was not usual, she knew, but she felt the Holy Ones would approve of her resourcefulness. It was to be, after all, the first wedding in this place of the whites, the first time the People would gather together for something joyful, rather than for another death, another counting, another ditch to dig or field to plow.

She remembered clearly her own *ts'aa*, the wedding basket that Deezbaa had given her, made of spliced sumac in soft colors of tan and red. She had worn bells on her ankles, and her grandmother's silver, and she had never felt more beautiful.

This wedding basket would be beautiful also, even though it was the shell of an armadillo. The bride would be beautiful as well, even though she had no bells to wear and little silver. There would be few gifts, no hogan, and not much of a wedding feast, but the People would find happiness and satisfaction in the old ways, and all would see that a marriage could happen, could bond clans together, even in this place of strangers.

She smiled to herself, feeling the sun on her shoulders and the light breeze of early summer moving up from the river. Dolii had come to her soon after the meeting of the council, half afraid, half defiant, to tell her that she would marry the man, Honágháahnii, of the Clumped Tree clan, if her mother would perform the ceremony.

"Are you certain, Little Bird?" Pahe had asked her daughter, holding her chin in her hand tenderly.

Dolii had evidently expected less tenderness and more protest, for her eyes welled up in gratitude, and she took her mother's hand and squeezed it gently. "I think so," she murmured. "Are all brides certain?"

"Hardly any of them," Pahe chuckled. "And yet the mothers

always will ask. He seems like a good man. Does he speak words of affection easily?"

Dolii nodded, blushing. "He is very gentle with me."

"That is good. Gentle is important," Pahe said firmly. "He comes from a good clan, if a small one. I am sure, in other times, I would have asked a large bride price for you and many suitors would have been turned away by your father. But here, none of that matters so much. If you wish to have him, then I will give my blessing."

"And you will make a marriage ceremony for us?"

Pahe thought for a moment. "I would never dare to do so in other times. But I have said I will do this in council, and so it does seem that the place to begin is with my own kin. What says his clan to this?"

"They are agreed." She grinned. "They did not think that one of their clan would ever reach so high."

Pahe nodded. "And if your father were here, he might forbid it. But we must take happiness where we can find it, eh? And if he makes you happy, then this is what should be. But, my daughter, just because a man wants to marry you doesn't mean he will take care of you forever. Learn to weave."

Now she had gathered the pollen, ground the cornmeal, and made a medicine bundle of a piece of her own wedding basket, a shred of her mother's blanket, and a remnant of Deezbaa's silver, the three most powerful symbols of continuity that she owned. She could remember some of the wedding chant and much that the singer did when he attended her wedding to Nataallith, and she could only hope that others who attended would speak up and add their memories to her own. In that way, they would create the Planting Ceremony, *ki'dilye*, male and female planting equal seeds, together. If there were errors, they would share them; and when the joy came, they would share that as well.

It seemed to Pahe when she thought of it that this must have been as it was when the Holy Ones first taught the old ways to the People, for they surely did not get it right the first time. She held the pot out before her, an armadillo shell transformed into a wedding basket for her only daughter. She felt the rightness of what she was doing, and she was deeply glad.

If only Dolii's brother could be here, she thought with a sudden deep sadness, and her father and her grandparents, and her friends— Ah, that road led to such sorrow as to make her eyes glaze and her hands still their movement. There was no time for sorrow now. No place for such coldness in her heart. She must do her best to fill the spaces outside and inside herself with what joy they could make for themselves.

The night came quickly, and with it, the People who gathered for the ceremony, many of them unknown to Pahe from clans strange to her. She was pleased to see that they were willing to take joy from anything that was available, surely a sign of a people determined to survive.

She had built a small shelter of boughs and hides and earth which was open on three sides for the wedding couple, and she set stones around in half-moons for seats for all who wished to witness.

She saw quickly that she had not brought enough stones from the river, for the clans who were related to Honá filled up all the seats and genially beckoned to others to join them. Pahe realized that to be both the mother of the bride and also the singer was impossible, so she murmured a word of apology to her daughter, hugged her, and gave her over to Honá's mother to be escorted into the wedding shelter.

It was dusk, and the glow from the setting sun made the air seem golden, the shadows long and purple in the folds of the hills. Pahe sat before Dolii and Honá with the wedding basket in her hands, and she sent a silent plea to the Holy Ones to witness and bless her efforts. She began the ceremony with a small welcome to the listeners, telling them how glad she was that they were able to attend, making a wry joke about the important work that waited for all of them—the digging of the ditches for the white soldiers—and to her surprise, they laughed readily enough, as though they were eager to continue the tradition of the singer beginning each Blessingway with laughter.

And then she began singing the song she remembered from her own wedding, the Blessingway chant of union and peace, all the while taking the pollen out of her pouch and sprinkling it in the four corners of the space between Dolii and Honá, telling of the beauty of the land and the richness of the fields and the herds, the strength of the corn crops and the clean, clear water of the mountains, weaving together plain words with words of beauty, song with rhythm, closing her eyes and listening to her own heartbeat and letting her words echo through her and flow out of her mouth, heedless of their correctness, thinking only of Dolii and Honá and the happiness that a good marriage could bring to all who knew them.

She took from her side her water basket. It was not old and traditional and covered with sacred pinyon pitch, as the chanter had at her wedding, but it was dear to her all the same. It had been her mother's water basket, and she had gathered bits of fleece from the sheep and seeds from the cottonwood trees to adorn the sides. She made a cross in the dirt between Honá and Dolii. "This place, where all lines come together," she said, "is the center of our earth. This center goes with us wherever the People journey, so long as they keep to the old ways. It is a place of connections, and so fitting for two people who will henceforward be connected for all the days of their lives."

Pahe gave the water basket to Honá, who took it from her with trembling hands. She smiled encouragement at him. He carefully poured the water from the basket on Dolii's hands, washing them in the water of life. When he touched Dolii's hands, she looked up at him with a profound tenderness and joy, and Pahe felt her eyes well up. When she looked around the circle of watchers, she saw that many were equally moved. So, then. This was the healing power of love. There was no greater miracle, she realized.

Honá washed his own hands then and took some of the corn mush from Dolii's wedding basket, eating it slowly. His kin then came forward and ate from it as well, and as they moved from their places, Pahe felt the tension of the ceremony dissolve, and the pleasure pull them together in one place of peace and joy.

A voice said then from one side of the shelter, "I am pleased to have such a fine grandson in our clan."

Pahe turned to see Manuelito standing at the back of the shelter, having approached silently while all eyes were watching Pahe. Behind him stood Juanita. And behind them were eight ragged warriors, all of them gaunt and unkempt, and two other women of the clan.

"My father!" she cried out eagerly, rising to embrace him.

Dolii rose and threw herself into his arms, and those closest to them gave cries of welcome also, rising and hurrying to touch Manuelito, to assure themselves that he was real.

"But when did you come?" Pahe asked him, when she could speak.

"Only a while ago," Manuelito said wearily. "We can tell of all that later. Now, let us remember what we are about. I am proud to see my daughter sit as singer for such a gathering—"

"I am ignorant about the proper songs and rituals," she said humbly.

"It does not matter if it is perfect," Dolii said. "What matters is that we can keep to the old ways and make a marriage."

Manuelito grinned at her with rare pleasure. "You have grown in my absence, Little Bird, and not only taller." He turned to Honá, who had stepped back respectfully to give the women and kinsmen a chance to welcome their headman. "And this man comes to join us. I am pleased at your choice, my granddaughter. He looks strong and capable, and he comes of a good clan."

Pahe knew that no matter who Dolii had chosen as mate, Manuelito would have made an effort to embrace him. She was glad, however, that in the case of Honá, the effort did not need to be extreme. She turned to the guests and said, "The blessings of the Holy Ones are already evident. Our warriors are returned to us, and our clan is whole once more." She held up the wedding shell she had decorated and handed it to Dolii, taking Honá's hand and placing it on hers. "Remember that in all fields, you plant equal seeds. One cannot thrive without the other. You are part of the earth and the sky, the land and the water, and the fertility of all growing things. May you each walk in beauty all of your days, and may you take that walk together."

The watchers rose then and came forward to give their blessings, and a few of the old ones, remembering how they had been asked to speak at other weddings, began to shout out advice about how to have children and grow old together with happiness. Dolii blushed prettily as some of the advice grew more ribald, and finally, Pahe said, "It is time to eat together."

They moved to the back of the shelter where she had prepared mutton stew and cornmeal, all that she had for the guests. As they served themselves, Pahe went to Juanita and embraced her.

Her stepmother looked as old as the most wizened juniper,

gaunt and hollow-eyed. Pahe said, "You must eat, my father's wife. It has been a long journey."

"Not as long as your mother's," she said sadly. "We heard of her death even on the trail. I wept for you both, my husband's daughter."

They clung to each other silently. Pahe felt the old woman's heart beating through her shrunken breasts, breasts she had always been so vain of in seasons long past. If Ayoi could see Juanita now, she would be finally rid of whatever small jealousies she had carried for so many years. For that matter, the two wives could have been more comfort to each other in the last part of their lives than in the first part, another blessing stolen by the *Bilagáana*.

Pahe pushed those thoughts from her head and tried to cling to the resolve she had formed when first they came to this place: to be grateful for the blessings they had left. Dolii was by the stew pot, serving small portions to the guests, and Pahe pulled Juanita up to take a bit for herself.

"It has been so long since I have tasted good mutton," Juanita sighed eagerly as she ate the few mouthfuls slowly, savoring the smell and flavors.

"I wish there was more," Pahe said, "but perhaps the next season will be easier."

Honá came from his kinsmen to say to Manuelito, "I am grateful that my wife's mother was able to sing us into union." He spoke formally, keeping his chest out and his head up, aware that all eyes watched him approvingly.

Manuelito grinned and put one arm around the young man's shoulders. "There is one tradition which you will come to be grateful to continue, my granddaughter's husband. The one which allows you to be deaf to your mother-in-law's words hereafter."

The people laughed then, and Pahe remembered in that moment why her father was such a powerful leader. He knew when to speak and when to be silent. He knew when to be serious and when to laugh. Those qualities alone, she realized, were sufficient to make men admire him. She murmured to Juanita, "We did not know he was coming. Did he surrender?"

She shook her head. "They will say that he did. But the white soldiers never could find him. He came because he could no longer feed us. Also, he had news that there will be a new white chief who is coming to inspect the camp."

Pahe turned to her in surprise. "How is it that you know things of this place that we, who are here, do not?"

"Your father has spies everywhere. Many have escaped, and the traders tell us that the new white chief who comes to this place is a great warrior, much respected by the *Bilagáana*. Your father means to meet with him and ask for our freedom."

Pahe's eyes widened in amazement. "But this is what was promised to me! He will succeed!"

"What do you mean?"

Pahe shook her head, half dazed with the news. "While we were on the journey, Coyote came to me and told me this thing. That if we kept to old ways, we would be returned to our lands." She looked at Dolii, who stood now near to her new husband, as he accepted the good wishes of other clan members. "And my daughter will live to have children," she added softly. "All of this was promised to me, and now it appears that my father will be part of this promise."

"This is why, then, you chose to be the singer at your daughter's wedding."

"There was no one else to do it," she said. "And the Holy Ones said that I was to be the one to keep the People to the old ways." She dropped her eyes. "It is not something I would choose."

"And yet, they came. And they listened." Juanita smiled. "You have fulfilled your duty."

Manuelito and Barboncito were talking together, their heads close, surrounded by headmen. Barboncito said something, and Manuelito looked at her and smiled. A flood of relief came over her, that her father was with them again. Now she would not have to carry the burden of the family alone.

That evening, Pahe took her father to visit the place where Ayoi had been buried by the white soldiers. It was a place of many deaths, and none of the graves had been marked, for that was not the way of the People. But Pahe knew where her mother rested, for she had placed a small stone over her feet, so that she would not feel restless and need to walk about.

Dolii and Pahe stood to one side, while Manuelito knelt and

examined the earth where his wife had been buried. He sat on his heel for a long while silently, and the only sound was the wicker of the torch in the night wind. Finally, he stood and said, "I have thought of her so many times since she left. But I never thought of her in this way. Always, in my mind, she was not only alive, she was still young and full of spirit." He picked up a small stone and set it alongside the one which Pahe had placed at Ayoi's feet. "Why did she do this?"

Pahe said quickly, *"Che'ééná.* The sadness for something which will never come back. She did not wish to live in this place." She did not want her father to know that Ayoi had died, believing that he would never return to her. "She spoke of it often. She said she felt as trapped as a fly stuck in corn mush."

Dolii glanced at her and was silent. Only the two of them could know the truth, and in that silence, they both agreed that the truth would die with them.

"I will miss her all the days of my life," Manuelito said soberly. "She was the wife of my youth."

As they walked away from the graves, Pahe said, "I had hoped perhaps that you might have had some news of Wasek." Saying his name made her throat thicken with sorrow, but she could not stop her mouth from saying it.

"I had hoped you might have seen him here," Manuelito said sadly. "There are so many of us here, I thought perhaps he might have made his way."

"I have asked at every fire," Pahe said. "No one has seen him or heard of his trail."

Dolii murmured, "Sometimes I can hardly remember him at all." She looked anguished. "I did not think I would ever forget his face, but it is hard to see him now in my mind."

"That will come and go," Pahe said, taking her hand. "When you have a son of your own, you will see him again in your son's strong legs and smile, I think."

Dolii squeezed her hand and asked softly, "How do you stand it, my mother? How do you keep the sorrow from killing you?"

"I do not know," Pahe said. "I put it from my mind many times every day, and every day, I think it will be softer. It does not go away. It only changes into something else."

Manuelito cleared his throat to change the trail of the talk.

"Many of the clans speak your name, as I go from fire to fire. They say that you are a woman of wisdom, like your grandmother before you."

Pahe laughed mirthlessly. "They forget how much they hated her. Barboncito has spoken my name, I think, and they are repeating what they hear."

"Barboncito has their respect," Manuelito acknowledged.

"He has been a good friend in your absence." Pahe nodded.

"He tells everyone of your promise." He corrected himself at her glance. "Of the promise of your vision."

"It was not a vision, my father," Pahe said firmly. "The Holy Ones have chosen to come to me, as they did to my grandmother before me. I do not know why, but I know that they have promised me that if I help the People keep to the old ways, we will be set free to go back to our own lands."

"He told me this as well," Manuelito said.

"My husband and his clan believe this to be true also," Dolii said softly. "There are many who believe."

"That is well," Manuelito said. "For we will need all of the faith we can gather together to make this promise come true." As they approached the settlement again, Manuelito turned and embraced Dolii. "Go to your husband now, Little Bird, and do not think of death any more this night. Think only of new life."

Dolii smiled shyly and moved away toward the small shelter that she and Pahe had prepared for her. There were few places of privacy in the crowded settlement, but Pahe had placed her sleeping shelter as far from the others as she could. It was lined with a new sheepskin, and the sleeping robes were clean.

"Be well, my daughter," Pahe murmured after her as she walked away. And then she took her father's hand and walked with him back to the lights of the settlement fires.

*   *   *

The headmen wasted no time in calling for council, now that Manuelito and Barboncito were together again. Everyone knew that the arrival of the new white leader might mean an opportunity for the People. Things could hardly get worse. Barboncito had information Manuelito had not: that the white soldiers had been put on half-rations recently so that more food would be available to the People.

The summer before, the corn had been eaten by worms, so nearly half of it was lost. Then in the fall, storms flattened much of the wheat. The white soldiers had to bring in many barrels of flour and more than two thousand head of cattle to feed the People and the few Apaches who were still left. The People had been adept at forging ration tickets so that they might get as much food as possible, but then the soldiers brought in metal tickets which they could not so easily copy.

The men had worked all summer digging irrigation canals with few tools, tearing mesquite roots from the tough desert soil with their bare hands, only to see the crops fail. And now, there was no more wood left for fuel, and the next winter would be on them soon.

"It is a good time for us to ask for what we want," Manuelito said. "They cannot feed us, they cannot take care of us, and many of them wish they had never forced us here."

"How many have escaped?" Barboncito asked.

One of the headmen said, "More than a thousand. And many more talk of it. The old ones and the singers say that the land is cursed with ghosts and evil, and that is why the crops fail and the sheep do not breed."

"The crops fail because of the worms, and the sheep do not thrive because of the water," Manuelito replied grimly. "The Holy Ones have not abandoned us, and the only evil here is that of the whites. We must walk out of here free, without the fear of being chased down once more. That is the only reason I have come. I understand that they have built a place for the sick? A place where the white doctors treat the People?"

Another headman answered, "Yes, but it is a place of filth and death. No one will go there willingly, for many who have gone never return. The People cannot forget that the soldiers shot and killed those who were too sick to walk on their way here."

"There is something else," Delgadito said. He was one of the headmen who had escaped once, then come back again, for his clan was hounded to starvation by the white soldiers. "The *Bila-gáana* tempt some of the young women with extra rations. They come back from the soldiers' hogans with bad disease. The chant-

318 ▼▲▼ *Pamela Jekel*

ers cannot cure it, and the sores disfigure their bodies. Their men will not touch them again."

Manuelito frowned silently. Finally, he said, "We must convince the new headman to let us return to our own lands. That is the only way we will survive."

But the council had not remembered just how slowly the white men moved. In 1866, General Carleton was relieved of his command, and the care of the Navajos was transferred to the Department of the Interior. Many investigations commenced and ended, plenty of paperwork and letters flurried around Congress, but less food, clothing, and tools arrived each season than had the season before.

When the summer came, Pahe spoke to many of the headmen and suggested that they might consider refusing to plant at all. Perhaps, she said, if they did not, the white man would be forced to let them go. If they refused to use the white tools and dig the white ditches, the Holy Ones might see that they were determined to keep to the old ways. Some of the headmen listened. When the winter came, many died and many more ran away. Smallpox swept the settlement, and some of the old and the young succumbed.

And still they kept the old ways as best they could. Pahe led many Blessingway ceremonies, chanted over the sick, and sang the old songs to the dying. Manuelito caught her a badger, and she killed it and made a powder of its dried eardrum, placing a pinch of the powder into her own ear. Deezbaa came to her and told her to do this.

"I was a hand-trembler," her grandmother said, "but you are a listener. Mother Earth and Father Sky will tell you where the sickness comes from, if you listen well."

And so, when clan members came to her with an illness, she listened for the *nitch'i*, the Holy Wind, the breath of the earth which also lived in all living things, to tell her why they were sick. Perhaps they had made a fire of wood struck by lightning, or they had eaten unclean food or passed too close to the burial ground without cleansing themselves properly after. Pahe listened to the sounds of the wind, the rocks, the birds, the animals, and they provided the clues.

The other medicine men, Hombro and Largo, no longer

frowned when they saw her going to a shelter with her basket of herbs and sacred medicine bundles, for they could not care for all of the People between them.

*   *   *

Aquila had been following the herd's movement for days, hoping that a lamb would die. She was hungry, and she sensed that her fledglings were hungrier. Her mate, the large male she had nested with for five breeding seasons, was also out hunting, and she could only hope he would have better luck than she was having now.

Aquila spread her primaries to their full extent, caught a thermal and soared higher, watching for movement below. It was a warm morning and would become hotter as the sun rose to the middle of the sky. Then it would be harder to find anything moving out in the heat. The rabbits and prairie dogs would go underground or under shaded cover, and without her mate to help flush them out, she would likely find nothing until dusk.

Again, she turned back to fly in large circles over the moving herd, watching the dust roil up from their hooves.

Aquila was a Golden Eagle, *Aquila chrysaetos,* a full-grown female with a wingspan more than six feet when extended. From the ground, she looked much like a vulture, but she was bigger, more powerful, and if you saw her up close, the eagle look of her eye with its deep socket and dark, lustrous pupil, was unmistakable.

Aquila lived in the canyons that surrounded the Rio Pecos, and until the coming of the white man and then the coming of the many huts and caves of his slaves, she had known a time of good hunting. She had reared five generations of eaglets in the same eyrie, a large mass of sticks on a high crag which she and her mate had built.

When man came to the land, the prey became more scarce, but Aquila had also been able to take lambs, on occasion, and scavenge those who died at birth or were too weak to live past the first few months. And so she had not moved her nest from man, for what man took from her was also provided by his herds. Now she was beginning to think that this might be the last season they could successfully live among these intruders. There were simply too many of them, and they watched their herds more closely every season.

Aquila noticed something now about the slowly moving line of sheep that riveted her attention. She wheeled to get a better position and saw that the goats, who led the sheep, were moving in a wide arc away from a place near some rocks. She waited until the last sheep had moved around that same place, and then she dropped from the sky, keeping her keen eyes on that place of rocks.

When she came in to land, she extended her talons just in time to snatch at a large rattlesnake which was lying across a wide rock, the thing that had caused the goats to shy around that escarpment, leading the sheep to safer ground. The viper was nearly as long as her wings, very thick and well fed, and a prize which would feed her brood of two quite adequately for the rest of the day, with some left over for herself and her mate. That this snake, an ancient enemy, had obviously feasted on the very rodents she wished to catch herself only made her eagerness to kill it more intense.

Aquila grabbed the snake with one talon firmly, but she missed with her second foot. She shot aloft once more, determined to carry the snake high so that she might drop it on the rocks below, but the snake twisted free, dropped to the ground, and coiled swiftly, buzzing its rage and eager to attack.

Aquila landed again, this time several yards from the snake, and assessed her position. The snake was bleeding, obviously injured, but not injured enough to be weakened much. It coiled and twisted, keeping its large triangular head always toward her, watching her approach with eager anger. Aquila sensed no fear in her prey, and this gave her pause.

She knew that this snake was likely the best catch she would have in several days, and her hunger made her less cautious. She knew that she must avoid its flat head, and she would likely not have more than one other chance. In the seconds that she paused, the snake suddenly turned to run toward the rocks, stretching out like an arrow and fleeing with all its fluid power.

Swiftly, Aquila ran at the snake and raised her wings, hoping that it would strike at her feathers if it struck at all, then brought the edge of her huge wing across the snake's back in a high, hard blow with all her strength, knocking the rattler flat in the dust. Simultaneously, she hopped onto the snake, snatched it with both feet this time, and flapped her powerful wings desperately up, keeping the twisting body well away from her feet.

Aquila flew up, testing the wind, searching for something other than rocks this time. Finally, she reached the place she remembered, a small copse of ragged juniper, twisted stumps, and jagged edges which the men had cut at and ripped until it resembled stakes jutting up into the air. She dropped the twisting viper directly over the jagged spikes of wood, watching with great satisfaction as it was impaled on two splinters, writhing and helpless.

Aquila soared over the trees, keeping a keen watch on her prey. It writhed, but every twist only impaled it more. If it managed to rip free and drop to the ground, Aquila would be on it in a flash to try again. She sensed that the reptile was weakening, and she knew that, as the sun rose higher, the heat and the loss of blood alone would do her job for her. All she had to do was wait.

But Aquila was hungry. She knew that her brood would be hungrier still. She could not depend upon the hope that her mate might well have already hunted successfully and was, even now, feeding them. She circled the snake again and again, making up her mind. When she saw that the snake had not moved in a few moments, she tightened her circles, and let her hunger make her decision. She flapped her wings more swiftly, and hovered right over the jagged spikes of wood, peeling the snake off the trees like a limp, long fish. She flew up again over the place of rocks and dropped it again, this time watching with relish as it hit with a smacking, moist sound, obviously wounded badly.

It should be dead now, she knew. It did not coil; did not attempt to move out of the sun. She made a few more tight circles over it, watching for any sign of life, for she knew that a serpent was a shrewd adversary with a terrible will to kill and to live.

Finally, Aquila landed close to the still-unmoving snake, inspected it with a cocked head and a piercing stare, and then moved closer to pick it up. As she bent to pluck it off the rocks, it suddenly coiled, arched itself up and in the air and struck with its last bit of strength high up on her leg where only small feathers protected her bare skin, close to where her leg joined her body.

322 ▼ ▲ ▼   *Pamela Jekel*

Its fangs sunk deep into her leg, hung there for just long enough for the rattler to pump a jet of poison into her artery, and then withdrew and fell back once more in a heap.

Aquila staggered back from her enemy, amazed and disbelieving. Suddenly enraged, she leaped upon the viper, but before she could rip it apart with her talons, she felt a rush of heat up her body, a quaking in her chest, and then an awful pain and pressure which made her open her beak and cry out in agony, something rare in an eagle. She took a step away from the snake, one more, and then fell down, her leg muscles no longer functioning. In seconds, she felt a great sense of constriction in her lungs; she could not move at all, and only her eye turned to gaze once more on the rattler, who stared at her with its flat, black-hooded eye, also too injured to move away. In the next moment, Aquila died, never turning her eye upward to the sky.

For long hours, the snake lay without moving. But finally, its cold, reptilian determination to survive prodded it out of the sun and it inched itself under the overhang of a rock, to at least be partially out of the heat. When dusk came, it forced itself to move once more, a few more feet into a crevice where it lay out of the coming night and the colder air. It lay there for five nights, never moving, letting its body heal sufficiently to travel. Finally, the snake moved painfully, slowly out of its hiding place and started back to its place of rocks and home.

As it passed the body of the eagle, now dusty and flattened by the wind and the sun but untouched by predators, the snake buzzed its rattles fitfully in a reflexive response to an enemy.

*   *   *

It was the month when the flowers blossom, May of 1868, when more wagon trains arrived at the Bosque, and the word moved through the settlement like a fast fire that the new white headman, General Sherman, had finally come to discuss the fate of the People.

The headmen were called to council, and Barboncito was chosen to speak for them. The old ways demanded that when a man wished to speak with particular eloquence, he must hold under his tongue a turquoise anointed with live pollen—or pollen sprinkled on a living animal. A coyote was best for that purpose.

Manuelito took his men out and caught a coyote. Largo gave up his sacred turquoise which he had carried all the way from the Black Mountain. The pollen was placed on the captured animal, Barboncito put the turquoise under his tongue, and he stuck his knife in his moccasin to walk to meet Sherman. Behind him followed the rest of the council.

They sat on the ground in a half-circle before the general, who sat in a chair alongside Colonel Tappan and Agent Dodd, with a low, flat table before them. On the table, a pack of papers were fanned out, something which the People had seen so many times before in futile treaty councils.

The men listened while Agent Dodd welcomed them, and they waited still when General Sherman asked Agent Dodd to give a report of the People and their conditions. Agent Dodd spoke for a while about the crops and the bad water, saying that more than two thousand had died of smallpox, chicken pox, pneumonia, or dysentery in the four years they had been imprisoned. Another thousand had escaped and never returned. Several hundred more had disappeared and, he said, no one knew where they were.

General Sherman asked Barboncito, "Are these figures correct?"

Barboncito, who did not understand the concept of a thousand, agreed that they were correct.

"So you are saying that more than a quarter of the Navajo have died since they have been under the care of the U.S. Army?" Sherman asked again.

After a brief discussion with the interpreter, Barboncito agreed again.

"What, then, has happened with the two hundred who had disappeared?" Sherman asked.

Barboncito said, "Many were shot by the Comanches. Others were stolen by the Mexican raiders. Others, perhaps, have simply gone into the hills to die."

Sherman frowned and wrote some notes on his papers.

Agent Dodd went on to say that many of the sheep had been lost, to disease, to Comanches, to the Navajo themselves, who had to eat them to survive. There were fewer than a thousand sheep left, perhaps as many goats, and as many horses. There were only twenty mules left; most of them had died from overwork.

"And how many sheep had they when they came four years ago?" Sherman asked.

Dodd consulted his papers and said quietly, "Twelve thousand, more or less."

"More or less," Sherman repeated gently. "That is appalling."

"Yes, sir," Agent Dodd said.

Sherman then said, "I have come to Fort Sumner to invite you and your leaders to go and see the Cherokee country. If you like it, we will give you a reservation there. It will be much easier for you to live there. There are schools to educate your people in English or Spanish and take care of you until such times as you can care for yourselves. We will be able to protect you there. We do not expect you to take our word for it. Send some of your wisest men to see for themselves." The general spoke for some time in that way, with calm words and fierce face, telling the headmen that they could choose a new reservation in yet another country far from where they were.

When the interpreter finally finished, there was a silence around the circle of headmen. There was no need for them to discuss the general's proposal. Barboncito was ready to speak for them all. He rose and stepped nearer to the table, keeping his eyes on the interpreter for signs of dishonesty. They had been fooled before by twisted words; he was determined that it not happen again.

"When the People were first created," he said, "four mountains and four rivers were pointed out to us, inside of which we should live. That was to be our country, and it was given to us by First Woman. The Holy Ones told us that we were never to move east of the Rio Grande or north of the San Juan rivers. We have done so, and we have died. So have our animals."

He looked around the circle of headmen for encouragement. Manuelito nodded at him, as did Delgadito and others.

Barboncito lowered his voice as respectfully as he could. "I hope you will not ask us to go to any other country except our own. It might turn out another *Hwéélte*. They said that this was a good place when we came, but it is not."

He bent and took his knife from his moccasin and threw it on the floor before the soldiers could react and move forward. "If you wish to send my people away again from their home," he said, "first take this knife and kill me."

Barboncito sat down again slowly, as though his limbs were aged and his spine weak. The silence behind him from the other headmen was total.

General Sherman then spoke again through the interpreter of the good land in the Cherokee country, how many Indian tribes had been relocated there with harmony and peace. He painted large word pictures of the trees, the fine soil, the good water. He talked of the crops and the herds which were being worked by the others who had been established there. He said again, how happy the People would be in such a place.

Pahe watched this Sherman soldier very carefully while he spoke, to see if she could see the lie at the time his mouth made the words. They had said he was ugly and fierce in the face, and they were right. She had never seen a man with such hard eyes as this general, and his beard made his mouth look like an angry ember among black coals. But even listening with all her heart and mind, she could not see that there was a lie hidden in his speech. If there was, it seemed to her that the general did not know it.

On the other hand, she reminded herself, many men of good intent had decided that the Bosque would be a fine place for the People to live, and they were just as wrong as though they had told deliberate and perverse lies.

Barboncito answered the general again, and each time, he said the same thing: the People do not wish to go anywhere but their own lands. They will die if they are taken from what they know.

Sherman dismissed the council after the long speeches were over, saying that they would meet again in the morning, and he would give his decision.

That afternoon, the settlement was aflame with the news from the council, that it was possible that they would not be returned to their own lands but would be taken someplace else instead.

Pahe sat by her fire, with her father on one side and Barboncito on the other, as kinsman after kinsman came and went again, asking for the story to be told once more. It was promised, was it not, by the Holy Ones, that they would be returned to their own lands? Three years, she had told them. The three years were up. She had said this, no? Coyote was clear, that the People would be set free? Was there any possibility that she had misunderstood the message? Had there been any further promises or appearances by the Holy Ones? Was she certain?

Was she certain? Was she certain? Was she certain? Pahe was so weary of answering those questions by the time night came that she was eager for her sleeping pallet and silence, but she could not rest. The singers were making a dry painting, and she had been called to help them remember the way it must be. She stood before the crowd of people who had gathered and said, "Changing Woman made the first painting out of clouds and then swept them away with her hands to the winds. We must do the same."

"And if we cannot find all the proper colors of earth?" Largo, the youngest chanter, asked her.

"Then we will do the best we can. We will make a place where the Holy Ones come and go, and they will know that we are keeping to the old ways."

When the dry painting was finished, Barboncito sat within its design, to pull power and strength from its symbols, while the singers sang and the dancers moved around him in unison. And then Pahe led the women to the most private cave for a sweatbath so that they might be a source of truth and hope for those who must speak to the white men.

*   *   *

The next morning, when council was called again, the People waited to see the white General Sherman as he walked outside the fort. Crowds of old women clutched at his coat as he tried to pass, and wept, begging him not to send them anyplace but home. Answering wails went up from the children, and even some of the men called out to him, forgetting their pride.

Sherman stopped and asked the interpreter what it was that the old women were saying, those who were pulling at him and weeping. "Is it more food they want?"

"No." The interpreter shook his head. "They are begging to be sent home."

"Home?"

"To their own lands, sir," the interpreter said, turning away from the women with shame in his eyes. "To where they were born. To where they buried their kin."

Sherman turned and stared at the mass of people around him, his mouth in a tight frown. Pahe was at the rear of the crowd, and she could not see him clearly, but she sensed a change in the man's body, as though he were a bag of flour which had sagged in the middle. He looked less sure of his steps, as he walked through the People into the council area.

The headmen were gathered once more to hear his words, and, once more, the general was flanked on both sides by his agent and his colonel and his interpreter. The table now before him had even more papers, and more soldiers stood as sentries to the rear of the council, as though expecting to be needed.

The white general began his words with a long talk about peace among men, much of which the listening headmen did not understand. But then at last he said something they were able to comprehend. "We are now willing to discuss the proposition of your people going back to their own country."

A great murmur of joy rose from the headmen.

General Sherman held up his hand for silence. "However, if we discuss this proposition, we must agree that there will be a boundary line, like a fence which you cannot see, which surrounds your lands at all times. You must not go beyond that line except for trading purposes. You must live at peace among yourselves, and you must not fight with other Indians. If others make trouble for you, you must go to the soldiers and you must tell them so. The commanding officer of the soldiers will punish those who make trouble upon your lands."

Barboncito stood in the pause and nodded vigorously. "We are well pleased with what you have said. If we go back to our own country, we will be willing to stay within this line, you say."

Sherman went on. "You must agree to stop all fighting. The Army will do the fighting. If you are allowed to go back to your own country, the Utes will be the nearest tribe to your boundary. If the Utes or the Apache or any other tribe comes into your lands for the purposes of fighting, you can drive them out, but only to the edge of your lands. You must not follow them beyond your boundaries."

"We understand," Barboncito said. "We will not cross the boundary."

"You must not permit your young men to steal from the Utes or the Apache or the Mexicans."

"We will not allow this."

Sherman let his gaze move slowly over all the headmen present. Most particularly did he stare at Manuelito, for, of course, he knew that this headman had been the last to surrender and the most firm in his resistance. "I will hear," he said, "from each man here, that this is agreed."

Manuelito quickly rose and said, "I will agree to follow these laws. I will agree for my clan."

"And the others?"

One by one the other headmen rose and said the same words. *"Hao, hao!"* "Yes, yes!"

As each spoke, the full realization of what was agreed rose from them like a heat, and they became more animated, unable to keep their faces solemn, and those who watched and listened to the council from the rear sensed the tremulous, unbelieving joy that came from them.

"Very well," Sherman said simply. "Your past behavior is taken from you."

"We are going home," one man said quietly, turning to his son, who stood behind him.

His son grinned broadly and left to tell his clan members, who were clustered outside the council tent. They whooped loudly upon hearing the news, and then others rushed to hear. Before long, the men inside the council could scarcely finish their business, for the noise of jubilation outside their meeting.

The headmen finally came out, looking dazed and unbelieving. But then the women rushed them, embracing them and weeping, taking their hands and leading them out in gratitude. Barboncito was almost buried beneath grateful kin, and Manuelito was laughing, trying to walk toward Pahe and Juanita with two dozen women pulling at him, taking his hands, weeping and laughing all at once.

They were going home. Pahe embraced Juanita, wept on her father's breast, and then, when Dolii and Honá came running to hear the news, danced with her daughter's hands in hers in a circle, shouting her delight.

*   *   *

That night, the settlement fires were high, for no one wished to hoard wood anymore. Whatever food had been saved was brought out for feasting, and clans pooled their meager stores to make a celebration. The children laughed and whooped, and the women danced with some of their old vitality. The men smoked and laughed and told evil jokes about the white men, taking rare relish in their words this night, for at last they were no longer afraid.

They were going home.

Pahe left the dancing and the fires finally and walked out into the darkness alone, telling herself that she needed to see to the flocks. Actually, she simply needed to be alone for a few moments, to let the joy and relief pass over her and through her, letting her tears of gratitude flow unimpeded.

As she came to the little valley where the herds rested, she stood on the rise and looked back at the settlement. The noise and gaiety of the People could be heard, she imagined, far out on the desert. Even the creatures must know that this night was one of freedom and hope.

The sheep made welcoming, warm sounds as she came near them, slowly moving apart to envelop her within the flock. She stood with sheep on all sides, listening to their sleepy sighs and mumbles and small complaints. This must be what it is like, she thought, to be a Holy One, moving through the villages, in and out of the hogans, listening at the fires and watching at the doorways, knowing so much more of their lives than those who lived them.

She bent her head, enormously comforted by the nearness, the smells, the sounds and heat of the sheep. She prayed silently to the Holy Ones that the wait for departure would not be long, that the walk would not be too arduous, that the People would arrive safely to their own lands.

And then it occurred to her: betrayal. Coyote had spoken of betrayal. Was it possible that the white man would promise one thing and then do another? Was it possible that once on the trail to the west, they would be shot by the soldiers? Then the *Bilagáana*

330 ▼▲▼ *Pamela Jekel*

could say that the Mescaleros had attacked, or the slave raiders, or a sickness had swept through the People and carried them off, every one. The white man could betray them and there would be no punishment, no one would ever know the truth.

Pahe began to shiver in the cold, despite the warmth of the sheep so close to her. She had promised the People that they would go free, if they kept to the old ways. If they were now betrayed, she would be blamed. She would be more hated than Deezbaa ever was in her own time. She might even be killed.

"You worry like an old woman," Deezbaa's voice grumbled inside her head. "More. I never worried as much as you do, and I am old as the rocks."

"Older," said Ayoi mockingly. "And you listen as well, besides. Do you think every time my daughter prays to the Holy Ones, she calls on you personally?"

"I know something of betrayal," Deezbaa huffed. "Most particularly, the betrayal of the *Bilagáana.*"

"Thank you for coming to me," Pahe breathed silently. "I have missed you both."

She felt the presence of both the women in her life so powerfully that it seemed they stood alongside her in the darkness. They were in the presence of the sheep, the sound of the breeze, the feel of the night. She was comforted, and she felt her power and strength return.

"Is there anything to fear in this news?" she asked them both directly. "Is there yet more betrayal to come?"

"Only the betrayal of time," Deezbaa sighed resignedly. "A betrayal which comes to all of us at last. The white man will keep his promise to let you go. The other promises will be meaningless over time. But then, so will everything else."

"Like an old turtle, she croaks of doom," Ayoi muttered. "There is much to be joyful about, it seems to me, my daughter. You will have eternity to think and wonder. This life is to act. So, why are you up with the sheep? The dancing is down below."

Pahe turned and watched the distant fires, the dark shapes moving in quick joy from shelter to shelter, the dancing forms and the noise of singing which still came from the settlement. There was a sudden shift in the bodies around her, a ripple of something sensed which moved through the sheep, and Pahe turned away from the settlement to where they had turned.

A coyote stood on the rise above the flock, gazing down at her. To her amazement, the sheep were suddenly silent, frozen and mute and staring at their enemy above them.

"O Holy One," she breathed, scarcely daring to hope, "is it you?"

The coyote did not move, did not speak, did not alter itself in any way. It watched Pahe intently, seemingly more interested in her than in the sheep. Pahe said once more, "It is I, daughter of Manuelito. Have you come to give me a warning?"

Again, the coyote did nothing. Neither did it flinch at the sound of her voice. Pahe suddenly realized that if it were only a coyote, after all, and she did not chase it off, it would likely attack the lambs. On the other hand, if it were a Holy One, and she chased it away, she would cause grave offense.

The People believed that if a coyote crossed their path, they should go another way. Or they could sprinkle pollen and ask the coyote's blessing. But she had no pollen, and she did not feel as if this were her truth. She stood for a few moments more, trying to sense from the sheep what she should do. As they became more restless, and finally a few of them bleated in anxious fear, she made her decision.

"Go!" she shouted at the coyote, waving her stick. "Go from here at once!"

The coyote stared at her an instant longer, then turned and melted into the desert night.

Pahe walked back down to the settlement, determined to keep her faith and hope intact. The Holy Ones made themselves visible by becoming clouds, sun, rain, and thunder, Pahe knew that much. In that way, the People would not feel alone. "Well, and if that was a Holy One, he must learn to speak more quickly or not come among the sheep," she said with some irritation. "I can only do what I can do."

She realized as she said it that she had her answer. The People would be given their freedom, or they would not. They would make the journey safely, or they would not. The whites would keep their promises, or they would not. She could only do what she could do, and that was to keep to the old ways, to try to keep her family safe, to keep hope in her heart. That much she could do, and that she would do, and if disaster came from that, she would die knowing that she had done her best.

She walked down in the darkness, hearing the chuckles of her mother and her grandmother in her head, as though she were once again a child, come into the hogan to announce what new victory she had achieved today.

Pahe came down into the light to the nearest fire, bent to take a piece of good mutton from the spit, shouted a greeting to a kinswoman, and hurried to join the dancers.

*   *   *

It took more than fifteen days for the wagons to come, and many of the People were not willing to wait so long. Some of them slipped away each night, ready to make the journey alone rather than wait another day for the white wagons to take them. At first, they had kept their excitement high, and the lack of food, wood, and decent clothing did little to diminish their joy. But, finally, as they saw that, as usual, the white men were skilled at talking and less skilled at action, they found the deprivations more difficult to stomach. "Would that it be today!" the old ones cried. "Would that it be tomorrow!"

Every day, there were fewer and fewer of the People for the wagons to carry.

Dolii and Honá had considered leaving with his clan, but Pahe forbade it. "I will not have us separated," she told Dolii firmly. "You will stay with your mother and your grandfather, and the rest of our clan, as we have always done. This is the old way, and we will keep to it."

"But my husband wishes to go," Dolii said. "Is it not also our tradition that a wife honors her husband's wishes?"

"Only if she can do so without leaving her own clan," Pahe said, shaking her head. "There are some things which I will not allow, that will not change. This is one of those things. I will not lose another child."

When she said that, Dolii dropped her head, nodding. "I understand."

Pahe took her daughter's arm urgently and added, "You will be safer with Manuelito and the other headmen, my daughter.

The raiders will not dare to attack the white wagons. If you leave your own clan, against all custom, the Holy Ones will see that we have not kept to the old ways. They might not keep their promise to me!"

"I will tell him this," Dolii said. "He will stay, I think."

"He will stay," Pahe said firmly. "There is nothing so strong as young passion. His desire for his clan will not be as strong as his desire for his woman." She gave Dolii a small, conspiratorial smile. "Make sure of that."

*   *   *

Another council was called so that the general could read the treaty to the headmen and they could sign. At that meeting, Barboncito stepped forward once more, for the women had pleaded with him to do so.

"What will the Great White Father do about all those of my people who have been taken as slaves?" he asked.

Sherman looked surprised at the question. "We have fought a great war against slavery," he said finally. "And Congress has passed laws against it. We are not aware of any Navajo being held by Mexicans, but if there are, you can apply to the judges of the courts and the agents."

When Barboncito still would not sit, but only stood with his head bowed, hearing the murmurs of the women behind him, General Sherman asked, "How many Navajos are among the Mexicans now?"

Barboncito looked up. "Over half the tribe," he replied.

Sherman sighed and looked away. "We will do what we can to have your children returned to you," he said quietly. "Our government hates slavery." His voice grew more loud and angry. "I hate slavery."

Barboncito nodded and sat again.

*   *   *

Finally, the wagons came, and the jubilation of the People rose high again. They did not need to be told to get ready for departure; they had been ready for years. The old ones and the young clamored for places in the wagons first, and those able to walk were proud to do so, wishing only the protection of the soldiers from raiders. The column would stretch out for ten miles across the desert, and they would move ten or twelve miles each day.

Dolii and Honá walked alongside the third wagon, where his old grandmother rode, pushing the herd before them. Manuelito rode with his few warriors to one side of the wagons; other headmen rode alongside their own clans. The noise and dust of their going, the complaints and cries of the herds that trailed behind them, and the laughter and shouts of the People made the wagon seem a parade.

Such a difference than when we came here, Pahe thought dazedly as they drove away from the Bosque for the last time. It looked so much smaller now. She looked back over her shoulder as she walked alongside Juanita, back to the little rise where her mother was buried, together with the many others who had died in the four long years they spent imprisoned.

She knew she would never see this place again. Her mother would rest alone forever. But at least she is still in my mind and heart, Pahe thought. Until I die, she will live. Indeed, she smiled ruefully to herself, it is getting quite crowded inside me these days.

Juanita saw the direction she gazed. "Your father will miss her all the days of his life."

Pahe looked at her, surprised. "She has been here all the while," she finally said. "I imagine she will be wherever we go."

"He says the same thing," Juanita said.

Pahe smiled. "The Tall One could rarely keep silent, when there was an ear to listen. So long as he listens, she will keep talking."

"Does your grandmother come to you as well?"

Pahe nodded. "I am a lucky woman."

Juanita shook her head doubtfully. "There are some who, so addressed, would not consider themselves so fortunate."

"Ah"—Pahe grinned—"but they do not have grandmothers like mine. There is only one Deezbaa."

"In that, we are *all* fortunate."

Pahe glanced at her stepmother, and when she met her glance, they laughed together, reaching out to hold hands as they walked alongside the wagon.

*   *   *

They had walked for three days before Barboncito came up to speak to Pahe from the rear of the wagon train. He rode on a large mare, yet his long legs still dangled down below her belly.

"Have you had any more visits?" he asked her boldly, grinning down on her as though she were an entertaining child.

She looked up at him, shading her eyes against the sun. "Believe me, you would not find it so amusing, if the Holy Ones came to you."

"I suppose not," he agreed. "But perhaps they have, and I have been deaf to their words. You have a more sensitive ear."

She did not respond to that. She pulled her blanket up to hood her eyes.

"And, likely, a more sensitive heart," he added.

She glanced up at him and saw that he still watched her. Something turned over gently in her chest, the smallest of revolutions, and she knew in that moment that he wanted her. She was glad the blanket hid her smile. Still, she did not speak.

"I wonder, daughter of Manuelito," he said then, "if you would welcome the attention of another man besides that of your own kinsmen."

She let her blanket slip down from her face slightly so that he could see her smile. "Perhaps," she said. "That depends on which man offered the attention, I suppose."

He rode silently for a moment, and she could not tell if he was annoyed or confused.

She was determined not to speak again until he did.

Then he kicked his horse and the animal jumped forward, as startled as Pahe was by his sudden movement. He rode forward to another group of women who walked ahead, and he did not look back at her. She was disappointed that he had given up so easily. Perhaps she had spoken too abruptly—

But then, she saw that he was turning his mare back to her, and he cantered up, wheeled the horse around, and was once more at her side, pulling at the reins to slow to her speed. "Perhaps you would like to ride?"

She stopped then and reached out her hand to pat his horse gently. "That would be good," she said.

He slipped off his mare, quickly boosted her up on the blanket, and took the halter in his hands. "She will be happy to have a lighter load for a while."

He walked along, leading the horse, and, finally, he said, "You know that my wife died on the trail."

She murmured, "So many did."

He was silent again for long moments. "I have thought to take a new wife when we come to our own lands once more."

She kept her back straight as she remembered how her mother looked when astride, for she sensed that many eyes were likely turned to them, for lack of anything more interesting to watch.

"If you would welcome my attention, daughter of Manuelito, I would speak to your father about taking you as my wife."

Now that he had actually said the words so baldly, she was startled by how swiftly it had come to pass. Almost deflated, she relaxed her hands and bowed her head. Passion was for the young, she supposed. A woman of her years could not expect the same courtship as a young bride might merit. But then, she thought, this is for me to decide. Not my father, not Barboncito, and not the People—but me.

"I feel as though I do not know you," she said quietly. "Perhaps we can become friends before you speak to my father."

"That is not the old way." He smiled up at her. "I thought you wished to keep to the old ways." He reached up and touched her leg with a light, almost incidental pat.

"Are you in such a hurry, then?" she laughed. "We are old, but we are not near death, surely."

He shrugged. "I have been near death enough in the last few years to know that it comes without warning, old or not. I do not need to waste time wondering if you would make a suitable wife. A better man than I has already proven as much."

Her heart warmed to him at those words. "There are some old ways which may not be useful anymore," she finally said. "Perhaps you are right."

He chuckled. "Words which please any man's ear. You are certainly not a foolish woman."

"No." She smiled at him gently. "I am not." She rode along in companionable silence for a while and then said, "I will welcome your attention. And we will see what comes when it comes."

"Then I will speak to your father soon."

She inclined her head in what she hoped was a picture of feminine pliability. "Whatever you wish."

He laughed aloud at that, for they both knew that such words did not come naturally to her mouth. They rode along then in silence, and he finally began to speak with her about the journey, his feelings about the clans, and his plans for the future, once they reached their own lands.

By the time the wagons stopped for the evening meal, Pahe felt she knew more about this man, the Bearded One, the man who encouraged her to speak out at council. Barboncito was a man with a heart strong enough for bad times and, likely, strong enough for affection as well.

As they started their fires and pulled out their cookpots from the wagons, Dolii came to her and said, "You should be well rested, my mother . . . riding all the day on such a tall mare."

Pahe grinned at her and rolled her eyes, saying nothing.

"What does my grandfather say?"

"I have not asked him," Pahe said, rather archly. "I am a grown woman, after all."

"But that is not the old way." Dolii grinned, vastly amused by her mother's predicament. "Surely you would not accept the attentions of a man without your father's permission."

Pahe sighed. "You are either too old or too young for this conversation. Come and help me find my roots, and stop talking to me about this man. It makes my head ache."

Dolii laughed. "Better your head than your feet, I suppose."

The two went out into the dusk to gather herbs and roots, as Pahe had done every evening they had been on the journey. As they walked and searched and bent and picked, they murmured back and forth as easily as the breezes moved past them. Some nights, Dolii seemed to be full of words; other nights, only Pahe wished to break the silence of the gathering shadows. This night, Dolii said, "You are lucky, my mother. You have something special about you. The People will remember you, even when you are gone."

Pahe looked up from the ground, surprised. "Well, and I do not expect to be going anytime soon, but even so, I would expect that everyone is special in some way. Everyone is remembered after they are gone, at least by their kinsmen."

"No." Dolii shook her head. "Not for long."

Pahe stopped and watched her daughter for a long moment. "You do not feel special in any way?"

Dolii was quiet. Then she said, "I used to feel so. When I was very young. I used to think that perhaps I saw things in a special way, different from the way others saw them. When I looked at the stars, I saw them clearly. Or the mountains or the canyons. It seemed to me that just as you could hear what few could hear, I could see what few could see."

"Really? I did not know this," Pahe said happily. "Why did you never speak of it?"

"Because it left me."

"It left you? You mean that you do not see things with such clearness?"

"Oh, my eyes are not diseased," Dolii reassured her. "But I do not see life with the same vision. Before, when I was young, the earth was endless, and I felt that I could see so many possibilities. That I could see like the hawk over great distances. That I could lay in the grass and see to the depths of the roots. The air was fresher then, I guess, and the land was quiet. Quiet and clear and waiting. I always felt that something was just about to happen, and that I could see it coming before most of my kin."

Pahe pondered this for a moment. Dolii talked often of herself, but rarely with such poignancy. This, too, was because of the white man, that she felt she had lost this special vision she once had. This, too, was taken from her.

"Pehaps when we return to our lands," Pahe said, "and we have gathered together again to heal, your vision will return." She opened her arms expansively. "I believe that it will. We are going home, after all, to the most beautiful place on earth."

Dolii smiled. "You have kept your faith through it all, haven't you?"

"No," Pahe said honestly. "I have only shut my mouth on my doubt."

*   *   *

They journeyed on, past the places they had passed before, and this time, they saw the evidence of many more whites on the land than when they had come that way four years ago. They walked, herding the flocks before them, watching always for the slave raiders, and every day, Barboncito found a reason to walk a while with Pahe or put her upon his horse that she might ride.

Of course, Manuelito noticed, but he only nodded approvingly at them both when he passed, moving up and down the line of wagons to speak to this or that headman. Pahe knew that Barboncito had spoken to him of her, and neither of them felt it necessary to tell her of their agreement. That was the old way, she knew, and yet it rankled her somewhat. When we get back to our own lands safely, she told herself, I will speak to the Holy Ones about this. Some of the old ways no longer serve, once the women have been made to be both father and mother to their children, to be both man and woman to survive.

*   *   *

The days passed and the weeks, and, finally, they crossed the Rio Grande. Once over the river, the wagons trundled into lands that lay at the fringe of *Dinétah*. As the familiar mountains loomed into view, the People began to hurry the flocks, to urge the mules and horses, and then they reached the pastures around Fort Wingate and stopped, the old ones and the young ones tumbling down out of the wagons to walk the rest of the way.

Pahe saw old women kneel, with stiff knees and painful grunts, to kiss the earth and lay upon it full-length, weeping with relief. The old men bent and scooped up handfuls of soil and grass, and they wept as well. Couples stole away to whatever small privacy they could find to consummate their pleasure at returning to land which was theirs, and the young ones ran like jackrabbits over the prairie grass, rolling in it and shouting with glee.

They were home at last.

*   *   *

That night, the fires were high and the laughter of the clans flowed back and forth, as they called to one another, taking great pleasure in their nearness. They knew that they would soon spread out once more to their old lands, and they would no longer be bundled together like fingers on the same hand. There was a sweet sadness in the coming separation, for they had grown dependent on each other and they both welcomed and mourned the parting that would come.

Pahe sat with Manuelito at his fire, greeting kinsmen who came and went, discussing the division of the flocks, the plans for travel, and even old boundary disputes which now seemed very important to resolve.

Barboncito came to the fire as the moon rose high, and he sat alongside Manuelito. No one seemed surprised to see him there, Pahe noted with shy pleasure. It was as though some collective decision had been made in the clans about her which she had not been privy to, yet she was strangely comforted.

When the men came to talk, Manuelito and Barboncito reminded them of their promises.

"All of the past is washed away," Manuelito said to them. "All our past behavior has been taken from us. And we are to send our children to the white man's schools."

"What does this mean?" they asked.

Manuelito did not know.

"And we are to become farmers. In ten years, we will be able to grow everything we need."

"How will we do this?" they asked. "We have less land, less grazing fields, and less water now. We must share it with the Apache and the Ute and the Hopi and the Pueblo, and we cannot steal or fight. So how will we become farmers?"

"The White Father in Washington will send us what we need," Barboncito told them. "There will be rations for everyone until the first crops come in. Every person will receive five dollars worth of clothing every year. And every man will get ten dollars worth of seed and tools. Every family will have one hundred and sixty acres—"

But the People did not know what an acre was, and they had no way to measure the land. They knew only that the sheep must be moved from mountains to meadows with the change of the seasons, and how did one divide mountains and rivers? It did not matter. They were home. They went from Manuelito's fire confused, but no less jubilant. They were to keep from fighting and stealing, they understood that much. The soldiers would no longer chase them, they knew that, too. And they would never again be forced from their lands.

It was enough. They were no longer Lords of the Soil, but they had survived.

* * *

On the third day of visiting headmen, Barboncito took a ram and tied him to a tree beside the fort. As the men came and went, Barboncito said to them, "See how he breaks his horns and bruises his head, fighting his tethers? This is what will happen if we fight the white man again. Go home to your lands and keep the peace."

That night, they sat by the fire as the last headman went away, and Barboncito asked Manuelito, "Will you go back to your old lands?"

Manuelito nodded. "And you will go back to the Canyon de Chelly?"

Barboncito looked at Pahe and said, "Yes. My clan would not be happy anywhere but there."

"But the soldiers burned the fields," Pahe said.

"Yes. We will have to begin again." He smiled at her intimately, as though her father was not there. "I hope that you will come with me."

Manuelito looked at Pahe and then down at the fire. After a moment of silence, he said, "I will go and take my rest now. It has been a long day."

Pahe said nothing. Her mind was suddenly whirling with confusion.

When her father was gone, Barboncito said, "I ask forgiveness for speaking of this so abruptly. But we will be leaving in the morning, and I want you to come with me and be my wife."

"Have you spoken to my father?" she asked faintly, unable to believe that it had come so quickly to this.

"Yes. And he has agreed, if it is agreeable to you."

"My father has agreed that I am to leave his lands and leave my daughter and go to live with your clan?" she asked, her voice rising indignantly. "But that is against all custom. It is the husband who comes to the wife's people—"

"I know this," Barboncito said patiently. "But these are new times. My clan needs me to lead them home and to help them begin again."

"And my people need me as well," Pahe said.

"Your daughter has a husband to care for her," Barboncito said. "Your father has a wife. You are the only one who has no one. Come with me, and my people will welcome you."

Pahe thought for a moment. He was right. Dolii would be kept busy caring for her new husband; perhaps a child would even come soon. Juanita would care for her father well enough, as she always had. She could go with Barboncito and, as his wife, be loved and respected among his clan.

But if she went with him, Dolii would have no reason to stay on her grandfather's lands—lands that one day would belong to her. She would be persuaded by Honá to go with him to his own people. The clan would splinter; they would be blown apart like tumbleweed, scattered into new lands, taking refuge with strangers.

Barboncito said she had no one. That was not true. She had her clan, and they were her responsibility.

Pahe knew what she must do. Changing Woman had told the women this truth: that they were the source of life, of the family, like the womb of the earth. The mother was the heartbeat of the clan. This was why she buried their birth cords near her hogan, that they would return to her. This was why the hogan was round, a circle, like the arms of a mother. The Holy Ones knew this, and the People must not forget.

"No," she said. "That is not the old way. We must keep to the old ways. The Holy Ones have told me this, and I have promised. There is a reason for all that we do. I will not leave my lands and the lands of my father."

Barboncito looked down at his hands grimly. "We do not have many years left for contentment," he said softly.

"I have enough," she said. "I will be content." She reached over and touched one of his hands. "Come with me. My father will make you welcome. I will be your wife, in the old ways."

He shook his head sadly. "I cannot. Perhaps when my people are settled, I can leave them. But not now."

She nodded. "I understand this." She took her hand away. "It is not easy to be a leader of men."

"I must listen to the heartbeats of many and be deaf to my own," he murmured.

She smiled at him wisely. "When you can no longer ignore your own, then come to me again. You know where I will be."

Barboncito rose then slowly and walked from the fire. She watched him walk away. He had now more than sixty winters in those knees, and they would no longer hold him as straight as before. But he had the heart and stomach of a younger man. She was proud that he wanted her and proud that she had something more important to do.

She took up her stick and stirred the embers of the fire so that they flamed up instantly and warmed her. They were a people who had customs for everything in their lives. Changing Woman said that she would write the laws that were to govern mankind for all time in the stars. She would not write them on the water, for it was always changing form; she could not write them on the rocks, for the wind would soon erase them. She wrote them on the stars so they could be read and remembered forever. The Rainbow way. This was the reason they had survived. Their beliefs kept them alive.

The old ones used to tell the children: "Walk in good and orderly ways always." It had been a long while since she had heard anyone say those words to the children. It was time they heard them again.

*   *   *

Manuelito managed to get one of the wagons from the fort commander, with the promise that he return it within the month. He persuaded the commander to give him all the rations due his clan as well as a small herd of beef to take with him, and before the commander could change his mind, he loaded the wagon with the rations, a few tools he was able to get from the soldiers, and the oldest and youngest members of his clan. They started for his land, six days ride from Fort Wingate, after saying hard farewells to kin and friends they had lived with, cheek-to-jowl, for four years.

Ganado Mucho, another clan leader, headed in the other direction to the Ganado Valley, which was outside the boundary lines set by the treaty. Barboncito gathered his clan and started for the Canyon de Chelly. Within days, the People had scattered. Those who had nowhere to go stayed within sight of the fort, expecting that the rations provided by the soldiers would be better than nothing.

But many more grouped together with relations, even distant kinsmen, rather than begin again alone. Pahe knew that her father had been ready to leave for his own lands the moment he set foot in *Dinétah,* but he waited so that he might see to the others. Now their wagon was crowded with grandmothers and grandfathers and children who were not of their immediate clan, but who had no place else to go.

"It does not matter," her father said. "We can use every pair of hands to some good."

As they crossed the valleys and wove their way through the canyons back to the old places, Pahe saw how large it all seemed after so many seasons away.

Dolii said it first. "I did not know how small we were until now that I see the largeness of what we left."

Pahe kept picturing her hogan in her mind, her mother's hogan, her grandmother's hogan, until the details of each was so clear and precise that she could smell the difference in wood smoke. Would they still be there? Perhaps the soldiers had burned them, as they burned the peach orchards, down to the ground. Perhaps they had been taken over by strangers.

If that were so, they would build new ones. But they would not go back to the soldiers, to wait for their pitiful rations. Manuelito would have to send many times to the fort for grain and rations, since it was too late to plant. It was curious that the white men did not think of these details when they made decisions. Every child of the People knew that when *Dilyehe* appeared in the early-morning sky, the little group of six stars, it was the end of the planting season, because it was too late to get harvest in before the first frost. One would have thought that the *Bilagáana* would have prepared for such things, but they seemed not to know or care.

"Will you go to the fort yourself?" she asked her father.

"I will not go there again," he said quickly. "I will send Honá or Tohat or another."

She thought of that for a moment. "Do not send Honá," she said then, quietly.

Her father glanced at her as they walked. "He will have to take his place," he said.

"Well and that will happen soon enough," Pahe said a little tartly. "Let your granddaughter know a little happiness first."

Manuelito laughed suddenly, his eyebrows raised in surprise. "And to think I was worried about the Utes! Let them come, then. Some of us are ready enough for battle."

Pahe's mouth twisted in an unwilling smile. "Yes. Let them come. I imagine there are some here who will make them wish they had never crawled out from their holes."

But still, they watched for raiders from every side, not knowing how much the Utes had suffered at the hands of the soldiers. It was certain the Mexicans had not. Pahe chanted to herself as she walked behind the herds, "In beauty it is done; in harmony it is written; in beauty and harmony it shall be so finished. Changing Woman said it so." It was like the beat of her stick on the ground, the step of her foot on the soil, the rhythm she kept as she moved toward the lands.

She thought of the corn seed she had saved, gleaned from the stables at the Bosque. Corn was the only plant that needed the People as much as the People needed it, for it could not reseed itself. The fields would be gone when they returned, but the land would be waiting. The spirit of the corn would be waiting in the soil for hands to bring it to life again.

She said to her father, "We must have a *Máii Bizéenaast'a*, the ceremony for a safe return to home."

"Will you lead it?" he asked.

She nodded. It no longer scared her to think of such things. And so that evening when they stopped, Manuelito and his men captured a female coyote. They made a circle and surrounded the animal, singing softly to keep her calm. Then Manuelito came and caught her fast. As he held her gently but firmly, Pahe walked to the center of the circle. She touched the coyote's jaw, and the animal opened her mouth. Pahe put into her mouth a small piece of white shell tapered at both ends with a hole in the center, the bead that was sacred to the ceremony.

When the coyote was released, she turned several times and then walked calmly to the west.

"There it is," Pahe said to the circle of clan members. "We will be seen safely home."

*   *   *

That night in her dreams, Narbona came to her and sat beside her sleeping robe. She sat up and embraced him, pleased to see how young he looked, as he had when she was a child. "Grandfather," she said, closing her eyes and holding him tightly, "I have missed you so many winters."

"I have been here, Little Bird," he murmured, patting her. "I look forward to seeing the old places again."

She pulled back and looked into his face. His eyes gleamed with the strength and virility of a young warrior. "Have you made a truce with my grandmother?"

"We are still negotiating." He grinned. "We shall be doing this until the rocks wear down to dust."

She laughed, full of pleasure at his words. "I have kept the old ways, Grandfather," she said. "I have tried to remind the People of who they are."

He nodded. "The Holy Ones are pleased."

"Is there something more I must do?"

He smiled sadly at her, taking one of her hands. "Tell them of your dreams. They will listen, I think."

"My dreams? But I do not remember them, mostly—"

"You will for many moons to come," he said. "When the dreams end, there is no more greatness for the People. Tell them that."

"They have scattered, Grandfather. I will not be able to speak to many as I did before. Some of them do not know their place, but they are determined to go somewhere and quickly. Anything to get land around them again which is not filled with soldiers."

"When a man does not know his place, there is no place for that man," Narbona said.

Pahe thought for a moment. Her grandfather's statements were either more profound than she could understand or they were empty. She could not tell which was the truth. Was it possible that the Old Ones, when they came back to the land of the living, were no more wise than when they had died? Narbona had always been a strong leader, but some would say that he had made some bad decisions, certainly about the white men. "What am I to do?" she asked him finally.

"Keep the clan together. Speak to them of your dreams. Tell those who will listen of the old ways."

This she could understand. She took his hand, and it slipped from her grip, and she saw that Narbona was not there anymore. She was alone. She felt a sadness well up in her heart, as though she had lost him all over again, and then she fought it down. He had come to her once. He might well come again. It was better than nothing.

*   *   *

They came on Manuelito's land from the east, up over the mountain pass and down the Tunicha Valley, pushing the flocks before them, letting the horse take his time with the wagon. From a distance, they could see that many of the hogans were still intact, and then they could no longer be patient, but pushed the herds and the horses harder, running ahead with eagerness.

Manuelito stopped the wagon in the first corral and tied up the horse, calling to his men to help the old ones and the young ones into shelter before they tended the stock. Pahe was coming from the rear of the herd, pushing some of the slower ewes ahead of her, when she saw her mother's hogan. Her eyes watered with relief. It was still standing. Some of the others had been damaged by raiders or the soldiers or simply the passage of time, she could not tell, but her mother's hogan still stood.

As she walked forward, she saw Dolii and Honá emerge from the hogan, and she came more quickly, thinking that perhaps they would prefer to take that one as their own. From behind Dolii came another man, a tall stranger with an unfamiliar blanket, and she took in a breath. Someone else was here before them.

As she got closer, she saw that Dolii was smiling, and she looked at the man she spoke to and stopped, her hand to her throat in shock.

She began now to run, pulling her blanket up to her knees.

The man turned toward her and shouted something she could not hear for the high, loud thumping of her heart in her chest. He raised his arm and the sun caught him in the face.

"Wasek!" she screamed, running faster.

He ran to meet her then and caught her up in his arms, whirling her around off her feet. "My mother," he said into her ear, holding her fast. "You are come."

"Wasek! Wasek!" She said his name over and over, pulling back to look in his face and touch his cheek. He was old and gaunt now, no longer a boy, all of a man and honed to a hardness she would not have thought possible in such a short time. He was alive, however, and he was returned to her. "How long have you been here? Where have you been? I asked the Holy Ones so often to keep you safe. Have you seen your grandfather?"

"I will answer all of these questions and everything else," he said, taking her face in his two hands and looking into her eyes. "I did not think to ever again see this face alive."

"Nor I," she murmured, beginning then to tremble with the pent-up pain she had carried for so many years. "Oh, Wasek! So many have died! But you are alive!"

A shout then from behind her, and she turned to see Manuelito hurrying toward them. Her son let go of her face and turned to meet his grandfather, the two of them lifting each other off the ground with the force of their hug.

"Wasek! Wasek!" she heard her father say. "My grandson is alive." And as he began to weep with relief, Pahe felt her own tears begin, the cleansing tears that fell unheeded down her face onto the soil. Dolii and Honá came behind her to embrace her, but she could not turn away from the sight of her son and her father, face-to-face, laughing and weeping with joy.

Pahe felt the earth firm beneath her feet, felt the heat and the strength of the rock beneath the soil, and heard the distant cry of the raven from the copse of juniper which stood near her grandmother's hogan. The wind, the breath of the earth, was blowing from far away, carrying the smell of sage. "*Shikéyah*," she murmured. "My home."

Epilogue

▲▼▲▼▲

And so the People came home again to make a new beginning. They arrived nearly as poor and empty-handed as when they had first come to the lands a thousand years before. They could not know that the Congress, which had promised them rations, clothing, silver, seeds, and tools, was also impoverished, struggling to bring a nation back from its civil war; they could not know that there were more than thirty tribes who had the same promises from that Congress, some more desperate than the Navajo. They had signed the white man's treaty papers, and they had been allowed to go home. In that, they felt fortunate.

In 1869, after long delays, the sheep promised the People finally arrived, fifteen months after the signing of the treaty. Thirty-five thousand were herded from Fort Union, but somehow in the three hundred miles between Fort Union and Fort Wingate, more than twenty thousand disappeared. Word went out throughout *Dinétah*, however, that the rest were coming, and the People came to the fort from all their hidden places. There were eight thousand of them left, and they owned less than two thousand sheep and goats. Now fifteen thousand animals were to be divided among them.

The sheep were the little Spanish *churros*, slim-legged, long-haired, and well suited to the Navajo lands. The People waited eagerly in their ragged blankets until they were called, one by one, to go into the corral and receive their sheep: two for every man, woman, and child. The fort commander, Captain Bennett, wrote to his wife: "I have never seen such anxiety and gratitude."

Dressed in flour sacks, living on rats and wild plants, the women set up their looms once more, and, within a year, there was a thriving trade for their blankets. With these blankets, their men brought back horses, always horses, for they must build their dignity again.

The men also went off to work for wages wherever they could find them, and the silver dollars they earned were sewed into clothing or fashioned into jewelry, and from those efforts, another trade was born—the Navajo silverwork.

In 1870, Barboncito died. Manuelito was now second in command of the clans after the older Ganado Mucho. Pahe's father took another wife and kept his clan safe for the ten years of the treaty, and by 1880, the People numbered nearly twelve thousand, and their flocks were more than seven hundred thousand, despite the fact that most of the promised rations, clothing, money, seeds, and tools never arrived.

In 1881, the Santa Fe railroad, crawling year by year from Topeka, Kansas, finally made it to Albuquerque, bringing with it the traders. With them came the calico, the colored yarns and dyes, the hammers, axes, wagons, pumps, windmills, and boxes of nails and lumber which would change the People forever.

Through all this change, Pahe kept to the old ways and counseled her clan to do the same. When the Indian agents came and went, insisting that the children must go to the new white schools to "learn paper," as the treaty demanded, she refused to let the children of Dolii and Wasek leave her lands, even though her father let his own young son be taken from him.

When Manuelito's son died of tuberculosis, a disease he contracted in the white school, she spoke loudly against the white ways and the white way of learning, and many heeded her warnings, keeping their children hidden from the soldiers who tried to force them to school.

By the time she had fifty winters, Pahe was known throughout *Dinétah* as a strong voice of wisdom. In 1893, when her father died and she had sixty winters, At'ééd Jóhonaa'éí Yidiits'a'í was one of the most beloved singers in the Navajo nation. It was said that when She-Who-Hears-The-Sun sat down in a hogan to begin a sacred ceremony, she turned first to the east and tilted her head to listen for a moment, and then to the west to do the same.

Some said she listened to the sun as it came and went, as she had been able to do since she was a child, and she let them believe this. But, in fact, Pahe was listening to Ayoi on her left and Deezbaa on her right, as they reminded and scolded and teased her to walk in good and orderly ways always.

Bibliography

▲ ▼ ▲ ▼ ▲

There are many books on the Navajo available to the re-searching mind, some of the best of which are more than forty years old. Ruth M. Underhill's *The Navajos* (1956) and Raymond Friday Locke's *The Book of the Navajo* (1976) are by far the best and most complete overviews of the *Diné* and their culture. How-ever, they are necessarily limited by the fact that at the time the authors took information from the Navajo, the People themselves were not as knowledgeable about their own past, and the authors had to deal with their own cultural prejudices. There is still a need for a new comprehensive history of the culture and growth of the *Diné*, written by their own historians.

Having said that, there are still masses of excellent sources available, and these are some of the ones I found most helpful. Of course, any errors or omissions in my novel are to be laid at my door, with the understanding that I am writing historical fiction rather than scholarly research.

Abbey, Edward. *Desert Solitaire: A Season in the Wilderness.* New York: Ballantine Books, 1968, 1971.

Amsden, Charles Avery. *Navajo Weaving.* New York: Dover Publications, 1991.

Austin, Mary. *The Land of Little Rain.* Albuquerque, NM: University of New Mexico Press, 1974.

Bailey, Garrick and Roberta Bailey. *A History of the Navajos: The*

Reservation Years. Santa Fe, NM: School of American Research Press, 1986.

Brown, Dee. *Bury My Heart at Wounded Knee*. New York: Pocket Books, 1970, 1981.

Brown, Kenneth A. *Four Corners: History, Land and People of the Desert Southwest*. New York: Harper Collins, 1995.

Evers, Larry, Series Editor. *Between Sacred Mountains: Navajo Stories and Lessons from the Land*. Tucson, AZ: Sun Tracks and the University of Arizona Press, 1994, by the Rock Point Community School, Chinle, AZ, 1982.

Greenberg, Henry and Georgia Greenberg. *Power of a Navajo*. Carl Gorman: the Man and His Life. Santa Fe, NM: Clear Light Publishers, 1996.

Griffin-Pierce, Trudy. *Earth is My Mother, Sky is My Father: Space, Time, and Astronomy in Navajo Sand Paintings*. Albuquerque, NM: University of New Mexico Press, 1992.

Hausman, Gerald. *The Gift of the Gila Monster: Navajo Ceremonial Tales*. New York: Touchstone, Simon & Schuster, 1993.

Kluckhohn, Clyde and Dorothea Leighton. *The Navajo*. Cambridge, MA: Harvard University Press, 1946, 1974.

LaBarre, Weston. *The Peyote Cult*. Norman, OK: University of Oklahoma Press, 1938, 1989.

Louis, Ray B. *Child of the Hogan*. Provo, UT: Brigham Young University Press, 1975.

Locke, Raymond Friday. *The Book of the Navajo*, Fifth Edition. Los Angeles, CA: Mankind Publishing Co., 1976, 1992.

Matthiessen, Peter. *Indian Country*. New York: Penguin Books, 1979, 1984.

Mayes, Vernon O. and Barbara Bayless Lacy. *Nanise: A Navajo Herbal*. Tsaile, AZ: Navajo Community College Press, 1989.

McAllister, Davis P. *Hogans, Navajo Houses, and House Songs.* Middletown, CN: Wesleyan University Press, 1980.

Newcomb, Franc Johnson. *Navajo Omens and Taboos.* Santa Fe, NM: Ryadal Press, 1940.

O'Bryan, Aileen. *Navajo Indian Myths.* New York: Dover Publications, 1993.

Reichard, Gladys A. *Spider Woman: A Story of Navajo Weavers and Chanters.* New York: MacMillan, 1934.

Roessel, Ruth. *Navajo Stories of the Long Walk Period.* Chinle, AZ: Navajo Community College Press, 1973.

Suzuki, David and Peter Knudtson. *Wisdom of the Elders: Sacred Native Stories of Nature.* New York: Bantam, 1992.

Tapahonso, Luci. *Blue Horses Rush In.* Tucson, AZ: University of Arizona Press, 1997.

Underhill, Ruth M. *The Navajo.* Norman, OK: University of Oklahoma Press, 1956.

Waters, Frank. *Masked Gods: Navajo and Pueblo Ceremonialism.* Athens, OH: Swallow Press, Ohio University Press, 1990.

Young, Robert W. and William Morgan. *The Navajo Language: A Grammar and Colloquial Dictionary.* Albuquerque, NM: University of New Mexico Press, 1980.

Afterword

▲▼▲▼▲

Every writer likes to believe that he or she writes in a cocoon of self-generated brilliance, that her creativity is hers alone, and that she is completely independent of not only the world but any supporting cast against which she plays her starring role.

That is, of course, only one of the more glaring lies we writers tell ourselves. Another would be that we write fiction and that therefore our characters are only creatures of our imagination, rather than parts of ourselves. And then there's the one about how we suffer so for our art, and thus should be excused excesses of drink, late nights, and ill-mannered remarks about other writers, agents, editors, critics, and the general public at large.

So much for illusions.

The fact is that writing is more craft than art and takes the discipline of an athlete and the circumstantiality of an IRS auditor. I have been writing for almost twenty years, and this is my thirteenth book. Finally, I do, indeed, feel circumstantial, and I have nothing more to say, at least for the moment. Also, at nearly fifty, I can no longer reconcile myself to deadlines. And so, for now, I will recede into a background murmur until the reservoir fills back up again.

> The finest flights of pen, they say,
> Are born from the disquiet minds.
> Those in a flutter and pother of heat,
> Who chafe at the tie that binds.

Those restless hearts of discontent
Who rail at the asinine:
Unreconciled, exacting, and vexed,
These write the memorable lines.
"But this will not do!" they are quick to cry
To a world more content or beguiled.
These friction themselves to frenzy or fame;
These drive the critics wild.
But critics aren't really people, you know,
They get their books for free.
And most spouses, kids, and friends
Prefer compatibility.
The attention's fine, and it's fun to fuss,
And for fussing, be raved and reviled,
But perfectionists don't age at all well.
Ah, to be reconciled!

Through it all, I have been blessed with family and friends who have listened, loved, and looked the other way. The cast has changed, but the support has been constant.

One of my most important research assistants for this book has been Geneva John, a young Navajo professional who came to my aid with vocabulary, hints on custom and usage, and general information about the ways of the People. I am most grateful for any errors and embarrassment she may have saved me, and, of course, any remaining flaws are mine alone.

As ever, I would like to thank (again and again) my wondrous agent, Roz Targ, who has been with me from the start, a committment that has outlasted many in my life. My editor, Ann LaFarge, is the backbone of whatever restraint my novels have, demanding always a good story, a tight scene, and a little less noise there, Pam. My family is, as always, the wellspring of my sense of safety and purpose, most particularly my sweet daughter, Leah, who will be pleased that Mommy can play a bit more now that this book is done.

My friends—Sandy Burns and Judy and Chris Ray and Gail Albert, Steve and Jo Burgwyn, Jim Greco and Pat Mowat and Kathy Magner, and to Dee Parenti, most especially, who has

been Leah's nanny (and now, mine) through many novels—
help make all my efforts easy by ordering my life with laughter
and love. My co-parent and once-husband, Bill, is still one of
my dearest friends, and in his love, sense of fair play, and
grace under pressure, I count myself and our daughter lucky
indeed.

And for my Jack, to whom this book is dedicated, who has
built us a home and a life rich with joy and blessings, let me offer
a song.

> It was my second marriage, and it was dying, too.
> You saw my empty eyes and held out a hopeful hand;
> My heart is dead to love, I said,
> It will not trust again.
> Find yourself another fool, if this is what you've planned.
>
> Before you go, you murmured, may I say just one thing?
> I'm not afraid of failure, and I'd like to be your third,
> I see some shine still glimmering there,
> Within your furious fist—wait!
> Just listen while I tell you about a thing I've heard.
>
> There is a mountain in Japan where red wildflowers bloom
> From ruddy soil, rich with clay and strong with silica
> Clay which makes the strongest bricks,
> When ovened hot and sure.
> And so beneath the mountain grew the town, Hiroshima.
> But men and bricks are blinks in time
> When war ignites the sky,
> Hiroshima was rubble in a flash of savage heat
> A no-man's land of wasted dreams and lives and souls
> A tomb for broken hopes, a desert of defeat.
>
> Until the rain came round again.
>
> And from the seared wreckage, the red wildflowers bloomed,
> For rain and seeds will not ignore the laws of botany.
> They raised their heads with heedless joy
> And opened to the sun;
> It was as though the earth itself bled in sympathy.
> I'm just a builder, then you said, but let me ask you this:

Should hearts be less resilient than a red wildflower seed?
I paused and heard you, took your hand,
And looked into your eyes.
We sat outside in silence, and I felt my sorrow freed.

I am grateful for every reader, every letter, every kudo and kick along the way, and I wish for all of you *hózhó*.